UNTETHERED

RHIANNON BLACKWOOD

This is a work of fiction. All characters in this publication want you to know that they are fictitious and to not come looking.

"It's only when you've lost someone that you realize the nonsense of that phrase "It's a small world". It isn't. It's a vast, devouring world, especially if you're alone."

-Clive Barker

"People tethered to things that hurt have to learn to get used to the pain."

Contents

I

A Very Long Day

Bone-white hair swept across the woman's figure in a long tangle that flowed into the muddy river. Her body was pale against the red of fallen leaves and easily spotted from the road above. Shane Walker took in the ghastly sight and sighed.

This was going to be a very long day.

He slipped down the frost covered slope, gripping onto thin trees to keep himself upright and nearly failing at it several times. Once on level ground, he felt the odd hush of the place, with only the sound of the slow current greeting him as he approached where she lay with her head resting on an outstretched arm, legs drawn to her chest beneath some grayish gown.

She was still and cold enough that the pulse he felt on her exposed wrist surprised him. He noted the light crunch as she disconnected from the ground when he turned her to him and began dragging away the stiff hair from where it clung to her face and black lashes. His first thought was that she looked much younger than someone with hair gone that white ought to, but his next one took longer to grasp because it wasn't at all logical.

He *knew* her.

Most people here in Elmwood had made up search parties to find her more than a decade ago, but they were just looking for a face on a flyer. For Shane, whenever he caught that face staring back at him from the faded flyer that still hung at the station, he remembered the pretty, black-haired girl who used to ride the school bus with him when he was a kid. Seeing that face had once been as much of his morning routine as coffee was today, and there was no doubt that it was the same one he was looking at now.

He had just found Nicolette Adair. *Cole.*

Unofficially, she'd been presumed dead, and she didn't look far from it. He shrugged off his coat and covered her. The ambulance he'd already radioed for was taking its time. He tapped her clay-like cheek, and an explosion of wings erupted from the other side of the water—a flickering shadow falling over the river as dozens of crows launched themselves into the sky.

Instinctively, he raised his arm, and leaned over her body as though expecting some attack, but the shadow only passed. Still, a creeping unease spread through him. Crows rarely sat silently in any number, and these hadn't made a sound.

He slowly scanned the trees behind him where they had flown off in the dull morning sun, unease sharpening into alarm as he turned back to the river and another woman's eyes met his.

She stood knee-deep in the water's edge, violently shivering. Deep wrinkles cut into the reddish brown of her skin, and beneath a blanket of gray hair, she looked to be wearing a garment of bone and feathers bound in twine that hardly covered her ancient body, but her eyes were sharp and furious as she began shouting at him.

He couldn't make out at first, but gradually he recognized his grandmother's language. *Looking at me, she probably figured I should understand her.* He winced.

"I'm here to help." He pressed one hand on his chest, reaching out to her with the other. "Do you understand?"

Apparently not, as with a look of utter defeat, she covered her face and sank to her knees with a hoarse, gnarled wail that echoed down the water.

The shrill ambulance siren in the distance seemed to join in.

Shane Walker's day was getting longer by the second.

2

Talia

I read somewhere that cats sometimes eat their young. Just swallows them up, bones and all. Maybe their mother is so distressed by new motherhood that she doesn't recognize that the small, squirmy things trying to feed off of her body are hers. Or maybe she senses something so wrong in them that she kills as a kindness. Whatever the reason, whenever I would feel down about my own mother leaving me when I was a little girl, I'd picture those tiny, mewling kittens being mashed up in their mother's jaws and tell myself that, well, as far as maternal rejection went, it could have been worse.

Cold comfort is better than no comfort at all to a lonely girl.

It was my mother who'd brought me to Elmwood a week ago. Well, not *literally*. Since she left, it had just been Dad and I living in our upstate New York home...until two months ago when he moved his girlfriend in. It was around this time that he figured out I'd stopped taking my medication. I didn't tell him that I'd been off it for about a year, that I'd started weaning myself off about six months after being released from Stillview—where I'd initially been told I'd be staying for only a couple of days. It had turned into weeks. Three of them. Twenty-three days actually.

I'd counted every dawn.

The months leading up to my involuntary stay in what everyone *insisted* I stop referring to as an asylum—those months moved quickly, too quickly for me to see what was happening clearly enough to try and stop it. I'd tried to summarize that time to the doctors at least, but each time I'd try to wrap words around everything, I failed to make them carry the weight of what happened.

It didn't matter. The point was that if I'd been a *normal* person, things wouldn't have affected me like they did. After all, girls throwing other girls under the bus for a boy they like isn't rare. Even if they had been best friends since childhood. Even if they both knew he had been lying. Friends betray friends all the time, right? And it doesn't cause normal people to have a complete breakdown. It doesn't land them in Stillview.

The rectangle of light above me hummed and flickered. Going by the nearly white trails worn into the fraying blue carpet and the OUT OF ORDER signs taped to screens of chunky computers lining a wall, which I guessed was yellowed with time and not paint, I'd be lucky if this library's internet worked at all. Once again, I asked myself who in the world didn't have internet at home these days and was sharply reminded of what a fine question that would have been to ask Vivian *before* I came to stay with her. I still would've chosen to come. She was my grandmother, even if I didn't know her at all, and coming here was one of the few choices I could still make for myself.

Vivian and Mom had been estranged since long before I'd come along, but it only took a couple of slightly awkward introductory phone calls and within days, I found myself two hours even more upstate here in Elmwood to claw around my roots and see what I could pull up. I thought if I recognized enough of myself in who my mom had been at my age, then maybe I was always meant to break. She had—at least, that was the theory. So maybe I'd been born cracked inside too. If that was true, then at least I could make sense of myself.

It would be a comfort, however cold.

I traced the thin lines of the scars I couldn't feel over the arm of my hoodie as I waited for my laptop to connect, reminding myself that in a few years, they'd hardly be scars at all. Just as the Wi-Fi kicked in, I caught a glimpse of blue jeans and flannel coming my way. I slipped my unconnected headphones over my ears and pretended that my homepage was the most fascinating thing I'd ever seen. For a moment it seemed like my giving the obvious appearance of someone not wanting to be bothered had actually worked, then a man awkwardly sat across from me, despite the room full of empty seats.

I began typing keys randomly in a last, futile effort to dissuade him as he cleared his throat loudly, but when that failed, he dipped his head down to catch my eye. He was around thirty, wore a gray wool cap on top of sandy-colored hair and his beard needed a trim. When he loosened his scarf, the stink of cigarettes wafted off of him. At his almost giddy expression, I braced myself.

"Hate to bother you"—his little smile told me otherwise—"but I saw that Vivian Adair's car dropped you off here, so...would you be *the daughter*?"

Being too young to be Vivian's daughter, I knew who he meant. I got that this was an out-of-the-way town that didn't see many new faces, so mine must stand out as much as my grandmother's old red boat of a Cadillac, but something told me he wasn't asking out of any small-town friendliness. I didn't say anything, unsure of the limited number of paths this would take if I said yep, I was indeed 'the daughter'.

"Talia, right?" He apparently took my silence as confirmation and slapped his knee. "I knew it! You know, she's sort of famous around here. Your mom, I mean. Well, not 'her' her, but her ghost."

"Her...ghost?" It took a second to be sure I'd heard him correctly, and in that second, he gave no sign that he had picked up on the fact that my being the daughter of a missing, *presumed*-dead woman would make bringing her up like this both creepy and cruel.

"Well, yeah," he said as though it were obvious. "We call her the Green Lady, and she's been haunting the woods since—"

"*Nope,*" I decided, snapping my laptop shut and sweeping it back into my bag while expertly encasing my instant panic in a barely perceivable rage.

"Okay, look..." He stood as I did, blocking my path and reaching his hand out just short of touching my arm, tapping it on the table instead.

I looked at his hand and then up to his face. This time, my expression was enough for him to creep his fingers back and raise his hands in a sort of mock surrender. But he was still in my way.

From somewhere behind the shelves came the shush from the librarian. Not that there was anyone else there to disturb, but I took the needed reminder that I wasn't completely alone with this absolute *creep.* I tightened my grip on the strap of my bag and slung it over my shoulder, pushing my way past him as I made straight for the exit. I heard him catch the door before it shut behind me. Great.

I guess I'd figured that by now, no one here would remember much about the woman who went missing from their town. It had been thirteen years after all, and it wasn't like looking at me alone should have been enough to jog anyone's memory. I didn't look much like my beautiful, dark-eyed mother. Once back in tenth grade I did dye my auburn hair black, but I still didn't see much of her in the mirror. The color never really washed out, still clinging to the ends that reached midway down my back.

Considering how she must've come to resent him, I wondered if she had been disappointed to see that along with the hair, I'd also inherited the storm gray eyes of my father. If so, that disappointment would only have deepened as my face too took on the more angular shape of his, and she realized the only time she'd see an echo of herself in the only child she'd pushed out into the world was when I smiled. Everyone said I had my mother's smile.

"Hey!" He jogged up alongside me. "So, let's start over. I'm Wes—"

"No," I said, and changed direction, stepping into the nearly empty street.

All I wanted to do today was get online, maybe check some emails, make sure the rest of the world was still there, yet I'd managed to not even accomplish that. I wanted to believe that this creep, *Wes* apparently, was a fluke. A sort of town idiot maybe. I couldn't afford trips to town to be a minefield of volatile social interaction, but exploring the place where Mom had grown up hadn't been soured by this alone.

On my first day here, I'd stopped in the only convenience store around. The cashier eyed me disdainfully the whole time she rang up my snacks. She was a round woman who could have easily been either twenty or forty, and I might have assumed I was being paranoid if she hadn't gone ahead and asked if I was "one of those Satan worshippers" with a nod toward the T-shirt I was wearing—it was black with a graphic of the cycles of the moon across the chest. I was genuinely unsure if she was making some sort of joke or if she really thought that Satan ran the moon these days, but going by the card-sized gospel tract with the word "REPENT" in bold type placed into my hand along with my change, I'd say it was the latter.

Whatever my plan might've turned into, there was no way I'd be staying in Elmwood very long.

"Just listen a minute," Wes said, exasperated as he continued to follow me. "If you're staying in that house, you should know...she's back in those woods. The Green Lady—*your mother*."

When all else fails, I default to manners in threatening situations. No matter how many times the idea was disproven, I still wanted to believe that it was harder to hurt someone if they were being kind to you. So I ignored him until he tugged on my bag, then I politely seethed, "Please let go."

"Fine." He released it, his mouth becoming a thin line. "But she'll try to drag you back into the dark with her, you know, she told me—" His mouth clamped shut and eyes went wide, a sheen of sweat appearing on his brow as he abruptly turned away. It wasn't until he rounded the corner that I realized my hand had balled itself into a fist, nails starting to cut into my palm.

I took a deep breath, then another, before marching off in the opposite direction, passing a schoolyard filled with the shouts and laughter of kids at recess and feeling sharply jealous of their normal, safe little lives.

I was supposed to call for a ride back, but that was when I thought I was going to be here for a while, and Vivian didn't own a cell phone. It was fine though. Walking helped clear my head, and I doubted even the nearly two-mile hike back to the house would be enough to wipe whatever just happened away.

3

Crossroads

The sky had been alternating between blue and gray, and now the clouds were taking their turn again, dropping the temperature a good ten degrees. I pulled up my hood, coiling my hair back into it as I made my way toward the main road. Once I made it to the bridge over the river, there wouldn't be any more sidewalk, just grass and dirt between the alternating fields of corn and soil on either side of the road. I didn't wonder why Mom had left this place—either time that she had done so.

It was just that last one that really stuck.

Elmwood was about fifty square miles of woods broken up by rural patches of farmland and houses. It hadn't been too difficult to be completely combed over by the hundred or so volunteers that had joined the search for her. They'd found nothing. Her car, still freshly packed from leaving her husband and daughter, was still in Vivian's driveway. She was just gone.

"...*not her but her ghost...*"

I rolled my eyes at the thought. If my mother really had died, she had gone off to do it somewhere else, and I doubt she would have come back here just for the luxury of haunting the place. She wasn't much younger than me when she left it the first time. She must've been a whole lot braver though. Taking off to start a new life in as far away a place as New Orleans had to be as scary as it was exciting. It was weird to think of my parents as teenagers, and it was weirder to know how in love they must have been to just run away together. She must have really loved my father once, after all.

I'd gradually hoarded pictures of the two of them from back when Dad had hair longer than mine. In them, Mom looked like I remembered her, wearing her slightly sardonic smile that matched my own. Dad was a musician who bounced around from band to band. She had some ambition to be a photographer. They were happy, but they were dreamers, and maybe those two things didn't sit well together for long.

I'd saved some of the black and white shots she'd taken of my father, but the ones I'd kept on my wall were what she captured randomly: strangers on the streetcar, at bars, in the park; photos of old mansions and mausoleums.All the random moments of life seen through her eyes, those were the ones I liked best.

The rest I kept in a shoebox. I'd looked at them so often, I didn't need to open it to see every image inside. All of the Polaroids and photo booth strips of her and my dad being together, being young. Happy. Fun. I kept it under my bed, a cardboard coffin for a life I hadn't been a part of but still somehow yearned for.

I did not bring that box with me when I came to Elmwood.

It stung that Mom had been reduced to a ghost story by some town yokel. If she were a ghost, she was all mine, quietly haunting my heart and infecting me with a grief whose reappearance I lost the ability to predict. Once the chemical fog of the medication had lifted, that grief liked to ambush me more often. It would strike quick—cutting deep before I even noticed what had called it close. I can't even blame the meds for screwing up my brain like this. I've always hated how easily I let things get to me. I just used to be quicker at burying them. Even thinking of her now had me squeezing my eyes tight to crush away the threat of tears.

It wasn't fair to still be mourning someone I hadn't known since I was six.

It also wasn't fair if I'd inherited her instability but none of her strength. Even as a teen she'd been bold, knew what she wanted and seized it. While I, on the other hand, found myself struggling with making decisions at all. Once I'd regained the right to make them.

At not quite eighteen, I hadn't had a choice about the asylum, which yes, I know wasn't really an *asylum*. Asylums hadn't had shiny brochures featuring rows of smiling doctors all dressed in neutral tones and a three-star rating on Google.

I hadn't had a choice about the pills either. They weren't going to let me leave until I agreed to take medication, to let it hook firmly into my brain and flatten me. That's the best way to describe it really. When the wholly unpleasant side effects wore off, I was left *flat*. I'd been expecting numb—numb would have been a welcome break—instead it was like someone had spread thin all that had gotten tangled up inside my skull with the back of a knife. Everything was level with a tautness to the edges I hardly noticed after a while, and when I did, it was like catching a shadow out of the corner of your eye. Easily dismissed and forgotten.

I stopped dreaming—I was grateful. But I couldn't paint anymore either, and that bothered me. Not that I was going to be using that art scholarship now anyway. I'd become pretty ambivalent about most things, like what I should wear or eat, or whether or not I could make it past the nurses and up to the limestone roof of that old hospital and step off of it without my pulse raising a single beat. That kind of thing was probably not the sort of thing the pills advertised, but I didn't mention any of that.

Instead, I said whatever I thought they needed to hear to release me, and once home, I began cutting those little blue chemical spheres out of my diet until they were completely out of my system. My head gradually filled back up with familiar, comforting clutter, and it was time to figure out how to move on with my life. Or how to begin it, really.

Only, every time I tried to consider something practical like college, or form any kind of plan, I hit a wall. There was this nagging sense that something was left undone and a fear that warned against trying to ignore it—that doing so would only prove to be an anchor around my neck. My dreams roared back as panicked vignettes where I suddenly realized I'd forgotten something vital but couldn't remember where, or even what, it was.

For some reason, thoughts of Mom roared back too. I began to wonder if this was how she felt before she packed up and left me and Dad. Alone. Stagnant. *Stuck.*

I shoved my hands in my pockets, grateful that my leggings were warm and my boots were comfortable. As often as my head needed clearing, it would be impossible to guess the number of miles I'd walked in the last year alone to do so. Back home, I preferred strolling cemeteries to the parks. Cemeteries always seemed safer. Once you stepped off the paths there, you would rarely see another person. It felt a little forbidden. I had always liked being where it felt like people didn't belong. Just the same, I would still carry this fancy little folding knife in my bag that I'd picked up at a Ren Faire when I was thirteen, just in case.

As the sidewalk ended, a truck rumbled by—likely to be the only vehicle I'd see the whole walk home. I paused over the bridge to look at the river, which I suppose was normally a prettier sight, but today it looked bleak. The lush spread of autumn-lit trees that flanked the water were all muted in the October light. From some hidden place in those rust-colored leaves, crows began their tuneless song, their grating call echoing from all directions despite there not being a single feather in sight.

The cawing began to swell louder, and dread began to bloom in my chest as the chaotic noise suddenly seemed to engulf everything. My hands covered my ears as I hurried from the bridge, panic rising with each step until I finally broke into a run.

I hadn't gotten far, when just as fast as it had come, the cawing ceased entirely. Standing in abrupt silence in the middle of a crossroad, I looked up at the completely bird-free sky and then back to the bridge, the pounding of my heart at odds with the tranquil scenery that I had just fled from like a mad woman.

It's okay.

Gradually came the distant twittering of sparrows. I focused on the yellow line of the road, and then on my breath, drawing it out and keeping it even. *I'm okay. A weird panic attack, that's all, but it's done.* Maybe it was the sight of the river that triggered it. I used to be afraid of dark water, and the old aversion to it kicked up now and then, though never like this.

Further down the road, yellow tape tied around some trees flickered in the breeze. I continued up the road at my city-dweller's pace, sidewalk or not. I'd promised myself that when I came here, I was going to leave all of my old stress behind so that I could move forward. That stress had gotten too strong and knew all of my weaknesses, so I would lock that mess away in its own little snow globe.

Here in Elmwood, I could find new stress, *exciting* stress, stress that I could still handle. But if even a small town like this could overwhelm me, then there was probably no hope for me. Maybe I should just stick to the house for a while.

I really needed to talk to Vivian about that internet situation.

4

Half Shuttered

The Adair house was set back about a quarter mile from the road, and because of the curve of the drive, it wasn't visible from where I opened the rusty blue mailbox to the cascade of envelopes and flyers. Gathering up the paper mess, I started down the path, and I wondered if I'd be here long enough to know how much of a nightmare it would be to keep it clear once winter hit. I tried imagining my slim, stylish grandmother out there in a snowsuit with a shovel, and I just couldn't see it. She seemed to tolerate people about as well as I did these days, so it was entirely possible she just didn't leave the house at all until spring.

Of course, I was still getting to know her. Vivian spent a good chunk of time as a mostly closeted alcoholic, which is what led to my mother's estrangement from her. From what Dad told me, Mom must've been pretty desperate to escape the life she had with us to ever return here. Then again, seeing as she disappeared the very same day, maybe she just needed that quick reminder of why she'd run off at sixteen in the first place.

But whoever Vivian had been, she was different now. For one, she didn't drink anymore. From what I could smell coming from her room, it seemed that she'd swapped martinis for weed. I still wouldn't

have called her *warm* exactly, but I wouldn't have described myself
that way either, so I couldn't really fault her for it. At least she was
making an effort to establish a relationship with my mother's only
living relative, just as I was.

It had been slow-going.

From the beginning, she asked that I not call her 'grandmother'
or any of its derivatives. "It's not a title I've earned, dear," she'd said,
tapping a silver spoon on a flowered saucer. "And it's too matronly."

Fair enough, as she was far from matronly. She must have been in
her late sixties at least but didn't look it. Her lightly creased face was
usually framed with strands of the silvery gold hair she kept pinned up
around it. It was the face of someone who had always been beautiful.
And not only had her figure managed to not be destroyed by the years
of drinking, but everything she wore seemed tailored to it. She lived in
long belted skirts, silk blouses, and layers of gem and crystal jewelry.
In the evenings, she changed into colorful kimonos and wrapped her
hair in a scarf, making her look like she'd be just as at home wandering
art galleries in Paris as she would reading fortunes out of a caravan,
but Vivian didn't have much interest in leaving Elmwood, or even the
house, at all.

Once I reached the curve, the house stretched into view. Whenever I
saw its weathered white walls climbing out of the fluttering sea of trees,
I pictured what it must've been like when the first round of Adairs
built it nearly two hundred years ago. The shuttered up windows on
one side gave it a half-derelict look, but for some reason I imagined it
as having been a happy home. Once upon a time.

It was a huge house, a mansion really, a place made for a family.
There were once probably a dozen laughing kids running up and
down the mahogany staircase, playing whatever games Victorian kids
played while old Mom and Pop Adair sat in matching rockers on

the wraparound porch, watching the butterflies dance in the garden. The home had been out of place, a cultivated square of civilization against the surrounding wild of the woods. It was still that at least, but these walls were no longer as welcoming, and if those children ever really existed, they had lived and died long ago, leaving none of their happiness behind.

Before last week, I had been there only once. When I was five, there had been a brief break in the estrangement between my mother and hers, and I had been brought along on a visit. I didn't remember too much about Vivian; it was the *house* that stayed with me.

To me, it looked like your standard haunted house from the outside. At that age, if a place wasn't lived in, it seemed safe to assume that ghosts had taken it over. A dead thing for dead things. But this house was only half dead. My grandfather had passed away long before, so she closed half of it off to save on upkeep. Each floor had a door that divided the house, like it had been built to be split up one day. The rooms beyond the closed dividing doors were still used for storage, but much to my disappointment, I hadn't been allowed to see them.

I'd wondered if the ghosts kept to their side of the house out of a sense of politeness or if they explored at night, looking into the other bedrooms as their warm neighbors slept unaware.

The living side of the house on the other hand, was stunning to a child whose apartment was filled with mismatched furniture picked up from garage sales. It was all ornate wooden things, richly upholstered and beautifully carved. The polished banister of the staircase was the same cherry brown as the paneled walls, and I badly wanted to slide down it, but I don't remember it as a particularly fun place. I *do* remember being fascinated by the walls; every room had a different motif. In some places the wallpaper was velvety to the touch, and in others it was uniform, intricate designs. The dining room had rose-colored, swirling, floral patterns threaded with gold that were almost hypnotic when the light hit it. I tried to replicate that pattern on my own boring beige walls that night with crayons that were then taken away from me for a week.

The many paintings and old photos in thick old frames that hung there were less exciting, though I could easily spot which of the children in those old frames were Mom. The large dark eyes and close-lipped smile had stayed just the same. Over one of the fireplaces hung a portrait of her as a toddler in a red holiday dress, a tartan bow in her black curls. She sat on the lap of a lady wearing a black evening gown with thick blonde waves that cascaded over her shoulder, pearls at her throat. She looked like someone out of a magazine, and I would not have guessed that it was really my grandmother. The woman in the portrait and the woman that lived with it had the same cultured, manicured appearance, but the one that sat on the sofa smoking one slender cigarette after another seemed far more uncomfortable in her skin. I don't know if she even spoke to me at all.

The visit had been brief. Afterward, Mom held me to her tighter than before. Maybe it was after this that she became quieter, that she would stare long at nothing. She would be gone within a year.

The house itself had changed little since. The garden that had once been so overgrown that I wasn't allowed near it for fear of snakes was now well tended to. It had become one of Sober Vivian's hobbies. Probably because that's where she grew her weed.

I got here before the first frost, and wild splashes of color still held on to thick- leaved bushes that rose neatly from urns along the little stone barrier wall. It was odd to me that the dining room, which offered the best view of the now thriving garden, had its windows shuttered. The light coming in through the pretty hatched glass had once made the wallpaper seem to dance, but now Vivian kept them shut year-round. All that sun gave her a headache, she said.

I nearly dropped all I carried while trying to dig the keys out of my side pocket when I reached the door. I'd heard that people in little towns often felt safe enough to leave their doors unlocked. Vivian was not one of those people.

There was the original door lock plus two deadbolts on both the front and back doors, not to mention an old alarm system. The house was more secure than any place I'd ever stayed growing up, and according to the crime report in the county paper, the worst things that had happened here this month were three DUI's and one case of vandalism involving garden gnomes.

Still, there had been several times where we'd been sitting in the living room together, watching the old wood-encased television, and she would suddenly hit the mute button and straighten up, glancing at the door, and ask me to please check the locks.

"You know, maybe you should consider at least getting a motion-activated light," I suggested after checking the locks for the third time that night, "if you're worried about someone sneaking around out there."

There was nothing for your average thief here, no cash that I knew of, and no electronics made this century. But maybe there was some kind of sad but brazen antiques junkie that would find it worth their while to trek all the way out here in hopes of getting their fix of unpolished silverware or some good old brass candlesticks. What did I know?

Vivian hummed, her eyes especially glazed. "I had them once. They were always setting them off."

"Who?"

"All kinds." She didn't turn away from her favorite fictional crime show. It was always on, and she watched it the old-fashioned way—where you had to sit through commercial breaks and opening credits.

I tilted my head. "Of what?"

"Oh." She glanced at me like she'd forgotten I was there for a second. "Raccoons or bats. Bears."

"Well." I'd never had to consider the wildlife in a place I was living before, but I was still pretty sure there were no bears in the small town of Elmwood. "If all of those things are out there, then it's probably unlikely any people would be."

"Yes, dear. That's why we keep them locked."

I kicked the heavy door shut behind me and made it to the alcove to the left before releasing a sprawling junk mail tide onto the polished circle table. Dropping my bag on one of the fading green chairs, I wiped my hands together with a satisfied sigh, ignoring the soft folding sound as several papers drifted down to the hardwood floor. After slipping off my boots, I turned past the staircase to head into the kitchen to scrounge for food.

As quiet as it was, I knew Vivian must be napping. She did that often—said she needed all the beauty rest she could get. When she was awake, there was music. Everything from Velvet Underground to Bessie Smith to Leonard Cohen spun on the record player that lived in the giant old console in her bedroom. She didn't like things to be quiet, and sound carried well in this house.

Often while I'd lie awake in the middle of the night, I'd hear her on the stairs. I wanted to think that maybe she was just going down for a glass of water or to watch some TV because she couldn't sleep either, but part of me just knew she was going to check the locks.

5

Divided

It was noon when I finished up my lunch. I couldn't help but know this because the clocks began to chime—a sound so jarring that as on edge as I already was, I actually jumped and sent my glass shattering to the floor.

There were six clocks by my count, and none of them were synced with the others, making the chiming a parade of various tones that lasted for several minutes. With the hollow reverberations of the final gong of the grandfather clock, I was reminded that beyond cleaning up the glass, I had absolutely nothing to fill today with. Or the next one. Or the next...

Had I gotten online, I'd planned to order some art supplies. Back when I was some sort of an artist, I never had a problem figuring out what to do with my time. I made art. It wasn't pretty; lots of broad, angry strokes over despairing, deconstructed heads, but it was art. Dad called it 'provocative' in a disturbed but encouraging way. He got that it was cathartic and had been rooting for the art school I was on track to get into. But since my brain got that chemical reboot, the part that used to be able to draw the dark things out of myself and give them shape on canvas so they wouldn't fester inside had gone into a coma. Now, I didn't remember the last time I'd so much as made a doodle.

A few days into my stay, boredom had driven me to try to find some pencils in the old writing desk that sat in the red room off of the entryway—the one with all the excessive seating and that painting of Mom and Vivian. Not having any luck there, I wandered to the once-forbidden dividing door at the end of the hallway. The one that lead to the dormant side of the house. It turned out, Vivian kept these dividing doors locked too.

She'd explained that the lighting didn't work over there, and with the windows shuttered, it was too dark to see, even during the day. And of course, she could never remember where the flashlight was. But as I opened the cabinet beneath the sink to replace the roll of paper towels I'd used cleaning up the glass spill, I saw it. There, all the way in the back, was an old chrome flashlight. It was heavy as a hammer, but it worked.

Boredom and the curiosity of my inner five-year-old made me climb the stairs and quietly open the door to Vivian's bedroom. I was greeted by the thick smell of old incense and hazy sunlight peeking out from behind heavy curtains. She didn't stir as I slipped the key ring off the hook, careful to hold my hands over the metal row of them to stop them from jingling, before just as carefully shutting the door behind me and creeping back downstairs.

The bedrooms had long metal keys resting in their locks, should anyone want more privacy. However, like my little knife, the security that came with them was false when there was a skeleton key that could unlock any of them. The key ring was a mix of about a dozen flat, stubby, modern keys and long heavier ones of brass.

At this point, I supposed I shouldn't have found it odd that Vivian had installed deadbolts on the dividing doors as well. I cycled through four keys before finding the right one for it. Then onto the original lock. The key with the longest tip also had the most ornamental handle. I'm a sucker for aesthetics so that's the first one I went with, feeling a stab of shame just before I turned it. I was being sneaky, but then, she didn't exactly say that I *couldn't* look into these rooms...just that they were too dark.

With the click of the lock, the door opened to cool, stale air. I stepped into the hall. To my right was a curved archway leading into a large room. I could only just make out the shapes of covered furniture beyond it in the light from the doorway. Vivian wasn't kidding about the dark. The shutters covering the windows weren't the kind with slats that allowed in slivers of light, more like small doors—all latched shut. The further I went in, the darker it got.

Just outside the reach of the dim, yellow beam of the flashlight, against the wall at the edge of that darkness, a shrouded figure stood tall and still. Maybe it was the eeriness that came with being in a room where everything was dressed as ghosts, but suddenly I was five again and afraid of the dark.

It would be possible, my asshole brain told me, *for someone to have slipped in through an unlocked window. No one would've heard them from our side of the house. They could've been here for days, longer even...*

But that's silly, my good brain argued. *Why would anyone break into a house just to hide?*

Not just hide. Wait. Wait for someone to open the door and let them into the warmth. Vivian has been here for years and even she thinks that someone is out there trying to get in...

No, asshole brain, not today.

I looked up at the hidden figure, swallowing down my almost certainly irrational fear as I reached out for the sheet and pulled, my breath catching at an unexpected sound coming from beneath it.

Beads.

Only beads dangling from the stained-glass bottom of a lampshade tinkled as the sheet fell. I exhaled, feeling silly. The metal string clicked as I tugged it a few times. No light happened, but the flashlight flickered. Maybe that was enough exploring for today anyway.

Something sticking out from under a nearby table caught my eye just as I went to leave. I moved the light on an old...cassette player? A small pile of paperbacks sat next to it. I squinted closer at the couple of vampire novels and a collection of poetry. Looked like I wasn't the only one that borrowed Vivian's keys without asking.

I shined the dying flashlight around the room. There were more chairs, a couch, another fireplace—and an eerie face manifesting from the darkness in front of me. My blood turned to ice.

It took me a very tense second to recognize my own reflection in a mirror that ran along the length of the mantle. I breathed a bigger sigh of relief and felt even sillier than before.

I didn't know much about where the Adairs had come from, but taking in the room, I gathered that apparently it was from money. They'd had a store in town. I'd seen it before in some sepia-colored photograph on one of the walls. Unless Elmwood had once been way more booming, that still didn't explain the house. Maybe they'd struck oil or gold somewhere before settling there, and there was a fortune hidden in the floorboards. At least that would explain all of Vivian's security measures.

The next room looked more interesting: floor-to-ceiling bookshelves lined with rows of leather-bound books broken up by decorative knick-knacks and statuettes. The books were old, some with unreadable titles. If I'd had more time, I would have liked to look through them and see if they held any of the family, *my* family, history. Being raised by a single dad with no extended family in our lives, it was pretty fascinating to be so close to any bit of my ancestry.

A huge desk sat uncovered toward the back of the room. Detailed carvings of leaves decorated the drawers and cabinets that were all locked when I tugged on them. On the carpet near my feet were a couple more paperbacks, discarded as though they had been read on the floor there. I wondered how many more traces of Mom I would find on this side where I imagined she came to hide from Vivian.

The flashlight flickered again, the light landing on an oddly reflective oblong box before it died completely, and I stood in nearly total darkness. And quiet. After unsuccessfully trying to smack the light back on, I somehow managed to make it back to the door without tripping, but I hesitated before closing it back up.

I didn't know when I'd have the opportunity to come back here and wanted to see more evidence of my mother's small rebellions. I wanted to poke around those shelves more too. I weighed the idea of lighting some of the many candlesticks stashed in the drawers against the flammability of the furniture coverings and my own general gracelessness when I remembered: my phone had a flashlight.

Okay, I'd just take five more minutes. Then I'd lock everything back up and return the keys, satisfied. Quietly, I rushed out of the room, using the banister to slide myself around in my socked feet, and grabbed my bag from the chair. After my hand searched its depths and inner pockets, I realized with something akin to horror that my phone was gone.

6

Come See

After dumping the contents of my bag on the table and frantically crawling around the floor for a few minutes like some sort of burrowing creature, I gave up. Fortunately, there was a little table topped with jade-colored marble along the wall of the staircase whose only job was to hold the cradle of one of the two house phones. This one was a silver and black square and had a built-in answering machine, making it the most advanced piece of technology in the house. The one in Vivian's room wasn't even cordless.

I awkwardly pushed my own number into the buttons, thankful that at least it wasn't a rotary dial, then listened for the melody of my ringtone. My heart sank when I didn't hear it. I was *certain* that I would've slid it into my bag along with my laptop if I had taken it out at the library. Well, mostly certain. Unless....

That creep, *Wes.* Could he have taken it without my noticing? Had I fallen for the old, Distract Someone By Making a Mockery of Their Likely Dead Parent in Order to Steal Their Mostly Worthless Two-Year-Old Phone, bit? Could he have reached into my bag when he grabbed hold of it, while I had been distracted by his disturbing lack of boundaries? No, he didn't strike me as smooth or nimble enough. It must have fallen out somewhere, maybe when I'd gathered up the mail? I could only hope that was the case, otherwise I'd have to retrace my steps all the way back to town.

The thing was, I hardly even used my phone much anymore, but the *idea* of it was still comforting. I cut people out of my life easily after Stillview, blocking my former friends' numbers and deleting my social media without regret. It helped with my anxiety at first. But I couldn't control the possibilities of who I might run into in the wild. Everyone became a potential source of panic. Someone might ask things or, maybe worse, *avoid* asking things. Their faces would be smiling but I would know better.

I started to not want to leave the apartment, but I didn't want Dad to worry, so I would make a point to occasionally tell him that I was going to meet up with some familiar name and spend time wandering around the city's huge cemetery instead. That was one thing I could appreciate about the town of Elmwood—I didn't have to see another person for miles.

The brilliant blue that had taken over the sky cast things in a more pleasant light. Rows of trees along the concrete lane were partially dressed in golds and greens, in roses and rusts. The sun was warm on my face and despite...everything, I felt a moment of surging content-ment. For just that moment, I thought maybe I could stay here and pretend there was no world beyond this place, just like Vivian seemed to do. There was too much looming from my past to have any hope of future peace, so maybe it would be better to just put everything off forever and let myself grow old alone beneath the shady watch of these old Sycamores.

I conjured an image of Mom looking down on an ocean of trees from some hilltop, walking stick in hand, her sardonic smile gone wiz-ened and serene. I still did that sometimes—imagined her as secretly alive somewhere; secluded and hidden. I wondered if that was the life she had longed for when she left me. A life safe from living.

I had read and reread all the articles on her disappearance. Most of them didn't say much beyond the "Local Woman Goes Missing" headline. In the beginning. Then as the time gaps between the articles widened, the picture painted was more grim: a depressed woman, an abandoned car with her purse and keys inside. There was never foul play suspected, not that the papers talked about anyway. That no sign of her ever resurfacing anywhere could be found, the insinuation became that she had gone off somewhere to die. Like some wounded animal.

Still, it was possible for her to have somehow skipped town and reinvented herself somewhere else. At least then she could be alive somewhere. If she was alive, then she might remember to miss me, and if she missed me, she might come back. This idea comforted me as a kid. I used to keep myself up at night concocting scenarios where she could both be alive...and forgiven for leaving me behind. Witness Protection program. Secret mafia boyfriend. She could have been kidnapped, brainwashed, and was now one of some cult leader's wives. Or maybe she had simply snapped and snuck across the border into Canada where she began taming moose and hunting men for sport. Anything was better than believing that she could be alive and just not want to be my mother anymore.

I was halfway to the road, nearing the curve in the drive as my eyes searched the ground, when I heard a small, out-of-place sound woven into the crinkling of leaves in a strengthening breeze. Birds maybe, but because of my asshole brain, I instantly started thinking of Vivian and her talk of bears. What does a bear even sound like?

I heard it again. It was definitely not a bear. It wasn't any animal. It was... singing? Or laughing? A voice, yes, but just as I tried to narrow down where it could be coming from, it was gone again. I started walking faster, just rounding the turn when a sudden wail from behind me caused me to jump and spin around to see no one there.

I stood still, heart galloping in my suddenly-too-small ribcage. Maybe the sound was being carried strangely because of the wind, but it hadn't been my imagination. I'd heard what was unmistakably a girl's voice, and it had been right next to me.

"Hello?" My voice came out more timid than I would have liked.

I waited for a moment before slowly turning back toward the road. I wanted to run, but something told me not to do that. Animals will chase you if you run, and I willed myself not to think about what else it might be if not an animal. Someone may be hurt. Or someone may be messing with me. I didn't know what else to do, so I resumed walking, calmly, keeping my breath steady. Three steps later, I caught movement out of the corner of my eye and froze.

There was a child standing just off the path. A little girl of maybe five or six with dark hair and a faded green dress. Her hands were behind her back, head tilted slightly as she watched me stop in my tracks. I had nearly walked right past her.

"Hello," she said, her voice sweet as a child's voice ought to be, but it didn't make me relax any.

"Hi?" I wasn't comfortable around children, but I was relieved that it was only another person there, no matter how small, and not a bear of any size. "What are you doing out here by yourself?"

"I was playing in the flower field with Starry Anna—that's my doll—while my mam went walking." The girl's accent was slight but surprising. "I don't like taking walks, they make my toes hurt." She held up a little Mary-Jane-clad foot off the ground to show me. "But now I've lost Starry Anna, so I took a small walk to find her and went off the path, just a *tiny* bit, and now I can't find it again."

I knew nothing about these woods and had no idea about any paths that may go through them. I could only assume this girl's family lived nearby, but she seemed awfully young to be left alone anywhere at all.

"Sorry, I haven't seen your mom. How far back is the path?"

"Hmm." The girl looked behind her and shrugged. "Maybe just...seventy-teen trees?"

"Right." I sighed. "Well, your mom is probably missing you. Why don't you come with me until we can figure out—"

"Oh no! Mercy me, miss." She shook her head, her eyes wide. "Horrible things happen when little children go off with strangers. Don't you know that? Starry Anna told me so."

"Starry Anna is wise. My name is Talia, what's yours?"

"I'm called Maevyn." She glanced behind her then turned to me with a smile. She was missing a front tooth. "Well now I s'pose we're friends...so it'd be alright if you come to help find Starry Anna!"

With a quick relieved grin, she turned, darting into the woods before I had the chance to tell her to stop. I called after her, but she had already been swallowed up by the trees. There was a split second of indecision, but I couldn't let a little kid wander lost in there. I ran in after her.

Green ribbon bounced down the back of her hair as her small shape skipped through the branches ahead. "Have you seen the flower field?" she asked, merrily glancing back at me without stopping.

"No. And please come back here—you'll get us both lost." I couldn't run to keep up with those little legs that were so much quicker at sidestepping around the trunks and roots of the wood's floor than I was.

"Oh, but it's so lovely there! There are primroses and daffodils, larkspurs and foxgloves, Queen Anne's lace and bluebells and forg et-me-nots..."

"Jesus," I muttered, ducking under a branch. I could still tell where we had entered behind me, but that was about to change as the ground began to slope downward.

"Once we find Starry Anna, we can have a dance." The girl bounded back to me, her eyes shining with such excitement that I guessed she might not have many real playmates. "Some of the flowers are taller than me!"

There was at least plenty of light coming in through the canopy of leaves above us, and I could see there was a boulder coming up below that would make a decent landmark. "Sure, but I want you to look around for a second and see if anything looks like something you might have seen before you found me, okay?"

"Just down *there* is the path, and a ways down it lies the field." She pointed ahead, tugging on my sleeve. I followed her, deciding that if I didn't see a path more than a few feet from the boulder, then I was out. I would go back to the house and call the police to let them know there was a manic child roaming the woods alone and hope for the best.

"See there?" she said rather triumphantly as the ground evened out to reveal a wide, clear path ahead. "That is my path and my mam's, and now it can be yours too!"

She skipped alongside me, humming a pretty, unfamiliar song. It would make sense if this path were connected to another property, but it would have to be set back pretty deeply into the woods for it not to be visible from Vivian's house. I suppose if there were a house nearby, it might explain why this girl's mother felt safe enough to leave her alone in some field. Her dress wasn't the sort of thing I would've even been allowed to play outside in. And wasn't today a school day? Maybe her family was one of those off-grid, homesteader types. I'd heard that out-of-the-way towns like this attracted them.

"Look!" Maevyn pointed to a circular stone structure in a clearing that looked like an old well—the sort of thing you wouldn't want a small child playing around, so of course she headed right towards it. I went to follow her, but once again, I was struck with that same inexplicable sense of dread as before on the bridge.

"Come see, come see!" she called. "It is here that leads to the flowering field with lilies and marigolds and chrysanthemums and poppies and...."

While she twirled about and recited what had to be every flower known to man, I was focused instead on the sky and the black birds flying in a twisting wave formation, dispersing themselves onto surrounding branches. There were dozens of them, but not one made a sound.

"Come now, miss." The girl's sing-song voice was in my ear now, but my eyes were still set on the trees that had gone black with those birds that sat silently, tilting their heads toward each other as though whispering secrets. I thought they were crows, crows as big as cats, but with a glimmer of color on the feathered backs of the too few that were not watching me.

Once more, that laughter-song I'd heard on the driveway whispered from somewhere. Then from everywhere. I whirled around to see Maevyn now at eye-level. Standing on the wall of that well. I hadn't noticed when I drifted off the path to be standing beside her, but it was a good thing that I had because the well was uncovered and easily wide enough for a person to fall straight into.

"Careful, Maevyn." I was more annoyed than alarmed, but more than anything, I was confused. "It's not safe, we should—"

The child's laugh reminded me of breaking glass as she stood on one foot and hopped along the edge. "Oh, but it is, miss. It is. Come see!"

She was reaching for my hand with hers, small and black with dirt. Had it always been so filthy? It looked like she had been digging in tar, but still I moved to take it, stopping when I saw her face. There was something that glimmered in her green eyes, something like mischief but much colder.

It's just a kid. A little girl. This is just some weird stress reaction that's making everything seem wrong.

Still, the way the girl's eyes held mine and the way her lips curled up made me want to back away. Slowly. But no, I needed to take her hand. Didn't I? I needed to follow her. I was looking for something, and she was going to lead me to it. That's right, I needed to find Starry Anna. I needed to take Maevyn's hand and then I'd find what I had been looking for. With great effort, I managed to drag my eyes down before my hand reached hers, which made me hesitate.

Maevyn's fingers were long, much too long. They curved in a twisting way that fingers should not. Strange that I hadn't noticed that before—but I could wonder about that later. For now, I just needed to let those black fingers twine around mine so that we could go down to the flower field. The flower field where we could dance. Yet dimly, I was becoming aware of a sound, sharp and bothersome. The more I tried to focus on what it might be, the louder it became until it was distracting enough that I had to look for what was making it.

"*Miss!*" Maevyn hissed as the sound sharpened.

It was *barking*. A black dog was on an incline above me. Soft dirt slid down between exposed roots as the beast stamped its paws at the edge of the steep drop as though it was desperate to get down to me, but was unsure about the jump. Behind it, a frazzled, irritated-looking woman emerged. One hand flew to her chest when her eyes fell on me, the other gripped the base of the dog's neck to keep it still.

She was calling to me, I thought, and frantically waving. She didn't look much older than me. She also didn't look like she should be here. Then I remembered that I probably didn't either. She was saying something, asking me if I was all right.

I could only blink.

I blinked again, this time with a growing awareness that I wasn't where I thought I was anymore. The path was nowhere to be seen, neither was the well, and in the place where Maevyn had stood was a pond, still and covered with the shadows of trees. I stood at the very edge, water seeping into the toes of my socks through my boots as though I had been there for some time. Behind me, in the mud, there were only my own footsteps.

I half stumbled back from the pond. I didn't see an easy way to get up the slope and had no memory of getting down it in the first place. The girl hurried to grip a skinny tree with one hand, extending down her free one to me. With her help, I was able to gracelessly scramble back to higher ground. Mumbling my thanks to her, I tried uselessly to brush the dirt from my leggings.

"There was—" I began to explain, turning back to that lonely little pond. "I...I thought I saw a little girl."

"No." She shook her head, worry in her hazel eyes. "Whatever you thought you saw in that water was no little girl."

7

Talking to Ghosts

So anyway, this is what it feels like to be insane.

Knowing that something had happened that also could not possibly have happened was viscerally unpleasant. I'd gone quivery and slightly nauseous and didn't trust myself to speak. If my mental health had just taken a flying leap into outright hallucinations, then I'd rather keep it to myself. And if that wasn't the case... then I'd almost rather not know. There was at least something definable about mental illness, something possibly treatable—whereas the alternative was, well, the alternative that *I* was fine, but reality had just been torn apart.

The fawnish color of the girl's skin was flushed. Her black hair fell loose across one side of her head and was shaved on the other where a row of silver circles wrapped the top of her ear. She was certainly looking at me like I was insane. I had the urge to tell her the truth, but I knew now there had been no lost child with a missing doll or a wandering mother with questionable parenting skills. No path either by the look of it.

Yet, there had been *something*. Something that wanted me to believe all of those things. Something that wanted to be seen as harmless. I needed this girl to understand all of this, but for the life of me, I couldn't figure out any way of laying the words out that wouldn't sound seven shades of crazy.

"Ponds in here can be deeper than they look, and mud can stick you right in them like glue if you let it." She swept her eyes over me. "You aren't from around here." It wasn't a question, and she didn't wait for a response before turning away. "Well, come on. I hate being this far in."

I didn't have to be told twice.

She was taller than me, but half hidden under a leather jacket that was at least two sizes too big. That jacket might've been older than both of us going by how cracked and worn it was in places. On its back, painted in a shade of blue that I just noticed matched the tips of her hair, was a centaur with its bow raised at a moon. The centaur was obviously a later addition going by the freshness of the paint. I focused on it, not wanting to look around and catch the eyes of something pretending to be a little girl looking back at me.

"You're lucky. I was driving home when Cinder started barking up a storm. I slowed down to check on her, and she jumped right out of the back of the truck." She patted the dog's side. "I figured she got a whiff of something by the way she took off."

Cinder was, if I had to guess, some sort of shepherd mixed with a wolf that was made entirely of charcoal. Her ears stood stiff and alert and her mane puffed out beneath them, billowing down her whole body so that when in motion, the thick, shaggy strands of fur gave the impression that she was dripping black ink. She would probably be more intimidating if not for the dopey expression that seemed to be the default setting of her narrow face. Seeming to know that she was being talked about, her tail began to wag.

"I chased her until I came across you"—she threw me a look over her shoulder—"talking to ghosts."

I wanted to tell her that I didn't believe in ghosts because that had been true when I woke up this morning. Now I didn't know what to believe. Suddenly I was thinking of Mom, and all sorts of new ideas about what might have happened to her were blooming in my head. My hands were clammy. I ran them down my hair, resting them at the nape of my neck, digging my nails into the skin just enough to keep any tears at bay.

"So, here's a tip: around here, anytime you can't see the road from the woods, it means you're way too deep in the woods. Oh." She stopped; the concern on her face told me what mine must've looked like. "You...okay?"

I didn't bother saying I wasn't. "Mostly."

"Well, hey look—don't be freaked out. I was kidding about the ghost thing. Mostly. People like to tell scary stories about seeing weird shit in the woods and fields. My brother used to talk to kids in our backyard that weren't there when he was small—really unnerved our folks. The unpopulated places around this town just have that creepy vibe and it's easy to let your imagination go overly vivid. It's normal even. To an extent."

What a strange and dangerous place it would be if something like Maevyn was just a regular occurrence. Oh, the little girl tried to lure you to a watery doom? Yeah, that's a Wednesday thing. Thursdays the trees pull up their roots and wander around in search of human flesh. Couldn't say what happens on the weekends—everyone just knows to lock themselves in their storm cellars at night.

"I'm Mattie, by the way." Mattie had a friendly face with a sharp jaw and rounded cheeks that probably made her look younger than she was. Her eyeliner looked like it might have been from the night before and her black nail polish was half chipped away. She looked like she fit in here in Elmwood about as much as I did.

"Talia." I unclamped my neck and shoved my hands into my hoodie. "I should... How far am I from Ide Road? That's where I'm staying."

"Shit," she said apologetically. "You're Cole Adair's daughter."

"How—?"

"Small town. Only a couple of houses out that way and the families living in them always have. And Vivian is—well everyone knows who Vivian is, especially since...well, since she isn't exactly 'social'. Gotta figure you must be family then. And...I remember seeing on the news that your mom had a daughter. I was only like ten at the time, and I still remember feeling bad for you. Kind of more surreal to come across you now."

"Yeah." I looked away. "I guess it's been that kind of day."

We resumed walking, Cinder trotting ahead. The light that broke through the trees made the shadows of the leaves still on the branches dance on the backs of their fallen family.

"So...the thing is," she said after a minute of silence, "stories feed stories, and a lot of them come from at least a *seed* of reality. Once people start trying to explain what they don't understand with nonsense, it gets all tangled up until no one can pick out what was real about them anymore. So, if you hear anything...*weird* about your mom from anybody just ignore it."

"Oh, you mean like she's some ghost?"

"That ferrety headcase already found out you were here, huh?"

"You make it sound like he was expecting me."

"Wes Samuel's got...problems. Years ago, he said that a ghost had chased him through the woods. Before that, the weirdest thing about him was that he liked to steal shit from people's sheds and dabble in shoplifting, but since whatever happened to him that night, he went a whole other direction of 'off'. Started breaking into houses and rearranging things. Rumor was that he got so bad he got sent to Stillview, but can't say it did him much good if that's true."

I frowned at the thought that if the timing had lined up, I could've been sitting next to him in group therapy. "So...why does he think his green ghost is my mom?"

"Timing. I guess." She shrugged. "Whatever happened with him happened not long after she went missing. I think he just slapped your mom's face on an old urban legend. You know the one where someone sees a woman by the side of the road at night, and when they look at the rearview mirror, she's sitting in the back seat? Well, our town's version is that she's also wearing a long green gown. Boom: Green Lady."

"Have other people seen her?"

"Oh sure. People *say* they have. It's a ghost story. And like I told you, the woods can be dangerous, so at least it keeps people out of them. Generally." She looked behind us as we finally stepped free of the trees. "You *really* don't want to go wandering around in there, especially this time of year."

No worries there. "Why is that?"

"Hunters." She headed toward a red truck parked across the road. Like her jacket, it looked well-worn, too big, but functional. "You know, deer, ducks, rabbits. It's a seasonal thing here. I hear the local kids even get to take off school once season kicks off to hunt. Well, I should say it's *supposed* to be seasonal anyway. I hear random shots echoing out here all year-round. Fall is just when you most see trucks driving by with something dead tied to them—which is always a good reminder to avoid the woods."

I risked looking back to the trees and wondered if other things in there had their own hunting season. My fingers touched a spot of rust on the truck's hood. I could be back home *tonight* if I wanted. Dad would come and get me if I asked. Only it wasn't home anymore.

Nothing had changed that. All that old stress would wrap itself back around me until I was back to being choked by it. I smiled ruefully that the idea of going back to where it felt like the walls were closing in an inch more each day seemed more dangerous to me than whatever had just lured me into the woods.

But more than that, an idea had begun to sprout beneath the fear still buzzing through me. The key to the mystery of what happened to Mom might exist after all. It reached out for me today.

I watched Mattie pop the back of the truck bed open to let Cinder hop in and wanted to tell her that I didn't think that Wes Samuel's being crazy necessarily made him *wrong*, but I didn't want to say anything that would make her suspect that he and I had Stillview in common.

"Point taken. No woods." I said. "And you've got me curious about these town ghost stories. Think I'll look into them whenever I make it back to the library." To answer the quizzical look on her face I added, "No Wi-Fi at the house."

Mattie was aghast. "Unacceptable. Look, Cinder is a good enough judge of character in my experience, and she went looking for you, so you're welcome to come over to my place and use mine anytime. I'm just half a mile up the road—which makes me your closest neighbor, by the way. Let me give you my number."

"Oh god—*my phone*. That's what I was looking for when I...got lost."

"You are having a day. Vivian must have one you can use right?"

"There's a house phone." It was a struggle to suppress the whine in my voice knowing that without my phone I would be alone at night with Vivian and crime drama reruns while who knew what stared from the dark of the woods.

"Just come over now then," shrugged Mattie, who sounded like the most sensible person around for miles.

"Thank you." I felt myself relax just a bit. "I think I'll take you up on that."

"What are neighbors for? Hop in," she said, followed by a disapproving sound as a white SUV climbed toward us. "Great. It's Walker. But it's fine. Probably." But quietly added, "*Shit.*"

The SUV had a blue 'Police' logo across its doors, and the driver had his heavy brows set close together as pulled alongside her truck. "Well now, Mattie Pratt," he said, "you wouldn't be having some trouble with what I just know is your *completely street legal* vehicle, would you?"

"Not at all—only stopped to give my friend here a lift home." She nodded toward me. "Thanks *so much* for the concern though."

"Hold on." With an easy smile, he waved me over to him. "Where is home?"

"I'm staying over on Ide Road," I told him. His smile faded.

"You're Talia Adair?"

I forced a laugh. "What—was there a town meeting about me?"

He put the car in park; something in his expression shifted in a way that made me immediately tense. He reached over to push the passenger door handle open. "I was actually just on my way to the Adair place. Why don't you ride with me?"

"Walker—it's fine," Mattie said, annoyed. "I *just* got the brakes fixed, and I'll get it inspected next week."

"Nothing to do with you, Mattie," he said evenly.

I didn't feel like I had a choice, but my feet stayed planted. "What's going on?" Then it hit me with a surge of panic. "Did something happen? Is it my dad?"

"No." His eyes softened. "No. It's...well, it's your mom. She was found this morning."

The breath fled from me, blood draining from my face in a hot rush when he said, "She's alive."

8

No.

She's alive.

For all the questions exploding around my head, none could drown out these words. They felt dangerous against the walls I'd put up long ago and I couldn't bring myself to let them in and settle as fact yet.

My mother was *alive.*

The questions began to tangle, but I could only sit silently, folding and unfolding the gas station receipt that Mattie had hastily jotted her number on before pressing it into my hand as I numbly got into the patrol car. It was probably just as well because I don't think this guy she called Walker, whose first name was Shane and would prefer I used it, had any other answers beyond what he'd just told me.

Mom was found unconscious, not in some foreign land but right here in Elmwood. By that river. When she woke, she was confused and spoke little, but what she did say was enough. She was missing *years* of memory. Not only couldn't she account for any of the time she'd been gone, but she thought it had only been a few weeks.

He was quick to tell me that temporary memory loss and confusion wasn't uncommon with trauma. He also said that she had no obvious signs of physical injury, but something about the way he said it made me think there might be some less obvious ones that he'd rather not speak of to me.

And she wasn't found alone.

An older woman was with her, but not only didn't she speak English, but after some translation they found she had no memory either. Shane didn't believe that she had been involved in my mother's disappearance. Or reappearance. She was just as confused and just as much of a mystery.

What had happened in the woods, that girl-thing *existing*, made more sense to me at that moment than anything he was saying. I could almost hear the crackling as my brain short-circuited.

Shane had a strong, clean-shaven jaw, high rounded cheekbones, and faintly slanted eyes that kept glancing my way. Maybe he was expecting a more joyous response to this impossible news, but the best I was managing was guarded disbelief and suspicion.

"I went to school with your mom," he told me, and I wondered if he'd been trying to see her in my face. "When I moved back to town, hers was the case I made sure to knock the dust off of first. I'd hoped to find something that got overlooked, but no luck."

"What was she like? Back when you knew her?"

"She was quiet. Nice, but quiet."

"Did you know my dad too?"

"No...but I do know your grandmother, so I'm prepared."

"*Vivian*," I forewarned. "She doesn't like to be called grandma."

"Yeah." His downturned lips lifted at the corner. "That sounds about right."

The house stood lonely and proud against the graying sky as we pulled up. The proximity of another person made me feel safe enough to look over at the spot where I'd first seen Maevyn as we drove past.

There was nothing threatening about it at the moment. I wished that made me feel better.

The curtain of the parlor window fell shut, and before we made it to the stairs, Vivian swept onto the porch in a long gray skirt. A thick turquoise medallion rested below the collar of her blouse. Her eyes narrowed on me. "You left the door unlocked." She turned to Shane impatiently. "Well? What else did she do, chief? Rob a bank? Why does she look so nervous?"

"Now, Vivian," he said politely, "as I've told you before, Ben Crowley is chief here."

"Well, you *look* like the chief," she said dismissively and I cringed. I didn't know if there were many other Native Americans walking around Elmwood, but if there were, I hoped to god she didn't call them all "chief".

"No ma'am, Chief Crowley is a shorter, bald man that I bear absolutely no resemblance to." His smile was the same one he wore when talking to Mattie.

Vivian clicked her tongue. "That doesn't seem right. He was here not long ago about Nicolette, and I'm certain he had a nice, full head of hair like yours."

I wondered if Shane noticed the unfocused look in her eyes that partly explained her end of the conversation, and that's what kept him remarkably patient. "You're thinking of my father. He was chief when your daughter went missing. He passed a few years back."

"Well, that's a shame. Such a good head of hair," she said distantly then waved her hands. "My mind takes strange avenues these days. Yes, I must've been thinking of your father. But now what did you do?"

"Oh." I realized she was talking to me, and I fumbled my words. "I didn't...it's not ..." I couldn't bring myself to tell her this thing that still felt like a lie. What if, like me, her grief sat in her for so long that it had become attached to who she was? So much so that even good news wouldn't be allowed in. I was still standing in the shock of it and didn't want to be the one to pull her in with me.

"Why don't we talk inside?" Shane suggested.

With a mix of confusion and hostility, Vivian stood aside, turning all of the locks once she closed the door after us, worry gradually invading her face. "Alright, what is it?"

He gestured to the red room where I was already perched on one of the burgundy chairs. "Maybe we should all have a seat."

Vivian straightened her back, her fingers closing around the stone of her necklace. "Perhaps you'd like me to serve tea while we're at it? It's *my* house. I know where all the best seats are—if I wanted to sit, I'd be doing it in one of them. Just get on with it."

So he did, in the exact same neat, professional manner as when he told me. I don't think Vivian had the reaction he was expecting either. She shook her head and told him that they must've made a mistake. Pointing her finger toward the back of the house, she told him that her daughter was *out there* and wasn't coming back, that she'd known it for a long time. She told him that, whatever they found, it was *not* her.

He calmly explained it to her again, this time taking out his phone to show her what I assumed was a picture. I wanted to see it too, but stayed put when I saw the twitch in Vivian's eye as she traced a finger over the screen.

"Her hair." She breathed out. "But what have you done?" She backed away until her eyes started to flutter. Shane was quick to catch her before she collapsed onto the rug.

I jumped up, unsure of what to do. Her eyes blinked back open seconds later, and Shane asked me for a pillow for her head. I grabbed the nearest one and plucked the phone from where it had fallen. At my touch, the screen lit back on.

It was my mother's face, that much was certain because it was exactly the same. She looked closer to my age than to what should've been her forty years, but her dark eyes were unfocused, her lips dry and cracked. I understood why Vivian was so confused about her hair; it was a frazzled mess around her face and as white as the moon.

From the floor, Vivian's voice trembled low.

"One of us died that night. Do you understand? And if it wasn't Nicolette then it must've been me."

Wisely, Shane had refused to let Vivian drive herself to the county hospital where Mom was. He had to repeatedly assure her that his car was clean of any vomit or 'drug needles' before she would consider letting him take us. Finally, he ended up giving her a gentle order to get in the car and, thanks to her being a little out of it due to the shock and probably at least a residual high, that did the trick.

The drive had been quiet except for her distant realization that "Richard will be there I suppose. I never thought I'd have to see that man again."

I wasn't sure who she was speaking to, but she was right. I saw my father's copper-bearded profile as soon as we got to the waiting area of Locksville Memorial. He was always smartly dressed and well-groomed, equipped with a natural charm that drew people to him—something that served him well as a musician-turned-club owner and that I inherited exactly *none* of. Today though, he looked like he just rolled out of bed. He smiled when he saw me. I tensed when we hugged.

He and Vivian greeted each other curtly. I was almost disappointed that he left the girlfriend at home. She was about five years older than me and looked like a low-rent version of Mom, but he didn't see it. Vivian, however, I didn't think would stop herself from pointing it out.

Thankfully, the wait was brief. A thin-faced doctor came and updated us on what he could about Mom's condition. There was no brain injury, but she seemed to have—what he would guess—was dissociative amnesia, but they couldn't be sure until she could be better evaluated. But someone was on their way to do that. From Stillview.

I was sure that Dad heard my sharp intake of breath before I clamped my mouth shut and looked away, avoiding that too-familiar concern in his eyes. I hoped he couldn't tell how my stomach roiled with panic, as though the broken state of mind that had brought me to that asylum in the first place could be conjured back by the mere mention of it.

The doctor was wary about her having visitors at this point. "We don't want her to be further agitated at seeing how...*changed* her loved ones are," he said, looking at me directly.

"Well, *I* still look basically the same." Vivian sat up and smoothed her blouse. "Surely I could see her just for a little while?"

A short laugh flew from my father's mouth. "Good god, Vivian. You know, if you're having that much trouble staying grounded in reality, maybe you should get evaluated too."

"You're being *rude*, Richard." She turned to me. "We have very good genes when it comes to staying youthful. You can just look at my own photos to see how well I've maintained."

"Well, she'd have to look at photos because it's not like you were around for her to remember. Care to remember why that was?"

"I was *asked* to stay away," she said icily.

"Don't pretend there wasn't a reason." He leaned forward but didn't raise his voice. "Or has your gin-soaked brain—"

"I don't drink *gin*. Ladies don't drink *gin*."

"*Ladies* probably don't get blackout drunk by the time school's out—"

"Enough," I snapped. To my surprise their bickering stopped, and the two looked away from each other like shame-faced children.

The good doctor, who had his mouth open the whole time, waiting for a moment to interject, saw his chance. "Er...I understand how difficult this is for all of you, but surely no one wants to hinder the healing process."

No one spoke.

So, after all this time, I *still* couldn't see my mother. If she still thought I was six years old, then I could see the logic in not dropping the bomb that was twenty-year-old me on her, yet there was part of me that was forever locked at age six. That part of me didn't care about what was best. She just wanted her mom.

"I need some air," I declared and hopped up before anyone could argue.

I was getting some air for a very long time.

After dry heaving a little in the bathroom, I drifted between the cafeteria and the benches outside next to the giant cement ashtrays. In part, I was hiding from the tension in the waiting room, but also from the idea of seeing *any* familiar faces from Stillview. Though I'd been indifferent to the doctors there, I knew that I'd feel the need to pretend to be well-adjusted, or at least sane, around one of them. I wasn't feeling either of those things enough to pull that off.

I'd been staring blankly at my reflection over the bright wrappings of the salt and sugar treats of the vending machine when I heard arguing and recognized Shane's voice. Stepping quietly down the hall, I stopped at the corner to get a better listen.

"She doesn't belong here," an older woman's voice clipped. "We have the room, and I've got the time to care for her myself."

"You're out of your mind," Shane said. "And so is she—by the sound of it. Not a great quality for a roommate, Gran."

"She is old, frightened, and alone," the woman said. "And she should be with her people."

"*We* are not her people. "

"We're just that, grandson. You know she'll end up in some state home if no one takes her in. You wanted me to translate what she said, but what if she remembers something later, after she's been sent away? Somewhere I *refuse* to go?"

Sounded like the woman Mom was found with wasn't going to be much help solving their conjoined mystery then. I peered around the corner, glimpsing colorful patterns of the oversized sweater of Shane's grandmother. Her hair was short and gray, and Shane towered over her, drawing his hand down the lower half of his face. I stepped back, not wanting to interrupt what sounded like a family drama moment. Not when I had my own.

The waiting room was empty when I returned. The last light of day was falling away outside of the windows. A nurse wearing glasses on a chain around her neck told me that the doctor was with my mother, along with Vivian and my dad. Before my mouth moved to form the question, she answered it.

"You'll have to stay in the waiting area unless you're called for," she said, barely looking up from her computer screen. "Doctor's orders."

"No problem," I said automatically, fully aware of how very much of a problem it was.

After thirteen years, I should have been able to wait a little longer, but after a while I began pacing, eventually finding myself away from the nurse's desk. Soon enough my hand rested on a cool metal handle, pressing my ear against the orange wood of the door with Dad's voice behind it.

After a few seconds, I heard her.

I couldn't make out words, just the still-recognizable sound and tones of my mother's voice.

I knew that she wouldn't recognize me, but maybe it wouldn't be so bad. Maybe she would just *know* me in some maternal, instinctive way. She might say my name. She might smile, or cry, and lift her arms toward me in a welcoming embrace. She might even tell me that she missed me, and that she never meant to leave me for so long. Surely then we'd be allowed that moment. I might still have to return to the waiting room after, but when I did, I'd be free of the ball of anxiety that had been tightening in my chest ever since finding out that she was *alive.*

I opened the door and there she was. She sat with her strange, white hair now loosely braided over her shoulder, falling to her waist. Her pale face didn't react, but I saw the moment those dark eyes sparked with recognition. Yes, I wasn't six anymore, so I was expecting shock, but that wasn't what I saw in those eyes. It was *repulsion.*

I wanted to tell myself that I was imagining it, but when she spoke from those lips shaped so much like my own, it was a simple, heavy sound.

"*No.*"

I felt traces of the smile that had started to curl my lips crash down as I tried to form words that wouldn't make it past the lump in my throat.

"Talia," Dad said from a chair at her bedside. The weary strain on his face told me that things already weren't going well before I barged in.

Vivian sat on the opposite side of the bed, her hand resting at the stone at her throat. I only vaguely recognized the doctor, but he didn't matter anymore. My mother was looking at me like I was some alien thing. At that moment, I questioned if maybe I'd forgotten if she'd always looked at me like this—like something she couldn't fathom and wanted to bury away.

Like something *wrong*.

Since she'd known him, Dad's face had gotten older and was now half hidden with a beard, but when she glanced his way, she didn't look at him with rejection. Yet, when her eyes came back to me, they stared like she was trying to discern what was so *off* about my presence. She began to shake her head. What else did she see? What flaw did that maternal instinct detect?

Her voice was more resolute when she spoke again. "No."

My hand hadn't even left the door handle, but the crushing tightness in my chest was spreading into my throat. I stepped back and was halfway down the hall before I heard the echo of the door close behind me.

9

Notes

The crisp air of the October twilight cooled the sting of tears as I started marching up the sidewalk, relieved that no one had followed me. I didn't have a direction in mind, but I also didn't know where the house was from here, and being nearly dark, it was the idea of that long driveway at night that made me slow my pace.

It wasn't until the glow of the hospital sign was behind me, and I started to regret that I hadn't grabbed a jacket, that reason began to sink in. I wasn't being fair. Whatever had happened to Mom, it wasn't her fault. Still, while I could never help the grief I had over losing her, I tended to forget that there was anger there too that would sometimes overlap it. I guess I always thought the grief was more deserving of its place, so I let it be louder.

But that anger lashed sometimes.

When it came to my disjointed collection of hallmark memories with Mom, those glimpses of bedtime stories and birthdays were anchored to darker things I could only almost remember. There was warmth of her smile here, but distance in her eyes there. She was comforting, then cold. I believe she was probably *at least* depressed, and like me, was trying to take some time to get her head together. But still...she had left *me* behind. However justified it might have been. And I let myself be convinced that she just decided to never return.

But I now knew something else intervened. Something with cold eyes and a child's smile.

It was fresh kindling for that neglected anger. I hadn't mentioned what happened today to anyone, as I had no desire to be escorted back to Stillview this or any day. But it couldn't be a coincidence that the Maevyn-thing had shown up, or that it had tried to lure me into the same woods Mom had gone missing from on the same day she was found.

Behind me, blue lights flashed. Without stopping, I turned to see Shane's car creeping up. I didn't want to talk, but I was still coming up with a good reason to refuse a ride as his window rolled down.

"I'm going that way anyway, and I've seen possums walking along these roadsides after dark that could probably take you in a fight," he told me, sliding his phone and notebook over to make room. It was getting too cold to be stubborn. I got in; the car smelled like stale coffee and nothing like the pine tree hanging from the rearview mirror. The smile of begrudging gratitude I attempted came out as a grim line.

"So," he said after some awkward silence, "take it you got to see her then?"

"Not exactly." My voice was tight, and I crossed my arms over my chest to try to warm away the cold beneath my ribs.

"My own mother passed a few years ago." The slants of his profile were lit green by the light of the dashboard. "Her mind went ahead of her. I knew it was gone for good, no matter how long the rest of her lingered. But with your mom, with time, there's a good chance she'll come back."

"Sorry about your mother." I stared at the last of the violet-streaked-orange glow of sky dropping into the trees. "But I never even got to know mine, and whoever she is now definitely wasn't glad to see me tonight."

Whatever he was going to say collapsed into breath. It was a few moments before he tried again. "I know that you were very young when she went missing. That had to be hard on you and your dad."

"Yeah." I pressed my head back against the seat and looked away.

When Dad picked me up from school that day instead of her, I'd thought it was just a fun switch up. He waited until dinner to tell me that she wasn't coming home that night. The next day, he said she was just going to be away for a few days. He might have believed that, but I think he just didn't want to have to break my heart. Even while he knew search parties had been forming, he didn't want to take that... *hope* away from me. I know he meant it to shield me, but telling me she'd be gone 'for a few days' for *weeks* only led to my imagination kicking open the door to anxiety.

It was when she didn't come home for my birthday that I finally made him tell me the truth. I knew it was going to hurt. I knew because of the heaviness in his voice whenever I asked about her. And the sadness in his eyes. But when he tried again to tell me that fairy tale about her having gone on some mystery vacation, that budding anger towed by grief stopped him.

"No, Daddy." I'd told him, "Mommy didn't like being here anymore, so she doesn't want to come back."

I'm not sure when I stopped waiting to hear the door open, the sound of her footsteps on my bedroom floor to tuck me in. Or when every woman with short dark hair in every crowd could have been her until I saw their face, and that thorn in my heart would twist again.

"Before..." I thumbed the scars on my wrist over the sleeve of my sweater. "When you knew her, did she seem...normal to you?"

"I'm not sure I knew what passed as normal for a teenager even when I was one, but she wasn't strange. Plenty of people who aren't 'normal' can sure seem it though."

I thought of the pictures I had under my bed, then the image of her white hair and eerily youthful face superimposed over them. I thought of fingers twisting like thin branches toward me. Ice slid up my spine. "Did you know these woods are supposed to be haunted?" I asked abruptly as the fields we passed gave way to trees.

"Oh, all woods are haunted. All the forests and all mountains, deserts and rivers. Depending on who you ask." He glanced over at me. "Before I came back here, I was a park ranger out in Colorado. I heard all sorts of stories."

"Did you ever see anything? Anything...unexplainable?"

"The sunlight can play tricks on the eyes the same way the wind can trick your ears, especially if you're lost and panicked—or as in a lot of stories I heard, you've had a few drinks."

"That wasn't an answer."

"Heh, I suppose it wasn't." His broad fingers tapped on the steering wheel. "Well, like most places around here, my backyard stops at the trees, and I used to see a wolf that wasn't there. A huge black one. This was when I was just a little guy. Told my folks about it, but they insisted that there were no wolves in this area and hadn't been for a long time. Just the same, they didn't let me play outside alone once I started saying that."

"Oh? And had little you had a few drinks?"

He half smiled. "It was probably just a coyote that I made bigger in my imagination."

"What about the Green Lady?" I asked, and his eyebrows raised. "She's a local."

"*Mattie* told you about that?"

"Only after I asked her about it."

"And I'm assuming you asked because someone approached you about that story?" he asked as though he suspected the answer already.

"Kind of."

"And was that someone named Wes Samuel?" He turned to me, and my face must've told him he was right. "That's...disappointing. He has a bit of a history of taking things too far with his stories, and I'd have hoped he knew better then to start it up again. Especially with you. If you see him on Vivian's property, give me a call."

I thought of Vivian and her locks. "Is he dangerous?"

"Everyone has it in them to be dangerous in the right circumstances, but no, I don't know him to be the violent kind, more misguided than anything. He's been warned away from trespassing there in pursuit of ghosts—or for any other reason."

"So just to be clear, you *don't* believe that my mother has been out there in a green dress chasing people through the woods all this time then?"

Catching the sarcasm, he let out a short laugh. "Well, tha*t is* probably the best theory I've gotten so far, but no. And I don't think the Green Lady is even really a local gal. She's newer, as far as town ghost stories go, but I've heard other versions in other places. The whole disappearing girl on the road thing. So, I guess I should add that lonely old roads are haunted too. I think the old urban legends get a makeover and spread faster these days. That's the internet for you."

"You don't believe in any of it, I take it."

"Well, there's too much of it. Slenderman. Mothman. Good old Bigfoot. I just hope everyone gets along—the old ghosts and new monsters."

The blue mailbox was in the headlights as we turned down the drive. I kept my eyes from the trees. Shane's notebook was between us, and while I mostly couldn't make out his scribbles in the dim light, one word was circled and stood out clear enough: "STORM". Below that, all I made out was "Billy Eddington".

The car pulled around to the front of the house, and he pulled a card from his wallet. "The non-emergency station number is on the front. Mine is on the back. You can use either one."

I took it and pointed to the notebook. "Are those notes about Mom?"

"Some of them," he said, flipping it closed. "But if you're going to ask, no, I still don't even have a guess. One theory is that she might have gotten mixed up with drugs. Might explain her mental state—except her tests were clean."

"Drugs? That turned her hair white?"

"Didn't say it was a *good* theory. Also, not mine. It's close, but I'm actually not the only cop in town."

"What's relevant about a storm then?"

"She said some things today—not a lot of them made sense—but it stood out when she said there was a storm in the house. I went ahead and assumed she meant metaphorically, but then she said that it chased her outside. It was the last thing she said she remembered about the night she disappeared—that storm. She seemed coherent enough when she said it, but I've been through her file enough times to know that there was no storm that night. Clear night, full moon. Fifty-six degrees low. Like I said she's—"

"Confused. Right." Of course, even if she could remember what happened, it wasn't like anyone would believe her if it involved anything like Maevyn. "What about the woman that was with her?"

"She's...well, I'm afraid there's a good chance she's senile."

"And who's 'Billy Eddington'?"

He sighed. I could tell he was reaching his limit with my interrogation. "An old missing persons case that this one got me thinking of. From my ranger days. Boy that disappeared from a trail."

"Who randomly showed up years later?"

"Three days later. It was a case that was closed, but it never really added up to me. I'm hoping I get to the bottom of what happened to your mom so this doesn't linger with me the same way."

"Do you think you will? Get to the bottom of it, I mean."

He paused and looked ahead then nodded to the house. "You going to be okay here until Vivian gets home?

I turned the card over in my fingers. In the dark, it felt like the house was looking back. I never did get to look for my phone, so I almost told him to wait with me, but I knew visiting hours at the hospital were going to be up soon. I hadn't had any time to really process any of this alone, and I really wanted a snack and a small breakdown before bed.

"I'll be fine. Thanks for the ride."

"And Talia?" he said as I stepped out of the car. "If you see anything odd, even if it's 'unexplainable', call me for that as well."

I leaned back down to look at him, tucking my hair behind my ear as it fell forward. "Thought you said you didn't believe in ghosts."

"No," he said, meeting my eyes. "I didn't."

10

Whispers

The hallway is narrower than it should be as I move toward the dividing door, my feet soundless on the rug. There is something in the house. I feel it. Something dead-eyed and long-limbed with sharp, grasping fingers. I want to warn Vivian, but then I also know that whatever I hear sliding thickly across the floor in her room isn't her, not really.

When I reach the door, a long white key sits in the lock and makes a loud click when I turn it. Too loud. It echoes like the ticking of a clock down the hall. The movement in Vivian's room stills then rushes along the walls. There is a clacking like hooves fumbling up the stairs—

The sound was a sharp thing cutting me from sleep.

My eyes blearily focused on the blue digital numbers of the clock on the nightstand. It was just after three, and the darkness behind the curtains told me that it was in the a.m. I could feel the weight of exhaustion still on me, so why was I awake? Then I heard it; the familiar chiming of my phone alarm carried through the silence of the house.

I kicked off the covers and clumsily scanned the floor in the dim lamplight as I followed the sound into the hallway. Then downstairs. Only when I got to the last stair, it stopped.

Moonlight filtered in through the arched window above the door, casting long lines of shadow on the wall behind me. With my hand still on the smooth wood of the banister, the residual fog of sleep fully lifted. Why would my phone alarm be going off in the middle of the night? Of course. I probably hadn't really heard anything at all, and this was just my sleep-drunk brain chasing a sound from a fading dream. I would've laughed at myself then if what was unmistakably my ringtone hadn't just sounded out from the other side of the heavy front door.

My phone had *not* been on the porch today. I would have seen it. Which could only mean that someone had left it there after I had come home. Or. They were still standing there with it. Waiting.

After four rings it stopped, and I stood in the quiet stillness of the house for a moment before I slid my feet from the step. I crept around the table, still cluttered with the mail from earlier, to the window that offered the most direct view of the front door. I didn't turn on the porch light. I didn't even risk moving the curtain, instead arching my neck to peer between it and glass, bracing myself for what I might see. But the nearly-full moon illuminated the porch well enough to show that there was no one there. No phone either.

I stepped back with an exhale and looked around, eyeing every piece of furniture suspiciously before running back to the stairs. I was halfway to the top, when the phone sounded again from outside the door, this time playing tinny music I didn't recognize.

"Not a fucking chance," I muttered to the dark and bolted to Vivian's room.

She slept soundlessly on her side, hair spread out across the pillow. I stopped myself just short of shaking her awake. What would be the point in frightening her too? The doors were locked; the alarm system was on; the danger was only outside at the moment. I had to admit that I was probably wrong about Wes Samuel not being able to pocket my phone without me noticing it. I wasn't sure what he was trying to accomplish here though. Maybe he was trying to lure me outside so he could tell me whatever he hadn't earlier. Maybe frightening girls was what he did for fun. Maybe he was actually a serial killer. Still, he was only a man—a creep—but a human one who couldn't get in, not without setting off the alarm.

Police. This is the sort of thing you called the police for. I picked up the receiver from Vivian's nightstand, my fingers hovering over the numbers. I'd never actually had to call an emergency number before. There was something about doing so that made everything more real.

A watery memory swam by of Dad's urgent voice saying he needed an ambulance. I shook it away.

No, I would be justified dialing 9-1-1, someone was outside the house after all. Only...I hadn't *seen* anyone, had I? In fact, I hadn't heard them exactly either. I'd only heard a phone. My own phone at that.

I set the receiver back down. How would this make me sound, especially if there was no one there? *Small town.* Once word got out about the paranoid head case at the Adair house, how quickly would the police come next time if Vivian or I really needed them? I remembered Shane's card on my dresser next to the cordless phone I'd brought upstairs before heading to bed.

After a full minute of listening to silence at the top of the staircase, I darted down the hall. All of the rooms here were decadent, and mine was no exception. Sage swirled with gold vines blooming with lavender and pink flowers papered the walls. Thick royal blues and jade greens wove together in the oriental carpet. A four-poster canopy bed large enough for me and three friends sat against the far wall, a blue velvet chaise lounge at the foot of it.

In the corner of the opposite wall was a double-doored armoire that was nearly big enough for me to stand upright in. Next to it, a vanity with a huge oval mirror encased in ornate, dark wood presided over a small bench with legs carved to resemble the bodies of birds whose wings held the red and gold cushioned seat—I'd stubbed my toe on those damn birds half a dozen times already.

I snatched the phone from where it sat, bulky and oblong beneath a tiffany-style lamp on the nightstand, quickly shutting the damask curtains on the way. I clutched the phone to my chest like a shield as I peered outside. No one was lurking near the front of the house or stalking about the lawn, however when I raised my eyes up the long driveway, there he was.

Little more than a shadow at this distance, but I could make out the male figure standing with folded arms. It *would* be useful if I were able to report that it was definitely Wes Samuel trespassing, as it was likely he would be gone by the time someone came—assuming anyone did. Knowing he wasn't down there trying to pry a window open made me feel a bit better, a bit braver. I had an idea.

I pressed in my own number into the archaic block in my hand and waited a few seconds for the light from my phone to appear in his, illuminating his face.

It was not the face I was expecting.

A dark-haired stranger looked down at the screen, then to me, as though he knew exactly where I was. His eyes were reflective as a cat's, his mouth twisted before the phone went black. I pressed the curtain closed, allowing a sliver of a gap so I could see that he was now walking casually up the pavement. His clothes blended into the night around him, but the face still turned to my window was so pale it looked almost luminescent in the moonlight, shadows filling in the deep hollows beneath his cheekbones making the angles of his face sharper and his upturned mouth sinister.

I debated trying to muster up enough authority in my voice to demand who he was and what he wanted, or threatening him with the police. Instead, I nearly choked on the short scream that erupted when the phone I'd been holding in a death grip rang, startling me into releasing the curtain, putting me fully in his gaze.

No sense in pretending I didn't see him now. I put the phone to my ear. He mirrored the movement, but when I hit the button to answer, whispers that didn't come from his mouth slithered out of the earpiece, overlapping and harsh, urgent and indecipherable. The man tilted his head and the whispers grew louder until the noise shot out of the phone in a shrieking wind. I threw it away from me, watching as the back of it popped off and a battery bounced out, silencing the noise.

He was gone when I looked back to the window. Either he was pressed to the wall of the house beneath me, or he'd been quick enough to run around to the shuttered side of the house. I wasn't sure which of those ideas filled me with the most dread, especially since I'd just broken the nearest phone.

I clicked the light on and knelt to find the battery. Once I got it back into place, I hit the dial button to do what I should have done in the first place and called the police. But the phone was dead.

I sat on the floor and waited. The house was silent, and after it had stayed that way long enough, I checked the window again to see the empty driveway. Eventually I crept back downstairs and boldly pulled the curtain away to see the porch, which was, of course, also empty.

With a bitter laugh, I slumped into a chair with all the frightened loneliness of someone who just realized they've been shut out in the cold, or more accurately, of someone who had just realized that they might truly be losing their mind.

II

Protection

The next morning it was Nico that woke me up from a rest so fitful it had no right to be called sleep. Her deep, tremulous voice floated down the halls wrapped in the off-kilter embrace of accompanying strings. The dawn light had just begun to drift past the edges of the curtains before all my tension let up enough to let me close my eyes. The alarm clock had apparently also died last night, but it had to be early. Too early, most definitely, for Nico.

Whatever mood Vivian must be in, it was no match for the surreal, either-I'm-on-the-edge-of-insanity-or-really-being-stalked-by-super-natural-beings-who-have-also-stolen-my-phone sort of cloud my own head was in. I rolled out of bed and trudged across the room, appreciating how thick the wooden door really was when I was assaulted by the full volume of Nico's voice singing about dancing demons and crucial paradies upon opening it.

Cutting down the hall to Vivian's room, I turned the music down. If ever there was a morning where I needed things to be calm and at least leaning in the direction of normal, this would be it. The chime clock on her dresser read just after ten. There was still plenty of day to look into these town ghost stories and see if any of them maybe matched up with any girl-like creatures or...ghost phones? Anything that might point to me not hallucinating. Mattie and her Wi-Fi could help there, and I could also look up some things about this town. See if there was anything strange in its history.

I wouldn't go to the hospital again. Not unless Mom asked for me. There was no point in seeing her until she was well enough to at least do that.

From the landing I saw Vivian pace from the parlor to the dining room, fully dressed despite what for her was an early hour. "Good." She stopped mid-pace when she saw me. "You're awake. But good lord, you look...Well, I've made a pot of tea, you'll need a cup. Richard will be here with Nicolette shortly, but really, if you're unwell..."

"What do you mean?" Surely, I'd misheard her over the residual Nico.

There was something different about her. Her hair was pulled into a loose bun, her peach blouse and burgundy skirt just background noise for the layered silver and amethyst necklace at her chest. Her eyes though, they were brighter, more alert than I'd ever seen them. I sniffed the air, noting that it was absent of the distinct weed stink that usually clung to the hallway.

"She's being released this morning." Her fingers repeatedly ran over gemstone rings. "It seems that doctor had quite the change of tune and now he thinks it's best for her to be around the familiar. He recommended she come *here* since Richard— Well, you can imagine why that wouldn't work out very well."

I wondered how his girlfriend would go over with Mom. Probably about as well as she'd gone over with me. It didn't matter though. Even if her relationship with Vivian hadn't been great, the Adair house *was* Mom's childhood home, full of triggering memories. Maybe the idea of having some of those memories recovered was why Vivian was literally wringing her hands right now.

A thunderclap of panic hit me as the events of last night surged forward with those of little Maevyn just a breath behind them. For a minute there, I'd let myself think having to deal with a dysfunctional family like a normal person was the crisis at hand, but Mom wouldn't be safe here, surrounded by the woods and whatever walked in them. But where else would they send her? Stillview? If what was wrong with her was because of wherever she'd been, then doctors couldn't help. Treating damage without knowing where it was coming from would be like smearing mud around with a dry mop in the name of cleaning.

I mumbled that I needed to get dressed, reordering my day in my head as I returned to my room to stare blankly at my clothes that only filled a fraction of my armoire. I needed to be here for a while today—at least to act as a buffer between Dad and Vivian. My stomach knotted at the impending tension as I threw on black leggings and a short floral dress. Some thick woven leg warmers too—if I were going to be miserable and terrified for the foreseeable future, I might as well be cozy. No time for a shower, so I washed my face and brushed the tangles from my hair to make myself presentable. I wished I could make myself look like a competent, stable daughter, the kind you could be proud of, the kind you wouldn't leave behind or have committed.

The girl in the mirror was none of these things. Rusty waves of hair still looked wild around my pale face. Bluish shadows under my eyes. I looked like some small fragile thing that had no business trying to handle anything on her own. I applied a layer of tinted Chapstick. Yeah, no miracles there.

The kitchen was the brightest colored room in the house. The pattern of yellow-papered walls dotted with little red flowers was broken up by decorative china plates. Copper pans hung above the ancient looking stove that I was afraid to use, and the window over the sink was stained in a peacock design that peeked over a roller blind. The window faced the garden, but the blind was never opened, and the back door at the end of the counter was always locked.

In the middle of the room, surrounded by cabinets, was a small table with tea set up on white cloth. Even with the stress of everything, I knew better than to expect simply a couple of mugs with steeping bags in them. Instead, Vivian drowned painted violets and roses that scrolled down the inside of delicate cups with steaming liquid from a silver pot. Honestly, I didn't really care for the stuff, but I was a big fan of caffeine. I stirred in several spoonfuls of sugar.

"Hemorrhoid cream," said Vivian. I glanced up to her. "For under your eyes. It helps with the bags. They show more with pale skin, and your skin is paler than Nicolette's was when she was young."

"Oh." I wrapped my hands around the heat of the cup. "That's all right. I just didn't sleep well."

Her spoon tinkled in the cup as she stirred it absentmindedly. "Well, I unfortunately slept well enough to have such *awful* dreams all night." She raised the cup to her lips, setting it down again without taking a sip. "She always had those dark circles, you know. She would say she had bad dreams all the time, though I wasn't sure what could possibly be giving her that much distress."

I chewed the inside of my lip, remembering some of what Dad had told me about Vivian. It didn't seem fair to know these secondhand stories when the woman in them didn't match up with the one seated across from me now. Still, that's not saying they weren't true, and it made me feel a little treacherous. Having tea with my mother's nightmare.

"Talia"—she looked at her hands— "the Nicolette in the hospital didn't have those dark circles. Her skin was as perfect as pearl, and she looked younger than she did before she—" Her fingers pressed to her mouth for a moment, then reached to unfasten a thin silver chain from her neck, a bit of rough-looking black stone swung from the end as she pulled it from her blouse. She laid it on the table. "That's for you. It's for protection. They're all supposedly good for some sort of protection, but that one is supposed to be the best. I've worn it every day for years."

"I didn't realize you were superstitious." I rolled the stone over with my finger.

"It's desperation, not superstition. Although one does tend to cause the other, I'll give you that." She looked to the window. "If you take a walk out past the garden and into those woods, you'll see crosses on the trees. Dozens of them. There are also some hexagrams, penta-grams, hamsas, a few eyes of Horus carved into various trunks...just to cover as much ground as I could. I was obsessed with protecting this house and myself, but I didn't know precisely how."

"Protection from what?" An iciness was reaching into my chest, the warmth of the cup in my hand evaporated. Vivian wasn't just more alert, she was *scared*.

She shook her head, rising to take out an embroidered cigarette case from a drawer. "I've never known. I was never afraid of the woods before Nicolette was lost, but after—"

She drew out a slim cigarette and placed it into a gold and white holder. Before lighting it, she clicked on the small fan on the counter to blow the smoke away. It was a considerate, if ineffective, gesture. I stifled a cough.

"I couldn't shake the sense that there was something...*sinister* out there. I knew it was insane, the things I thought. But who could blame me after what happened? I was eventually able to convince myself it *was* only insanity, but still took precautions in case I was wrong. After seeing her in the hospital yesterday, I'm glad I did."

Fear rolled into relief at the idea of an ally. I wanted to tell her every-thing, all I had seen and heard, to let her know that her instincts were well-founded. But I hesitated. There was no putting that elephant back once it was released into every room. I couldn't blame her if she didn't believe me, even if what I said would prove she wasn't crazy. Everyone knows insanity is hereditary.

"What made you stay here then?" I asked, safely.

"I can't sell this house. It's my husband's family home. He was adamant that it stay in his family. To leave it would feel like I was betraying his memory."

"You thought she would come home." I realized.

She took a long drag on her cigarette. "Yes. Yes, I suppose I was afraid she might after all."

"Vivian, what..." I began cautiously, "what *do* you think happened to her?"

She abruptly snuffed out her unfinished cigarette. "I can't say. And I can't say what's going to happen when she comes home." She gave her hands a quick wash then refolded the dish towel, draping it back over the stove handle. "But I can tell you that I would feel much better if you would wear that necklace."

"You really think this will protect against anything?" I slipped it over my head, the stone cool against my skin as it slipped into the neckline of my dress.

"Well." Vivian sighed. "I suppose that depends on what the danger really turns out to be."

And as if on cue, there was a knock on the door.

12

Below the Surface

Unfortunately, Cole Adair was not very present for her own home-coming. Her white hair loosely braided to the side, she was a wavering figure next to my father. She stood frail in a peacoat that had been thrown over clothes that I recognized from a box kept in the back of his closet. Dad had never been able to get rid of them. The way they hung on her now, it was hard to believe they'd ever been hers.

No one spoke until Dad ushered her in, and he greeted me with "Hey, Doodlebug" and a hug I half-heartedly returned. He only broke out the 'Doodlebug' when I was sick or sad. Or apparently when I'd been stuck in an asylum, which I guess was a combination of both.

My mother drifted around the room, eyes on the ceiling, the walls, the furniture, and then on me with a curious tilt to her head like a bird as she said in a voice like a cracked china cup, "It's the wrong place for you, you know."

"Cole, you remember," Dad said wearily. "I explained that Talia has been staying here with your mom?"

"It's the wrong place for anybody." She shrugged, glancing at her mother, who closed her mouth over whatever words had wanted out.

"Are you feeling...?" I trailed off as she began smelling the couch and running her hands along the walls.

"I've got your old room ready for you," Vivian said as though offering a dish of cream to a cat, rolling a chunk of amethyst between her fingers. "It's probably still a bit dusty, but the bedding is fresh."

Mom's head turned slowly. "The key," she told the grandfather clock beside her. "I would need the key."

"It's unlocked, of course, Nicolette." Vivian's tight smile was back. "If you'd like to rest."

Mom whispered something, perhaps to herself, perhaps to the clock, and shrugged off her coat before folding it in a meticulous bundle and sliding it under a chair. "Rest it," she told it, and headed toward the stairs, pausing as she passed, her dark eyes flitting over my face with what might have been curiosity, then traced her hands along the banister and hurried upstairs, a flustered Vivian following at a safe distance.

Dad started to head after them before thinking better of it. Instead, he ran his fingers down his beard, as was his habit when he was troubled. I doubt his hand had left the beard much since yesterday; it rested at his chin now when he turned to me. "This is a terrible idea."

When I was little, before mom left, I fell into a lake and Dad had been the one to pull me from the water. I almost drowned, so it's probably best that I remember nothing about it except for the feeling of being lifted, of being somewhere cold and dark, then being brought into the light. The instant relief of that safety. Of being held.

That's what he'd always been: safe arms around me. I never felt like I wasn't the most important thing to him growing up. Then something changed. I know that something was me.

I don't blame him for Stillview. But things weren't the same between us in the aftermath. That feeling of sanctuary when I thought of him was replaced by the sense of his disappointment in me. The worry.

And I couldn't *stand* it. His hovering concern, my having to lie to him about the medication. So I pushed him away. I think he figured that meant I didn't need him anymore and was free to start up with that knockoff of Mom. I'd been inching my way toward leaving anyway, and his moving her in with us was the shove I needed.

Now sitting in the kitchen of my new, in-between home, I drank my room-temperature tea as he explained that the doctor had called him at dawn to tell him that he was discharging her this morning.

"I would've brought her home with me. For a while anyway. But the doctor said it would be best if she were someplace familiar." I was sure I heard a hint of relief there. "Thing is, this doctor was different from yesterday. Same guy, but...different. When I asked him what made him change his mind about her needing to stay for observation for a while, he threw his hands up and laughed saying, 'Why do I do anything?' So, for some reason I'm not filled with confidence that this is where she needs to be. Especially with you here as well.

"I *know*"—he held his hand up as I opened my mouth to object—"that you don't want to come home. You know how I feel about you being here. I've said my peice on that. But she's *clearly* not well. She hardly spoke at all yesterday. I was tearing up just to see her, and she just casually says, 'Hello, Rick.' Like no time has passed. She doesn't seem to hate me, which is better than before, but she barely asked about *anything*. Not about me, not you. Nothing."

I flinched at that. "Does she even know who I am?"

"She does...but I'm worried, Tali." And he was, I could see it in his tired eyes, the same gray as mine. Maybe the same tired too. "I don't want you to be hurt if she doesn't understand..."

"Doesn't understand what a mess I am?" I fiddled with the delicate curve of the teacup's handle. I knew I'd earned the way he saw me.

"Look," he sighed, "I sat with her all day yesterday. Mostly she was in a daze. But I could tell there's something happening just below the surface, and I would feel a lot better if she were somewhere with people better trained to handle whatever bursts through."

"Like a hospital? Like *Stillview*? Jesus, Dad, throwing pills at someone isn't always the answer."

"Talia—"

"And if she's *here* there's a chance she'll remember who she is." I paused, looking at the puddle of amber left at the bottom of my cup. "I know that it might not happen. Maybe she won't come back like she was, but...if she wasn't happy, maybe that could be a good thing."

"You don't remember..." His brows furrowed. "Before she left—she was...she wasn't *well*."

"Like me."

"No. Not like you. I'm worried you're expecting her to be someone she never was."

"I just want her to be *okay*," I said honestly. "I'm not expecting a miracle, I'm just...Hope for the best, expect the worst, right?"

He rested his cheek in his hand, abandoning trying to convince me otherwise. "I guess that's a healthy way to look at it."

"You know me, full of surprises."

A smile invaded his beard. "Well." His sigh morphed into a yawn. "Cole may be indifferent to me, but clearly Vivian isn't, so I don't want to hang around to add to the stress. I also don't want to be all the way back home if something happens, so to compromise I'm sticking close by at the town inn for a few days. Promise to call me if anything happens?"

"No phone, remember?"

"I'll pick one up for you—bring it tomorrow. Safe to assume you're going to be sticking close by here in the meantime?"

"Everything here is close by, so yeah."

"You know what I mean. It's not a great idea to go wandering around alone right now when we still don't know what happened."

"Not many places to wander anyway." I walked him out to the porch, and a door slammed shut upstairs. Vivian shouted something, her voice angry. A moment later, another door slammed.

"Already going well. Which reminds me, that old lady they found at the river with your mom? She got discharged too. Apparently, that cop, Walker, took her in. Maybe it's just him being a nice guy, but that seems a bit above and beyond."

"Maybe he's hoping she'll remember something helpful."

"Maybe." He lingered, looking up at the windows upstairs. The sun made his eyes look more blue than gray and brought out the silver that had begun taking over the copper in his hair around the temples. "I think I'll bring my violin when I come back. Play it for her. She used to love that."

"So did I." I smiled. Dad could play anything with strings, but there was something exciting about the music that trembled out of that violin. The lively songs were fine, but to me, the violin was made for the dark and melancholy. When I was little, the way he pulled the most solemn notes out of it with one long pull of his arm was almost like magic. I just then realized that I wasn't sure when he had stopped playing it.

"I've never really given up on her, you know."

"Neither have I," I said, both of us knowing that had been the problem.

13

Poor Pretty Thing

There was a photo in a gilded frame on top of Vivian's dresser of her with my grandfather on their wedding day. He was a stoic-looking man with kind eyes, a good bit older than his elegant wife. It was only after he died that a freshly widowed Vivian had first come to Elmwood with ten-year-old Mom.

The inherited Adair house did nothing for Vivian's grief or her boredom, according to what Mom had told Dad. She dealt with the burden of being saddled with her husband's estate, as well as single motherhood, increasingly with the aid of a martini or spiked tea in a dainty cup. She didn't attempt to make the place more contemporary, only bringing the parts of herself that would fit: the photographs and collected pieces of art. But anything she added was only swallowed up by the vastness of the house. That's what happened to Mom too, by the sound of it. She almost got swallowed up by this house. By the loneliness and her mother's instability.

The first thing I'd wanted to do when I arrived was to see her bedroom. I figured that would be a good place to find some idea of who she'd been. Of course, I had to ask Vivian to unlock it first because, as she explained while flipping through the brass keys on their metal ring, she liked to keep all of the rooms not being used shut and locked. It was one less thing to worry about, she said. What the worry of an unlocked bedroom could be, I didn't ask.

The filigreed handle of the key she gave me was cold in my hand, matching the chill of the room it opened. I pulled my sweater closed and made my way to the bay windows to pull the curtains open, greeted by the garden, fire-colored leaves of the trees below, and a nose full of dust. The air smelled dimly of cedar; specks swirled in beams of light that landed on the bare bed. Odd little porcelain figures of animals dressed in aristocratic finery and wearing human masks were arranged on a pale chest of drawers.

A couple of books wrapped in brown paper sat abandoned on an otherwise empty desk. I flipped open the one with the word "English" drawn on its front in bold black marker. The inner cover had a list of handwritten names, the last written in sharp, curved lines: "*Cole Adair*". I rubbed the dust from my fingers.

Across the room, a harlequin doll, porcelain like his roommates, sat on a neatly stacked bookshelf which, unlike those in the rest of the house, had slightly more modern titles under a thin layer of dust webs. There were gaps where some of them had been removed, likely hastily thrown into a suitcase. I very much wanted to know what books had been considered too precious to be left behind. I pulled out a Maurice Sendak title I recognized—I knew she had gotten another copy of this one at some point. She used to read it to me.

Like the rest of the room, the bookshelf was made up of remnants of childhood mingled with scraps of budding adult. Magazine cutouts of bands tacked to the wall next to kitten posters, all yellowed and curling at the edges. I ran my fingers along the remaining cluster of dresses and plaid skirts, denim and flannel, that still hung in the closet before randomly plucking one out to feel the soft fabric on my cheek.

To the side of the vanity mirror, among the few accessories that were scattered on the table, was a little wooden box. It played a pretty little tune when opened and held a small, single rose. Time had turned it soot black, but it somehow still had a breath of sweetness. I left the box open but stopped short of touching the flower. It would doubtlessly crumble at the contact after all this time in its musical little tomb.

As I looked through the drawers and under the bed, I felt like the desperate invader I was, rifling through a ghost's past uninvited. Whatever I was looking for, I didn't find it. It was full of objects, but the room was empty. It was no wonder she could leave most of it behind, none of it felt personal. It was as though she hadn't really lived here at all.

The music box's song slowed then stopped, and I sat on the bed and wept like I hadn't in a very long time.

As I stood in front of the door again today, even knowing I didn't need a key now, it felt even more impassable. I raised my fist to knock a couple of times before actually doing so. No answer. I knocked once more before cracking the door open.

The room was pretty much the same as I'd left it, with the addition of the mint-green bedding Mom was lying curled up on. She silently faced the window, eyes open. Someone had covered the vanity mirror with a matching sheet.

"Hey..." I was suddenly aware of the awkwardness of calling her 'Mom' after all this time. "I just wanted to see if you needed anything."

"Don't," she whispered.

I almost closed the door then, but I had to at least *try*. I walked around the bed, watching as her gaze shifted to me. For a second, I thought I caught the warmth of recognition in the damp-earth color of her eyes.

"Do you know who I am?"

"You're his daughter," she said in her cracked-china voice.

"Well, I don't think you can put all the blame on him. Come on, who else am I?"

"My poor, pretty thing." She smiled, just a bit and a little sadly, but she smiled and it *hurt*. "How cruel. These tricks."

Sharp warmth from my chest bled up into my throat, pooling into a lump.

"I hate the beard." Quickly her smile screwed to the side. "A hiding thing. A lie. It all comes back again. Slow as a serpent freshly fed." I swallowed the lump as she pointed to the window, no longer smiling. *"Don't."*

With that she rolled her back to me which I took to mean that she wouldn't be elaborating. I turned to leave with a resigned sigh and caught an odd shaped shadow move under the bed. A trick of the light, surely, but I knelt and peered beneath where the blanket hung unevenly off the mattress anyway. There, almost out of reach, was a book. Soft dust gathered under my fingers as I managed to slide it out. It was red and leather bound with the word *Folklore* in faded gold print on its spine. One of the missing books from her shelf.

I doubted she'd mind if I borrowed it.

Downstairs the dining room was invigorated with sunlight and crisp air from the garden from the now open windows. I let my fingers trace the patterns of intertwining gold blossoms of the rose and gold wallpaper for a moment before rushing to check that the doors were locked. Thankfully they were, so at least Vivan wasn't dropping all of her practical protections in favor of the gemstones and crystals now that her daughter was back safe.

She'd been what I would describe as panic-cleaning all day. Since she refused to let me help her, I fixed us a lunch neither of us were hungry for. After she checked to see that Mom was sleeping, we sat at the dining table that—until today—had been a storage place for stacks of magazines, sorted mail, and other orderly clutter with only bird songs from the garden filling the silence.

"We'd argued that night," she said finally. I stopped peeling the crust of my sandwich. "*The* night. I'd hoped enough time had passed to grow some common ground between us, but we weren't made for each other, my daughter and I. Motherhood wasn't a natural state for me, and everything I did..." Her fingers ran across her gemstone rings. "After my Ed died and it was just the two of us, I was made even more acutely aware of how much she and I didn't understand each other."

"But"—I was careful to keep the accusation from my voice—"she was just a little girl then."

"Oh yes, but after a certain age there's only so much you can do. She was born willful. I knew she would always do as she pleased. It didn't help that Ed spoiled her. Once he was gone, I didn't know how to *be* with her. I should have been better, but I lost track of us." She began folding her napkin on the polished surface of the table. "I drank. More than I should have at times. I'm sure *Richard* told you that."

"Yes...but that was because that's what she told him." I felt my cheeks redden, not liking how what I knew felt like gossip. "She said that was why she left...that the drinking made you cruel."

She looked thoughtfully at the napkin and then folded her hands and looked at me for a long moment. "I made mistakes. No doubt about that. But I don't ever remember being purposely cruel."

"Well, probably because you were drunk," I said without thinking, but Vivian smiled.

"There she is, there's your mother in you. She was just as blunt when she had been avoiding saying something."

"I didn't mean—"

"I'm not *saying*," she continued over me, "that I didn't say some regrettable things. Or that I'm not sorry for them. But I said plenty of things while stone sober that weren't meant to be unkind—she just didn't take well. Nicolette saw things very differently than I did. Things never settled well in me after my Ed. That's not an excuse, but drinking...that wasn't what made me a bad mother. It was absolutely everything about me."

"Doesn't seem like the drinking helped though." The words again snapped out of me as though I felt the need to push my mother's side of things.

"No, dear." She sighed. "My ways were not always useful, but I got set in them. I didn't want her roaming those woods. She was always taking walks out there, but I worried there could be, oh I don't know, *vagrants* camping there. And then there were the men out hunting who knows what. But I couldn't watch her all the time, and my daughter was clever. I'd actually thought to be glad that at her age at least she wasn't going out with boys, so that one snuck up on me. Your father. I had the studio in the city, and some days I would be gone well into the night, and she...did what she pleased. And then she was gone."

"Studio?"

"Oh, she didn't tell you about that? Well, I suppose that's not as useful as my drinking habits to a girl looking to be interesting. My portrait studio. I'd moved it out from New York. Just a vanity project, but it got me out of the house once in a while. I'd taken the camera up while modeling—I even tried to show her how to use it once she expressed an interest. The modeling," she said to answer the question that must've been on my face, "was how I got around Europe. I suppose *that* chapter wasn't dark enough to be relayed either."

I'd never heard of anything good about Mom and Vivian's relationship, but I suppose it made sense that it was there. No one can be awful all the time, it takes too much effort.

"Anyway," she said, collecting our barely touched dishes, shooing my hands when I tried to help, "I don't like talking about the past. I'm not proud of who I was with Nicolette. I was honestly surprised that she wanted to come back into my life at all when she did. That's why I was going to let her stay here when she'd asked, though I didn't agree with what she was doing."

"You mean leaving?" I followed her to the kitchen.

"I mean leaving *you*. I was never fond of Richard, but he was a grown man. I told her children need their mothers, such as we are." She shook her head and rinsed the plates and glasses, handing them to me to dry one by one. "I wish I could tell you anything useful about what happened that night, but the fact is my memory is hazy. Yes," she said before I could, "because of *the drinking*.

"But at the hospital last night, when I talked about my garden just to fill the air until the doctor brought up what was supposed to be her *eventual* discharge, he asked Richard and I each about whether we would be able to take her, and I said that of course—if she needed me to. I was her mother. Then she looked over to me with the most peculiar expression and said, 'Such as you are.'"

"So"—I set the last glass in the cabinet—"doesn't that show she's still in there?"

"Yes, but behind what?"

14

The Door

Mom must've taken one of the sedatives she'd been discharged with because she slept the rest of the afternoon. After lunch Vivian went to nap, and I tried to digest everything she'd told me about herself and Mom. I thought of her here alone at night as a kid and whatever sanctuary she might've found in the woods while Vivian was away. The idea that maybe the reason she spent time hiding and with her books under a desk– why she had been in such a hurry to leave here, had less to do with Vivian than I'd thought, hadn't been lost on me. What if she had seen something out there that scared her away?

I stuck around the house so Vivian could rest and not worry about Mom being alone. The afternoon light was already fading, so my plans on researching what I could about the town and its stories would have to wait until tomorrow. There was no way I was going outside the house after dark. I passed the time with the television on in the background, flipping through the book from under the bed.

It was mostly very old fairy tales or *Tales of Faerie* as it was written on the oddly weighted paper, along with some history of and descriptions of plants and mushrooms. The illustrations were what held my attention, the details and the way they curled all along the page, even in some of the lettering.

Over the sounds of whatever show was on, I heard a door open upstairs followed by hurried footsteps. "Talia!" Vivian whispered harshly from the stairs. I sprang up to see her staring at something down the hall. She waved me up without turning. I reached the landing and saw the dividing door was wide open to the sleeping, dark side of the house.

"Did you do this?" she asked, equally panicked and annoyed.

"No," I answered with a blush of anxiety, even though I really hadn't been guilty...this time.

"The key isn't missing. Nicolette is still asleep. I just checked."

"Maybe she could have taken and replaced it. You sleep pretty heavily."

"But why—" she began, then she laughed under her breath. "She used to do this. Sneak over there in the dark. I never knew why. It would frustrate me to no end when I couldn't find her, so I started locking the doors. Well, I suppose this might be a sign that she's remembering...well, it's a sign of something."

I couldn't argue with that.

There was something in the walls.

I lay in bed listening to the scratching sounds in denial before reluctantly blinking my eyelids open. I'd fallen asleep fast and early and would still be there if not for the persistent noise. The full moon's light flooded the room well enough to let me see that whatever it was wasn't in the room with me, thankfully. I hoped it could be a squirrel. A possum maybe. I'd even take a swarm of rabid bats. But that wasn't the week I was having. Reluctantly, I pushed the warmth of my blanket aside and swung my feet to the carpet.

My sleep-heavy legs staggered across the room, and I held my hand to the wall it seemed to be coming from. No movement, so at least whatever it was wasn't close to clawing its way through the wood yet. I pressed my ear to the wallpaper as the sound scraped closer, gasping when it dragged over my door. It kept going. Whatever it was wasn't coming from *inside* my wall, but on the other side of it. In the hallway.

When the sound had been stationary and, I hoped, far enough away for a few minutes, I cracked the door open enough to see my mother, her forehead pressed against the wall, face hidden by the loose curtain of hair so white it seemed to glow against the dimness of the hall. She was hissing "*izzit..izzit...izzit...*" as she ripped chucks of green wallpaper away. Shreds of it trailed down the hall from her room, past Vivian's, to mine. She wasn't peeling it away in long strips, but small fingerfuls at a time, as though she were being cautious about revealing what was beneath.

I moved closer to her frantic whispers until I could make out the words. "*Is it?*" she was asking as her fingers began to dig into the plaster as though she were trying to force her hands through. "*Is it?? Is it??*"

"Mom?" I said gently. I'd heard you needed to be careful when waking sleepwalkers, and I hoped that was all this was. There was no reaction. I tried again, a little louder. "Mom?" And then, "Cole?"

But she carried on undisturbed. Digging and digging. As my eyes adjusted to the low light, I saw dark smears on the white of the plaster. *Blood.* She was shredding the skin of her fingers open as she clawed in an increasing frenzy at the wall. I grabbed her shoulder without thinking, and she swung around, a glint of metal in her hand.

She clutched a narrow knife at level with her wild eyes. I felt the sting on my forearm where it had sliced and a warmth spilling down my skin. I must've cried out because Vivian's door swung open and she rushed toward us, her face going pale at the scene before her.

"Nicolette!"

Backed against the banister, pressing my hand to the wound, I was unsure of what to do. I knew it was an accident, that she didn't even know who she was right then let alone me, so I didn't move. With the heightened awareness of a wounded animal, Mom's eyes flicked to where Vivian stood then back to me.

"Is it *here?*" she demanded of Vivian in a hiss. "The bridge of its eyes? It's been *changed.*" She slapped the defaced wall behind her and turned to me whispering, "There's a cage in its veins. The door..." She spun around, glancing around her. "The door..." she repeated, seeming to come back to herself in waves as she looked from me to Vivian to the knife in her hand.

"You were having a nightmare," Vivian said finally, moving cautiously toward her. "That's all. You were having a nightmare." She gently placed one arm around Mom's shoulder while she plucked the knife away from her unresisting grip.

"Talia, dear," she said over her shoulder as she led Mom away, "there's a first aid kit in the hallway cabinet."

The two of them disappeared into the bedroom of dancing figurines and old books, the room of the ghost that now lived in my mother's skin, leaving me alone.

The cut was a bit longer than the few dozen lines it neighbored. Brighter than their pale pink. *In a few years, they'll hardly be scars at all.* But this one might stick around for longer. It could have used a stitch or two, but it would stop bleeding on its own soon. I expertly cleaned it, taped it down with gauze.

I don't know how long I was sitting on the couch staring blankly ahead, adrenaline working its way into exhaustion, before Vivian emerged from upstairs holding the key ring and a small oblong box she handed to me. "This was in her room. I've never seen it before."

It was beautiful, laid with an intricate, swirling pattern of mother-of-pearl. Inside was a soft bed for the dagger my mother had cut me with; its wooden handle was carved leaves wrapping a slender blade. I'd seen the box before, as a glint caught in a dying flashlight. There must be a back staircase in the shut-off side of the house, I realized. Mom had gone over there to get this. Somewhere in her cloudy head, she sensed she needed to protect herself.

"I looked through her room after I got her into bed and made sure there was nothing else like this. Nothing else she could..." She frowned at my arm. "I'll need to call the doctor."

There was a heaviness to her voice that told me she wasn't referring to my arm. I knew if they thought Mom was a danger to herself or others, then she'd be put away. I'd lose her again.

"It's just a cut—I'm fine. She didn't know what she was doing, you saw that," I insisted. "She wasn't trying to hurt me."

"Well, she did." She snapped the box closed. "And that wasn't your mother."

"No, but wasn't that the point of her coming here? To remind her who she is?"

"That's what the doctor hoped, but that woman upstairs is not Nicolette."

"How would you know?" I snipped. "You didn't ever really *know* her."

"Neither did you," she said, her words a calm slap to my face.

"Whoever she is, it's all I have left of her. If you send her away..." My voice began to crack. "Look, if anything like this happens again, you can have her carted off to Stillview and I'll understand, but just give her another chance. Please, Vivian."

I knew I was putting her in a tough spot between alienating me and keeping me safe, but I just needed time. I didn't know what I could do, but I was certain if I could find out what happened to my mother, I'd be able to find the answers needed to fix her. Well, as certain as I could be of anything.

"All right," she said finally, as though she already regretted it. "But I'm keeping her door locked at night, and I want yours kept the same way when you go to bed from now on."

I agreed, though I doubted I would ever sleep well here, or anywhere, ever again.

15

How Curious

In my dreams it was cold, and the shadows hissed my name like a song, morphing into something familiar and as clear as a bell until it pulled me awake. The room was bathed blue with moonlight, and the chiming of my phone reminded me that nightmares no longer stayed in my head, and I was either as mad as my mother seemed or in a danger I couldn't define. Either was apparently something I couldn't escape from. Because the chiming, dear god, was coming from in the room with me.

Someone had been in the house. In my room. It had to be that man from last night. My eyes popped open wider as my exhausted mind clicked together that if he had gone through the trouble of sneaking in, the chances that he had just kindly returned my phone and left were slim.

There was no obvious movement around me—no odd shapes in the shadows. The chiming alarm was coming from the armoire, which was very unfortunately by the door. I could get to it quick enough, but since I'd locked it, it would cost me several precious seconds to get it open. I assumed that's what he was waiting for to pop out. The sound of me trying to escape. Whoever he was, he had gone through the trouble to build fear into this room while I slept. He could have shown himself, been standing over me when I opened my eyes, or pushed a pillow into my face when I was sleeping to muffle any sound. He *could* have done anything, but instead he was hiding. Using the phone to scare me first.

The cut on my arm throbbed.

I didn't wait to find out what he planned to do next. I tossed the blankets aside and ran. Only, thanks to my eyes not leaving the armoire doors as I did so, I didn't notice that I'd launched a pillow from the bed in the process, which I then managed to trip over with both feet, sending me careening to my hands and knees. I completed the journey to the door in a rising crawl.

The chiming stopped.

The doors of the armoire stayed closed. I didn't turn from them as I stood and felt for the key in the lock, but finally grasping it, I paused. Every bit of sense seemed to be gripping beneath my skin and pulling at me to turn the lock, to move, to *flee*. But I hesitated.

What would I do when I fled? Go to Vivian and tell her there was someone in the house, only to find that there wasn't? What was she going to do if she thought I'd gone delusional? She'd feel outnumbered here, that's what. Was there a way to explain *why* I assumed there was a man with my phone hiding in my closet in a way that made me sound even a little bit sane to the police, to Shane, or anyone? Word would get to my dad. Even though he likely couldn't have me committed again, he'd see me as even more broken, and that *look*, that disappointed concern, would never leave his eyes.

If whoever this was wanted to murder me without much fuss, he'd have done it already. He could still murder me, of course. I'd already been knifed tonight by my own mother, so what a cherry on the end of things that would be—but I couldn't take the uncertain tension about my own sanity anymore.

Trying to calm my breathing in hopes that my heartbeat would follow suit, I let go of the key and switched on the light. Nothing came bursting out at me. I moved to the armoire, slowly aware of a fork in my dread; if my phone *were* in there alone, I'd really have to face the possibility that it'd been there all along and that I'd made up the rest without telling myself. I yanked the doors open, jumping away from them as I did.

Nothing. There was nothing besides a few clothes swinging on hangers. My hand went to my chest, the laugh at the tail of my relief over how I must have looked just then was cut off with the resuming of the chime. I'd been wrong. It hadn't come from the armoire, but next to it, over the vanity table.

It came from the mirror.

I turned slowly toward it, my hands flying to my mouth to poorly block my shriek at the man standing next to the bed behind my reflection. I whirled around, my toe getting caught hard on one of those damned carved birds at the foot of the chair. Through the sharp, wincing pain, I could see no one was behind me. No one was in the room, but I wasn't alone. I shifted my weight off of my throbbing toe as I turned back to the mirror, and there the man still stood. Though 'man' would not be very accurate.

While he resembled one in form—tall, broad-shouldered with the appropriate number of limbs—his otherwise normal face, with its sharp cheekbones and the curved line of his lips, looked as though someone had smudged it. Inky veins of shadow drifted like smoke from eye holes that blended with the pale, gnarled skin of what should have been a forehead.

I stood rooted and unblinking as with a roll of his neck, the blurred features shifted, the tendrils of shadow receding into his eyes as the rest of his features settled into their proper place, leaving him flawlessly smooth. Only the terrible perfection of his face didn't make him any easier to look at because now I could more easily focus on the rest of him; how his ears rose to tapered points and sprouting from the black of his hairline were a pair of dark horns striated in silver, curving and arching around, ending in points at the top of his head. Yet these things weren't as unnerving as his onyx eyes and the ghostly pale pools at their center, which were set unmistakably on me.

I felt I ought to scream now, this seemed like a perfectly acceptable time to do so, but just as the thought came, he brought a slender finger to his lips, and I swallowed down the urge. Instead, forgetting my unbalanced stance, I wobbled forward, toward the mirror and further away from where he was reflected, my hands grabbing the chair back to stop me from hitting the floor again.

"Well. As graceful as a bat. Perhaps." His voice was tattered velvet over his grin. *"You should sit."*

"Not real." My words weakly stumbled from my bone-dry mouth to the creature not far enough behind me, but even I didn't believe them. I gripped the chair but decided against taking advice from the reflection. My breath was my anchor. I focused on it and the gallop of my heartbeat to keep myself from blind panic. I didn't dare to take my eyes off of the mirror. "You're...not really there."

"Oh." The grin lingered as he stretched his hands out before him and gracefully flipped them over a few times. *"I'm here enough. Real, enough."*

"Fine." I nodded and kept nodding, reason bleeding out of my head. "Fine. Fine."

"It is. Now," he said, taking a step toward me. Oddly, the prickles of fear that started up my spine as he did so faded as quick as they came. *"I am called Noc. Archcarver and Shadow Warden to your Kind Neigh-*

bor, *the graciously Grim King Orias of Midnight: Lord of Shadows and the Riven Court of Umbra, but Noc...will do."*

"What"—my voice was barely over a cracked whisper—"are you?"

"Archcarver and Shadow-" He sighed. *"Do you really need me to say it again?*

"No—no," I said. Not having understood it well the first time, I had little hope for the second. "But, like, WHAT are you?"

"Oh." He studied me with the moons of those midnight eyes. *"Your forgetful kind has many names for mine. Monsters. Spirits. Faeries. Demons."* His grin widened. *"Gods. But none of these names matter more than the one I've chosen to give to you, Talia Adair."*

He spoke in an accent I couldn't place; there was nothing harsher in it than a husky edge to his tone. Yet hearing my name from his mouth, a chill moved through my heart. Demon certainly seemed to suit him best, nothing spritely there. But, nothing completely monstrous either.

"*I* didn't choose to give you my name at all," I told him, and he smiled fully, showing his white and slightly sharp teeth. At this, the familiar burn of irrational anger began to pull at me. It didn't just kick in to counteract grief but also terror. Apparently.

"No. You know what? This is fine. I think...I'm dreaming." I announced this as though saying it would make it true. Boldly turning to the empty spot in the room where he should have been, I explained rather loudly, "I am *stressed* out, and now I'm having some very vivid, very *weird* fucking dream."

"And. Am I the sort of creature you have such dreams about then?" the amused voice from the mirror asked.

"No..."

"How curious," he said. *"It would seem then, that you are awake."*

I turned back to the mirror to see him sweeping his eyes over me from head to toe. I couldn't suppress the shudder and hugged my chest, suddenly aware that the fabric of my top wasn't as thick as I would have preferred it to be just then. Some brave, logical part of me took more details of him in, wanting to force him to fit in with the world I understood.

Despite the bestial features, he did at least look like a *civilized* being. The dark clothes he wore were suitably bizarre; a long fitted coat that looked to be edged in small flat feathers, a soft looking waistcoat over a high-collared shirt that was open to the hollow of his throat, and tall boots that made no sound when he stepped. For a second, I had the horrifying idea to reach behind me to where he looked to be to see if my hand would pass through him, but I didn't risk it. If he were solid, if I *touched* him, I did not think I could stop myself from screaming then.

"Okay." I was nodding again. "Okay. Then maybe I just finally really am completely insane."

"*Oh, by the Dark, all the stars in every sky,*" he muttered, glancing up at the ceiling. "*How much easier this would be for both of us if only that were true. Howbeit, here we are both present and sound.*"

"Well, to be fair," I said, annoyed at the lack of sense at this moment, "that's just what a hallucination would say."

"*If you so wish.*" Amusement faded from his face as the room dimmed. "*To be mad, it would be easily granted, but that isn't my errand. Not this night. And you haven't the time to waste on reveries.*"

He clasped his hands behind his back and turned on his heel. The room reilluminated as he paced toward the bed. "*Something lost was returned to you by way of water, was it not?*" he asked, looking disinterestedly at the photos on the wall.

Christ. I'd almost forgotten. "My mother."

"Your mother," he said with a shake of his head at a photo of some long dead relatives at a picnic, *"was stolen from your realm and in mine given sanctuary by the most merciful, Grim King Orias. Protection was promised to her. And I"*—he turned back to me—*"am that protection. Protection that reaches to everything of her, including you, Talia Adair."*

"Stolen," I repeated. I saw no weapon, but the ominous air around him said he probably didn't need one. If something like him was the protection, I didn't want to imagine what the threat looked like. Or what a "Grim King Orias" was.

"By the most vile, cursed beast to have ever been formed over the Veil, from Hell, Faerie, or the Slumbering Dark. He drove a sword"—his voice rumbled—*"through the Kindly King Orias in a frenzy of vengeance to steal her once again. Your clever, sweeting mother. Tricking something from him, a...sort of key."* For a moment, his tone switched to what could have been either admiration or disgust. *"And with it, she was able to open The Veil enough to drift back to this soil on the waves of Moon Dark Sea. At a cost, as you would have noticed."*

The image of blood dug into the walls flashed in my mind. "A cost...is that why she's—?"

"Addled. The key she held seems to have left her with a disordered mind. Worse, the shadows of my realm do cling and so were half pulled from their place as she left it, tearing a hole in the Veil between our worlds. Now any manner of your Kindly Neighbors and creatures whose names no longer exist in your tongue can ebb through from my lands. Into yours. So, I have come. To keep these things from her."

"But," I said thinking of Maevyn, "isn't *everyone* here in danger then?"

He shrugged. *"Others are not my errand."*

"Well, what about this...beast? The one you say stole her, what if he comes to find her again?"

"*Oh.*" His smile was like a knife. *"I do hope he tries."*

"You said you were a protector..." I dug back through the jumble of his words. "A 'warden', right? Then those other...grim...kindly...the *Neighbors*..." I pointed at the reflected window behind us. "Shouldn't you—?" He raised a dark brow. "*Couldn't* you stop them from coming through?"

"*Perhaps.*" He folded his arms, leaning against the bedpost behind me. *"But you have my protection, as does your mother. And hers. Protection that is easily carried out within these walls. Howbeit, though multitudes of creatures of Dawn and Dark may walk as they wish on your soil, I on the other hand move in wind and shadows and on the breath of dreams. I cannot enter human lands, not fully, without being summoned. If you wish me to warden the whole wood, you might do so.*" He drummed his fingers on his sleeve. *"If you like."*

"I might...you mean, *summon you*?"

"If you like."

"No thank you."

"Well. Then you ask the wrong question." He pushed off the bedpost and approached me casually, my heart quickening with his every step as I was locked between the mirror and what, part of my brain tried to remind me, was someone not actually there. I focused on the cool of the wood beneath my palms, the soft rug under my feet. He seemed taller than seconds ago, the black depths of his eyes on mine. *"Cleaning up a spill of blood"* —his voice was soft as he gazed down at my arm— *"does nothing to stop the bleed."*

My whole body tensed as he was now close enough behind me that, were he really there, I would feel a breath on my bare shoulder. "Can the tear be closed?"

"*Yes. But my telling you how*"—he smiled at my reflection—"*will cost.*"

"What kind of cost?"

"*For this, only a promise.*" His fingers moved as though to brush a lock of hair back from my neck, then stopped short, closing around only air, and pulling back. "*You must promise to speak of me to no one. I must be your dearest secret.*"

"Why?"

"*To tell you my motives...*"

"There's a cost. Got it." I certainly wasn't going to figure any of this out alone, and it wasn't as though anyone would believe me about a demon in my bedroom anyway. "All right. I won't tell anyone."

"*No.*" He shook his head while holding my reflected stare. "*Promise me. You must say the right words, make an oath of it.*" Up close I could see the details of his horns, the thin silver that flowed into the fine edges like liquid mercury and the delicately carved symbols scrolled around each one. "*Swear secrecy to me, and I will tell you what can close the path.*"

"Er, I promise you...Noc"—his name felt strange on my lips—"that I won't tell anyone about you." His mouth twitched and I thought to add, "As long as you are protecting this house and everyone in it."

There was a faint red glow in his pupils, then a silvery flicker across the pitch of his eyes. "*It's a bargain struck.*" He grinned and the knots in my stomach tightened. "*Now.*" He clasped his hands together. "*What opened the path can close it. What was taken must be returned. If you find the key she used to escape, it could close the path it opened.*"

I hoped he wouldn't nickel-and-dime me on any follow up questions, because it felt like my promise should have bought me more than: *key used to open thing, also locks thing.*

"Okay...does it *look* like a key?"

His grin faded. "*Perhaps. However, since he does not wish it to be found, least by me or mine, it's likely to be something nondescript. A glamoured thing for certain. A lackluster amulet perhaps. Or a rather plain scepter.*"

"So." I had surpassed fear, veered off into frustration, and landed in absurdity. "You don't know where it is *or* what it looks like?"

"*Finding the key*"—he smirked—"*is not my errand.*"

His eyes narrowed and he tilted his head, as though he heard something I couldn't. Then he was across the room, at the window. I gasped. Already on edge, seeing the blur of inhuman motion he became had me gripping the chair again to keep myself from bolting to the door, like every instinct I had in that second commanded I do. My shock must have been apparent, because when he turned back from surveying the outside, his black eyes widened at the sight of me.

"*Oh.*" He held his hands up as though to steady me like I was some skittish little animal. Though to be fair, that is what I felt like. "*Apologies, dear Talia,*" he said with what could have been sincerity if not for the bemused glint in his eyes. "*You are still...alarmed by me.*"

I allowed my eyes to squeeze closed for a few seconds, when I opened them, he hadn't moved and almost looked like he was trying not to smile. He moved toward me with exaggerated slowness, oblivious to the fact that doing so made him even creepier.

"*Your ilk does not place much value on words, but they are law in my realm.*" His tone was soothing as he loomed over me once more. "*You have my word that I will protect you from harm. So long as you do what I ask of you.*" His eyes flashed. "*But our time this night grows short.*"

"Wait. My mother. What was done to her, the way she's...'addled'. Can you fix it?"

"*Yes...*"

"Oh. Let me guess," I said, exasperated, "not your errand?'"

"And. You would not like the cost."

I raised my chin up. "Try me."

He licked his bottom lip and stared at mine for a moment, his expression unreadable. *"She would have to come back across the Veil. Back to the Lands of Midnight."*

"No." I said resolutely. "I just got her back."

"Did you?" He shrugged again. *"You are her blood, but not her keeper. That cost is not yours to bear."*

"She's my *mother.*"

"And do you think that makes her yours? Curious." Before I could respond, he held up his hand. *"This key is most like to lie in the forest. But beware and be wise and do not trust all you see. Or who you may meet."*

"But...I'm supposed to believe you'll be keeping me safe from a distance?"

"You see me only half here, like this, so you doubt. But I can keep you from harm. From my kind. As long as you don't stray too far from where she is. If you want me to be more of a force, summon me then. I would be much more...effective, were I wholly there."

He smiled just a bit when he spoke, but something flickered in his eyes that made those pricks of fear dance up my back in full force. "You're here enough."

He chuckled, stepping back and becoming less, well, less. With a faint crackling sound, he was fading. *"Do remember"*—his voice fractured into an echo as the edges of his face began to trail veins of shadow into the air— *"your dearest secret."*

"Wait!" I called, but he dissolved into fading black tendrils, leaving only a faint scent of burning embers and rain. I moved to where he had been and sighed to the empty room. "You still have my phone."

16

Don't

The next morning found me sitting on the floor, next to the bed I'd barely slept in, with the book of folklore. The book was old, the stories older. Still, there was no mention of Midnight Lands or of any Veil or Grim, Kindly Kings. It was mostly accounts of goblins, redcaps, will-o'-wisps, and other faery things—none of whom acted in *any* sensical way. They were far from the idea sold to me as a kid of delicate beings no bigger than a hummingbird, dancing in circles wearing rose petals.

These tales painted this wildly uneven picture of creatures that could be benevolent, but also insanely easily offended, while the people they encountered were mostly unaware of the seemingly random rules the things lived by. The punishment was always far greater than the crime when it came to accidentally pissing off a faerie, often ending up in some horrible, life-ruining curse. Or Worse.

Reading the book stopped just short of being helpful to me. There were mentions of luring away and drownings by different types of faeries, but their reasons for doing so were vague. Did they *eat* the people they killed or was it just recreational murder? And stealing babies, that was popular, but again—why?

Noc had referred to this Veil that divided our worlds. Maybe this one was once more infested with creatures from the other side of it, but nowadays the ones that inspired these faery tales were now just kind of...tourists. No point to their visits really, just shitty, kidnapping, casually murderous tourists who once in a while would do some housework in exchange for some milk and honey.

Noc had stayed aloof when it came to what he was, casually dropping words like demons and gods while implying that they were all one and the same. What if he was right? If they had always been here, then what if once upon a time we *had* worshiped them? Why would they have given that up? Maybe something happened to push them out, to make them smaller to us.

Whatever the reason, they weren't gone enough. And if they had many names then I wondered how *faery* got attached to the idea of harmless little things beloved by children. But then...maybe that was the point. A bit of rebranding on the part of the gods and demons of old so people would forget to be afraid of them. Then forget how to keep them away. How to protect themselves from them. Forget they were ever real.

I wondered which kind of beast had taken my mother. A gnarled little man like the ones illustrated on these pages? Or something that didn't look anything like a man at all? Maybe something that very much did. I thought of those figurines in her room; beasts masquerading as humans. I wondered what Mom had seen him as when he stole her away, and how scared she must've been when his mask came off.

After I dressed, with a sheet over the mirror, in what was basically my fall uniform of leggings and layers, I went to check on Vivian. I'd assumed she was still asleep as the halls were devoid of music, but she was downstairs, already set to liberating every surface, frame, and odd bit of art in the place from any fleck of dust that may have possibly settled there. After watching her run the feather duster over a blue glass ashtray for a solid minute while staring at the stairway, I offered to help, but she shooed me away.

"I just need to keep my hands busy. I may try to clear the garden of the branches that came down in the storm later on," she said, moving the duster along a picture frame, her waist cinched by her floral, green apron.

"Storm?" There weren't many hours between what happened in the hallway and Noc, but I didn't know that I could have slept through anything that could wake even Vivian.

"I don't know how you missed it. All that howling wind. It was frightful." She glanced at me as she moved the duster on to a vase. "You must have been exhausted, you still look it. But at least *she's* back to being calm today. If you want to help, I suppose you can collect the tray from her room. Assuming she's done...well, assuming she's done."

I understood what she meant when I saw the food tray sitting neatly on Mom's desk. Bits had been peeled away from the toast and rolled into dozens of little balls, arranged in a spiral pattern.

Along with her shifting stare set to the garden, she wore an over-sized black sweater I recognized from her closet and some ripped jeans. Minus the black bob, she looked like every picture I had seen of my teenage mother. Only more sunken. Her legs were curled under her on the window bench. I sat on the other side, placing the book between us.

"Mom," I tried, and she flinched slightly. "Who is Noc?"

"Knock, knock," she said to the window. "The old wooden clock. The mistress has lost her head. Best to make haste through the door in her place, to pull her sweet children from bed."

"Okay." I blinked, pushing the book closer to her. "I know that you...aren't *you* right now. And maybe you don't even understand what I'm saying, but I want you to know that I'm going to keep you safe. I'm going to close that door you came through, but before I do, I'm going to try and figure out whatever one of these things"—I patted the book—"can make you well and—"

Her hand had drifted down to cover mine. Somehow her fingertips showed little trace of the damage I'd thought she earned them last night. "I missed everything," she said mournfully in a cracking whisper as she looked down at our hands. "It wasn't *meant*."

My heart tore wider than before. I placed my hand over hers. I wanted to trust that this was a moment of lucidity, but I didn't want there to only ever be *moments* where we understood each other, so I couldn't just enjoy this one. "Mom, do you know where the key to the door is?

Her lips trembled, a tear spilling down her cheek. I thought I saw something come into her eyes, some sort of focus, as she leaned forward....and yanked the book away. Clutching it to her chest she shot up, ran over to her bed, and rolled smoothly beneath it. A few seconds later, I heard tearing. Little slow bits of it.

"Right," I said and collected the tray. Just before closing the door behind me, the tearing stopped.

"Talia." Her voice sounded perfectly normal from under the bed. *"Don't."*

The tearing resumed.

I leaned against the torn wall in the hallway for a few moments before going to the kitchen, then dug Shane's number from my bag.

After the demon in my room *dissolved* last night, and my wits were more about me—as much as they could be after that anyway—I came up with more than a few questions for him that I probably couldn't have afforded to ask. Like how did he get my phone in the first place, and could I please have it back now? But the more pressing question was the reason I was dialing Shane up.

According to the book, faeries seemed to often take the form of either the young and beautiful or old hags to trick what they wanted from humans. What if the old woman found with Mom was just the first creature to follow that torn path after her? Followed by Maevyn and who knows what else. If so, not only could Shane be in danger, but he might be harboring someone that might know something about either un-addling Mom or finding this key.

When his phone went to voicemail, I turned the receiver of the landline around to start punching in a text before catching myself, which reminded me to drink something caffeinated before calling Mattie.

"I can just walk," I said more out of habit than anything when Mattie offered to come pick me up. "You said you're just around the corner?"

"Yeah, but it's a long damn corner. I'm leaving now."

She hung up before I could argue, only to call back minutes later telling me I'd have to meet her at the road.

There was something odd in her voice that made me ask, "Why?"

"Well, there's an entire...*tree* blocking your driveway."

It must have come down in that storm I'd missed, but it was already noon, and I needed to be back here before dark. Maevyn had appeared in full daylight; I didn't want to see what came at night.

"Give me ten minutes," I told her.

I let Vivian know about the tree. She didn't seem too surprised. Apparently, she usually had to call the town's tree-removal service at least a couple of times a year for this kind of thing, though usually it was just for downed branches. I started to wonder if maybe I should wait after all, since now she would be stranded there alone with Mom until the tree was removed, but she wouldn't hear of it when I offered to stay.

"Oh." She waved her hands. "Don't worry about me. You go spend time with someone sane for a while, or at least someone mad in a better way. You're young and should have a variety of madness in your life. It's useful."

I doubted that very much.

17

Exactly No One

Stepping into the fresh air and light felt surreal. I stood on the porch with my bag slung across my back, noting that, despite the litter of branches, the day looked *normal*. Uncomfortably so after all that happened last night. I think I half expected darkness to have seeped out of the house to cast a shadow over everything. But there was nothing foreboding out here. Only another beautifully crisp October afternoon, just cool enough to warrant the long burgundy cardigan I'd grabbed on my way out.

Back when I still had a best friend, this was the time of year she and I would get together and watch movies that were meant to be scary, but the characters were usually too unbelievably dumb. The fun in them came from her and I yelling at the people on the screen, hurling insults, and sometimes even rooting for the monster to take them out of the fictional gene pool.

I was thinking of this as I trod up the pavement, my eyes darting to either side of me at every twittering bird, wondering if in some alternate universe I was up on screen and she was yelling at me to turn around, go back to the house. Of course, if she were watching me as a movie, she was probably curled up next to *him*—the boy she stepped on our friendship over, squishing it into the ground with her heel for good measure and never looking back.

"You know, her mom went crazy before she disappeared." She would remind him in the same dramatically concerned manner she had when she told everyone who would listen back at school. "Talia's always been a little out there, but nothing like how she is now. I've tried to be there for her, but she's just gotten absolutely delusional. I just hope she gets the help she needs..."

She had been so cool and convincing when I overheard her saying it that I almost thought she really believed it. Except I knew she was only making sure no one would believe me if I tried to tell what her new boyfriend had done. It would work too. Small towns have got nothing on high school when it comes to the quick spread of rumors. Mattie had been right: people ate up a morbid story with a seed of truth in it. And my mother *had* really gone missing after all.

I'd easily imagined what was being whispered about me in the halls. Then after a while, I couldn't tell if it was only my imagination. *The apple didn't fall far from that tree,* all their eyes seem to say. *And if the tree was rotten, the apple would be warped inside. At least the tree had the sense to die.*

"A fine day." A man's voice startled me from my thoughts, and I snapped my head towards it. "For sorrows."

He leaned chestnut waves of hair against the trunk of a tree with his eyes shut. I'd somehow nearly walked right by, though everything about him stood out. He was dressed out of time: his hands hidden in deep pockets of high-waisted pants, a green coat stopped above the ankle of boots that came to his knee, a shirt hung loose and open at his chest. He reminded me of a toned-down version of someone from one of those New Romantic bands from an eighties-themed night, minus the makeup. It didn't escape me that, like Maevyn, he was just off of the driveway. Like Maevyn, he had been waiting.

I didn't even have the urge to run, which I thought was rather brave of me, though I did wonder if Vivian or Mattie would hear me if I opted to scream. Not that there would be much point to that. If I wanted answers, it would be foolish not to take advantage of not having to go hunting for someone who might have some.

"Trust me," I told him as confidently as I could, "you don't know my sorrows."

"You are her child, are you not?" He squinted his eyes in the sunlight and pointed his stubble darkened chin toward the house.

Whoever he was, whatever sort of 'Neighbor', he was striking. Not for the perfect slants of his face but for the spark in his eyes. I don't know what I had been expecting, probably something more obvious, like Noc. More monstrous. And far less photogenic.

He looked me over. "Well, 'child' no longer, but her daughter just the same."

I stared, trying to find something more otherworldly about him besides maybe his clothes. Was I trying to make a monster out of what might only be a man? Or maybe he wasn't even there at all, and if someone were to spot me there, they would only see me staring dumbfounded at a tree.

"And yet," he continued lazily in a variation of the accent that Noc had, "though she sits back once more at that house, where you can see her, *speak* to her once again, each time you do so, I suspect you don't feel any less motherless—as though she's not there at all, not really. She's like a lovely monument to her own absence." He pulled a burnished silver flask from his pocket and sipped from it, wincing slightly. "And nothing is as it seems."

There was something disarming in the depths of his voice, and with every word there was less and less of a chance that he could just be one of those roving vagrants Vivian seemed to believe dwelled out here. My mind kept drifting back to what looked so much like a little girl, until she abruptly did not, reaching for me with those twisting hands.

"Who exactly are you?" Really, I wanted to know *what* he was, but I was stalling for my own sake, stretching out the illusion that this could somehow be a normal interaction. Once you go and ask someone *what* they are, in any situation I would think, you remove any chance of that.

"Oh, I am *exactly* no one." His lips curled further upward. "But I am called Hawthorne. You"—he slid his flask to some inner pocket in his coat—"don't favor her much. Cole's beauty is dark, melancholy, but spirited. You're more like a fox, graceful and haunted. Hunted."

"What a completely odd thing to say to a person." He'd know that, of course, if he really were one.

"But nonetheless true."

"Sure." I nodded. "So, how do you know her then?"

"I met her here, in these woods. Long before the idea of you was formed."

"And...do you meet many young girls in the woods?" I took a step back, folding my arms over my chest. Mom had run away from here when she was sixteen, and he was well enough older than that.

"Well, I *live* in these woods," he said and smoothed his hair from his face. Several rings glinted from fingers on what was thankfully only a normal, human hand. "So, it's the only place I meet anyone."

"Are you like some kind of hermit?"

"Something like." With the heel of his boot, he pushed himself from the tree and sauntered over, stopping just at the edge of the path.

It was then that I noticed the golden hilt of the actual *sword* he wore at his side. "*You* haven't told me your name."

I certainly hadn't. He was almost close enough to touch, and I was suddenly very aware of that closeness, that his scent subtly wrapped around me: mossy and leather and some kind of spice. Seeing now why his eyes were so striking effectively killed any doubt about what he was; each of them held two colors moving against the other like oil and water refusing to mix. One half-blue, the other a sparkling green. An azure sky over an emerald sea, each half-moon of color swirling against an invisible divide, giving his gaze a liveliness all its own that I couldn't seem to break from.

"Talia." It felt like I'd let my name loose more than merely speaking it, snapping the tension.

"*Talia*," he repeated, tilting his head, seeming to taste each syllable as the colors of his eyes *rotated*. "Well, Talia, now we are well-met. If you wonder what Cole made of me, you might ask her someday. With my help, she might even be able to tell you."

"Your help?"

"Nothing—no medicine or prayer can help her now. She's been someplace that leaves a stain, filled with creatures that throw curses for fun. I've sought you out because, luckily, I know of a talisman that can erase much of it and return her senses...such as they were. I'll take you to it, but first"—his voice was as soft as a breeze—"I just need your promise that you will keep it a secret."

Oh good, this again. At least, thanks to Noc, I understood that promises were not taken lightly when made with those from over the Veil. Maybe Mom's failure to realize this long ago had been the first step on the journey that eventually led to her going into hamster mode in her childhood bedroom.

"Did my mother promise to keep *you* a secret?"

"Well, no, I didn't ask her to." He gave an annoyed half-shrug. "But *you* are not her. *You,* I don't know. I need your word. Secrets for secrecy. That's the bargain."

At least the currency was something I could afford. I looked toward the road where Mattie was waiting. What's one more thing I can't speak of to sane people? "Fine. But tell me why first."

"Because you aren't the only one after it, I suspect."

I so wanted to believe that Noc had omitted that there could be a way to fix Mom that didn't mean her being lost again. After all, he hadn't exactly been forthcoming with anything. I needed what Hawthorne was offering to be real, just as badly as I needed to believe Noc had been honest about my being protected from things like Hawthorne. But...if that protection were real, then even if Hawthorne was lying. I'd be safe. Right? And if he weren't lying, then I'd finally get Mom back. I just could not risk passing that up. "All right. I give you my word."

"And I take it." His eyes flashed a circle of gold around the warring factions of his irises for a half of an instant as they rotated once more. "Walk with me."

He offered me his arm and visions of trees full of silent black birds and the girl who really wasn't one flooded my mind. I stepped back, my doubt going to work. "Couldn't you just *tell* me where to find it? My friend is waiting for me, and I don't like the woods."

"Well, I can't walk the roads. How vexing. I told you I would bring you to it, not discuss the *secret thing* openly." He glanced at the sky with a sigh. "We'll make it an exchange of promises then." Pressing his hand to his chest and with a touch of sarcasm, he hastily proclaimed, "I, Hawthorne of Dawn, promise you, Talia of This Speck of a Town, my protection in these woods as long as I'm at your side. Do you accept this bargain?"

I threw my hands up. "I guess."

And with another glimmer of gold in his eyes, I now had the vows of protection from *two* sort-of-men that I had no reason to trust. Reluctantly, I traded my doubt for hope that maybe combined they might actually be worth something.

18

A Bad Idea

This is stupid. With a deep breath, I wrapped my hand just above his elbow, feeling the raised lines of stitching on the soft leather of his sleeve. With my other hand, I felt that my knife was still in my bag. *This is the epitome of all things stupid, and I probably deserve to get eaten by something.*

"Why can't you walk on roads?" I asked as he led me into the trees, yellow-orange leaves crunching under our feet.

"I just can't anymore. And shorter ways are usually found in the wood anyway. Well, shorter for me, but not safer for *you*, so stick to your roads—when unaccompanied. There are hidden pathways that weave through this world like spiders' webs, and all it takes to find yourself on them is a wrong step at just the right time." His stride was leisurely and his feet light on the ground as it sloped downward, deeper into the shadows of the woods. "Sometimes it's only a fateful misstep that finds one astray, but more often, it's a lie that *lures* them."

Not something someone who had just basically agreed to be lured into the woods wants to hear. Knots reformed in my stomach as I saw the boulder ahead and realized that we should be near Maevyn's path, yet there was no sign of it today. Instead, the trees were becoming less dense as we walked, gradually becoming a canopy over a wide, somewhat overgrown trail.

"So," I said, swallowing down the dry ball of panic that wanted to rise, "did my mom take a wrong step, or was she lured?"

"Have you ever been in love, Talia?" That caught me off guard. I was strangely embarrassed by the fact that I hadn't. At my silence, he went on. "Love has the reputation of being sweet—one of the very roots of all that is beautiful. But really, it's this evasive, fickle thing. Powerful. And dangerous. At its heart, it's really...a kind of sickness. Faerie have much in common with love."

"You lost me at the end there." I stepped over a crumbling log.

"*Love* has led many away to that rotting world. Love, or rather the yearning for it." He took a twig from a pocket and put it between his lips, exhaling a breath of amber-colored smoke that smelled strongly of cloves with something acrid beneath it. "Those who dwell over the Veil in the Everlands of Dawn and Midnight are older than love. At their hearts, they can be colder than the grave. But they can be the fleeting promise of love for those who are looking. The promise of wealth for the gold-hungry. A playmate for a lonely child. But promises unspoken aren't promises at all, only tricks and one-sided games. And tricking the hapless into ill-made, forever-binding bargains is the faeries *favorite* game."

I was getting that not directly answering any question asked of you was a close second. "Are you saying she was tricked?"

"I'm saying she made a misstep. And *then*"—there was tension in his smoke haloed voice— "she was stolen."

"Stolen by—" The words caught in my throat. Stolen. I didn't like speaking of my mother as though she had been an unattended bicycle. I released his arm to press my fingers to my temples, as though I could massage in some semblance of logic. "Okay. So, my mother...," I attempted again, pushing out what two days ago would have been a ridiculous statement, "...my mother was basically stolen by faeries." I was hoping saying it would somehow make it sound more plausible. It did not.

I studied him closer, his sun-kissed skin and richly dark hair streaked with gold, his rounded ears. Aside from his kaleidoscopic eyes, there was nothing about him that gave away that he was anything more than human. Those eyes though were enough. "And that's what you are?"

"Is what what I am?" He gave me a sly smile.

"Please don't make me say it. It's just you don't look..." I was trying not to be offensive in any way, but also trying to picture him in tights and pointed shoes. "I mean, you're tall and you...you have stubble. And normal hands."

"I'm a man of Dawn. And some say a charming monster. Or just a bad idea in general." He arched his brow and exhaled a puff of smoke in my face that made my eyes sting. "You don't even *fathom* what is under the hills or waters, do you? You have *no* notion of what exists beneath all the little folds of space and time that make up the Veil between our worlds—even though this very town, which as I recall doesn't even have *a bar*, sits along one of those folds."

Faeries, ghosts, gods, and monsters—at that moment the logical part of my brain that would rail against these things finally decided to just lie down and play dead, and most of the fear I had been carrying was smothered under it as I accepted the world I thought I knew was forever gone. This is what, in therapy, they call a breakthrough.

I'm not sure what it would be called over the Veil.

"Its proximity to the Veil makes those here not pay *Kindly* Neighbors like me much mind—even though being along a fold means enough of us pass through the place." He rolled the twig between his fingers. "And the faery sort are bad enough for you, but then there are the demons. I think that even these days humanity still fears *them*. Thankfully for you, they at least only come when called."

Or when they are some sort of demon-guard protecting your lost mother against worse things, apparently, but I couldn't say that. Not without breaking my word, and I did not want to find out what the cost would be for doing so. "Well...yikes," I said instead. It was the most honest take on all of this, really. Fucking YIKES.

"Yikes, indeed." There was a sparkle of what might have been amusement in his eyes. "And then there's what's *beyond* the Lands of Midnight."

Birds trilled from the trees as we stepped around a fallen, lichen-covered tree, and a faint, sickly sweet smell carried through the air. I didn't want to think about what could outrank demons, or if they too could eventually slip through the tear I meant to close after this detour to save my mother's mind.

"Midnight is a place where you're from, not a time? Your land is divided by hour?"

"It depends."

"On what?"

"Where you are," he said a bit impatiently. "Dawn and Midnight are Everlands. As in *forever*. There was Meridian too, but it fell, leaving way for Twilight, which is quite a bore. But then there are all the places that move through them. And the ephemeral seasons and ones that can be anywhere, except when they can't."

I nodded as though I understood so he would keep divulging, hoping he'd get to something useful. "And *beyond* the Midnight Lands?"

"The Slumbering Dark," he said, and I recognized the phrase from last night. "But that isn't where your worry should lie at the moment. Cole would have saved you from ever knowing things like it. Things like me. Just like I know she wanted to save you from things like her.

But now you need to understand some things quickly, like that this pretty thing"—I felt the icy wisping of fear return along the back of my neck as he raised his hand and with a twirl of his wrist showed that, instead of a twig, he now held my knife—"will do nothing much."

He opened the blade and flipped it back and forth. "It's not even the right metal."

He tossed it back to me, and I thought of the strange little knife in my mother's hand as it sliced my arm. The one she'd hidden years before but left behind along with the faery tales when she ran away, imagining she didn't need them anymore where she was going. I shoved it back into my bag and continued to follow him up the canopied path.

"How much further until we get to this super-secret mystery talisman then?"

"Not very. Through the way here and just past the golden goose. Then there will just be the matter of it being given to you." His pace slowed. "None of my kind can just *take* it, thankfully; it's...corrosive to them."

He was becoming winded as we walked. Maybe smoking wasn't the best habit for whatever he was either. He took another swig on the flask, groaned softly and began to stagger. I instinctively took his arm to help steady him. The cool skin of his hand pressed over mine, his expression pained as he closed his eyes and, in that instant, he looked almost like a corpse: sickly pale, his downturned lips colorless, cheeks sunken. I recoiled, but in the blink of an eye...he was the handsome man from before.

"What—?"

"Tired," he explained quickly. "Just being here is exhausting. " His smile was strained as he pressed the flask back into the chest of his coat, and we continued on our way.

"So, what kind of metal protects against—" I stopped myself from saying *you*. "From things like faeries?"

"Sometimes it's iron, sometimes silver. Or sometimes it's obsidian and sometimes it's a certain wood or herb or scent or sound. It depends on which of my kin you're dealing with. But this talisman you're seeking repulses all of them."

"Why? I mean, *what* is it?"

He laughed bitterly under his breath. "It's a complete abomination."

I waited for him to elaborate. When he didn't, I rerouted my question rather than give up on the subject entirely. "If none of you can touch it, then where did it come from?"

A cool breeze made a few waves of hair dance around his sad eyes. "It came from something that shouldn't have been. Something made to hurt. Only it works... *differently* for her."

"Hawthorne." Since he was at least less aloof than Noc had been—and wasn't charging me—I decided to try being direct. "Why was my mother stolen?"

"Because..." He looked so tired then and shook his head. "Because where I come from, the Everlands and all their Roving Courts of seasons and countless other pockets of horror and bliss—each with their own charms of course—all of it, *all* of it is *rotting*. Rotting, but never dying. Never truly changing thanks to this"—he gestured all around us—"this Ruined World. Those on the other side of the Veil have always had their teeth sunk into this realm because they still see it as part of theirs, subtly harvesting from this land to feed theirs. And so things have gone in horrible harmony since the sun first began casting shadows."

"Harvesting *what?*"

"The lost," he said, and my throat tightened on the cascade of questions I would have asked when he grabbed my shoulder, his eyes widening at something behind me. Spinning me to face him, he leaned down, stubble lightly scraping against my cheek.

"Listen to me." His voice was low and urgent. "Continue on. You see the path now, yes? Follow the turn and you will come to a road, past the golden goose there will be a house, and in that house there is a girl, and she holds the talisman. Do not stop for *anything*, do you understand?"

"What? No. What the hell's a golden goose? And what happened to you protecting me?"

"Yes, well...a lesson about faery bargains." He barely lowered his eyes from what he saw—what he was plainly scared of, which in turn terrified me—to shoot me an apologetic half-smile. "Be careful that the word binds both ways. Mine was that I'd protect you while I'm by your side and...I am sorry, but I'm about to not be. That bargain dissolves, but I warn you, the other we made does not." He pressed his finger to his lips as a reminder.

I twisted my arms free and gave him a useless shove that barely moved him. "Are you serious? *Faery bargains*? What happened to 'I'm a man of Dawn'?"

"Just follow the path," he said distractedly. "And...*don't* give your name away so easily next time—you give a measure of power with it."

And with that nugget of advice, he was off. I turned in time to see the back of him running into the trees and caught just a glimpse of what he was after—it looked like the flowing green of a woman's dress, dark hair curling down it.

She disappeared into the trees with Hawthorne close after her, and I'd bet my weight in faery promises that I'd just gotten a glimpse of the Green Lady.

19

Little Dove

The path was soft gold and green, lit by hazy, uneven slats of sunlight swirling with flecks of pollen. My heart was pounding as I stood there alone. Maybe I could make it back to the driveway or to the road where Mattie was probably wondering why I was taking so long. What if she gave up and decided to walk up to the house herself to find me? What if Hawthorne was the type of creature that just collected girls from paths and dumped them in the woods to be picked off by greedy, hungry things—and he was waiting for her?

No. Sure, I didn't *trust* him, and he seemed like he may even have been a little drunk, but despite being one of them, he didn't exactly speak fondly of the rest of those Neighbors of mine—and didn't seem happy to see the Green Lady either. Maybe he was chasing her off. Whatever his reason, I was now abandoned and lost on some fold that I was just told could lead to some vampiric realm I'd have no hope of escaping.

At the sound of a branch snapping close by, I quickly headed in the direction Hawthorne had been leading me, apparently looking for a goose, and very much wishing I had some iron.

I wasn't walking long when I heard it. The singing.

A man's song carried in the cool afternoon air. Any hope that it might have been someone else lost or led here shriveled up as the notes of the song became clearer, and I stopped dead.

"There once was a bonny lass...who danced with kindly folk...she followed them around the stones...and down into the moat..."

I knew that melodic voice could be coming out of something horrible and considered hiding, but that would mean leaving the path. Hawthorne had been explicit about not doing that, and besides, I had a feeling whoever was singing likely knew these woods far better than I did, and his voice was coming closer.

"Her laughter only echos...her eyes no longer see...but still she dances gracefully...beneath the Moon Dark sea..."

I tightened my grip on the strap of my bag and forced myself forward but froze when the singer emerged ahead, leisurely stepping from behind a dead tree with branches as wiry as he was. He was not much more than a boy really, maybe a few years younger than me, with choppy straw-colored hair and a lopsided smile.

"*There* we are now, little dove." His eyes were green and bright. "You weren't where you were meant, but all's well now—I've come to guide you true."

"Er, I already know where I'm going, thanks," I at least half-lied as he strolled next to me. There was nothing about him that was intimidating in itself, but everything in me went to high alert.

"Mercy me, miss, I can't have you be going on alone." He stepped ahead to face me while walking backward. His clothes hung a bit loose on his tall-but-slight frame, and at his side, attached to the belt beneath his tattered black vest, was a long dagger. "All manner of sorts would mislead you."

"Yeah. That's what I keep hearing." I moved to step around him. "But I suppose you're the good sort, right?"

"Please, miss." His arm shot out, barring my way. "Indeed I've already made a rotten mess of this errand, and I mean to make it right. You seek something vital, and can help marvelous much there."

I blinked, stepping back. "Is there, like, a forest billboard about me up somewhere? How do you all know I'm *seeking* anything?"

"You're on this path. You were being led. The only kind that let themselves be led anywhere are either lost or looking. You said you weren't lost, so must be looking."

"Well, if you don't know what I'm *looking* for, then how would you lead me to it?"

He rubbed his hand along the back of his neck. "What you seek is lost to me and mine. But...we *know* it. Oh, we know it, miss. And *I* know more than any about where it lies. I do mean to make sure the right hands find it."

Did he speak of Hawthorne's talisman or Noc's key, or did every otherworldly thing come with their own unique side quest? I needed to find that key, but since I was already heading toward the talisman, it seemed wisest to keep going for it first. Besides, I was quite done following strange men around for today.

"Okay, look," I said firmly, "*my hands* and I are already on their way to something. If you want me to find something else, you'll have to wait your turn."

I knew he wasn't what he appeared to be, and I was bracing for whatever he might do at my rejection, but his eyes only grew more pleading, almost desperate. "O mercy me, miss, you must come. There is danger if you don't."

At this point, my staying on the course I was put on was really just my sticking with the devil I knew, or rather that I knew just well enough anyway, but I was afraid of where I'd end up if I didn't stop second guessing myself. "Sorry, but I'm not going to leave this path."

"Ah, little dove." His pleading tone evaporated and he slid on a crooked smile. "If only you had said that the first time you were asked to do so this day."

I went to step around him again but a tree was in my way. I stepped back into another tree. I turned. The path behind me had reverted back to untamed woodland, but the path ahead was still clear. Except for the singer. He followed my eyes as they fell back on his dagger.

"Well, I get lost as easily as I get found apparently." I sighed at the implied threat and forced my mouth into a complacent grin. "Is it far?"

"Not by much," he said, still smiling, "so long as you stay close. I'm always lost yet am always right where I need to be."

"Fantastic." I rolled around Noc's vow of protection in my head to check for loopholes as I reluctantly followed him into trees that quickly grew dense enough to have me slowing down to step over trunks and roots. I soon began to lose sight of him.

At first it was only a moment or two before I would again see the back of his vest or the white of his sleeve. We hadn't been walking particularly fast, but I soon was unable to keep up with even the sounds of twigs snapping under his boots and had to stop to listen for his footfalls.

"Hey!" I called. I should have gotten his name, but then he would've asked for mine. "Wait up!"

"Only just ahead, miss!" His voice was too distant.

I looked behind me to confirm that I had no clue where I was, no idea which direction to go, and that my agreeing to follow Hawthorne in the first place had indeed been only the second most stupid thing I could have done today. I stilled. My panic at not being able to hear him anymore only intensified once I could again.

"My mother loved a fine man...who lived across the sea...my mother loved a cold man...who had no love for me...she took me to the water...and

wrapped me in his coat...and there beneath the crashing waves...she slit my fair young throat..."

I tried reassuring myself that I was protected by Noc, though I definitely didn't feel very protected at the moment. I felt the cool handle of my knife, but assuming Hawthorne had been telling the truth about it being useless, the better plan was for me to run for it and hope for the sound of a passing car that would tell me where the road was.

The smell of decay hung just under the coolness of the air. Trying to tell myself that dead things in a wild place were probably normal only made me panic more. I needed to move. Now. Wherever the singer had me going wasn't an option, so I picked a new direction and started running my way towards what would hopefully be out of the woods—figuratively and literally. Unfortunately, it was impossible to be stealthy with this much fall on the ground, or so I thought until he swung around the trunk of the tree in front of me.

I screamed, which he seemed delighted by. "You *do* get lost easily, miss." He laughed.

"Is this a game to you?" I demanded, my trusty anxiety-led anger derailing my panic.

His laughter ceased. "No, miss. I guided you from the path you were put on. My memory dims, but I still know how quickly paths grow dark when you're on the wrong one—something the one who you followed first this day knows too well."

"I take it you know Hawthorne then?"

"My lady!" he said incredulously. "How do you dare so lightly speak the name of the Green Man of the Briar? Did your lady mother not warn you that Thorny Jack is ruinous and sly? The things he could do to both of us if he thought we were meddling with his plans. The shadows would sing nightmare ballads for ages!"

"Wait." I held up my hand."I'm sorry—*who?*"

"*Hawthorne,*" he hissed, his eyes wild and flitting to the trees around us.

"Right." I felt around again for the handle of my little knife, deciding it was better than nothing. "Because none of you can have just one name. Or answer a question simply, or be even slightly helpful without there being a catch."

" I do," he said in a low voice, narrowing his eyes to the ground. "I do have one name that I recall."

"Well, you can keep it." I started to back away, but his hand quickly closed tightly on my wrist, and I had an instant of blind panic as memories swarmed me like hornets.

"But it's already been given, miss," he said with a shake of his head as I tried to pull away from him without success. "I've been muchly changed since last we met . Reordered. Reshaped, but still myself. Still *Maevyn.*"

"Nope," I said with quick, false certainty. Having had enough of this sort of indecipherable nonsense, I was putting my foot down. "Maevyn was a little girl. Sort of."

"As was I," he scoffed. "Then I was gathered. Harvested with others. Now I'm more than what I am and barely anything." He tapped a finger to his blond head. "But hers is the name I remember most, so I keep it close."

I'd read something of shape-shifting faeries in that by now shredded book. They tended to be the drowning kind. And Maevyn *had* tried to lure me down a well, so that tracked. Now, this one held me in a grip I couldn't break out of as he tugged me to him.

"Onward, miss," he said cheerfully, tightening his hold on my wrist. "I'm to set you on the right way at last."

"You can't just—" I protested, though he pulled me easily along as I tried to twist out his vice-like fingers. "I'm...*protected!*"

"Are you now?" he mused from over his shoulder. "Well, I'm not *harming* you, am I?"

Well, Noc did say I was protected "from harm", which I guess would rule out my being drowned, but just my luck if I got kidnapped on a technicality. My bag kept flopping against my back as I stumbled along, still trying to wrench myself from his grip, but this latest Maevyn was surprisingly strong. In a few strides, he'd already dragged me into a wide, hushed clearing.

"I am...*not...,* " I said, hoping to dispel what would be the weirdest legacy, "...going to be stolen by faeries."

Just as I was able to shove my hand in my bag and close it around the knife's handle, he stopped. "Faery?" He looked down at me, confused, yellow hair whipping around his face in the breeze that rustled through the leaves. "How odd. No, miss, *those* are faeries."

He pointed his chin at the ground beside us, and there, slipping by as green as the grass they stood in, were a group of creatures no more than a foot high and a couple of fingers wide, heads like fine flower buds. They made their way, glancing up at me with mild interest in their slanted eyes. They wore the most delicate looking layers of leaf-like clothing around their slender forms, some with their wavy fingers wrapped around tiny pouches like they were off to the shops.

"And those." He looked to a patch of wildflowers, which moved when the three female figures attached to them turned; their skin, brown and mossy, bloomed bright with yellows and lavenders down their backs as though they'd been sitting still so long nature had coated them.

"Ah, and those as well." He pointed up to the trees where those now familiar black birds sat silent. But one was perched on a branch low enough for me to see that those feathers that shimmered like an oil spill were not feathers at all, but a tiny human-like figure with iridescent skin riding upon its back.

My knife forgotten, I crouched down with my hands over my mouth. One of the grass faeries stopped for a moment, angling its little alien head up to me, hair as fine as corn silk around its face. It grinned before returning to the others on its disproportionately long legs.

"That's a faery," I said to no one. "These are *faeries*."

"Well, of course they are." Maevyn pulled me back to my feet. "They're always thicker near an opening—lucky they aren't swarming really."

"But...then what are you?"

"Remnants. Barely remnants," he said distantly and resumed towing me along like I was a leashed animal. "A patchwork of forgotten shadows, ripped and carved and shaped into something new."

They definitely didn't cover that in the book.

"Where are you taking me?"

"Only keeping you safe and away from what comes for your lady mother." his long legs pulled us swiftly through the knee-high grass. "I mean to keep you *hidden*."

"I don't want to be hidden from what's coming for her. I'm trying to *stop it*—if you really want to help me, then let me go."

"*Help* you?" He covered his mouth over the shrill laugh that escaped him. "Oh, little dove. The path we're on, I can't stray from, but I muchly doubt you'll find it... helpful."

I was gradually becoming more aware of the movements in the trees, on the ground, and in the air. The sparkle and glisten of various shapes flitting by. I could just focus enough as I was rushed by to make out faces that looked to be etched out of the woodland around me. Some of the forms looked like human bodies twisted with nature, others looked far more insect-like. My attention was only pulled from the creatures by my nearly tripping over my own feet because of how swiftly he yanked me along.

I could barely process that he had somehow gotten much taller as I stumbled beside him, towering over me now. Cold from the grip of his fingers began to seep through my cardigan. Wherever something like Maevyn considered "safe", I was certain *I* would not, and the chances of ever finding my way out of these woods shrank with each step. There was no time to bother with my knife. Without thinking, I stopped trying to pull myself away, and rushed forward before he could react. I had just enough time to plant one foot steady, and kick him solidly with the other.

I put all my energy into it, so when my foot connected with his shin, I might have broken my own toes. But it worked in stopping him—just not in any helpful way. He seemed more annoyed than anything as he yanked me off the ground by my wrist and held me at eye level. Just then, and too late, I saw there was something wrong about the shape of him. He wasn't only taller, his arms and legs were too long, too thin. His face grew longer too, gaunt and perplexed, as he stared at me with paling green eyes.

"You *struck* me." His voice contorted with bored malice. "Oh, I wish you had not done that."

He let go of me at last, and the second I landed on my knees, I propelled myself back on my arms and feet, but there was no way to move quick enough to escape those increasingly claw-like hands as his limbs continued to grow longer, stretching thinner and serpentile. My terror left me transfixed on the ground as his eyes sank into his head, replaced by holes that bled black, the same black that spread out of his mouth, moved up his fingertips, and then his arms.

"We all play our part, miss." The thing hissed from somewhere in its depths. "As will you."

His claws reached out, but something flew in front of my face, forcing me to block it with my arms. That snapped me out of my terror daze. I swatted what was scratching at my hands, striking the black bird there—its wings flapping inches from my head. I backpedaled away, but I wasn't its target. A dozen more swarmed and cawed around the creature that was Maevyn, diving at him as he clumsily swatted them back with those spindly arms. More birds joined in, until they were swirling around him, a tornado of beaks and feathers.

I didn't wait to see what happened. I flipped over and bolted for the trees.

20

Talisman

I ran fast, stumbling over roots and logs, being scraped by branches and not daring to look back until the burning of my lungs forced me to slow, then finally stop. With my back to a tree, I strained to listen over the sound of my own panting. My legs were shaking, and my toes throbbed, but I couldn't rest for long. I had to keep going until I made it out. I had to get out of here before dark.

When my breathing calmed enough, I walked in the same direction I'd been running,though I knew going in a straight line away from the clearing didn't necessarily guarantee that I wouldn't end up back there again the way these woods worked. After every few steps over the undergrowth, I'd pause, listening for anything that might let me know where the road was. Now knowing Maevyn could shift appearance, I wouldn't even be able to trust anyone I came across—and that was assuming those birds and their riders hadn't taken him apart.

Midstep, I heard distant, rushing water and focused on the sound. No. Not water. *Whispers.* A low flood of them came from ahead. Cautiously, I followed them as they faded in and out like waves hitting a shore until I nearly stuck my foot in a pond that the trees abruptly opened to. Mostly bordered with rocks green with moss and muddy, half-rotted piles of leaves, the water was still as a looking glass. An old log decorated with gray mushroom caps stretched part way across.

After getting a good hold on the nearest branch, I peered over to see a patch of turquoise sky reflected through the branches above me.

"*I am so dreadfully curious,*" echoed Noc's voice, startling me back, "*why, after learning of danger now here, a clever girl like you would go off into the forest with an unfamiliar man. What strange desires must dwell in your heart to court fate in such a manner?*"

"Well, which time?" I snapped to the water. "Because the second one I didn't have a choice about—but the first one I followed because *someone* assured me I was *protected.*"

"*I did.*" The water rippled slightly with his voice. "*And you are. Though it is more difficult protecting one against their own foolishness.*"

My cheeks grew hot. "You told me I was protected. If I thought that wasn't true, I wouldn't have gone into the woods with anyone. You lied to me."

The water stood silent as I glared at it, though my anger was really at letting myself be manipulated. After debating a few moments on whether or not I even trusted him enough to ask him to point me out of here, I decided that I firmly did *not* and without wasting another word, turned briskly, smacking directly into Noc's very solid chest.

"How can you imagine," he asked, his midnight eyes impassive and his hand around the small of my back to stop me from stumbling into the pond, "that I would break our bargain? Our word is law. Do you not remember?"

He was at least a foot taller than me even without the horns and was no apparition this time. Also, no less flawless, accompanied by the not unpleasant air of amber on a storm wind blowing past a pit of burning leaves. I yanked my hand away from where I'd grabbed onto the soft sleeve of his arm with my sore wrist.

"Oh, I remember." Maybe it was seeing him in the light of day that quelled my fear, or maybe I was just completely burned out on that particular emotion, given the events of the day. "But I guess between my almost being kidnapped, *again* I might add, this time by some giant, shadowy...insect monster, I must have lost sight of your good intentions."

He straightened and flicked his tongue over his lip, evaluating me with a tilt of his chin before looking out over the pond. "So twice you were nearly ripped away from your freedom and twice those attempts were thwarted. I may not walk here easily, nor be able to use all of my strengths, but my kind can exude influence over lesser beasts to do my bidding. Which in your case, it seems they have. Twice."

"Those birds...?" I realized.

"Protected you. It would seem." He leaned against a tree and folded his arms. The fine silver of his horns glinted in the sun. He oddly did not look out of place out here in the middle of the woods wearing his strange, almost aristocratic clothing. A horned god among the trees.

"That...Maevyn. What is he? She? They?"

"An ort. Shadow-shaped things from those in my realm that once were. Made useful again." He half-smiled wistfully. "Nothing of anyone leaves the Midnight Lands."

I brushed some hair back from my forehead, noting the amount of twigs and leaves that clung to it and feeling the sting of the scrapes on the back of my hands. "So, it's like a ghost?"

"It is like an *ort,*" he said. "They are a cacophony of small voices, forced into a choir of purpose. That one's purpose is you." He looked to the sky and chuckled. "Maevyn. It *named* itself. Fascinating. Its master must have taken great care when carving such a dutiful minion."

That fear I'd been lacking pulled at me. "What do you mean, *I'm* its purpose?"

"None may leave the Midnight Lands," he said again, "unless they are sent. Orts that began as humans can still walk this soil easily. More easily than I. You are to be protected, so that ort was sent to patrol the paths nearby. It had been...*corrected,* since the first time it failed."

"It tried to steal me."

"Well. It may be overzealous. It maybe thought perhaps you are safer across the Veil. If you are foolhardy enough to freely follow a stranger into the forest, it may be correct."

"So, you protected me...against my protection?"

"I am *protecting you.*" He leaned forward. "Would you prefer I ceased doing so?"

"I...no."

"Now." He narrowed his eyes. "What did he promise you then? Hawthorne. I do hope there was a better reason than most of his ill-fated women have."

"He..." I swallowed, remembering my promise to not speak of the talisman. "He promised protection."

"But you already had that." He stepped closer. "What more?"

I didn't know what the fine print of the word I gave was. I said I wouldn't speak of the talisman, but maybe I could speak *around* it. "He said there was 'something' that could help—" *My mother,* I wanted to say. But I couldn't. I literally couldn't. My mouth locked down each time it went to form another word.

"Oh, by the Dark—you made a bargain." He smiled, but there was something just under it that wasn't amused at all. I wanted to tell him that I hadn't exactly meant to, but I couldn't say that either. I couldn't say anything, about anything at all.

He held up his hand. "And now. You've *broken* a bargain." He tsked with a shake of his head. "Dear Talia, you are bespelled. While I could leave you like this, forever silent, that would serve neither of us. He offered you something that could help, yes? Help *her?*"

I nodded.

"Let me tell you why you believed him." He turned briskly to the pond. "He lulled you to him with his voice, his beauty. He *charmed* you. Just like every fool girl before you. Just like your mother."

I shook my head. I hadn't been charmed...I'd been stupid.

"You," he said over his shoulder, the air about him going darker, "are fortunate that he doesn't hold the sway he used to. That he is weakened. You are *released* from your bargain."

"I..." I tested once I felt my mouth subtly unlock. "He said—"

"He *lied.*" His voice was a silencing rumble. "You must learn faster. I warned you not to trust anyone you met or what you saw. Whether through what they seem or what they say, it's easy to mislead when orts can be anyone they once were. When Faerie can use glamours to seem pleasing. Always look twice and never make a promise unless you are prepared to suffer for it."

"He said he could fix her—heal her. That there was a talisman that could bring her mind back."

"He said he would—" He spun back to me, his lips pressed together tightly. "If you were not charmed, then why do you think you simply *believed* such an obvious ploy?"

"It wasn't that I trusted him," I said sheepishly. "I guess it was that I just...needed to believe there was something that could fix my mother."

"Oh. I do so enjoy when one of you thinks you can just *wish* something true." He rolled his eyes. "Hawthorne is a dual creature. Lying is his nature. He is vicious and cruel in his delights, revered as he is feared for his strength in his lands, yet all he ever needed when it comes to humans was his silver tongue."

Leaves crushed beneath his boots as he moved closer, resting his arm on a branch just above me. "I told you we have many names, Talia—that's just what happens when you've always been. But be it Hawthorne or Thorny Jack, or the Prince of Briars—whichever name he allows you to have—know that *he* is the beast that stole your mother, and he means to do so again."

My stomach dropped. "But.... he knows right where she is, if he wanted to take her—" His eyebrows raised. "Right. Protected. He couldn't get to her because she's protected inside of the house."

"What a *fascinating* journey to an already present conclusion. She is the reason I am here, protecting her from *him*. But it looks like he is seeking witless help. Tell me." He leaned closer, locking my eyes with his. "What did he tell you about this 'talisman'?"

"Not much. That it was corrosive? That none of his kind could touch it, but he already seemed...unwell himself."

"Clever." His eyes glanced away. I thought, for a second, he looked...surprised. "Clever lad. The key I spoke of and his *talisman* are one and the same. He was leading you to what you already seek."

"But why would he do that?" I asked. "And how could something be corrosive to him if it was his?"

"Because it's part of his own curse. And true enough, it *is* poisonous to others. Look what it did to your mother. But more than that: it is a wellspring of *power*." He paced a few steps away, fists clasped behind him. "When objects of power change hands, the magic drifts along with them. Magical things cannot be stolen and still retain their strength. So it seems she did not trick it from him after all. He gave it freely, but the trick there was his. He used her to smuggle it here for him. That must be why he approached you. He needs *her* to be the one to return it to him, so he can regain all of its power. *Here.* On this side of the Veil. And who better to try to convince to place it back in her hands than her doting daughter?"

"So...he wanted to bring me to this talisman, because he needs me to bring it to her...so she can give it back to him? But if I just *find* it on my own, *you* could still use it to close up this tear in the Veil...even though no one *gave* it to me?" I paused. "Look, I'm no expert in magic, faery or...otherwise, but you know that really makes no sense."

"Hmm." He closed his eyes and leaned back on the tree. "Having a human try to make sense of magic would be like your having a baby drive a speeding car; it would be amusing at first, but ultimately someone would suffer for the trying. Likely the baby."

"You have *cars* where you're from?" I said, briefly picturing him behind the wheel of anything.

"Not at all, but we do have analogies." He gave the smallest shrug. "The thing must be given to keep its *full* strength. Though that does not mean that its power is otherwise completely nullified. In the right hands, it would still do much damage, things are just much more powerful when they are where they belong." He sighed, his lip curling up. "Or. When they are summoned to where they could be useful."

"Again, really, no thanks," I said, folding my arms over the chill I'd begun to feel now that the adrenaline had burned away. "The one thing just about every one of you Kindly Neighbors of mine that I've met seem to agree on is that I shouldn't trust any of you Kindly Neighbors."

"Ah. I would, in your position, probably put more faith in the one who has rescued me more than once and who has not absconded with any of my kinsfolk. But then, I do not believe I would ever find myself in your position."

"No. I suppose you wouldn't. I don't know how anyone from your Everlands bothers trusting anyone."

"*Midnight,*" he said patiently, the moons of his eyes on mine again, "is *my* Land. My kingdom. Perhaps one day, I will show it to you."

"If you know Hawthorne's plans," I said, ignoring the lick of ice up my back, "then why doesn't your king just send one of these orts to drag *him* back to your Midnight Lands?"

"It is difficult to trick a trickster. I can only keep him and the rest from entering the house I am watching over."

"Right. Well, speaking of tricks, there was an old woman found with my mother...is she an ort?"

"The lady's handmaiden," he said dismissively. "Human and hardly missed."

"Are you protecting her too?"

"From what? Carrion birds? No. I am watching over your mother. That house. I am able to keep watch over you out here as well by spreading my energy thin. But I cannot protect you from your own heart." He looked at me curiously. "She would tell you, I think. There is nothing more treacherous than one's own heart."

"I'm not sure if you can understand this, but if Hawthorne stole my mother and means to do it again, there's a *pretty* good chance he's not my type. He's not going to 'charm' me."

"Oh, apologies." A grated edge lurked beneath his smooth tone. "If a deer knows the arrow is being shot, it does not mean it can *certainly* dodge it. Still, one imagines the warning helps."

"Well, that last 'arrow' I ran from has left me lost. I don't suppose I could have my phone back so I can get myself out of here?"

"Your phone? Alas, it is no longer such a thing. I have been finding the noisy little thing amusing. Why"—he leaned forward to pluck a leaf from my hair—"are there so many images of cats inside of it?"

"You've been looking through my phone," I said, remembering that along with what was probably an oddly prolific number of random cat photos stored on the camera roll, there probably was a smattering of selfies too. "Fantastic."

"Your greater concern ought to be closing the Veil. It's safer for all if the Kindly Folk remain unseen when they...visit. Yet while the Veil hangs open, they are exposed to human eyes. And if *someone* were made strong enough to do so, well, they might tear that opening even wider. I wonder how many from my realm would come before *their* safety would no longer be in question? And your mother. What might he do with her when her part has been played, I wonder. Keep her as a trophy or...discard her"

"So..." I waited a moment for any expression of concern to come over him. It didn't. "You're going to help me *stop him*, right?? "

His pale irises seemed to say: *for that, you're going to have to do some summoning.*

"You—" I sighed, exasperated. "What am *I* supposed to do to stop him?"

"Get the key—his cursed *talisman*," he said in an infuriatingly off-handed way. "Let him take you to it. Then break free of him. Bring it where her water-torn path was made, where she was found. Once there, call me. Then I will be able to use it to seal the way, locking Hawthorne safely in Midnight."

"I don't suppose," I began, already knowing the answer, "that 'calling' you could be as simple as borrowing someone's phone?"

"You call to me," he said, "as you would any. By name."

"And—I have to ask—that wouldn't be anywhere near the same thing as 'summoning' you, would it?"

There was a sharpness to the edges of his grin. "To call my kind, you use our name. To summon is another game. A bit of blood. A bit of flame. Intention. Or desire. And yes, a name."

I took a step away from him. "I already have your name. Think I'll skip the rest."

"No. You need my *true* name."

I'd barely parted my lips to question what he meant, and he was behind me, his long fingers on my shoulder. I couldn't help but flinch at the unexpected contact as he gently spun me around to face the pond. I went to push back against his hands but froze when I felt his breath against my neck. He spoke something that I felt enter my head as though it had not been heard but pressed directly into my mind:

Only, I didn't know what it was. Every time I tried to focus on what he'd said, my mind skipped over it, like a tiny spot had been made just for it, then instantly buried over.

"You will not know it," he said, mouth still at my ear, "until you need it. Once you speak it, it will be gone. Take care, dear Talia. I do look forward to seeing how well you dodge."

Something dark bounded through the trees on the other side of the water. I couldn't make out its shape at first, but then it barked. "Cinder?" The big inky dog was soon at the edge of the pond, baring her teeth.

From behind me came a crackling sound. I turned to see Noc was gone. The smell of smoke and rain lingered. The branches of the tree he had been leaning against had withered along with those of the trees next to it, becoming intertwined with each other as they drooped.

21

Never at Night

When Mattie caught up with Cinder, she waved her hands at me, and then to the pond in an aggravated way, before bending over to catch her breath. Cinder's tail began to wag, her pink tongue panting from her mouth.

"I can explain," I called out, walking around the pond to her, nearly slipping every third step or so on the mossy rocks. "I mean, probably not very well, but I can explain."

She wore the same leather jacket, this time over a faded black crop top with the word "Ministry" scrawled in white lettering. She gave me the same sanity questioning look she'd given me when we first met that became more annoyed-disbelief the closer I got.

"I was already creeped out waiting out here, and then Cinder jumped out and dove straight into the trees. *Again*," she said, irritated. "She's never behaved like that before...well, *you*. Now we're all right in the middle of these goddamn spooky woods that I told you I hated being in AND warned you to stay out of." She pressed her hand into her side and winced one eye shut, scrutinizing me with the other. "You...look like you got into a fight with some shrubbery."

"There was this..." I began searching for the right way to word this. I was pretty sure it wasn't: *There was a man who said he could take me to a magical talisman that could help my mother—oh, my mother was kidnapped by faeries by the way, that's why she's crazy right now. But it turns out this guy was actually the faery that stole her in the first place, and then this other guy, who was actually an ort trying to save me by dragging me into some Hell world, got attacked by faery birds sent by a demon who is protecting me and Mom from the first guy. So ANYWAY...*

"You okay?" She cast a suspicious glance to where I'd come from, and then back to me.

"Yeah." I didn't even try to sound convincing. "I just....I was chased by someone, and I got lost." All more or less true, but I still couldn't make eye contact while I said it. "At least that's the short version."

She stood straight and pulled out her phone. "I'm calling Walker directly. Then you're telling me the long version."

"Don't call Shane. Not yet. There's...no point." I grimaced, knowing how I sounded. How I looked.

"There's no point," Mattie repeated, narrowing her eyes. "And why would that be?"

"He probably won't believe me." I drew in a long breath to steady myself against all of the ridiculous sounding things I was about to say to both warn her and explain myself. "What I ran away from wasn't really a person so much as it was something...else."

"Oh. Okay." She looked at me for a good, long moment before nodding slowly and putting her phone down. "So, you've been running around in here being chased by what? Another ghost? Look, if you're going to tell me any other concerning thing about you, I'd really rather you wait until we're out of here. And preferably in a well-populated place. Cinder"—she placed her hand on the dog's head and clicked her tongue—"ride?"

Cinder perked up and dutifully turned to begin trotting back the way she'd come. Mattie followed, and after a second, so did I.

"I know how it sounds, but you said to yourself that weird things happen here all the time, and that those stories people tell have a bit of truth to them, right?"

"I *also* said—and this should have been the main takeaway—to *not* go wandering around in here in the first place. It was very sound advice."

"Yes, but the danger goes far beyond hunters. These woods really *are* haunted by something, Mattie. By a lot of somethings, actually. And they're worse than ghosts because they can really harm people." I decided to go all in. "That's what really happened to my mom."

"What. What really happened to your mom?" I could hear her trying to force patience into her tone at the mention of my mother, reminded perhaps that I was just a crazy girl to be handled gently.

"Well—" I began, but collided with her back as she stopped suddenly, nearly knocking us both over.

Ahead of us, Cinder whined, her ears lowered as she stepped her paws back. Before I could ask, Mattie shot me a look that told me to keep quiet. I leaned around her to get a better view at what the dog must be seeing, but was halted by Mattie's leather-clad arm across my chest. Her blue tipped hair hid most of her face from mine as she grabbed my arm, yanking me to the ground with her. Cinder wedged between us, pressing her body and head as low as possible, soft brown eyes flitting nervously around her.

What? I mouthed to Mattie, before I heard the odd cacophony of noise approaching at a distance. Hard as it was to isolate and identify a single sound of it, after a few moments, I recognized that it was music, or some bastardized form of it anyway. More like an *invasion* of sound, offensive and wholly unpleasant. At least, at first. The closer it got the more bearable it became. Whimsical and violent. Exciting. What sort of instruments could even concoct such a bizarre melody? How many players were there? What did they look like?

Curiosity gnawed at me until I popped my head around the tree we crouched behind to see a dozen or more knee-high creatures parading through the trees on misshapen legs with their misshapen instruments, their skin in shades of greens, grays, and browns. Some were clothed in cloaks, pointed hats, and boots; some wore hardly a thing at all, but their knobby bodies were all stepping in static time with the disjointed tune. Most of their limbs were disproportionate, hands too large at the ends of long, stick-thin arms, but it was their faces that made me quickly duck back. Flat, pinched, bloated, or craggy– they were dissimilar in every way but in the viciousness of their features. Noses that were too narrow or too broad, eyes that were too elongated or squinted, and their mouths—their horrible mouths with lips either bulbous or thin—all stretched too wide into smiles over rows of jagged teeth.

Goblins. There were bits about goblins in the book, but I didn't need to have read it to know to fear them. Mattie's face said she felt the same. Even Cinder seemed to know to keep still and quiet as the monstrous little band passed, their music becoming almost pleasantly eerie as it came closer.

Mattie had one hand over her own mouth and one on Cinder's back, and the three of us crouched lower behind the tree, still as stones as the music grew louder, mixed in now with guttural laughter and voices whose language I couldn't decipher. I didn't notice when the delightful and grotesque goblin tune seemed to settle into me and became strangely beckoning. I began to imagine myself dancing and twirling, unwinding finally from every care, and knowing only wild, untethered joy.

For an instant I nearly forgot myself, overcome with the desire to spring up and join the horrible parade, but I snapped out of it when Mattie painfully gripped my arm, seeming to sense what I had been feeling, perhaps feeling the same thing herself.

We did not move or speak for several long minutes after the creatures had passed, and there were only the familiar nature sounds of birds and bugs. Mattie released her grip on my arm, and we all raised ourselves up from the ground.

"Okay." She said, quiet and painfully calm. "Tell me everything."

I laid it all out almost apologetically. Well, the important bits. I told the story around Noc the best I could—I just reassigned some of his words to Maevyn. Which I was pretty sure dangerously bent the rules of my bargain, but I seemed to get away with it. The broad strokes I hoped would be enough: creatures from some neighboring, shadowy world were seeping into the woods through a vague kind of door, and they were going to get a lot worse unless I found a vague kind of talisman to use as a key.

"So," she said after a long silence, "Wes Samuel wasn't crazy."

"Not about seeing the Green Lady anyway."

She nodded. "And this woman found with your mom…?"

"Another stolen person. She may know something, but it sounds like her brain is broken too."

Cinder led us out of the woods, but instead of heading toward her truck, Mattie took out her phone again. She didn't look at it, probably soothed enough by just having an instant tie to the normal rest of the world as she looked down the empty road, then to her truck, chewing her lip and shaking her head.

"I think I'd thought I'd feel better having someone else know about this," I told her as she began pacing, her fists on her hips. "But now I just feel guilty."

"No, no," she said, still pacing. "My brother always said that it was easier to believe that Elmwood was no weirder than any other town as long as you never actually *went* to any other town. Stories *were* just stories. But still there were kinda these unspoken rules and things that everyone just accepted without openly agreeing about why."

"Like no going into the woods?"

"Not alone." She nodded. "And *never* at night. But warning kids from wandering the forests has been a thing since there were kids and forests. Most of the homegrown stories I heard came from my brother because I was homeschooled, but I still remember them: the glass horses, the skeleton bridge, the ghost drums, the Sometimes House...."

"I....the *what*?"

"This place over on Gilings Road that you could only see *sometimes* on certain nights when the moon was full and the light hit it just right. Supposedly. We rode our bikes there once, and he showed me a vine covered post that was supposed to have once been a mailbox as proof that it was a real house once. No word on the inhabitants."

"Probably for the best," I said fiddling with the frayed red hem of my sweater. "That story at least seems tame. Even the Green Lady wasn't too spooky. Kid stuff."

"About that..." She chewed her lip for a few moments. "I kinda sugarcoated her last time. The *real* Green Lady story is that if you're in the woods alone at night, beware of a creaking sound that seems to follow you, because you might be unlucky enough to have your path suddenly blocked by the body of a hanging woman swinging out in front of you. Long green dress, long black hair—and if her eyes land on you then someone you love is going to die...or is it that you are going to die? I'm not sure."

"Well, that's...awfully specific."

"I just figured the story around what Wes said had gotten really bloated, but now..." She paused. "There were other things too. Just here and there. Weird little things that didn't seem to be related to each other. You know, until now."

"Such as?"

"Like sudden, violent storms that strike without warning, only over very small parts of town, that don't move, just suddenly dissipate. And mists that would roll around the woods at night once in a while, glowing greens and blues and not behaving like mist."

"Meaning...?"

"Well, I've only caught it once, but it didn't gradually form and hover like mist does, it more...gathered itself up from the ground and rolled off in different directions almost like it was..."

"Alive," I finished for her. "Weird, but not weird enough to not be explained away as weather anomalies—assuming those storms didn't rain frogs or anything."

"Not that anyone's noticed. There are also occasional sightings of black wolves, even though officially there hasn't been a wolf of any color in this part of the country in more than a century. Never been actual evidence of them though. No torn apart deer or pets. Or kids."

"Yes, intact children are what most towns want to maintain their image I'd think. The other kind—bad for tourism."

"*Tourism,*" she scoffed with a half-smile. "No one comes to this place without a reason. This time of year, it's to pick apples. And those people pass through. The town keeps to itself—"

"And the people who live here always have. Right. Hawthorne said this place was a fold along the Veil between our worlds. Maybe that makes people blind to the weird stuff. But I think to our neighboring monsters, Elmwood is just a door, not a destination, or you'd have more missing people."

"That makes sense...but I think it's safe to say that they're making themselves at home now."

I thought she was referring to the goblins, but then she stopped at her truck's door and folded her arms, staring past me until I followed her gaze. Nothing unusual, just more trees, but embedded in one of them was the blue of a mailbox. The tree Mattie said had been blocking the driveway hadn't fallen, but stood wide and unusually pale where the road should have turned, its naked branches twisting, reaching into its neighbor's leaves. I cautiously went over to it and put my hand on its smooth bark. It was cool and solid.

A breeze kicked up, dead leaves skittering across the road sounding almost like whispers. Cinder barked once, snapping me out of it.

Shading her eyes from the afternoon sun with her hand as she surveyed the tree, Mattie declared, "I say we get the fuck out of here."

I nodded. "And I vote you drive very fast."

22

Odd

Mattie wasn't the type of person that came to mind when I thought of homeschooling. She didn't wear a shapeless, homespun dress and hadn't tried to convert me to any lord or savior even once. I told her this on the short drive to her house with Cinder panting contentedly between us. It seemed we had both silently agreed to speak of normal, human things until we were in the safety of four walls and a locked door.

"I tried to go to school for fifth grade," she explained as we drove over a crossroad, heading to her house before deciding what to do next. "I insisted on it. But while I was ahead of all the other kids in some things, other things didn't make sense at all. Social things mostly."

"Yeah, I can see why you wouldn't fit in around here," I said, patting Cinder's fur absentmindedly.

"You mean because I've got some extra melanin, or because I'm not an asshole?"

"Both I guess. Also, your whole, you know..." I waved one hand over her aesthetic.

"Eh. There's some of that particular close-minded, small-town charm for sure, but it's not all bad. My brother had a nearly foot-tall mohawk, but he had a couple of close buddies here, so I guess it's a matter of finding your people. At least my parents do fully appreciate how lucky they are that neither one of their kids really fit in here."

"That's nice of them."

"It was. What about you? Got a booming social life back home?"

"Nah. I stewed in my own self-loathing there, mostly."

"So...artist?"

I laughed and realized I hadn't done so in quite some time. "Good guess."

"Google," she admitted, and I panicked for a second before telling myself that my medical history wouldn't be online and neither would the gossip, at least I hoped so on that last part. "Sorry, that sounded creepy. It was just after I met you the other day, I looked up your mom's disappearance and your name came up too. You had an art show at fifteen?"

I shrugged. That art show was my dad pulling some strings, though he didn't admit it. A woman saw some of my stuff he'd hung at his club and wanted to put some in her gallery. She was pretty and my dad...well, let's just say it didn't feel earned. Even with the gifted art program, the scholarship, I always felt like I was tricking people into believing I was talented. It still mattered though. The art. To me.

"So, what made you come here when you did then? Vivian?"

"More or less." I tugged at a leaf tangled behind my ear. It crumbled as it broke it free. I began combing my fingers through my hair which still caged bits of leaves and twigs, and possibly the odd bug—the idea of which alone was making me itchy.

She looked over to me skeptically. "You had a bad breakup didn't you."

"What makes you say that?" I asked, but in a sense she wasn't wrong. Not really. It was worse, I thought, to lose someone whose friendship was supposed to outlive all your shitty boyfriends. Definitely worse to be lost by them for one of those shitty little boyfriends.

"Like I said, people don't really come here, not to stay. Not unless they have ties, and even then it's only when they need to regroup from something out there in the big wide world. Like a breakup or a breakdown."

"A little from column A, a little from column B then." I shifted uncomfortably in my seat. Invading faeries, ghosts, and goblins, but my own mental failings—that was the scary topic. "I think I just wanted to know more about where I came from before figuring out where I should be going—if that makes sense."

"Looking back when you're trying to go forward is a good way to smack into a wall." She turned down another stretch of empty road. "But I think I get it. I was actually going to transfer to a state university next semester for a fresh start of my own, but I suppose I'll have to see if the world gets taken over by monsters first."

"Oh, hey—don't go canceling your future yet," I said, trying to assure us both. "I just need to find that talisman."

"We. *We* need to find that talisman." She glanced over to me, a touch annoyed. "I'm involved too. So are my parents. So is your...Vivian. And everyone else here. It'll take more than some borrowed Wi-Fi to figure this out on your own, so I'm helping you."

I wanted to say I could do it on my own, that I'd be fine. But she was right. "Sorry," I told her. "I mean, thank you. But also, sorry."

"Don't be. Even if I did want to just leave, my family's got deep roots here that are worth protecting. After all, one day *this* will all be mine." She gestured dramatically to the rows of apple trees we passed that the air was already sweet with.

"The...apples?"

"The *orchard*," she answered. "Pratt Orchard has been around for two hundred years, and we're just past the busiest part of the season, so thank god my parents decided to go to some festival or other for a few days. My dad has high enough blood pressure as it is."

Mattie's house was pretty and pleasant. Blue as a robin's egg with scalloped white trim, and flower boxes on the windows planted with colorful things. On the hood of a red car in front of the garage, a fat gray cat slept soundly. A weeping willow grew in the corner of the fenced-in yard, an old swing set sat in its shade.

Inside it looked comfortable and lived in, quilts thrown over couches and chairs, a shaggy rug in front of the fireplace where Cinder immediately plopped down after loudly lapping up some water from a bowl in the kitchen. It was all so...wholesome. Normal. Yet, despite how she clashed with the backdrop, Mattie still looked like she belonged here.

A picture on the wall behind the stairs showed her as a preteen in a plaid dress, smiling from behind glasses, her hair in thick waves. Next to her stood a lanky kid with bright blue hair, smoothed down to one side, that perfectly matched his tie, and though I couldn't see it, I knew it also matched the blue on the back of the familiar looking leather jacket he wore. That must be her brother. I pointed at the middle-aged couple wearing matching holiday sweaters and warm smiles flanking them.

The woman's hair was in a soft brown bob; her hand rested on young Mattie's arm. The graying, rosy-cheeked man had his arm proudly around the tall boy's shoulders. They reminded me of Sunday school teachers and were both as pale as I was.

"You're adopted?"

"Careful." Mattie leaned her head out of the closet she'd been rustling through. "I can't take any more shocks today."

"Haha." I smirked, then saw the shotgun she carried. "What are you going to do with *that?*"

"Help us both not die, hopefully."

"I'm not sure that'll do any good."

"You said metal harms faeries, right?" She zipped the gun up in a carrying bag. "What do you think bullets are made out of?"

"*Some* metals hurt *some* faeries. *Maybe.* And that's not all we're dealing with." I never asked Noc how he had gotten my phone in the first place. For all I knew something unseen could have gotten into my bag to steal it and deliver it to him. If that were the case, I wasn't sure bringing guns out there was the best idea. Things were going bad enough without us accidentally arming some pixies.

"Better than nothing." She shrugged. "We're on our own unless we can convince Walker of what's happening."

"Okay, so, we find him first. I want to find out more about this old woman anyway. But I have to get back to the house by dark. I don't think I could convince Vivian to leave for anything, and my mom, well...she's safer where she is unless she snaps out of it. You up for a slumber party?"

"You do realize that with that tree we'll need to *walk d*own that driveway to get to your house, right? And you didn't even make it halfway before some hot possible faery showed up to ruin both our days." She disappeared back into the closet, coming out with a sleeve of arrows and a bow that was large enough to be just as intimidating as the gun.

"Whoa there, Katniss," I said taking in her arsenal. "Pretty sure I never said he was 'hot'."

"You said he was attractive. More than once. Which I thought was pretty odd, considering everything else, so I assumed it was relevant."

"No, I..." But I realized that I couldn't remember exactly how I'd described Hawthorne to her at all. It was a blank spot in my memory. He'd warned me against giving my name, that it would give others a measure of power over me. I wondered if this was part of some hopefully benign spell he was able to use on me because I'd given him mine.

"You also said his voice was 'lyrical' and he smelled like a 'sunlit field after a day of leisure and delights' so...yeah." She sniffed. "Odd."

Definitely a spell then. I drew a deep breath and exhaled a slow fuming sound. "As long as I was clear about the dangerous and untrustworthy parts, yeah, fine, he was also a very pretty man," I said through my teeth. "At least that's how he appeared."

"You know," she said thoughtfully as she looked over her table of weaponry, "whenever I'd see Vivian driving around in that old Cadillac, I'd think, 'Now there goes a woman who probably has like a hundred of those fancy bald cats and a panic room.' Don't suppose I was right there?"

"No panic room. And unless she's hiding them on the closed up side of the house, no cats. I'd think I'd have smelled them by now."

"That's a shame. A hundred of anything could be weaponized. Well," she sighed, "I *have* always wanted to get a look at the Adair house."

She shoved a pile of notebooks onto a chair to make room and pointed me to another one. I pulled out my laptop, grateful that it didn't seem to have been damaged in today's woodland adventure, and there we were—just two girls cramming folklore that might help them stop a localized apocalypse on a Friday afternoon. It was a relief to finally know for sure that I wasn't crazy. Or at least that I wasn't crazy alone.

23

Poisonous

On the phone, Vivian had sounded as normal as could be when I'd asked if she'd called anyone about what she still thought was only an inconveniently downed tree. She said the tree-hauling service guy must be too busy to pick up today, but she was sure she'd get through tomorrow.

"Good," I said. "I mean, it's good you didn't need to leave today anyway. I'll still be back before dark, but please keep an eye on the locks. I think it's good...bear...weather."

She was silent for a few moments before clicking her tongue. "Honestly, Talia, I haven't gone senile since yesterday. You enjoy whatever you're getting up to with your little friend and don't worry about me."

"This him?" Mattie asked, spinning her screen to face me once I'd hung up. There were several images of sculptures of a male face made out of leaves staring back at me.

"Is that who?"

"Well, this is what came up for Green Man."

"Green Man *of the Briar*, and no. That wasn't him. Or it's not a very good likeness anyway."

I'd jotted down any name I'd heard in reference to Hawthorne for her to look up, while I focused on the unspoken terrors like "Noc" and "Orias" and "ort", none of which had yielded any results. Neither had Maevyn or the Everlands.

Mattie got a break first in some old Irish poem about a Thorny Jack, who lured people...not to their direct death but to their *ruin*. It was said that he was fair of face and full of charm and often traveled along the edges of forests. He called on both high-and low-born ladies, favoring the beautiful, and none could resist him once he had his sights set on them, for he came from the Unseelie Court of Faerie. He would seduce many, taking their hearts and souls to Hell, leaving them cold and "Jack-fallen", or mad with pining, until they wasted away.

Following that thread led to a shanty that told of a man called Jack Thorn who made a deal with the Devil to give the souls of fallen women in place of his own. Then there was a snippet of a Welsh tale that mentioned a sinister, inhuman creature called Jack of Thorns who would call a woman to him with his song and beauty, only to wrap her in his thorn-covered arms and drag her into the earth to warm his grave-cold heart, but I'd like to think that was a metaphor.

"Wow," Mattie said. "Cannot *wait* to avoid that guy at all costs. He's like monstrous fuck boy."

"I don't think we have that option, and a what?"

"A slutty guy who uses women? Tosses them aside like they're nothing, you know? A fuck boy."

"That isn't—" I blinked at her. "He's like a *faery*."

"Fine. A fuck *faery*. If these women are *wasted* by him, he must be using them for something. Taking something from them. Maybe it's sexual energy, like an incubus. Oh, or maybe..." She raised an eyebrow. "He's not magic at all and he's just really good at—"

"Yes, Mattie, I got it. *Thank you,* but...actually maybe you're not far off. Maybe he infects them with something? Poisons them with—"

"His enchanted faery wood."

I threw my hands up, which made her clamp her lips together with an apologetic nod. I might not want to think about his methods, but I already knew he *had* given my mother something poisonous. I could only hope that Noc wasn't the be-all and end-all source of magical knowledge, and the talisman was a poison that could be cured.

My budding dream was that if her mind was fixed, we could go somewhere away from all of this. Maybe to New Orleans, where she'd once been happy with Dad. Or...well, anywhere. We could go anywhere together, once we were finally safe. Assuming it was possible to *be* safe.

Interesting that all of these faery stories just faded away over time, if the faeries themselves did not. Maybe they just got better at covering their tracks and started leaving no one behind to tell their tale. How many people still disappeared without a trace all over the world?

A sudden clanging of church bells made my hand fly to my chest to keep my heart from jumping out. "*Je-zus!*"

"Sorry," she said, turning her phone alarm off. "But dark falls fast this time of year, and I didn't want to go down a rabbit hole and lose track of time. We can't be the only ones around here that've been noticing things getting weirder, but Walker's phone keeps going to voicemail, which...worries me. I think we should go to the station to see if someone there could track him down for us."

"What do you think the chances are that the phones are just being weird because of the storm last night?"

"What storm?"

For once I found the idea of going into town comforting. Buildings, cars, and even people would be a welcome sight. But as we drove up the main street, it was quiet. The library was closed despite the weekday, along with a number of other businesses. No children in the school yard today, and the few people that were around seemed hurried. It reminded me of what a city looked like when it was getting ready for a big storm. But that could've just been me doing what my old therapist would call projecting.

I was about to ask Mattie if things looked odd to her too when, without warning, I lurched into the door as she whipped the truck over a curb. "What the hell—?"

"Tiny detour," she announced, throwing her door open.

I quickly shut Cinder in the truck and followed her into a quaint little hardware store that smelled like sawdust and glue. The bell jingled above the door as we entered.

"Hey!" She marched up to a man heading into a back room.

Wes Samuel jumped and spun around, pointing his finger my way. "*You!*" He looked more disheveled than last time, his eyes wilder. "You had your chance. I told you—I *told you!*"

I shot a questioning look at Mattie.

"He made it sound like seeing the Green Lady was a current event when he accosted you, right? Well, if he knows how to find her, maybe she can tell you something about what we're looking for—or about this green briar man. Didn't you say the guy left you to chase after her?"

I had and he did, but if she'd been haunting the woods all this time, stalking people and occasionally hanging from a tree, I wasn't sure she would be the kind willing to help us, and if she were willing, I wouldn't want to even *know* what she'd charge us.

A gruff voice came around the counter. "Calm down, Wes."

"Dad—I was just..." His eyes flitted from me to Mattie.

"Mattie, you leave him be now," the man scolded as Wes ducked back through swinging doors.

"I just need to talk to him for like one minute," she said.

"Well, he's in no state for it," he told her, mildly exasperated. "What do you girls want?"

"It was me that wanted a word with Wes," I volunteered, thinking fast. "I'm...researching? Urban legends, small town ghost stories, that kind of thing. School project. He seemed...knowledgeable—and eager to help me the other day."

The man's face soured. "So that's what set him off. Bringing up all that stuff. Now he's running around those woods again, not sleeping, and worrying his mother."

"Actually"—I stepped forward with a tight smile—"the truth is, Wes might have... 'picked up' my phone the other day? Accidentally, of course."

His cheeks flushed red. He muttered under his breath and pushed through the doors behind him. "Aw, hell," we heard a few seconds later. "Well, looks like he ran out the back. Like I said, he ain't actin' right."

Mattie and I turned in unison and ran outside. I followed her down an alley to where the back door of the shop hung open. There was no sign of Wes, but there in the playground across the street sitting on a swing, was Maevyn.

He had shriveled back down to the little-girl version, only now she was misshapen, arms just a little too long, mouth too wide, and where her eyes should have been were large holes so black no light or life could possibly exist in them. Except she was definitely alive. Or at least animated. She sang in low, sharp whispers that I was thankful I couldn't make out from where I stood.

"You see her too, right?" I asked.

"I do..." She shuddered. "Which one is she again?"

"Maevyn."

"The lost girl gone bird boy?

"Yep."

She nodded. "And, uh...those other things?"

I hadn't seen it at first. A vibrantly colored mass of movement crawled around the bars of the yellow climbing structure, undulating up the slides. They appeared to be vines, with wide leaves of dark greens and midnight blues that flowered into petals of purple and gold. Only they weren't plants at all, of course. Plants do not have so many viny black legs. Or large crimson eyes. There was what looked like a sort of webbing cast beneath them, and as I stared, I caught the sounds of chattering and squeaking. *Gnawing.*

"Bad," I decided. "Bad, those would be very bad."

"Step back," an even, familiar voice said. "Slowly. Both of you."

Shane stood in the doorway behind us, casually dressed in jeans and a gray shirt, eyes fixed on the playground, and one hand on the holster he wore at his side beneath his denim jacket. Without hesitation, we backed into the shop with him. Once inside he bolted the door.

"Well, you saved us a very short trip to the station," Mattie said, her eyes on the bolt.

"Just as well—there's no one there," he said with a calm that *had* to be at least a little forced. "Phones seem to be down too. I was on my way to check up on the Adairs when I saw the truck up on the curb with Cinder still in it. Whatever...*that* is out there, I know I can't do anything about, but I also know it has just about everything to do with your mom, Talia."

"You're not wrong...but she's not going to be much help. That woman you found with her may be though. Senile or not."

"Oh. Turns out *not.*" Shane's eyes widened. "Luckily my grandma speaks Oneida well enough to understand her, but I was hoping something was lost in translation when she told us that a few weeks ago she'd run away from one of those Indian Schools and gotten lost in the woods. First problem there of course being that those assimilation schools haven't been around here since the fifties—bigger problem is that she *wholeheartedly* believes that she's twelve years old. You can probably see why I suspected she wasn't all there. But due diligence had me spending yesterday going through archive records anyway. I wasn't expecting to see the name she gave me, but there it was: *Kehente Scanadoah*—a kid that went into St. Thomas and never came out. And if she were telling the truth about that—"

The doorbell jingled, and Shane's hand moved back over his holster. He pushed open the swinging door enough to peer out then waved us back to the front of the shop where we were greeted by the appropriately suspicious eyes of Wes's dad. An older man with a tan jacket approached the counter nervously. He gave Shane an absentminded nod of greeting but said nothing when he got to the register. It seemed pretty obvious he was waiting for us to leave before getting on to whatever business he had.

Mattie and I went to her truck while Shane lingered inside. I assumed he tried to warn them both to go back to their homes and families. Maybe to leave town altogether. But something pulled inside my chest. I remembered what Hawthorne told me about those here in Elmwood not paying attention to Neighbors from over the Veil. From what Mattie'd said, it was like they'd all been acclimated to dismissing all evidence of them.

Shane came out running his hand through his hair with a shake of his head. I took it whatever he told the men hadn't landed. "I'm not used to feeling helpless, but everyone is on their own for now. When was the last time you talked to Vivian?"

"She and Mom are safe. It's this Kehente woman we were on our way to see. I need to find out everything she knows about how she and Mom got back here."

"You...might want to know about where they were first."

24

A Wrong Thing

Cinder's breath was my closest companion, but not my dearest one, as we followed Shane's SUV out of the town square. I turned and rolled down the window, letting in the strengthening undercurrent of chill in the air as the sun slowly fled.

I wouldn't have described myself as much of an optimist before but look at me now—finding new things to hope for on a regular basis. Right now for example, I was very much hoping that this Kehente would be able to tell me what happened to Hawthorn's talisman. I hoped Noc would really be able to use it to put everything back where it belonged before anyone would get hurt. I hoped for all of this, even as my mind drifted back to the image of Maevyn on the playground, looking like Hell's scarecrow, and to the pile of children's shoes under the merry-go-round I had tried very hard not to see.

The trees sailed by as we drove silently up the road. If this Kehente woman was no help, then I knew I'd have to go back in there and try to find that path Hawthorne had me on. Or whatever a 'golden goose' was. Maybe it was another bit of supposedly harmless town folklore involving a bird that spat out golden eggs on midnights when the moonlight hit Farmer So-and-So's chicken coop just right or something, but I was afraid that more likely the 'golden goose' was just one of like seventeen other names for some awful faery thing. And in that case, even if it started out looking like a bird, it would end up really being some twisted creature with a bad disposition and a horrifying mouthful of sharp teeth. *So, a regular goose then?* I cackled in a probably unhinged way.

Cinder and Mattie both turned my way. I probably made things weirder when I abruptly went quiet as I noticed a yellow, boarded-up building that looked like it could have been a convenience store once. The sign had a picture of a goofy, cartoonish bird with its wings open as though it were pointing to the letters that read "The Golden Goose".

Shane's house was just past it.

We rolled up the gravel of his driveway and stopped behind where he parked in front of his garage. The attached cabin-style house sat on a small hill. The woods came closer to it than they did to Vivian's place, allowing pinecones to litter the yard from trees that reached over the stone fence. Cinder bounded out of the truck the second the door opened and happily began sniffing around before bolting after a squirrel, prompting Mattie to chase after her yet again.

"Right there." Shane pointed to a spot in the woods as I came up beside him. "Earlier, I'd come out here to tinker on my car a bit to clear my head and almost cracked my head on the hood when a loud crow called from what sounded like right over my shoulder. But when I spun around, I saw—I *thought* I saw—a jacket. A bright little blue jacket tangled high in the branches. Just *there*. I saw it just as clearly as I'm seeing that damn dog squatting on my lawn now, and all of a sudden, I...*needed* to get a closer look.

"I heard Gran call my name, but I didn't even look her way—I just headed toward that jacket. Then she said my name again, but this time she sounded angry. You'll be meeting her, my gran. She doesn't get angry. So, I turned to her, but she was looking at the tree too. But when

I looked back, there was no jacket, just the biggest damn crow I'd ever seen. It just *stared*—didn't do that little tilt of the head from side to side like crows do—just sat stone still with its black eyes on me." He looked at his boots for a moment before turning to me. "In my gut, Talia, I already knew that wherever your mom had come back from wasn't a place on any map. Two women missing nearly a hundred years between them showing up on the same day, one white as the moon and the other wearing bones, was a pretty good sign of how wrong things were, but that jacket had cinched it for me."

"Really? 'Cause for me it was the goblins." Mattie was trying to wrestle a pinecone from Cinder's mouth behind us. "What was up with the jacket?"

"It's an unpleasant mark on my memory." He paused with a frown at Mattie. "Did you say *goblins*?"

"Long story—though not as strange a one as it would have been a few days ago," I told him.

"Right. Well. Unfortunately, all of this is still explainable," he said. "But that doesn't mean you're going to like the explanation. Or know what to do with it."

"Way ahead of you on that one," Mattie mumbled.

"I don't suppose my mom had anything on her when she was found that you maybe didn't mention? Or maybe you noticed something near her that looked...out of place?" *You know, like a run-of-the-mill scepter...*

"Other than Cole, the only thing out of place was Kehente."

"I mean something smaller." At least I sure fucking hoped so. "I think my mom carried something back with her that I need to find."

He looked at me curiously. "*She* wasn't carrying anything."

We were greeted at Shane's door by a short woman with a quick, warm smile, wearing bright blue earrings that dangled beneath the tip of her smooth salt-and-pepper hair.

"This is my grandmother, Lydia. Gran this is—"

"Yes, I remember Matilda, the apple girl." She looked at me. "We were wondering when *you* would get here."

Once inside, you could really see where Shane ended and Lydia began. The walls were hung with tapestries and the odd mounted mask along with a few paintings. There was a lot of functionally beige furniture covered by splashes of colorful throws and pillows. And rocking in a chair by a fireplace sat the oldest woman I'd ever seen.

She wore a shapeless house dress in bright, geometric designs that did nothing to hide her frailty. Her hair was in two long, gray braids that had to outweigh her. The crepe-paper skin of her hands gripping the arms of the chair showed every blue vein, yet on her thin, creased face, her eyes were sharp as they fell on me.

"This is our Kehente," Lydia said and took one of the blankets from the couch to drape it over the woman's knees, whispering something to her. Kehente pushed the blanket down with a scowl and said something I couldn't understand in an unexpectedly strong, clear voice, and Lydia answered back with a dismissive wave of her hand.

"My own daughter, Veronica, she was a good woman." Lydia sighed. "I passed along stories of spirits and their worlds, skin-walkers and Jogah, forest drums, and Deer Woman, all of our stories. But she left them behind, along with the rest of her heritage, and never passed them on to my grandson."

"Even if I grew up hearing them, my understanding would still be right where it is now when I saw what I saw today, Gran."

"Maybe so. But if you believe in other worlds and what comes from them, even for a little while when you're young, it opens a door that never quite closes all the way. It's easier on the mind, I think, to have that door ajar when you're faced with the things you forgot were real to you once."

"Yeah, safe to say our doors are all off the hinges at this point," Mattie said.

I sat close enough to where Kehente was rocking to make out the age spots around her forehead when she began speaking directly to me in an almost musical dialect. Lydia's own clipped tone translated her words from beside her.

"There are paths that run behind this world like rivers," she began. "And paths that climb through it like ivy. These are paths that we don't see, and you do not know it when you are walking them. Those paths do not end in any good place. When they end at all.

"The thing that put me on one of these paths had a face as rough as bark, and his wooden arms carried me into the sun of a twin world where I played with other children in a field and danced with spirits that wore changing faces—young and old at once. I felt sure I must be in a dream until I moved beyond the field and saw a glimpse of a village that was alive, though it rotted.

"In it were beasts that were some measure of human and some measure of animal and some measure of something very old that came from beneath the earth and deep in mountain caves. Then a lady found me and took my hand. She was beautiful because she looked like my mother, but her skin was cold. She took me to a place where everything was made of smooth stones and reaching trees, and for a time, I forgot that I'd been afraid.

"There were no more children in this place, but tall and shining people so finely dressed that I thought they were kings and queens from story books. They filled a hall so vast that I never saw the end of it. The cold lady dressed me in silk and flowers. She told me that if I did as I was told that I would be rewarded, so I filled the cups of the shining men and women and no matter how many I filled, my jug never emptied. And the people grew stranger. I'd see a glimpse of green skin or antlers, legs like flower stalks, and clawed hands. Still, I wasn't afraid when I saw these things. I felt less and less of anything as I drifted through that hall.

"When I saw Cole, I knew she didn't belong there. She had life and kindness in her eyes that made me want to warn her, but I was no longer sure of what she needed to be warned of. And she wasn't there alone. She was with one of them. He was called Hawthorne, and he was different from the others. He took my jug away. Let me sit with him. Talked to me. He warned me that I would die if I stayed in this place, but if I did what he said, he would free me. I don't know why I believed him.

"Then something came for Cole. He looked like a man, but I knew behind his face was something I never would want to see. It felt like he had walked in every bad dream I'd ever known. But Hawthorne made me a quick bargain, so when the man-thing took Cole to the dark lands, I went too. I stayed with her until Hawthorne came and brought us to the black water of the sea. He *promised* we would return to our own lands. He gave Cole something to protect us. Then we drowned our way home."

"Kehente?" I asked, forgetting in my urgency that she couldn't understand me. "Do you still have what she gave you?"

She understood well enough. Her eyes flashed angrily, and Lydia's voice rose over her own. "I promised her to return it only to him. I don't think she knew what would happen to me once we came out of the water. But *he* did. *He* knew I would not survive the freedom he promised for long."

Be careful the word binds both ways. Yep, that sounded enough like Hawthorne—tricking good girls into bad bargains.

Kehente reached into the pocket of her dress; her delicate fingers pulled out a small leather pouch. I heard Shane begin to say something, but she cut him off via Lydia. "I *will* keep my promise to her. He will come for this. But then it's her he'll be after."

Her hawklike gaze didn't move from my face as she unwound the twine cord from around the pouch and beckoned me closer, leaning forward and opening her palm as she shakily dropped the contents into it.

It was a stone.

Not much bigger than a walnut, rough and streaked with green, laced with silvery grooves that caught the light. But it was still just...a stone. I reached out, under her protective gaze, and touched it. An odd uneasiness ebbed into me. The feeling was akin to what I'd felt when I'd opened my dad's bedroom door once without knocking and saw him and whatever woman scrambling for the sheets, or when I'd heard my English teacher crying in her classroom and accidently made eye contact. A bit of sorrow and a bit of shame that comes with seeing something not meant for you.

"You feel it," Shane said. "Don't you?"

I nodded, remembering Noc telling me the talisman was still capable of being powerful in the right hands. Those hands clearly weren't mine because I could barely stand touching the thing.

"Feel what?" Mattie leaned over my shoulder. "It's *a rock.*"

"It's a wrong thing." Lydia frowned. "A dangerous thing that doesn't belong here. She doesn't want to keep it. But she won't give it up either."

"When we first brought her to the hospital she had to be sedated. She was combative and surprisingly spry." Shane rubbed his jaw with the back of his knuckles. "They were finally able to cut away the mess she was wearing, but even then, she wouldn't loosen her grip on it. I got the idea to hum this lullaby my mom used to sing. It calmed her, but the way she looked at me...it broke my heart. Then she opened her fist in my hand, and as soon as that thing touched me, I felt that *wrongness*. That...sorrow.

"I closed her fingers back over it, and she seemed relieved before she finally drifted off. I think she wanted to make sure I wasn't going to steal it if she slept or let anyone else take it. But I didn't think she had to worry about anyone else wanting that thing."

"I do," I said quickly. "Shane, it's, well, it's *literally* the key to what's happening."

"Cole told you about it?"

"No. She's still...the same. He showed up in the woods today. *Hawthorne.*"

He drew a breath and nodded. "Was he like the thing we saw earlier?"

"No..." I was still looking at Kehente's weathered face as she resumed rocking, trying to pull a twelve-year-old out of her skin with my imagination. "Not on the outside anyway."

"Okay." He nodded again. "Then I've got some questions for him—whatever he is—before anyone gives him anything."

"If you want him to show up, you could leave out some cream. Or an infant, " Mattie volunteered, picking at her nail polish.

"They're faeries, at least some of them are," I explained. "He was just one of the less obvious ones I've seen so far."

"*Faeries?*" Shane almost laughed. "Eh—I don't think..." But he trailed off, eyes drifting to the picture window.

Cinder, who had been politely sitting on the rug next to Mattie, began to bark, and Kehente was up like a shot, rushing past me. Shane moved to stop her, but he wasn't kidding about her being spry because she was already flinging the door open wide. He was at her heels. Mattie and I followed, and all of us stopped in our tracks when we saw Hawthorne.

25

Half Nothing

He stood at the edge of the walkway, eyebrows arched as Kehente yelled what I'd guess, based on the amount of vehemence in the finger jabbing came with it, was likely a string of curses.

Shane tried to put himself between the two, but Hawthorne only stepped around him.

"Oh, but little Kehente, you *are* free," Hawthorne told her over his shoulder.

When he saw me, my breath caught. Knowing who he was now didn't make him any less striking, but it wasn't the sharp angle of his jaw or the shape of his lips, it was the way his whole *being* commanded attention. Even Cinder was wagging her tail at a near blurring speed as she sniffed at him.

"Damn. That *is* attractive," Mattie said louder than I think we both would have liked.

"You understand Kenhente?" I asked as he sauntered to me.

"Of course. She is *quite* angry with me."

"Yeah, I think we all got that, buddy," Shane said while extending his arm to keep Kehente at a distance. "Why might that be?"

He assessed Shane with a glance. "You'd be surprised how many people find getting what they ask for upsetting, *buddy*. She wanted to return here. I saw that she was returned."

Kehente continued yelling at him until Lydia appeared behind her, placing her hands on her shoulders in a soothing way. Without taking her eyes from Hawthorne, she gently pulled the older woman back to the porch.

Hawthorne raised his chin at Kehente's stone-containing fist. "I do believe that's mine, by the way."

"Hawthorne." I caught his oddly soothing scent as I looked into the warring colors of his eyes. I shook it off and glared at him. "Then why didn't you just ask *her* to give it to my mother?"

"Well, as I just said, she is quite angry with me, *Talia*." He smirked. "And once I discovered it with her, I knew something had gone awry and that Cole would need it back. I feared the girl might not be able to give it to her. Or willing. So, I looked for Cole and found her back at that house she used to run from. I saw that she was sure enough bespelled, and I gathered *you'd* want to help her too."

"Bespelled as in...cursed?" I asked

"Something like a forgetting curse probably. Orias gets possessive and he does *love* a curse."

"Orias—" I began, almost forgetting to feign ignorance. "You didn't mention an Orias."

"No." There was a touch of acid in his voice. "He's a king of the Everlands—of Midnight to be precise and of Nightmares to be even more so. And he's apparently even sent minions to meddle. They're littering up the woods"

I had to force myself not to glare at him as I kept up the facade. "But I suppose that talisman of yours will be able to get rid of them, right?"

He narrowed his eyes at me. "What an *odd* assumption."

"What *is* the thing?" Shane had moved next to me so subtly I hadn't noticed until he spoke.

"It's a rather impressive gamble," Hawthorne replied. "And though it *is* mine, it no longer belongs to me."

"Make less sense," I told him. "I dare you."

"*Does* it have something to do with what's happening to my town?" Shane demanded.

Hawthorne considered the question for a moment before answering a begrudging, "Yes."

"Sorry to interrupt." Mattie crept over with her eyes not wavering from Hawthorne's face. "Hi. I'm Mattie."

She offered him her hand, and I had to stop myself from slapping her arm away from him. My mother's abductor smiled; his face was instantly a beam of friendship and warmth. I didn't think I could hate anyone more.

"Hello, Mattie." He practically purred her name and took her hand and swept his eyes over her. "Well. A doe in wolf's clothing."

She looked unnervingly focused on the bow of his mouth. "Thanks..." she breathed, a dreamy smile rising on her face until I elbowed her. "Oh." She blinked and shook her head, still holding his hand. "Um, is there any way we could move this inside because there is something watching us, and it's freaking me *right* the fuck out."

We all turned. Something quivered along a tree on the far side of the yard. It was blueish gray and would almost pass as bark if not for the movement. Angular shapes folded away from the trunk, leaving some shimmery substance behind. The little things were vaguely more human shaped by the time they reached the ground and spread along the yellowing grass to the next tree, coating that one as well with their diminutive forms.

"That's not...usual," Hawthorne stated.

"You don't say," Shane said dryly. "And if you had to narrow it down, what about it stands out to you, my friend?"

"*Friend*." Hawthorne side-eyed him while watching the cocooned tree drop the rest of its dying leaves at once with a light *swoosh*.

Cinder whined and backed into Mattie's legs.

"Well, for one, the Weaver's handmaidens don't usually work in the Dying Season. Obviously."

"Huh," was all Shane offered in response as pea-sized bits of red and purple began bruising along the branches. Leaves erupted next, dark magenta and easily wider than both of his hands pressed together but still delicate. The patterns on their surface had the look of lace even at a distance.

Flower buds sprouted next, but before they bloomed Mattie's voice was urgently whispering, "Guys, I meant *there.*"

We all turned to see a woman standing at the edge of the tree line. Only it wasn't a woman in anything more than shape and what passed for attire. Its flesh was pale, nearly translucent but for the indigo veins, and draped with porous swathes of pale pink membrane. Gossamer gills curved down, circled her head and down her neck like a mane, framing her narrow face with its elongated black eyes.

I must've really been desensitized by now, because I felt more fascination rather than fear as Shane began to herd Mattie and I back to the porch where Lydia and Kehente were already retreating inside.

"Hawthorne," Lydia called, "you're welcome here too."

"Just *move.*" Shane was practically shoving us now. Once he backed inside, he shut and locked the door, leaning a chair against it for good measure. He sat there rubbing his hands on the knees of his jeans a few times before hopping back up. "So," he announced to no one in particular, "that was a faery."

"That looked more like what happens when a human fucks a mushroom," Mattie said and I slapped her shoulder. She followed my eyes to her hand which was entwined with Hawthorne's. "Oh..."

She reluctantly let him go and he winked at her, then explained, "That is a faery creature. As am I. Or so I was. Now, I'm half nothing."

He moved to the window. How odd it was to see something like him in a normal home, like seeing a dog wearing a dress or a queen in sweatpants. "Her kind usually exists on the edges of things along the Midnight Lands." He looked worn then as he gazed out at whatever creatures were making themselves seen. Even weariness on him translated to brooding charm. "But coming *here* like this..."

"The Midnight Lands is that—" Shane began, but then Kehente said something edged in razors and plopped herself back in the rocking chair with her arms crossed. It was an odd thing to say of someone with this many wrinkles, but she appeared to be pouting.

Hawthorne kneeled down and softly spoke to her words I couldn't understand as they glided out of his mouth as smooth as cream. Lydia seemed to lap them up too. Even Cinder was enthralled, tail whipping side to side as she stared up at him.

After a minute of watching with fairly well-veiled apprehension, Shane leaned close to Lydia, keeping his voice low. "Remember, she can't hand it over to him yet, not until we know more."

"Oh, he doesn't want it," Lydia said.

Shane opened his mouth, aborted whatever he was going to say before starting again with a simple, "What?"

"It's not *mine*, I told you," Hawthorne said, without turning. "I am *trying* to make the girl understand that."

Kehente said something, finger raised, and Hawthorne huffed. "I can't make a bargain I can't keep, and you would *not* want me to craft one I can, my little bobcat. Look where that got you last time."

The argument I could only half understand went on until Shane, looking at the end of his superhumanly long patience, tapped my shoulder and gestured for me to follow him. I tugged Mattie's sleeve, not wanting to leave her with Hawthorne.

"We're just going to take a minute to..." He didn't bother with the rest; the older women barely acknowledged him. "I think," he said once he led us through the garage door in the kitchen, "it's time to compare notes."

26

A Darkness Walks

Shane's garage was cool and smelled vaguely of woodwork and grease. A shiny blue car that must be his tinker toy was its only occupant. He locked the door behind us.

"I...I don't know what happened back there." Mattie wandered puzzled past the workbench littered with oil rags and sawdust lining the wall. "I knew what he was, but I wasn't ready for him being so...I mean, it's like all sense flew out of me when he looked my way. Maybe I shouldn't have looked directly at him? And I definitely shouldn't have *touched* him."

"Or continued to touch him," I reminded her.

"I got *distracted*," she said through her teeth. "*Monsters are distracting*."

"Everyone just handles fear differently," Shane offered. "Some people lock up, some people fall apart—"

"And some people just go and hold hands with the magical lady-thief?" She hugged her chest and leaned against the bench beside me. "I didn't like that. That...that lack of *control*. If that's how good he is then we're probably screwed."

"Good he is at what exactly?" His glance bounced between Mattie and I.

"Charm," she answered. "It's like...*a spell* or something. You know me better than to think I'd ever go that stupid for anyone in any normal circumstance."

"That I do, Mattie." A small smile cracked along his face.

"It's something between magic and hypnosis, I think," I said. "I felt it when I first met him too, but I guess that wears off. Or he's just not bothering with me anymore. He's been coming around our world *charming* women at least long enough to have garnered a bad reputation of mythic proportions."

"Oh yeah, the legend of the golden rod." Mattie huffed.

"He ruins women," I explained to spare myself from Mattie doing so. "Makes them love him. Leaves them insane with wanting him until they die. That's what he did to my mom. Minus the dying bit. So far."

"Where are you getting all this?" Shane asked.

"We found some stuff in old stories online, and"—I spoke carefully, just skirting the edge of the truth—"I've had run-ins with Maevyn—that thing from the playground—since Mom was found."

"Sounds like you've been popular." Shane's brows rose. "And you didn't think to call me?"

"No one in their right mind would've believed me before now. I wasn't even sure *I* believed me for a while," I admitted. "Anyway, it talks a lot. And sings too. Unfortunately. But Hawthorne's reputation where they're from is something much worse than that of a charmer. And he didn't rescue anyone—he used Mom to escape. I think he's some kind of criminal over there."

"Over there..." Shane said distantly. "The Midnight place?"

"They call it the Everlands." I attempted to clarify. "There's also the Lands of Dawn and Twilight and, I don't know, maybe the Land of

Tuesday and the Island of December or something. I kinda got that it's all different facets to the same nightmare world that sits right next to ours."

"Well, seems he's here." Shane scratched his chin. "So, it seems his escape worked. And apparently, he doesn't even want that stone Kehente has been waiting to give him, so why is he sticking around?"

"Because apparently *Mom* needs to be the one to give the thing back to him to activate whatever power's inside it, and that if that happens, we would all *definitely* be screwed."

"Oh in all sorts of fun ways," muttered Mattie.

"He'd be more powerfully...charming?" Shane asked.

"No...actually *yes,* that too probably, but I don't want to find out what else he'll be able to do," I said. "That stone of his is a talisman...a kind of key, and the door it opened allowed Mom and Kehente to escape back here, only it *stayed* open. Now even the things spilling over to our world are in danger until it's closed. The talisman is a kind of poison to them, so I've more or less been enlisted to do the job. I just need to bring it back to where she was found and...that should seal it off."

"I still don't get how that rock is key," Mattie said.

"Maybe it makes more sense once you see the door." Shane shifted his stance, his eyes betraying the calm in his voice. "Whatever that stone is, it feels so...wrong. It, and all the things I've seen having anything to do with it, feels *alien*. But also very, very old. And dangerous, almost casually so."

I nodded. "Hawthorne told me there were *always* folds between our worlds that people can wander through. Or be lured into—I think he was telling the truth there."

Mattie grimaced. "Like strings on a web."

"Yeah. I'm afraid of how much sense that makes." He puffed his cheeks out as he exhaled what felt like a confession. "I've seen them before. Once. Not here. I didn't know what I was seeing. But if you told me that the place they come from is closer to Hell than it is to this...Never Never Land, I'd take that bet."

"Oh," I said as it clicked. "Billy Eddington?"

"Billy Eddington." He paced around the other side of the car. "Four years old. Disappeared off a trail in a state park back in Colorado within *feet* of his family. No trace. Dogs and helicopters found nothing.

"People getting lost on those trails is easier to do than people realize. We usually found them relatively quickly, especially when they did the smart thing and stayed put once they realized they *were* lost. A handful of times, I'd join a search-and-rescue that took a day or more, but we always found them, usually a bit worse for wear, but we found them.

"Then three days into this search, I look up, and way up in the branches of a sequoia, I see the bright blue of a little jacket. Above that, a little dangling leg. I knew for me to be seeing what I was seeing meant some animals had likely gotten to the boy. Maybe a hawk had snatched up that leg from the rest of the remains and brought it to its nest, but I knew then that whatever else we found of him wouldn't be...whole. Only, when the climbers made it the more than hundred feet up that tree, he was so much still intact, just sitting on a branch and leaning against the trunk, that the guy that reached him first was worried he'd wake up with a start and fall. But Billy wasn't going to wake up. just as inexplicably as he was up that tree, Billy was dead.

"No one could say how a boy barely three feet tall made it nearly four miles to that tree, much less got up it. Then there were his feet, he hadn't been wearing any shoes—his little sneakers that were the same bright blue as his jacket were missing—we never did find those, yet his feet were clean, without a scratch on them. No one could make a case for foul play, and exposure was the official cause of death. Even with my fellow rangers talking among ourselves, no one could put in even a clear *guess*. Not one that wasn't rooted in some supernatural folklore."

"Like faeries," I said.

"Apparently. But not then. Not yet. Not for me." He stared down at his knuckles as he rolled them on the hood. "I shook my head over it for a long time but had to accept I'd never really know what happened to that poor boy. Especially when two years later, I saw him again.

"I'd just gotten out of a bad relationship and needed some solitude for a few days, and knowing the park like I did, I had my favorite spots that were away from the campsites where it could just be me and the stars for a while. One night I woke up before dawn. Wasn't sure why, but I was suddenly wide awake, and it was *quiet*. The insects and frogs that had sung me to sleep had gone completely silent. I didn't know what time it was, but the smell of smoke was still in the air from my campfire, and the moon was still pretty high when I unzipped my tent.

"I was just off of a clearing, and I could just make out the shapes of deer there. Maybe a dozen. Everything was silver in the light of the moon, but when my eyes adjusted more, I could see clearly that they were all *staring* in my direction. For a second, I thought I'd just startled them. But it wasn't the deer that made my insides clench up, it was the smaller figure with them. A small boy wearing strange clothes, some sort of...fraying suit with short pants that showed the pale off his legs in the tall grass, and little sneakers I knew would be bright blue in the light.

"I knew, somehow, that it was him. It took me a minute to really register that his eyes were gone. His...his cheeks, they were fleshless—I could *see* the whites of his little teeth through the tendons of jaw. But I still knew it was him. He looked at me while he raised the bones of his fingers up to one of the deer's noses to pet it, then—lightning quick—he grabbed its antlers and swung himself up to its back. He didn't look back—thank *Christ*—as the deer leapt away, carrying him into the trees."

"Jesus." Mattie shuddered and rubbed her hand over the bristles of the shaved side of her head.

"I didn't go back to sleep. I didn't try to make it back to my car in the dark. I lit another fire and kept my gun in my hands until the sun rose. It was that morning that Gran called me to tell me my mom was sick. Much sicker than she'd let on. Two days later, I was back here in Elmwood. I never went back to Colorado. Never told anyone about that night. I tried to convince myself as time went on that it had been a nightmare. Until a few days ago, that's what it had been.

"I don't think what the *charming* man in my living room is, or what any of them are, matters—not as much as knowing what kept them all at bay until now. Because that seal was never airtight. I believe they've always walked here, and there's a darkness that walks with them. So, if you really think that rock really is the key to closing them out, given that it's all we have to go on, just tell me what we need to do."

"Okay. Then I need to get it *away* from Kehente."

"Actually," said Hawthorne, "Kehente will be giving it to Cole."

He stood casually in the corner of the garage opposite us, hands in his pockets. The door we had come through was still shut and presumably locked. That he was just *there* all of a sudden was startling, but after a second, not surprising really. At least for me.

Mattie shrieked, just a little.

27

Thorny Jack

"I know, I said I'd bring you to it," he said with a wave of his hand. "But Kehente doesn't trust handing it over to anyone but Cole."

"But she trusts *you*?" I asked.

"Better to say she understands me."

"Well, trust *me* when I say that no one I don't know is getting anywhere near my mother." I shot a conspiratorial look at my fellow humans. "She doesn't even remember you. I can bring it to her—*alone*."

"Oh, but my little fox"—his mouth crept upward—"she doesn't remember *you* either. Wasn't that the point of bringing it to her in the first place? But going anywhere alone isn't wise since the woods seem to be shifting."

"What the hell does *that* mean?" Shane asked.

"That the way home is no longer where she thinks it is. And I'd advise against anyone stealing *any* talisman. Giving such a thing acts as a sort of contract, but taking it is a sort of curse."

"Then why are these things out there then?" Shane folded his arms. "Looking for something you stole?"

"I didn't *steal* it," he said with mild disgust.

"Okay, but since it's currently in my living room, I think it's fair to ask you again: *what* is it?"

"To *me*, a curse. To the gentry of the Everlands, half of a bargaining chip between the lands of Dawn and Midnight that was never meant to be in the hands of a human woman. But to that human woman...it's something that can undo some of the wrongs visited on her by that gentry. Namely, the curse she's under."

Shane's head bobbed along with what passed for Hawthorne's explanation, eyes getting smaller as it went. "Well, that explains just about nothing."

"Fine," he said curtly. "Just think of it as a kind of...artifact. From a darker time."

"Sounds like it's something everyone would be better off without," Mattie said, averting her eyes.

Hawthorne's smile was bitter. "Certainly she would be better off, unless you want her to have her mind back."

"You *did* tell me it was protection," I said and hoped he hadn't heard me telling the others that I knew what he really wanted it for. "So, I should be safe enough to bring it to her on my own."

"The girl won't be swayed into letting it go. Alas." Already too close for my comfort, he stepped closer. "And none of you can find their way through the woods now without me."

I knew I had to tread carefully here, or not only would I accidentally break my bargain with Noc—which would probably mean something far worse than losing all my words—but I'd reveal too much to Hawthorne, who might figure out that I meant to take his talisman and essentially turn him in.

"Look. I ran into something on that path. An ort called Maevyn. He told me you weren't to be trusted, and I should keep you from my mother. Sure, he could be lying, but considering how you *ditched me* out there, it's fair to say you're not the most trustworthy guy either."

"Really?" He turned his chin to the side and rested his hand on the wood of the bench behind me. I focused hard on his jacket. It was a muted green with textured, fine, raised lines of brown stretched out in patterns that reminded me of leaves on a forest floor. I caught a sweet scent under the lichen and leather. "This *Maevyn* warned you about me, told you to keep me from her, and spoke *my* name, specifically?"

"Yes." I swallowed audibly. I could feel the tension filling the room. He leaned over just enough so that his golden-brown hair, which looked much darker indoors, brushed against my forehead. From the corner of my eye, I saw Shane soundlessly sidestep closer.

"And what else did this shadowling say? About *me*. Specifically."

"Well." The material on the lapels looked durable, yet supple, without any of the stiffness leather usually had. Noc's jacket was the same. "That you were just...the worst. That you were cruel. A liar. A thief. I believe the word 'vile' may have been used more than once. That you destroy women. That you steal them from their families. From their *children*."

I knew it was careless to scapegoat Maevyn into being the one to carry my own words as well as Noc's, but I needed to say them. When I finally met his eyes, all amusement had faded from them. He still put on an easy smile.

"Well then. It seems that it knows me well indeed. Though it did make some distortions. Not that I blame it, they're only carved from shadows, you know—and shadows don't hold things well. Orts are mostly mad after a time." He stepped back. "And are a curious thing to listen to, since they're made by demons and all."

"Demons?" Mattie's eyes flashed wide at Hawthorne before landing on me. "You didn't mention *demons*."

"And due to certain...trespasses," he continued, "those demons tend not to be able to leave the Midnight Lands. Even when they manage it, they're still tethered to them. But some can shape the shadows of the once living, or for some even more unfortunate souls, the *still* living to be their far-flung minions: *orts.* The more powerful the demon, the more complex the ort. These shadowlings are designed to do the demon's damage for them. Interesting then, that this one only stopped you just to gossip about little old me."

"Okay well first of all, 'shadowling' is way too adorable a name for him. And he didn't just talk, he tried—"

"To lure you across the Veil? Well, of course it did and yet"—Hawthorne turned his palms toward me in a dramatic swooshing motion—"*here* you are. Believing even in part what it told you. Odd, that."

He doesn't believe me. I might be able to still turn it around if I choose my words a bit wiser. As long as Shane and Mattie were still behind me, I could still pull this off. Maybe they could help distract him while I—

"Not that I trust him either," Shane said to me, throwing a glance at Hawthorne, "but it seems maybe no one has reason to trust anything coming out of any shadow things either."

Well, shit.

"When we saw it earlier it didn't look too 'well crafted'," Mattie said, finally risking a longer look in Hawthorne's direction. "Didn't look very shadowy either. She just looked...wrong. Like a stretched-out ragdoll.".

"As I said, shadows don't hold much, not away from the dark. They unravel eventually. To be reshaped, it would have to return to its maker. Did it say anything more?"

"Aside from a few disturbing ballads, no," I told him. "*Alas.*"

"Pity. And it was so *chatty* about me. But aimed for you, it seems, which means a demon is aiming for you."

"What would *a demon* want with Talia?" Shane asked from my side.

"Who knows?" He leaned on the car and pulled out his flask. "Better question: *where* is the demon? Though summoning demons is a lost art, some fools still manage it. Once they're here...*yikes.*" He smirked at me, taking a sip.

I forced my expression to stay neutral. "Well. I'll be sure to be on the lookout ."

"Yes, *do*. Especially since Orias is allowing Midnight fae to just...meander all over this place, he risks the wrath of Dawn by over-stepping the truce."

"Truce?" Shane asked.

Hawthorne sighed. "There are...rules when it comes to what's allowed—especially here."

"I thought you guys have always 'harvested' from our world," I said. "What—is there some sort of guideline on how much they can take in one gulp?"

"Yes," he said simply.

"I'm so confused," Mattie said.

"Think so now, just give him a minute," I muttered.

Hawthorne sighed more wearily this time. "Once upon a time, your world was ours. Or I should say it was more *obviously* ours. Before we receded behind the Veil. There was a war there a long time after that that almost ended everything. *Everything.* The truce created a frail balance between Midnight and Dawn, and if that truce were to crack...that ancient war could restart. With war comes all kinds of hunger. And when more of *your* kind went missing to appease that hunger, your authorities and rulers would come looking. Hunting. In droves. With pitchforks in hand. Normally the paths through the Veil would evade you, but if they were left open, like this one here in your town now, well...they'd find us. And that wouldn't go well for your lot either."

"Well, we don't need to go looking now, do we? You're here." Shane was reigning in exasperation with every word. "And these days people have a lot more than pitchforks going for them when it comes to defending themselves."

"You misunderstand." He looked at us with his strange eyes and took another swig, wincing before returning the flask into his coat, his hand lingering there. "War, within our realm, or with yours, knocks that precious balance gained by the truce off. And the more the war grows, the louder the echoes of that havoc knock on the door to the Slumbering Dark, and once that primeval, chittering chaos within that void wakes...that's all *any* living thing will know in the end." He looked at the ceiling and shook his head, his voice losing its silkiness to strain. "I just need to get to Cole—get the...*talisman*...to her—and this can all be righted."

"So, the fate of all of us depends on your faery land drama." Mattie eyed him with thankfully less affection. "And you just want to get your rock to Talia's mom?"

Hawthorne considered her for a long moment, tapping his fingers along his lips. "Once Cole has it, the curse upon her will lift. Once that curse is lifted, I can get word to the Dawn Lands to come fix whatever mess Orias is letting Midnight make here."

"And once this talisman fixes Cole, this demon king guy is just going to back off?" Shane asked.

Hawthorne nodded. "She was only given to him in the first place as part of the tithe the truce grants him, and he would replace her easily enough."

"Given? Oh, I thought you said she was *stolen*," I snipped.

"She was. By him," he said and for a moment the cool exterior faded, and there was a glimmer of desperation in his eyes as he gritted out, "*from me.*"

I glared openly at him. "And why? Why would an entire *king* just swoop in to steal my mother?"

"I know it's hard to believe, but there are some that find my very existence unpleasant. Some in Midnight find it unbearable. So, they find ways to sleight me. I sleight back. It's an endlessly long, boring game."

"And what did you do to get him back after he 'stole' my mother from you?" I asked, distinctly remembering Noc's voice trembling with anger as he told me how Hawthorne had driven a sword through his king, which seemed to cross the line of 'a sleight'.

"Nothing I'd want to undo. Nothing that warranted sending even one minion after me, much less to ripping the door to his kingdom off its hinges in pursuit."

"So, in other words," Shane said, rather too diplomatically for my liking, "he wouldn't break an ancient truce over a girl."

"He has no reason or right to come here after her. Which is why I suspect there's something more to it, but until Cole is mended and I can reach out to Dawn, I'll stay as lost in this as you all."

"If you so badly want her to be healed," I goaded, "then *just* let me take her the damn thing."

"The truth is Talia"—he closed his eyes and lowered his head, running his hands through his hair and looking like every word added weight to his bones—"I almost didn't make it over the Veil. Until I saw Cole yesterday, I didn't even know for certain that *she* had. It had all been a gamble. Now, I *can't* return to the Everlands as I am. But, if she is mended...so might I be. Only then can I warn Dawn of what Orias is doing here so the tear can be mended and this door closed."

"But not the rest of the doors?" Shane asked. "So, shadows and ghosts and whatever else will just keep coming, taking people, whenever they feel like it—just not *here?*

"Things will return to normal, yes," he said softly and ran his hand across his stubbled jaw before sitting down heavily on a nearby stool. "If you want to change the natural course of the entire realm, you'll need more than a day, more than *me*. But your little town can be saved. So can Cole. But apparently, only if *Talia* allows it."

His silver tongue was working; I sensed that Shane and Mattie were being swayed by his words. I tried to remember everything I'd said, if it was too much or not enough, if I didn't tie my little lie about who told me what with a neat enough ribbon. Whatever my misstep, my barely a plan was crumbling. At this point, even if I *was* given the key, no one was going to believe I'd be just fine getting it back to Mom alone. *Especially* with a giant mushroom-person currently propagating itself along Shane's backyard. And even if I convinced them otherwise, Hawthorne would follow me.

With that thought, panic began to brew, but my frustration stamped it out. "You know this is all because *you* took my mother in the first place. Why couldn't you have just left her where she *belonged*?"

"Because I love her." His voice was tremulous. When he looked at me, the colors in his eyes rotated.

Angry laughter is a disturbing sound, but there I was, making it anyway.

"Well, fortunately you don't have to believe me for it to be true." His wry smile was weary as he stretched his long legs out in front of him. *"I love her."*

My nails bit into my arms through my sweater beneath my tightly folded arms. "You must define love very differently over on your side of the Veil."

"Perhaps, but it is love nonetheless." He shook his head, looking in that moment younger, more human, through the sorrow on his face. "I gave all I had to save her, little fox."

"You gave her ruin and a magic rock," I bit out.

"It is my *heart,* you daft thing." Hawthorne breathed out, and before I could question what he meant, he was dragging his hand over his shirt, opening it to the side to reveal a jagged, sucking rip in his chest. No blood fell, held in place by some invisible barrier that revealed the gory black fist-sized hole there. His breath shuddered, his lips as gray as the rest of him. He was the living corpse I'd glimpsed earlier.

"I gave her my very heart."

28

Noc's Work

I had to admit, the heart thing was a good trick. He likely used it on Mom too—just some dramatic flair to achieve a goal—but convincing everyone else that's all it really was wasn't going to happen. Especially after the three of us spilled inside into the living room to find a heart that looked human enough, *real* enough, beating steadily in Kehente's hands.

Mattie gripped Shane's arm with a shuddering yelp. I think someone spoke, but it all became white noise until I found myself in the bathroom sitting for a while on a mat embroidered with little red birds, my back against the tub, waiting for the wave of nausea to pass.

Throwing any blood wrapped organ, especially a living one, into an argument was going to have a lot of sway. And Hawthorne's point about Maevyn had already been a strong one, especially after he pointed out to everyone what orts were. Once you introduce the word 'demon' into a conversation, people were generally not going to side with whatever was doing its bidding, and it wasn't like I could just volunteer that it was that demon and his attack birds that had saved me from some King of Midnight's grab-happy ort twice now. Or that he'd been protecting the house and Mom from being invaded by the things "meandering" in the surrounding woods. And from Hawthorne.

Unsurprisingly, once the need for shock value passed, he'd recovered—once again sun kissed and robust as he explained that as long as
we stuck together, he could get us all safely through the shifting woods
to Mom. I knew it was a gamble of my own, but it was my only chance
to be rid of him, so I agreed.

Yet again, I found myself following a faery into the trees like a fool.
Yet again, allowing him to lead me on a path that wasn't really there.
Only this time, it didn't feel *as* foolish, or at least I wasn't shouldering
the responsibility of being foolish alone. I now had what at worst was
the comfort of stupidity in numbers.

"So what is that anyway?" Mattie asked Hawthorne as he sipped
from his flask. "Some kind of potion to keep you alive?"

"Whiskey," he answered. "So, kind of."

In addition to having Cinder by her side, Mattie also insisted on
bringing at least the shotgun, which was in a sling over her shoulder,
even though Hawthorne expressed doubt that stopped just short of
concern that it would do much good. "If you can strike a creature from
the Everlands, you *might* kill it," he'd told her. "And you'd better pray
that's what happens. And that there are no others."

Shane was staying close to Kehente. She was dwarfed by his borrowed jean jacket—cuffs that didn't reach her hands flapped as she
shooed him off whenever he tried to help her step over the odd tangle
of roots. With a raise of Hawthorne's hand, the talisman—his fucking
heart—had thankfully shrunk back to a stone, which she'd buttoned
into the jacket's front pocket.

Lydia walked behind them, and I trailed alongside her. Though I
didn't feel invulnerable, knowing I was protected made me feel safe
enough to keep as far as I could from Hawthorne. It was clear that no
one exactly *trusted* him, but we all were in silent agreement that we
didn't have much choice but to follow him for now.

He'd reminded us that once the stone brought Mom around, she could tell us the truth of what had happened to her herself if we still didn't believe him. Another gamble on his part, sure, and I didn't argue. There was no way I could secretly let Mattie or Shane in on my real plan anyway, since apparently Hawthorne could walk through the damn walls.

Ahead, Kehente muttered something to Shane, or maybe to herself. It would have been easier if she'd turned out to be some Everland thing herself, but not only could she clearly hold the stone, she seemed more...*together* than Maevyn had been. Each iteration of the ort had it playing a part that came undone at the end. But Kehente, she was more childlike than crazy. Maybe it was the almost violent focus of her emotion, her stubbornness. I couldn't blame her for her angst. If she was just a little girl wrapped in wrinkles. If she had most of her life stolen in a long day.

"Is she always so...angry?" I asked Lydia.

"She is always sad," Lydia corrected. "But sadness doesn't get you anywhere, so she leans on anger."

"What will she do? Once she doesn't have to worry about that stone anymore and this is all over?"

"She was a *child*. A child wanting her own mother when she found yours. And the things she's told me...seeking fingers and black, laughing eyes..." There was a secondhand sadness in her eyes when she looked at me. "She was stolen away in parts. In pain and pieces. What was done to her means it will never be all over. You probably already knew that."

"Oh, except my mom *can* be freed from that place once Kehente gives her that rock." My sarcasm was aimed at the back of Hawthorne's head as the spice-smelling smoke of his cigarettes drifted back to us.

"You don't believe that," Lydia said matter-of-factly.

"Do you?"

"I believe that he believes it. I believe that even *you're* hopeful for it to be true. People tethered to things that hurt have to learn to get used to the pain. I understand that when pain is so entwined with hope it is *binding*." She gently placed her hand on my arm. "Shane told me that she had left you. My own daughter was always leaving me, but I think the hurt goes deeper when it's a mother that leaves. There's a wrongness to it that warps the heart."

"Yeah, well Shane didn't know the whole story." I pulled away. "I grew up thinking she'd abandoned me, but she didn't...she needed *help,* but she didn't get a chance to find it because—"

"*Kehente!*" Shane called.

I saw him start to rush from our group into the trees when Hawthorne intercepted him, blocking his way. "Well, aren't you the noble one? Like a...stoic bear. Sorry to impede your heroism, but I don't have the time to rescue two of you people."

Shane ignored him and explained, "She was right *there*, then all of a sudden I didn't hear her footsteps anymore..."

"That child..." Hawthorne rolled his eyes with a huff. "Everyone hush and everyone *stay.*"

He turned to study the trees off of the path with a tilt of his head. With all of us standing still, there was a heavy quiet I hadn't noticed until now. No birds or the buzz of insects.

Then he moved. His feet barely made a sound as he rushed past Lydia and I, stopping at the bottom of a sickly looking birch behind us. Its yellow-brown leaves were half gone, but the ground surrounding it was bare—without even grass, just cracked dry earth and...feet. Claw-like feet, with thin and curling toes that looked like roots at a glance, sat at the base of its white trunk. Hawthorne tapped a finger on his lips for a moment before raising his boot and kicking it hard in the center.

There was a soft thud as the thing that was wearing a tree's shape coiled around itself like a fist and fell with a shudder.

The serpentine body of the creature had skin that mimicked birch-bark, but those feet weren't its only pair. Like a centipede, protruding from its sides was a ladder of skinny limbs mostly ending in points. Its face reminded me of a possum's, only flatter, vaguely more human, except for a gaping mouth filled with short fangs. With horror, I realized that it wrapped around Kehente up to her shoulders. I could see her blinking eyes through a gap in its arms.

"Oh, what the fuck," Mattie half whined.

"Mishmosh," said Hawthorne

"*What?*" Shane asked as he ran to help pry Kehente from the apparently dead thing's claws.

"A sort of fae that's the result of many varied unions." Hawthorne made quick work of cracking the legs open. "At least part Lindworm in this one's ancestry, I'd wager. It was likely looking for a quick meal. Or companionship. Or a fancy combination of both."

Once the dazed woman fell free, Hawthorne snapped his fingers a few times by her head until, with a sudden start, she came back to herself, eyes going wide as they darted to the fallen creature. She tried to squirm away in a panic, but Hawthorne held her.

"Calm yourself." He firmly took her hand, pulling her close to one of its larger intact limbs that ended in a small grabby fist that had turned black. With a tap of his knuckles, the fist broke off and landed in her palm. Her free hand covered her mouth as the fist corroded and flaked away, leaving only the pouch in its place.

"You really ought to know better, little bobcat." He patted her head, his hand coming away with a gooey trail of Mishmosh spit, and turned to me. "See? She was *protected*."

"She was traumatized," Mattie said flatly, "as am I."

I looked down at my own hand that had only briefly held his heart and then to the huge lump of gray creature on the ground. So, now I knew what happened when an Everland creature touched it. I was even more convinced that getting it to Noc was the right thing to do. That door needed to be shut quickly. I didn't ever want to find out what a whole Lindworm looked like.

We hadn't resumed our trek for long when the tangled path we'd been walking converged with one of pavement. At the end of it was a house. A house that might not look amiss to anyone seeing it for the first time. A house we shouldn't have reached by foot yet, but there it was.

It still looked like a half asleep thing, with shuttered windows and peeling paint, but now there was the fun addition of countless black vines. Thick and thorned, they stretched up along the face of the house, branching out finer and vein-like as they went, reaching across the upper windows, wrapping across the roof, netting the porch within them. Like a barrier.

I knew I was looking at Noc's work.

"You know, actually," said Mattie after a moment, "this was exactly what I'd always pictured. Only, you know, with those bald cats."

Shane looked back to me, then to the house. "That's a complication."

"No," Hawthorne said, flicking his smoke to the ground as he pointed. "*That* is a symptom."

"Everyone hang back for a minute," Shane ordered, and began to step ahead, giving me a stern look when he noticed I was suddenly right beside him.

"*I'm* the one that lives here," I told him, stepping right over the authority he was trying to infuse the situation with.

I didn't know what would happen when Hawthorne tried to enter, but my whole plan hinged on the fact that Noc wouldn't allow it. Maybe the vines would simply close up and block him, or perhaps something more binding than that, but I didn't want anyone else caught up in it—an idea that grew more urgent when I noticed that in the mostly leaf-barren trees that surrounded the house, black birds the size of cats were silently gathering.

"Oh, then I'll accompany you," said Hawthorne over my shoulder. "Chivalry, and all that."

Before I could come up with a way to stall him, Kehente stormed past to the front steps. The rest of us surged in an inelegant blob after her until we were crowded on the porch—Hawthorne casually following at his own pace.

No kind of alarm sounded. No swarming of beaks and feathers. The vines that had snaked across the door didn't move. It wasn't until I pulled my house key from my bag that they receded with the sound of twisting wood. The movement made me recoil for a second. Then I turned the key in the lock. The door opened, as doors normally do, and then...nothing.

Well, nothing climactic, nothing *unusual*. I was half expecting to see Noc standing there, ready to magic Hawthorne away to some Midnight Lands prison, but it was only the entryway I was ushered into by the tide of bodies that flowed in behind me—Shane, Kehente, Lydia, Mattie, Cinder...and Hawthorne.

He stepped over the threshold without any bother, even wiping his boots on the mat before closing the door behind him.

Shit.

I gasped. "You can't—you can't just..." I began, but after taking in the confused looks around me, and his raised brow, I had to change my objection. "He's not...*invited.*"

"That's vampires." He winked and swept his eyes over the room.

"Talia," Shane said, the look on his face redirecting my worry.

I'd been very wrong about there being nothing unusual beyond the front door. The entryway was normal, but the rest of it...

Paintings and portraits were skewed along the walls by what I first thought were more vines, but these were different. Thicker and stretching out from the shuttered side of the house, branching down the wood paneling. They reminded me more of *roots*. Then the smell hit, dampness with something lightly acrid behind it. Though that might've in part because of all the mushrooms: ghost white or in shades of oranges and purples, some fanning out sponge-like from the photo frames, others umbrellaing along the furniture.

I dropped my bag, rushing to the stairs, but stopped at the scream of a tea kettle followed by its quickly dying wail. "Vivian," I whispered. Peering down the hall, I saw the kitchen light, and beyond that, the dividing door was opened to complete darkness.

Shane signaled to the others to wait there and followed me. Dread and hope did an uncomfortable tango in my chest as we approached the cheery yellow of the kitchen that was at odds with the fractured mess inside it.

The plates on the wall were pierced with roots that continued along the ceiling, porcelain shards lining the floor. The stained glass once over the sink was now in it, jagged colors glinting off the chrome. Knives scattered the counter and floor from the overturned knife rack.

In the center of the room, at the table covered with a white embroidered cloth stained with splotches of bright red, Vivian's shaking hand was pouring tea from her silver pot.

29

Her Ghost

Her hair hung loose around her shoulders, framing her twitching eyes in frazzled white-gold. A soft green cardigan hung in disarray off her shoulder, partly tangled with the straps of her apron. She smiled around the cigarette in her mouth when she saw me, an uneven look in her eyes.

"Talia, dear"—she set the pot down mid-pour, tapping ashes on the tiles below—"would you like sugar? Officer Walker, let me bring you a cup."

Shane and I exchanged glances as she went to the counter where several mismatched, already-filled cups sat, some half broken, some no more than handles drowning in saucers full of the dark amber liquid.

"Are you hurt, Vivian?" he asked gently when she handed him one of the more intact cups, which he immediately set back on the counter while holding up his hand in what felt like a warning.

She didn't answer, but went to refill the kettle, the water tinkling on the stained-glass shards in the sink as it overflowed. When she turned, I saw what Shane must have caught first; jutting from the top of the reddening pocket of her apron was a handle of carved wooden leaves and, piercing through the bottom, a silver blade.

"Vivian." He tried again, this time more assertively. "Is someone hurt?"

Dread took the lead, and I stepped around him. "Vivian, where's Mom?"

Her shoulders slumped. "I locked it away. In Nicolette's room. It was never her. I *knew* it wasn't her, but I thought...I thought—"

"The key, Vivian." I cut her off, trying to not let myself think about what Hawthorne being able to enter the house meant, or what could have made Vivian so...addled. Maybe something had happened to Noc. And if not—well, I wasn't going to let myself get on that train of thought if I didn't need to, and the simplest way to *know* if I needed to was to get to Mom, or at least, get to the bedroom mirror and hope that calling Noc worked there. "Give me the key to her room."

"It's not *her*." She turned, her hand covering her mouth after every sentence she rattled out. "I should have tried to make you see that, but I let myself think...maybe it could be. Somehow. Maybe I'd been wrong. Oh, I'd been drinking then and maybe...maybe I was *wrong*, but I wasn't. Part of me knew all along I wasn't crazy, but...I *wanted* to be. I wanted to be crazy so she could still be alive."

"Oh yeah, you're sane as a hatter," I said, sniffing a tea cup for whiskey.

"Ms. Adair"—Shane slid into his authoritative tone—"I need to make sure your daughter is okay, and it'd be a whole lot easier to do that if you'd give us the key to her room."

"My daughter is *not* 'okay'!" She raised her voice, almost disgusted, as though we were willfully not understanding what she was saying. "My daughter is *dead*."

"Vivian—" He sounded like he was going to scold her, but stopped to listen to the thumping of what could have been footsteps overhead until the sound morphed into a rumble that seemed to come from the walls around us.

While I knew it wasn't possible for her to have hurt mom, she must've hurt something. My skin crawled when I noticed the door to the garden was unbolted. My patience eroded. "We don't have time for this. Vivian? I need to get to Mom. Now. Before something else does. Give me the key or...or Shane is going to break down her door."

The doors were heavy enough that his shoulder would break before the door would, the look he gave me said he knew that too. "So, you're saying that Cole is dead, but you still locked her in her room—that where we are here, Vivian?"

"I don't *know*." She looked to him and back to me, trembling. "I never *knew*. She *was* dead...then the next day she was...she was gone."

I went to turn away, deciding that I'd have better luck just *knocking* on the damn door on the chance that she would scamper out from under her bed to open it for me, but I stopped. A needle in her nonsense had found its way through and pinned me before it fully registered.

"Vivian." My exasperation faltered, making room for something worse. "Why do you think Mom is dead?"

Her expression was blank as she stared through me. "We argued. That night." Something cold came with the familiarity of those words and the way her sapphire eyes were starting to glisten, the tremble of her voice. "We argued. And then I left. There's a bartender over in Locksville—you know Locksville? Makes a good negroni. Or did back then."

She reached into her pocket, the one that wasn't red, and pulled out her cigarette case, even though a cigarette was still burning on the side of a saucer. "When I came home, I had another drink...maybe two. I may have forgotten she was even there, but then I saw her in the garden. I think she...she...*accused* me of stealing from her. She was so angry. She was yelling these things, I don't know...I don't know when...or why, but the garden shears were in my hand..."

The truth just sounded different, and her words resonated with it. My mouth dried and my throat tightened. The more I tried to swallow, the harder it became. My mouth fell open to let more air in, which dried my mouth, which tightened my throat...

"I remember the blood. I can still see her laying still on the wood-pile. But even though I woke up the next day with blood on my hands...she was gone. *Gone.*" She made an odd little smile. "I looked. I waited. Then everyone looked. I still waited. Without a trace of her, I convinced myself it hadn't happened. But she was still gone. That no one found her meant...it *must* not have happened. But I never *knew.* Sometimes, I'd think I'd see her out there. Beyond the garden. In the woods. Always wearing that grass-green dress. Always the same."

The warmth rushed out of my cheeks, drained from my chest.

"I started to think she might come back. It'd be what I deserved—if whatever she was came back to punish me. If not for what I did, then for who I'd been."

Not her but her ghost.

"I've been afraid of my own mind ever since. So, I didn't drink. I made the garden grow—grow over the memory of what may have happened there. But all the while, I waited. When you said you found her, I let myself think it might be true. Even if that would mean that I *had* imagined that night—that I'd gone mad and imagined murdering my own daughter. That would be better, but...it was a lie. Some trick I tried to let be true, but it wasn't. It wasn't her. It wasn't..."

No. Whatever she killed that night *couldn't* have been Mom...but it might have been something pretending to be her. Maybe that blood on her apron now came from that same thing. An ort. The same thing she'd locked upstairs. The thing that had been pretending to be Mom all along.

"Alright, listen to me." Shane deftly plucked the knife from her pocket and lowered it behind him with one hand while raising the other level with his head to draw her attention to it and away from his disarming her. "There was *no* body. There was *no* blood. They had dogs that picked up no scent, no place to dig. You did *not* kill her, Vivian. Not that night, but if she's hurt now then *let me help her.*"

"She was there." Vivian pointed to the door. "Today. There were monsters in the garden, and she was there too."

My eyes were on the knife, the knife that what I'd believed was my mother had cut me with. The blade was fine and silver, red pressed into where it met the fair wooden leaves. Rumbling came again like the groaning of a storm suppressed by the walls.

"Now that's more like," said Hawthorne casually. He strolled through the kitchen as though he did so every day, nodding to the knife. "Familiar too. Holly and silver. That will do a good lick of damage. It's why I gifted it long ago, though not to *her.* "

Under his gaze, Vivian flinched and moved her hands down to the sink, then to the cupboard below, hauling the rest of her along until she was on the floor, crawling behind the table, eyeing Hawthorne as she climbed back into the chair and gripped her cup like it was a kind of shield.

"So, the lady of the house herself," he observed, grimacing. "A bit touched, isn't she?"

"That trick you pulled earlier in my garage"—Shane turned, keeping the knife down at his side—"could you do it again to get into a locked room?"

"This is a changing place. What's opening the doors between our worlds is also keeping the ones upstairs here closed, and it'll take more than *a key* to open them." He pressed his lips together, turning to me. "Perhaps you should try."

"I..." I jumped as Cinder's tail brushed by me, her nails clacking across the floor, whining toward the back door. "Why me?"

"Why. You." He said mockingly.

"Talia dear," Vivian said, "offer your handsome man-friend a cup, don't be rude."

"Yes, Talia, wouldn't want to be *rude*." Hawthorne grinned and leaned against the sink. "After you didn't even invite me in."

"Hawthorne..." I stared at him, the impulse to hurl a cup at his head only a dim glimmer in my mind. "Could an ort be used to fool a faery? Could it fool *you*?"

"An ort like the one I 'ditched' you to go after earlier? I certainly would have believed she was someone dear to me." His grin faded. "So yes. Especially if the ort had been carved to fool one *specifically*. Demons delight in such cruelties."

"But you said an ort can be carved from a still-living person?" I asked, trying to sound casual despite my dry, heavy tongue. "It wouldn't mean the person they were impersonating was dead...right?"

"Oh yes. Those are the ones still aware of themselves enough to pray for a truer death. They're like marionettes who forget and remember over and over again the fact that they have strings."

"How...?" My lungs felt like they were deflating. "How could you tell that she was an ort?"

"Well, mostly because women from this side don't tend to hold up that well over the centuries."

"Hey, so whatever you all are doing here, can you do it quicker?" Mattie leaned her head in the doorway anxiously. "I don't know what she's saying, but Kehente is starting to get...squirrely."

Vivian appraised Mattie's shaved hair and piercings. "Oh, offer your little she-biker friend a cup too I suppose. It's wonderful to have friends. I always told Nicolette that she needed to make friends, try to fit in more. Instead, she found *Richard.* You'll be better, Talia. Won't you? You'll make friends with the right kind of people."

Mattie blinked rapidly at Vivian, clicking her tongue as she mounted a response, but when she saw the tablecloth, the deranged tea party, she stepped back.

The rumbling now came from Cinder, eyeing the door intently. She barked twice as the breeze kicked up, lifting the curtain over the broken window. The men both moved to peer outside.

"Why...?" was all Shane managed.

"Well. That's not good." Mattie's voice was concerningly resigned.

30

Stitches

I wanted to snatch the heart from Kehente, run upstairs, press it into Mom's hand to see if she...*shriveled.* Instead, I went to where Mattie stood in the dining room, looking out of the hatched windows into the garden. There the sky was sinking into a deep plum, reaching into a crimson that stretched into hazy orange and yellow. I'd paid enough attention in my time here to know that was not the direction where the sun set, and I'd seen enough sunsets to know this one looked wrong, but not as wrong as the three figures that were approaching from the now completely foreign tree line beyond the garden.

The first one looked like a child that had been overstuffed with a monster. Her limbs were stretched thin and ended in blackened finger bones so long they each had had a couple of extra knuckles—guaranteeing that she would look ridiculous trying to hold a teacup, but since Vivian had gone full tilt into madness, she may well still offer her one if she made it inside.

Her dress clung to the bones of her torso, thick black cords stitched bloodlessly through fractured pale skin, but at least her face was familiar enough. It seemed Maevyn had been reshaped once again.

The second figure was a gamine woman with a wild tumble of dark hair and a green gown that was at least two centuries late. I didn't think she resembled Mom too closely, but the coloring was there. The beauty. Only the Green Lady had a more raised chin, an almost regal bearing. They certainly had a different stride. The Lady moved like static, etching in and out of sight in jaunty steps that weren't nearly as unnerving as the blood trails rising red from the hollow of her chest and rising in smoke-like tendrils around her grinning face.

She was probably just as terrifying when she was hanging from a tree and chasing boys down in the woods, but Wes Samuel seemed to have finally gotten over it. He was disheveled as ever but looked strangely at ease between his companions.

The garden at least looked *great*. Quick blooming with flowers that had never grown there, or anywhere, before. And those birds, *Noc's* birds, still merely decorated the stone fence. They did not seem interested in Maevyn and company in the least.

I hoped Hawthorne was right about Mom's door opening for me. I knew Noc was the one holding it closed, supposedly keeping her safe. I had to hope that, but before I could see if I was right, Mattie yanked me toward her.

"What the hell is happening?" she whispered, pointing to the kitchen.

"There was blood...and this...holly knife..." I sputtered, suddenly too overwhelmed to string together a linear version of events. "Apparently Vivian might have...kinda...killed one of them."

"She killed—?" She shook her head, deciding on which question was the most urgent and going with, "*Where* is your mom?"

And I suddenly wanted to cry. I blinked away the burning in my eyes. "Could you just...just wait with everyone while I find out?"

"Uh-uh. No way I'm going into the *knife room* with someone who may or may not have just *murdered something* with one of them."

"C'mon, you have that thing," I sniffed, pointing to the shotgun.

"Yeah. I don't actually want to *shoot your grandmother*, Talia," she hissed.

"Wouldn't that fellow be one of your townsfolk?" I heard Hawthorne say, and I peered around the doorway to see him glaring at the scene outside over Shane's shoulder. "And that—would *that* be your 'stretched out ragdoll'?"

"Yeah," Shane answered grimly. "Yeah, on both counts."

"But my, that ort does seem *lively.*" He didn't turn, but I could feel his eyes cut into me from the side. "Only, as I said, to be revived it would need to return to its maker. With all of those Stitches about, it not only shouldn't have been able to cross through the Veil and back...it shouldn't be able to be here at all. "

Shane looked at him. "Stitches?"

"Those birds. Their riders," he said, stepping closer to the window, "they stay close to openings between the realms, and when a shadow creature manages to slip out, they...*stitch* them back in. But also, they're spies for the Queen of Dawn. They likely honed in on my heart like a beacon, but I've managed to keep them from finding *me.*"

"They're what saved me from Maevyn..." I said, moving between he and Shane, hoping they were talking about some *different* otherworldly birds, but no.

He turned, looking me up and down with fresh scrutiny. "It's not their nature to *rescue* hapless humans. Likely they saw that ort with you and tried to stitch it back where it belonged."

I blinked. Noc said they were doing *his* bidding...or had he only implied it? Just went with a useful narrative to something that was already there doing their jobs anyway, knowing I wouldn't know the difference?

"Then why are they just sitting there?" Mattie asked from behind us. "With, you know, all of the 'slipping out' going on right in front of them right now?"

"The same reason that the ort is not acting—I would wager." He tapped his ringed finger on his bottom lip and seemed to speak more to himself than to us. "If they're here like this...then Dawn already knows...which must mean..." He went rigid. "Oh. You pretty little fool."

I didn't even see him move, but suddenly he was backing me against the kitchen wall, his dual eyes glaring down at me. "Enough of this game. Tell me. Who lies in wait for me? What bargain did you strike?"

Panic locked my tongue. What bargain *did* I strike? Cinder began to bark, but with a look from Hawthorn, she retreated into whining concern. I caught Mattie slip her gun case down her shoulder and subtly reach inside it.

Vivian only shrugged from her chair. Sipping her tea and muttering in an I-told-you-so tone, "Monsters in the garden."

"You'll want to step away from her now." Shane's voice was a calm threat, as was Hawthorne's smile as he turned to face him.

"We're all *allies* here, Shane Walker, remember? We *all* want to close the tear in the Veil. We *all* want to save Cole, but this treacherous child has her own plan for that, don't you?"

His hand was on the wall, blocking me between his arm and the counter. Before I crumbled into anxiety, anger rode in with its shield of bravado. "*Back. Off.*" I told him as forcefully as I could with my voice barely making it above a whisper.

"*Answer. Me.*" His words fell like silk.

As soon as I realized I was staring into those gold-rimmed irises, I shoved his chest, remembering the hole there and hoping it would hurt. It did. He hissed and staggered back.

"If I have to ask you again to back away from her, I won't be as polite." Shane didn't move, but his look was calculating. I saw his fingers tighten around the holly knife.

"Oh, but I'm not harming her. Nothing has *harmed* her...so long as she was doing what she was told—isn't that right?"

I bit my tongue.

"I'll bet." He stepped around the table. "Some opportunistic demon got you to strike a bargain, to uncurse Cole, doubtlessly—which I offered to do *for free,* by the way—in return for you giving it my heart. But *all* demons are sworn to the Midnight King. So, to make a bargain with a demon is to make a bargain with the Midnight King—*the one who cursed her in the first place.*"

"I miss the part where you mentioned why you're so convinced she's some demon's accomplice?" Shane asked.

"Orts aren't clever and they are *mad*. The longer they are, they go even *more* mad. They aren't made for espionage, just quick tricks and easy grabs." He answered without looking away from me. "So, I had to wonder why *an ort* would tell you that this 'key' could close up this tear and send all us bogies away. Why *an ort* would tell you that it must be kept from Cole. Why *an ort* would tell you to...what was the plan? To deliver it to Orias himself?"

Safe to assume he'd heard *everything* in Shane's garage then. I didn't trust myself to lie, so I only shook my head.

"So, you think these Dawn folk, those orts, some demon, and... *Wes Samuel*...? Are all working together. With Talia." Shane moved a step closer.

Hawthorne pointed to the window. "*That* is the show of unnatural alliance between two lands that have come together here for the same purpose. Some demon's manipulation of Talia was just a piece of that plan." At my silence, he chuckled mirthlessly. "The Veil is open because it is being *held* open. Dawn hasn't returned shadow creatures to the Midnight Lands from this town because this town is being woven *into* the Midnight Lands in return, I'd wager, for ME."

No. Noc was there to protect Mom. But...hadn't he sent me into the woods to find the thing that could help him capture *Hawthorne*? Hadn't he made sure I knew that *Hawthorne* was the criminal, the villain of my mother's story, and the beast that had attacked his beloved king on whose orders he had come at all? And yet, Hawthorne could walk right into the house he told me was specifically protected against him doing so?

Noc had lied. Of course. He was *a demon*, after all. One on a mission. Not to protect but to *pursue*. That's why Hawthorne was allowed to enter the house—this was a trap, and my mother had been the lure. Or what I'd been made to believe was my mother.

Nothing, of anyone, leaves the Midnight Lands

My heart collapsed in its cage of bones.

31

A Wise Ploy

The life, the *escape*, I'd let myself hope to have for Mom and I danced away from me in cruel flashes. I hadn't realized how much I really had let myself believe in it until I felt it being ripped away now.

All of this had been Noc's elaborate deceit, and I'd just been a pawn in one of those faery games Hawthorne had warned me about. Mom had never really returned from the place Hawthorne had taken her. Was she still trapped in the Midnight Lands, or had she drowned or withered down to nothing in her attempt to flee them? Either way, just like that, she was lost once more. And even if she were dead, she'd been made *useful* again.

Orts can be anyone they once were.

Noc had even told me *to my face* not to trust what I saw, what anyone seemed or said, almost mocking me with the truth. He'd wanted me to find Hawthorne's heart but must've known giving it to Mom would have given away what she really was, so he convinced me to keep it from her.

At least Vivian hadn't really killed her daughter thirteen years ago, but whatever she'd locked, dead or dying perhaps, in her bedroom was *a trick*. And not even a very convincing one in hindsight, one that never even tried to act like a real person, and I was so caught up in trying to save her, it never occurred to me that it was because she wasn't one.

"And what makes *you* worth all this?" Shane's eyes narrowed on Hawthorne.

"Well, I am a criminal. No. Worse." He ran his ringed fingers through his hair and closed his eyes for a moment before grinning. "A *renegade*. I escaped the Dawn Queen to come here. I cut out my Dawn heart so that I would never have to return. But the Queen...is *fiercely* possessive. More than even I knew, for her to pair with Orias. It may not be too late for me to stop this, but first Cole needs to be saved."

"Talia," Mattie asked, her hand never straying far from her bag of violence. *"Are* you working for some demon?"

"I'm not working for *anyone.*" There was still a threadbare chance that was true enough, so I confessed nothing,

"So what do we—?" Shane began, before being cut off by a chittering echo.

"Son of Dawn and Earth." Maevyn's voice was a chorus of whispers anchored in the sing-song tone the last iteration I'd dealt with had favored. "Come see. *Come see* your lady love, her arms grown cold from lacking, her heart grown colder still. Colder even than yours."

Cinder growled and Mattie began tugging her from the room.

Hawthorne reluctantly went to the window where he laid his hands on either side of the sink and dropped his chin to his chest. Shane took this chance to move back to me, and without looking, I slid my hand down his fingers and around the holly knife's handle until he released it to me.

"Who is the Green Lady—that woman—really?" Shane asked.

Hawthorne drummed his fingers. "A cruelty. A remnant." He turned, his eyes were an equal measure of rage and sadness. "A *puppet.*"

"Mercy me, mercy me," crooned Maevyn in a voice that fluctuated between the little girl's and the young man's as she lifted herself to the windowsill with unnaturally long arms and perched there with two blackened fingers resting on the side of her cheek. "Did I seek you out before, Heir of Shadows? Was that my doom once? As it was for all of your sweeting lovers? Or am I here now for the first time? I can never tell where I am in the circle of things."

"Oh, so am *I* who you seek now?" asked Hawthorne, looking my way.

"We are all *your* creatures, my Gloaming Lord, after a fashion. And there is none I seek now that everyone is in their place, even you little dove." She smiled at me. I should have expected that, like everything else about her, her teeth were also too long, too thin. Too many. "I only await the calling of my name."

"Don't we all?" Any trace of what had been in Hawthorne's eyes moments ago was gone. "If only to learn who calls it."

I heard the quiet clicking a second after Shane did, and he was already slamming the opening garden door closed, holding the knob as it turned and bolting the lock just in time. I didn't even want to know what was trying to come in.

Hawthorne turned toward the sound, and I would've taken that as my chance to back out of the room, but Kehente appeared in the hallway behind me. She got a look at Maevyn and froze in what would make sense to be terror, but looked more like fury.

"Ah, Handmaiden." Maevyn's finger bones clacked as they pointed at her over the sink. "My lady's decoy—wasn't *that* the wise ploy?"

"*Monsters in the garden!*" Vivian scream-sang into her teacup.

Kehente turned to Vivian, then back to the horror at the window, and finally to me. She whispered urgently, her dark, fierce eyes not leaving mine as she fumbled into the jacket pocket. When she looked down and saw the silver blade of the knife I held, she paused, then grabbed my other arm and shoved the pouch in my palm with a nod. Before I could question her, she was already shoving me out of the kitchen ahead of her.

I didn't understand why she was finally surrendering it, but when I felt its weight not only in my hand but in my whole *being,* that tugging down of any contentment, I wondered how she could bear to have held it for as long as she had.

The door at the end of the hallway still yawned into darkness, so I didn't protest as she pushed me down the other way, back into the parlor where Lydia was patiently sitting on the couch, twirling a mushroom in her fingers.

"Finally had enough of it?" She glanced at what I now carried, and the old child answered by pointing impatiently at the stairs.

"She tried to go up there, but she said the whispers told her not to. I don't hear them, but I think they're right. Whatever happens with your mother, it should be *you* that closes that door. Do I want to know what's going on in there?"

I looked back toward the kitchen, anxious that Hawthorne would be coming to stop me at any moment. "Definitely not," I said, shoving the holly knife as far down the side of my boot as it could go. I put the pouch in my sweater pocket.

"I'm sure I'll find out anyway." Lydia frowned at the bloom of moss spreading on the rug. "But she needs you to go. Now."

I wasn't sure if she meant Kehente or Mom. I looked up the stairway as the house groaned. I'd experienced firsthand that what Noc and Hawthorne both said about bargains being law was true enough, which is why I'd kept my mouth shut.

The addendum I'd pinned at the end of my promise with Noc was the only way our bargain bound both ways, and that meant even if he'd been lying about everything else, he'd still be bound to his part. I'd said I wouldn't speak of him as long as he protected this house and *everyone* in it. Since now here we all were, it was apparently the only time I'd get any real use out of his "protection".

I just had to hope that it was enough.

32

Were I Not a Demon

The landing was hushed. Even my footfalls seemed to be immediately swallowed up as I stepped into the hallway. On my left, closest to Vivian's room, the second dividing door was opened inward. Black veins stretched along the ceiling from the complete darkness beyond it. There, the silence was most unnerving. I felt if I reached my hand into all that dark to swing the door closed, it wouldn't be a hallway, but something thick and cold. Something that pulled back.

Not that I had any desire to put any part of me close enough to do that. The other doors were closed, and from behind each of them, even the closet, came sounds that shouldn't be there. Thumping, scraping, and...music. So strange, so distant that you would think it was coming from outside, but I knew better. I immediately stopped trying to listen when the tune began to become familiar.

The only silent door was Mom's. I made my way to it and didn't hesitate before turning the handle. I wasn't surprised that it was unlocked. Unlocked for me anyway. The room seemed to have escaped Noc's renovations, and there was no one in it. I turned the lock behind me and pulled the sheet from the dresser mirror. My own reflection was startling; my hair still full of bits of leaves, a couple of tiny scrapes coloring my cheeks and forehead, and a wild determination in my eyes I wasn't familiar with.

I moved my head from side to side to try and get a better view of all the reflected angles of the room, but it appeared I was alone. "Come on..." I whispered to the glass. "Where are you?"

"*I am here.*" Noc's voice came low and from nothing.

"What, are you shy now?" I stepped back and looked around the still-empty room. "You've been busy—*love* what you've done with the place, by the way." He didn't respond, but I felt a stirring in the air and caught a flickering of shadows from the corner of my eye. I knew I should be careful, but I was burnt out on playing this game.

"I appreciate all of the attention to detail that went into carving the ort sent to play my mother. Coloring her like a ghost? How fitting."

"*A ghost?*" His voice swirled around me. "*No. A dream come true? Perhaps. But I've told you, she was never yours, much as you wanted her to be. So much that you would have followed that dream into the fire. It's only when realizing the dream was true, that you find you no longer recognized it. Yet it has been her, with you, protected by me. Just as I promised.*"

"Except"—I searched the space around my reflection—"you're lying. It was *you* that sent Maevyn to get me. *Twice.* But even if you could eventually twist this house to your liking, you couldn't steal me away as long as I was inside of it, could you? You couldn't break the bargain made."

"*Lovely as you are...why would I wish to steal you away?*"

"For *bait*. It was Hawthorne you were really after all this time, wasn't it? My mother, that *ort* you put here in her place, was meant to fool him into coming for her. But maybe you figured if you had me dragged into Midnight, he'd have to follow, since he needed me to be the one to collect his heart for her. Or maybe it would just be easier to get me to do what you wanted if I were stolen to where you could…"

I stopped myself from thinking what Noc would do to me if he were able.

"*Carve you?*" he whispered harshly, filling in those ideas for me. "*Shape you. Bend you to my every desire. Oh, yes. I could make you a pliant thing to do my bidding here. Or. I could make something new from you and send that instead while you festered in my bed…*" The hunger building in his disembodied voice made me shiver. "*While I can see the fun in that, what would be the point, when my errand was to protect Cole here?*"

"Because it wasn't. Your 'errand' from your Creepy…Night King—"

"*Grim King of Nightmares and Warden of The Chittering Dark,*" he corrected.

"*Fine.* Him. The guy who's been allowing the Midnight Lands to take over Elmwood? He sent you after Hawthorne. *You* sent me after some magic 'key' as a pretense to get me on Maevyn's hunting grounds. You used me."

"*Well. That much*"—there was a spectral sigh—"*at least is correct. I am using you, but not as you think. I say yet again, I am protecting you.*"

"It doesn't count if you're protecting me from *you*!" I seethed. "You've wrapped your world around this place, this house is half sunk into you, you're in *the walls*. Remember how you told me none of your kind could enter? Well, Hawthorne is *here*."

"*He is not my kind.*" His words sliced through the air.

"Whatever he *is*, I think the only reason you haven't snapped the trap shut on him is because you can't. Especially not without this." I raised the pouch in my fist. "As far as I can tell, you're the only one of 'your' kind who actually *wants* this thing."

Then I thought I heard the quietest chuckle. *"Yes, since you decided to bring him so dangerously close, despite my warnings. Well. That and that woman's utter lunacy downstairs. I've had to hide Cole away. But, you're right. I do want that repugnant thing you hold. I want to render him powerless. To bind him. To return him to where he belongs. Because then your mother will be safe. Safe as she ever was."*

"Stop." I pressed the pouch into my dress pocket. "I'm not playing this game anymore. If she's truly alive and well, show her to me."

"A clever demand. Yet, I believe you will give her the very thing I've warned you not to. Tell me, do you think this little hovel of a town will thank you for your cleverness, when they're being mated off to shadow kin? When their nightmares become flesh. When their children begin changing. While you can still speak, will you tell your new friends here that you could have helped close the door and stopped it from happening, but you decided, in your cleverness, to rob them of their chance at freedom all because you let yourself be tricked by the dangerous creature you were directly warned would doom you all?"

I knew, I *knew* he was lying. Well, I *mostly* knew. But I couldn't afford any doubt. If I could just give Mom this damn faery heart that was making my own feel even heavier than it already was, I'd have my answer, but of course, he knew that too.

"Just prove *anything* you've said is true by showing me my mother"—a pounding sound reverberated in the air—"safe and well."

"And round and round we go. For her to remain safe, she must stay hidden. Whether you believe me matters not, keeping her safe is my duty. And what you hold is poison. He is poison. We don't have much time. I am afraid there's no way around it now," he said impatiently. *"Talia, you must summon me."*

"Look"—laughter slipped over the start of my words—"I may be crazy but I'm *not crazy* enough to ever *summon you.*"

There was a pause, then he asked, slightly annoyed, *"Why do you do that? Why do you play yourself off as mad? Because you believe others see you as different than themselves, or because you see others as different than you?*

A memory surged forward, my face in a different mirror, blood on porcelain. *In a few years...*

*"I'll tell you a secret, even the sanest and most clever of you secretly think they are broken in some way. Some are better at keeping it hidden, but all of your ilk feels that crack that someone else made in them. I speak from a palace of knowledge on this. That is just where my kind thrives, in those cracks in the light of humanity. You would all be so much less fun without them, you know. So, consider that what you think of as your being 'crazy' is only your being human, so would you **stop** disparaging yourself in that way? I find it tiresome,"*

For a second there, his words disarmed me. They were almost some version of kind.

"All the parts have been played well enough—you have done well enough. If you would only summon me here, this will all be over." Even disembodied, the cool midnight of his voice was rich enough to almost feel as it wove its way into me. *"One small incantation and all of this will be gone from your life. If that is what you wish."*

"In other words, once I've given you what you've wanted since the start, that's when you'll return my mother to me, right?"

"If that is what she wishes. By your own tale, all I want is Hawthorne. Summon me then. Give to me what he foolishly gave to her so that I can take him away. Unless, you wish him to stay with you."

"Of course I don't—" The pounding noise came again, but more muted. "Look *no one* is summoning *anyone*. I want to see her, or you don't get his heart."

"*Oh, that bloody heart.*" He sneered. "*If you only knew how many had lost themselves in pursuit of it. And now, he's able to use only the very idea of the vile thing, even in all its naked gore, as leverage. You see only what he wants you to see.*"

"And *you* say only what you want me to hear. I could argue that using someone's mother to manipulate them is just as *vile* as anything he's done. Maybe it's not even really his heart—he does have some...*deranged* aversion to it if it is. But I'll bet he'd take it back though, even from me, to get rid of *you*."

In my ear came a sudden, bestial growl. I jerked my head away from it, but my body was held in place by two hands on my shoulders. Noc's eyes were on mine in the mirror, but he was more than just a reflection now. His head bent down to the level of mine, his slightly sharp teeth bared near my throat in the mimicry of a smile.

"You know," he said smoothly, keeping his eyes fixed on mine in our reflection, "it is said when bargaining with the Fae, you must make sure it binds evenly both ways. You were to keep me secret. You have. I was to tell you how to close the path. I did—and if you *give me his heart*...I can. And so that bargain dissolved."

"But..." I swallowed hard to keep the desperation from my words. "I've still kept my end, so you still have to protect me and everyone in this house..."

He slowly shook his head. "Do you know what is said about bargaining with a demon?"

I couldn't speak. The slow sucker punch of where he was going with this was pressing the air from my lungs.

"*Not to.*"

With that, he raised his finger and a thunderous crash boomed so loud I felt it in my teeth, bringing with it a blinding flash of blue light. I shrieked, jumping back against him, my heartbeat a stumbling gallop. Spots of light danced in my eyes, but there in the mirror, seated on the edge of the bed, her face pale and calm, was my mother.

Noc's hands pulled away as I took a step toward the mirror, blinking down at the rug crunching under my boots, at the debris of silver shards of mirror glass. My hand went to my face to check for fresh cuts from what had to be an explosion. Finding none, I carefully turned, looking behind me at the empty bed, and then back to the mirror frame that now held...well, not a reflection anymore, but a sort of window.

Through it, the bedroom was recreated, only there, pale flowers bloomed across the wall, the spines of the books were lined with moss, and the figurines on the shelves...were dancing. A miniature ball set to the thin strands of sound coming from the music box was in full swing.

"What is this?"

"What you asked for. You wished to see her. She is there."

I moved closer and waved my hand in front of the scene. If she saw me, she didn't show it. There was a nest of what looked to be twigs in her lap and with a lobotomized look of serenity she rhythmically snapped them in her fingers.

"That's...not what I meant."

Snap.

"You wish to speak to her?" He turned, leaning against the dresser and gesturing to the mirror/window behind him. "Step through. I'll not stop you."

"But this doesn't prove anything. Plus, she seems...worse?"

Snap.

"Oh, but she is better off than the last one Hawthorne claimed as his. With revealing his heart, no doubt there was a story: a tale of his great *love* for Cole." He shook his head, smirking. "He would not have told you of Joanna. If he did, he would only tell you how he loved *her* with all of that vile heart of his as well. He would have left out that in the end, that *love* damned the poor girl to spend her days pursuing him, always just too far away to touch. Cursed to never reach him. *She* went mad, of course. Until that elder Adair woman freed her with the stab of her blade."

Snap.

"And created the Green Lady." I looked to the window, hoping the wraith of a woman was still grinning from the garden and not the parlor. "She's haunted the woods for thirteen years, but as something more dangerous than a ghost. She did something to that man out there that cost him a chunk of his sanity. If orts are made with a purpose, what's hers?"

"Isn't it clear in your cleverness?" he mused.

"*You* made her," I realized. "'Carved' her. Why?"

"That man."

"Wes Samuel?"

"He hasn't our limitations. And was already cracked enough to let in the dark."

Snap.

"I don't understand."

"No." He ran his tongue along his lip and stepped toward me, while I stepped back. "But that was by my design. You said you'd keep me a secret as long as I protected this house and everyone in it—that *was* clever. Or would have been. Were I not a demon."

I stepped back again, he moved forward again. Another game. "Yet, I *did* watch over this house. I *did* protect Cole. And you. But not because of any dissolved *bargain*. Lies are also a form of protection, dear Talia. You would not have gone after the key and left her here if you didn't think you and she were safe. There *were* truly things stalking you in the wood that you didn't realize, things far worse than a few goblins. I kept them from you."

Snap, snap, snap.

Mom began to hum and Noc closed his eyes, rolling his neck. "Demons have been made out to be so purely evil by the mythos your people came up with to explain away mine over the last thousand years. Give or take. Things like faeries, unfairly, are not seen as even half as bad, when we're really all branches of the same mercurial tree, but you never hear about the Kindly *demons* do you?"

"Are—?" I retreated another step, the back of my legs hitting the bed. "Are you going to tell me that's what you are?"

He tilted his head. "There is no morality in our motives when it comes to humankind. No malice. No love. Only what we desire Often, what is necessary. *She* is necessary. *You* were desired. So I gave you my word that I would protect you—so long as you did *what I asked.*"

Fuck. I half fell, half sat on the mattress. *Fuckityfuckfuck.*

A wicked smile spread on his face as he placed his hand beside me and leaned over, forcing me back on my elbow to keep as much space between us as possible. I hadn't noticed the flecks of silver in his eyes before, but they were all I could see now. They matched what spiraled through the onyx of his horns, around those strange runish symbols carved into them, which were as black as the hair that fell over the pointed tops of his ears, as he looked down at me. Distantly there was that hammering sound, but it was drowned out by the not-unpleasant sensation of currents tugging at my skin, like little licks of electricity, and the smell of smoke and amber dancing in a storm.

"Talia Adair," he said with a tilt of his chin, a pinpoint glow of red appearing in the milky, blue-haloed pupil. "I want *you*. To summon *me*. This is what I ask. This is what I desire."

Fear drowned out any sense and my tongue moved faster than my brain. "No way in hell." I was impressed I got it out, honestly, considering I didn't think I'd been breathing for some time. I continued not breathing as Noc's smile faded, but then, he...*laughed*.

It was so sudden that I think it even caught him by surprise. It was not a sound I would have imagined him making: guttural, but genuine laughter not rooted in some lofty retort.

He further surprised me by sitting himself on the bed next to me, one arm on his lap and the other on his knee, as he continued to chuckle over the s*nap, snap, snapping* from the mirror window.

And then from his fingers: *snap*.

With that snap, the bedroom door swung open, but not here.

On the other side of the mirror, the other room, Mattie wandered in looking bewildered until Mom turned to her.

Snap.

33

Nothing of Anyone

"Oh...kay." Mattie looked around the room with her hand over her mouth, tilting her head at the woman on the bed whose fingers stopped midway between halving a black twig. The woman's eyes focused, turning hard and cold. I realized then with a mix of relief and horror, that this was *not* my mother.

"Don't—" I shot forward to warn Mattie away, but Noc's hand clamped down on my leg.

"You're Talia's mom, aren't you?" Mattie asked, then after looking over her shoulder, stepped back out of view. Relief at the possibility that she'd recognized the danger was gone as fast as it'd come when I heard the door click shut and saw her walk closer to what must still have been a mirror on her side. Her eyeliner was a mess.

"*Hell* is but an underberg of the Midnight Lands." Noc didn't face me, but the pressure of his palm was enough to keep me pinned, his fingers resting on my inner thigh. "But for you, it means something. The truth of us—of those across the Veil—was jumbled up over time. Lost in translation between the realms as we shaped your early civilization, but no part of Hell has ever been told as kind. Yet, it isn't even a real *place* for you. More a state of being. A misery of your own construct."

"What are you doing?" I hissed, frantically pushing at his forearm. "Let. Go."

When I tried to stand again, something about the room *shifted.* Every shadow reached outward for an instant before receding just as quickly. I didn't have time to question if I'd only imagined it—Noc grabbed both my wrists in one hand.

His sudden touch on the bare skin of my arms is cool. Before I can try to squirm away, he's slamming my hands over my head. There's no time to panic before his free hand is on my hip, locking me in place as he slides his body over mine.

"You wanted to understand"—his voice is rough, his breath hot on my throat—"my motives." The scent of roses and fire emanates from him, but there's something else hidden beneath it, something that is turning my stomach. The weight of him shifts. He releases my wrists, but I'm seized by an awful familiarity. My thoughts are butterflies caught in tar.

No, no, NO.

I think of Mattie, Shane, and of those little shoes on the playground. I think of my mother, alive somewhere and trying to come home. The wings tear free. I try to push his shoulders back, but his fingers are turning my chin, and his mouth is on mine. I twist all of the strength of my body against him. He doesn't budge and when the heat of his tongue slips easily over mine, I go still.

He wants me to fight him. He knows he is stronger, that I'll tire and have to give in. There's little chance that Hawthorne or a knife-wielding Vivian will burst in and rescue me. I have to create a distraction that might give me the chance to land a good enough shove that will allow me to free myself.

So I return his kiss.

He doesn't seem surprised. This annoys me. It really annoys me. It annoys me so much that the anger I can always count on to show up doesn't disappoint me now. With that surge of illogical rage, the weight of him lifts like a nightmare in the waking light.

I was sitting just as before, his hand on my knee, as though nothing had happened. "What"—I pushed his hand away and was on the other side of the room in a heartbeat—"the *fuck* was that?"

He didn't rise but kept his amused eyes on mine. "A desire."

"Not *mine*." I inched my way further back.

"No? Are you sure?"

My back is on the mattress, his teeth scrape the skin below my ear, hands caress their way across my hips, fingers dance their way downward. I am helpless against these tingling jolts his touch is tricking out of me. And it is a trick. It has to be, because I'm moving with him until he pulls back his eyes lit red with—

Nope.

The room slammed back into place around me. I was still standing against the wall. He hadn't moved from the bed.

"Will you..." I said, shaking off the illusion. *"Stop that!"*

He laughed. Again, it was unnervingly sincere. "Whatever your secrets, your desires, your regrets, your shame. It all twists and rises to form the path to your own suffering and *this* is what you people call 'Hell'."

"What does—?" I blinked at him. "*Why* are you going on about Hell right now?"

"You," he said icily, "are the one who brought it up."

He rested one booted ankle over his knee. Relaxed. Like a coiled snake.

I stepped a wide circle around him to get to the mirror/window. Ort-Mom's dark eyes followed Mattie as she cautiously approached her. I pushed on the glass with both hands. "Stop this. You said I could go through."

"I changed my mind."

He is looking down at me, his lean, muscled body pale as bone, all traces of the civilized man he'd pretended to be gone. His nails dragging up my side as he moves, his lips murmuring some guttural thing in my ear, his hand warm around my throat...a trick.

"Godammit!" I whirled around to face him. "Is *that* what you want from me?"

"I have told you what I want. I have *asked* you for it." He rose, and the shadows rose with him, the darkness making me feel smaller, and the fear which began crawling under my skin collected at my neck, slithered down my back, and began to bore its way into the core of me.

"Let me try once more," he said, still coming toward me. "I am now *asking* that you *give me* Hawthorne's heart. Is there a way 'in Hell' you would do that?"

He is behind me, gripping my hips as tightly as I'm gripping my pillow.

He is beneath me, his forearms holding me to him, his teeth in my neck, my toes curling into the sheets. A trick.

A trick.

A trick.

He stared intensely down into my eyes as I blinked away the forced fantasy. I was grateful for the riptide of sadness I felt then. It wasn't mine, but it was muting the jarring horror of what he was doing and preventing me from being launched into a panic. It was the melancholy heart of a dramatic faery that had begun to pulse in my pocket.

"*No,*" I said in a voice ten times bolder than I felt.

"Really?" His smile pressed together, a chuckling rumble rolling in his chest. "It would *pain* me to rescind my protection."

He angled his chin toward the mirror.

Snap. Snap. Snap.

I turned to see Mattie backing out of view. Ort-Mom was standing now. The snapping still came from the nest of twigs as they untwined from each other from the pile at her feet, unfolding again and again, until each was a bundle of needle-sized legs scattering out along the floor, up the walls—away from the alabaster woman in the center of the room.

Mattie began shrieking when, with a sickening, wet sound, the thing's mouth tore and pulled back—a wide, toothy wound across the mask of my mother's face. My hands clamped over my own shriek as her eyes sagged and slid down her cheeks. And *snap snap snap,* something rose up, distorting her chest, her throat, until the white of her hair split like a seam as a black mass reared out, spilling over and enveloping the rest of the pale mask of my mother's body.

And then Noc, his voice a cool blade, asked, "Will you still refuse me?

I was unable to look away, so he helpfully swung me around by my shoulders and forced my hands down. His gaze bore into mine, and I wanted to tell him I would give him anything he wanted if he made this stop, if he saved Mattie and made all this go away, but the latched-on melancholy pulled hard as if to remind me, *Demon, you little fool.*

Once he had what he wanted, there was no saying he would stick to his word. And once he had what he wanted, there would be no saving any of us.

I shook my head and whispered. "I refuse you."

The screams behind me abruptly stopped.

His hands released me, his smile widened.

"Do you dance?"

"I..." The absurdity of the question overrode the urge to look behind me, instead studying the curve of his mouth. My voice squeaked, "What?"

"Do you *dance?* I like to think you would have, in my Court." There was a velvety purr in the way he said that last bit. "But perhaps you prefer the little Hells you create for yourself. I'll leave you to them then. What a pity though." He traced the tip of his finger down my jaw, lifting it up toward him. His steadiness made me realize I was shaking. "There is not more time for us."

The bricks scrape my elbow as I struggle to maneuver away from the boy as he's kissing me, sloppy and forceful in a reeking halo of beer and patchouli.

When I try to shove him away, he could have apologized then. Said he didn't mean it. We could have laughed it off as his being drunk and never mentioned it again. In the hundred versions of the "what if" scenarios that would play over and over again in my head afterwards, that's where things usually ended up—a few uncomfortable conversations and things went back to normal. We went back to being friends.

This moment should have been awkward. Not violent. Not this.

He doesn't let me shove him away.

He grabs my wrist and I know now he'd been wearing a mask all this time. He was never really my friend at all. When he backs me more tightly against the wall, his arms on either side of my head before gripping my face so I can't turn away, my arm so I can't run, he's tearing that mask off.

"C'mon," he whines breathily. "You like me. Don't pretend you don't."

But I don't like him, not like that. I tell him this.

"You're just saying that because of Ashley. You don't want to make her jealous, but Tali, she's already jealous of you. But you don't need to prove anything. You know exactly what you are."

I want to tell him that he doesn't know me, that he doesn't know us *at all. I want to yell this at him, but instead I am pinned beneath another unwanted kiss, one that is harder to get away from because of how hard he's now holding both arms.*

I'll find blue marks the size of fingers there tomorrow, little echoes of brutality.

My knee catches him by surprise when I bring it up. Hard. As he doubles over, I shove him and run back up the alley he'd told me was a shortcut. I'm already to the street when I hear him yelling, "You bitch! You crazy fucking bitch!"

My heart is a sledgehammer against my ribs as I make my way back home, zig-zagging up my normal route here and there in case he's following me. Fear of what he might do if he were to catch me, what he'd tried to do before I got away, making me run in bursts. I try to articulate what I'm going to tell Ashley about this boy she liked that we'd both thought was our new best friend.

Ashley has always made me feel normal. She was the same kind of shy, the same kind of awkward that blooms in loneliness, and that makes me hold fast to our friendship when it hits the speedbumps. I am protective of her. Even when it hurts. It's the boys that make it hurt. Because Ash doesn't ever just like a boy, like I do now and then, she obsesses.

She's developed a talent for changing her skin. When she has a new boy, I get over the stab of rejection, of ignored calls and texts, by delving into art. Ash always comes back, a patchwork of discarded obsessions, but still at her heart, the sister I never had.

But she was different with him. She couldn't become something he wanted when he didn't seem to want anything. That only made her fall harder, sulking behind his back when he remained completely disinterested in anything more than friendship. Then tonight. An invite to some club he said he could get us into, and Ash was grounded. He pleaded with me to come anyway, he said it would be utterly boring if he went alone. It was boring anyway, until the alley.

By the time I get home and lock the door behind me, it's too late. He didn't follow me because he had gone straight to Ashley's and told her his version of what happened. All lies, but mixed with enough truth to make my heart twist to hear it told back to me in my best friend's voice, a voice shaking with hurt and anger. At me.

I'd mocked her, he'd said, before throwing myself at him. He tried to push me away, but I snapped. Became violent. I believe that Ashley won't take long to see through this fiction, once she thinks about it with a clear head. But she blocks my number. Looks past me in the hallways.

I wait. I wait for her to come back like she always did. Instead, she tells everyone that I was stalking them, that his choosing her over me has sent me over the edge.

As the days go by, the rumors build and the whispering starts. I'm determined to show that I'm fine and sane and strong. But behind closed doors I dig my nails down my arms, the burning my blood-dotted skin brings is more urgent than the storm in my head. When I focus on that burning, there is a brief, precious quiet. I force myself to go to classes. I wear long sleeves and don't make eye contact. I won't let them know they have hurt me. Real or imagined, I hear the whispers behind my back. Under my desk, I pinch my legs hard enough to leave black welts.

Weeks later, I'm in the cafeteria alone in a corner, scribbling thick black lines while my eyes flit around the room and...land on him. With Ashley. They aren't supposed to be here. I moved my schedule to avoid this very thing, but they're here. They don't see me, or they're ignoring me, either way. I decide to leave, but just as I get up, he looks at me...and smirks. He clasps his hand over hers. She looks down and smiles, the trail of her gaze along the table is awkward. She's trying not to look at me.

And what coils around my heart, tighter each day until I can't help but look at it, is that...I know she doesn't believe him. She has sacrificed me for him anyway.

I go home. School isn't over, but after today I don't care. Dad is at work. The apartment is empty. I delete Ash's number and toss my phone on the couch. Walking through the kitchen, I pluck a paring knife from the wooden block and head to the bathroom. Sitting on the floor, each breath is a pulling ache in my chest.

There will be worse days ahead. But this is where they start.

In a few weeks, I'll be at Stillview.

When I am soothed, my heart like a stone, I stand, holding a wet cloth on the lines I made on my shoulder until the light spill of blood is gone, and look at my face in the mirror. Such a normal-looking face, no one would have ever guessed that there was so much gone wrong behind it.

"What's wrong with you?" I ask, my hands on the cool porcelain of the sink. "What the fuck is wrong with you?"

Pounding begins to shake the mirror, and I look away. The face in the mirror does not. A trick. She smiles, and around me the room snaps back into place.

The mirror was still in pieces on the carpet. In its place was nothing but an empty frame. The room felt strangely hollow. I took a slow breath. It hurt. Too familiar. Too fresh. The scab I'd built up over the last year had been scraped away. The pain and cold fear of being truly, inescapably alone cut me down quickly. I sank to my knees, a low wail rising from my lungs.

The pounding came again. Someone was trying to get in. It didn't matter. I should have never come here. If I'd been stronger, *normal,* I would have been able to shrug everything off and keep going. Somewhere there was a version of the world where I'm in college and I'm making normal, college girl mistakes. I'm making friends, dating, getting drunk on the weekends, and maybe sleeping with a teacher's aid. I'm *living.* Without one foot in the past, I just. Keep. Going.

But instead, I'd doomed an entire town. I convinced Vivian to let what I thought was Mom stay, even when she knew something was wrong. And because of that, Hawthorne stayed, so Noc focused his plans here. If she had just been shipped off to Stillview, Noc's schemes wouldn't have worked, at least not *here.*

And I got Mattie involved. I didn't even know if what I saw through the mirror was really her or an illusion, but wherever she was, she was still in far more danger than she would've been if she'd never run into me.

I ignored the pounding door and sobbed, sitting on the glass strewn carpet. Until I saw a pair of eyes staring at me from under the bed.

34

Rot and Bloom

Reformed once more as long-lost Nicolette Adair, the ort's lips parted in surprise when she saw that I'd noticed her there. She unfolded herself from the fetal position and began army crawling her way toward me. Defeated as I felt, I think it was only survival instinct that made me automatically back away from her, ignoring the glass under my hands.

She stood, pulling the oversized collar of her sweater back over her narrow shoulder from where it had fallen as she cautiously scanned the room before coming closer. Gone was her shark-eyed look from the scene in the mirror, replaced with fear—and what I swore could be disappointment.

"Uh...Mom?" I attempted, but she only offered me her hand. No, still not *Mom,* but at least a safer rendition of her, I hoped. I really didn't have anything more to lose if I was wrong here, so I took her hand. She pulled me up, looked at me with her default confusion. But if she *were* the same ort I'd believed was Mom all along, then the one in the mirror had been a complete illusion, which would mean...

Someone pounded on the door again. I dared to hope as I unlocked it that it might be Mattie on the other side. Instead, I threw it open to Kehente, alone in the quiet hallway. She muttered something, then saw who else was in the room.

Her fingers barely reached out of Shane's jacket sleeves as she raised out her arms to throw them around who was obviously close enough to the real Cole for her. She spoke urgently, but Ort-Mom seemed to understand her as well as I did. Finally, she landed on the right word and rolled her eyes to me, slowly enunciating *"KEY"* while jabbing her finger in my direction, then pointing slowly back at the ort.

She repeated this motion until I gently stopped her wrist. This was what I had come here to do after all, and it would probably be good to have a witness. One that was more trustworthy than me when it came to explaining what happened here.

I reached into my pocket. The stone felt heavier and, even through its leather bindings, warm in my hand. I felt a pang of guilt, knowing what would happen when the ort touched it. It didn't occur to me before now that she might not know what she was, what she was made from. It might not be her fault that she was essentially a pawn too. And she hadn't really done anything to hurt anyone, not on purpose.

But it was time to put all illusions to rest. I took her palm and set the pouch in it before she could consider jerking away from me. But she didn't react at all. Not at first.

Then, slowly, she brought it close to her chest. I braced myself for what might be about to happen, but she only let out a little gasp and kind of fell forward, catching hold of the dresser before she made it all the way to the ground. She kept her fist closed as she steadied herself then looked at it with disgust before tossing the pouch on the bed.

"Nope," she said confidently and backed away, perching herself on the window bench. It looked much darker outside when she turned to the glass behind her. It must not have been any less nightmarish down there judging by how quickly she then scampered away from it too.

This didn't seem like an ort's reaction to its fellow shadowlings.

My breath caught in my chest. "Mom??"

This time her eyes snapped to me. There was focus there and, at last, *recognition*. Once that set in, her face became a flipbook of emotions. Shock. Relief. Anger. Sadness. I was most sure about the sadness because of the tears that welled in her warm, dark eyes, but I only got a glimpse of that trace of humanity before the curtain closed again, her expression reset into an impassive mask.

But it was enough. This *was* my mother. Noc really hadn't been lying about that, only...everything else. He'd taken advantage of my brief doubt and whipped up a *real* ort-mom in the mirror as a last-ditch effort to trick me into summoning him—something that might not matter soon if Elmwood got annexed to the Midnight Lands. I guess I shouldn't have been surprised that demons were opportunists. But I now had to grudgingly admit that Hawthorne really had been telling the truth all along.

"You..." she began as though she didn't trust her own voice. "You shouldn't be here."

"Yeah, right there with you on that one." All the years I'd spent dreaming of ways I could see her again, and now...I didn't know what to say. I'd been foolish enough to expect an instant bond once, and I wasn't making that mistake twice, not when I couldn't even be sure how much she remembered.

"And you"—she looked at Kehente by my side—"shouldn't be...old."

Kehente's brown-spotted hands went to her hips and she inhaled deeply, but I was quick to jump in before she launched into whatever tirade she meant to go on. "Do you understand what's been happening?"

"I think so." She looked pained at the sight of me, but at least she didn't look away. "I was trapped in a kind of dream, but I couldn't gather enough of myself together for things to become coherent. Some parts are still blurry, but enough sense is settling back to see that everything is doomed, so...thanks."

Beside me, Kehente resumed what I'd interrupted. Something I'd guess was an attempt to explain everything she had gone through since a cursed faery heart was placed into her then twelve-year-old hand.

Mom must've understood her, because she let her finish, then gently took her hands in hers. "I'm so sorry, Kehente. But it was all I could do to save you. I knew there was a chance I'd survive without it, but we couldn't t cross the sea without—"

We were all jolted by a loud, harsh noise. Not a storm rumble or lightning boom this time. It was a succession of three loud snaps: little explosions that I knew were gunfire. As though it had punctured the sound bubble we were in, it was immediately followed by a too-sudden clamor of shouts and barking over a loud crash, then more shots.

This reunion and all of its questions and apologies would have to wait. "Grab the talisman," I ordered Mom, then clarified, "Hawthorne's *heart*. You have to give it back to him, he's...I think he's our only chance," I conceded. It took her a second, but when it looked like she understood enough to want to refuse, I ordered, "NOW."

She pressed her lips together but snatched it up. I grabbed Kehente's frail arm as carefully as I could, while still ensuring that my urgency wouldn't get lost in translation, and ran out the door. She let herself be towed along, yanking Mom along with surprising strength as I pulled us toward the stairs.

There were cool rushes of air in the hallway as the doors folded inward when we bolted past. I didn't risk losing the seconds it would take to look and see where they opened to. A good call, I decided, because by the time I turned to the landing, the stairs were gone, replaced by a mossy stone drop-off. It was roughly the same height

and angle the stairway had been and wet, on account of the bubbling
stream of water flowing down it.

The rug squished beneath my boots, and I couldn't help but turn
toward where the water was coming from. A cave-like entrance had
replaced the door to my room, but really, the music and cackling
echoing from what I hoped was far, *far* within it told me that it wasn't
my room anymore, though I could still make out the shape of the
door frame within the rock wall. Probably everything I had in there
had been converted to moss or stalagmites or creatures that would be
close to, but not quite, giant bats. The low, deep snarl from something
that wasn't attending whatever Town Takeover Party was going on
in the background reminded me I shouldn't spend too much time
wondering about it. It sounded closer and, very unfortunately, large.

I wasn't the only one who had heard it. No one dared make a sound.
I quickly lowered myself and scooted down, grabbing onto the dry
stones away from the center to stop from sliding, making myself the
anchor to help Kehente down part of the way, and Mom slid below
me and did the same. Once the old woman was safe at the bottom, we
followed, our feet landing with a small splash in the pool that reached
around either side of what was once the stairway.

On the dry ground, moss and mud had replaced the floorboards.
Some of the photographs were still half visible from between the dirt
and rock wall. Above us, the ceiling might still be there, I thought,
behind the canopy of branches and ivy. *A terrarium.* That's what it
felt like we were in: a big box of wood and green, thriving things with
a few decorative humans thrown in for drama.

The lighting of the house was uneven, and I realized I couldn't
tell where it was coming from. The lamps were dead, so the power
must have been cut. The layout of everything was still recognizable; the
walls and furniture were still where they ought to be, only more...in

bloom than they had been. In some places you could still make out the pattern of the rug, the fibers mingled with the new undergrowth and mushrooms. All around us the damp, green smell of forest almost masked another heavier scent of rot.

Over the trickling water, I heard a ticking I might not have noticed if I weren't focused on Mom as she stood ankle-deep in the pool of the entryway, silently tracing her fingers along the glass face of the grandfather clock. A lump formed in my throat over the jumble of questions I had surging around my brain, but before I could go to her, Kehente tugged my sleeve and pointed to where I had left Lydia in the parlor.

The room looked scorched by an angry black tear that went from the fireplace to the center of the room. A trail of the frayed, colorful fabric of her sweater poked out of the broken bones of the couch that led to the room's large, smashed windows. And it wasn't just the glass, the wall around the frames had been broken through—from inside.

The cold that had been sitting in my stomach twined its way through my chest. No, this wasn't like a terrarium. Those only had one opening, didn't they? There were many here, both seen and unseen. What was coming through them were vampiric, overreaching things with appetites. After feeding on the matter of the memories on the walls, and the walls themselves, what would come next from the darkness? What would it hunger for?

35

The Cage

A growl from beyond the still intact front door—which stood as a proud, ridiculous reminder that this house didn't completely belong to the wild yet—gave me enough of an answer. I wasn't remotely curious to find out what had made it, which worked out well since at the same time, a barking erupted from what was hopefully still the kitchen. With barely a glance to each other, the three of us moved quickly toward the least threatening sound.

Kehente and Mom were pressed at my back as I halted midstep at the door. I wanted to be able to say that nothing prepared me for the sight of what was happening in there, but with everything that had taken place in the last hour alone, that simply wouldn't be true. Which was probably why I was incapable of panic when I saw Hawthorne in the wreck of the overturned tables and toppled chairs, his fingers dripping red while holding his sword out at his side. The Green Lady, still grinning and with thin strands of smoke drifting up from a gap beneath her breastbone like algae dancing in a current, came toward him from the opened door of the garden.

I was even mostly unphased when I could so clearly see that she stepped over the crumpled pile of Wes Samuel. At least I was at first. He was face down, his hand still holding a pistol. Something in my brain began to twitch at the sight of the blood stretching out from beneath him, slowly pooling in the lines of the tiles.

"Oh, back off you bloody, cursed *thing,*" Hawthorne whispered harshly, deftly stepping over a chair leg while backing away from the Lady's reaching arms. That swagger was gone, and as he came closer, I could see the focus of his glare, his lips pulled back from his teeth.

I could well imagine what he must be feeling to have this thing wearing the face of someone he'd loved, *Joanna,* if Noc was to be believed on this, mimicking something like old affections. Her movements were twitchy, uneven. Steadily up the exposed skin of her arms and neck, dark veins were branching out, but the mockery of her still-beautiful face gazing at him with serene eyes that clashed with that demented smile seemed to do what it was intended to.

She was sent to hurt him, after all.

His hands tightened on the blade's handle, but he didn't raise his sword. His face was a mask of anger and agony. As far as I could tell, he really only had one option here, and it spoke to Noc's cruelty, knowing it would fall to Hawthorne to be the one to have to choose it. *Or maybe not,* I thought as Vivian ran in from the dining room, hurling a teakettle over head with one hand, wielding a frying pan in the other.

Hawthorne quickly put himself between my grandmother and the ort, but not before the kettle struck the thing square in the chest, making a hole there with a wet tearing sound as though its flesh were made of paper. It lodged there for a moment before slowly sinking into the tar-black of her insides.

I think it's safe to say that none of us expected that, not even the Green Lady herself. She stilled, looking down as those black veins spread quickly from the hole and wrapped down her arms, up her face and even over the green of her dress, connecting and weaving together until that darkness was all she was. But she came forward still, a lady-shaped shadow still bleeding slow trails into the air from her thorax as she staggered toward Hawthorne.

I leaned to grab Vivian's arm and pull her back to where I was anchored by my own grip on the doorframe, ducking as she swung the frying pan my way. Her wide eyes blinked into fast relief when she saw it was me and rushed over, putting her pan-free arm around my shoulder. It was a protective gesture, but the first time she'd ever shown me anything close to physical affection. I was glad for it, because the shadowling hissed out a screech that was by far the worst thing I'd ever heard in my life. It cut through me, nearly causing my knees to buckle, but Vivian held me tight.

"Curse the devil who fouled you," Hawthorne uttered before the silver of his blade easily sliced the ort diagonally. Each half spilled onto the floor into a silent, black pool of itself that ended up in the shape of a woman lying still on her side.

For a few moments, no one moved, then Hawthorne dropped to his knee, his bloody hand releasing his sword with a clatter. He looked tired, then corpse-pale. Gingerly, his fingers reached to touch her, barely brushing across her shadow cheek as it wafted away, the whole of her swirling and dispersing in the breeze that blew in from the still open door. His hand recoiled to cover his mouth, but he stayed on the floor.

Seeing him there alone, I had the surprising urge to put my hand on his shoulder and say something comforting, but Mom drifted past me, her bare feet hardly avoiding the broken bits of teacups strewn among the silverware. I don't know if he'd realized we were even there, but *her* he seemed to sense. He rose with a graceful spin, the illusion of life springing back into him, bringing his beauty back with it. His dual-colored eyes immediately sparked warm with hope. His shoulders raised as she cupped his face with one hand...and soundly slapped him with the other.

The impact turned his head, but his smile was beaming when he turned back to her. "There you are," he said, and god—he looked so genuinely glad to see her, and not in a greedy, lecherous kind of way. It was more sickening than that...he really did look like a man in *love*.

He wrapped his arms around her waist and moved to kiss her, which I'm sure would have looked like a completely romantic moment if you were lucky enough not to know the backstory, but he stilled when he noticed the silver knife point in his chest.

I don't know when Mom had lifted it from my boot, but she must've hidden it in her sleeve in case the slap didn't get her point across. Which clearly it didn't. Beside me, Vivian tsked the same way she did when she disapproved of something on one of her ancient television shows. I was a little glad that whatever Hawthorne's feelings for her, anything he mistook as genuine on her part was probably some form of Stockholm syndrome.

He looked down to the thin blade over where his heart should be and the small dot of blood it was drawing through his shirt. With one eyebrow quirked, raised his eyes to hers. "Ah, my first gift to you." He smiled. "But it will do no good where you're aiming it...because of my last one."

"It's symbolic." The smile she returned was devoid of warmth. "You *tricked* me. You lied."'

"Did not," he said, then tilted his head. "Wait, to who?"

"Let's start with *her*." She pointed my way. But she wasn't talking about me. Kehente shuffled forward, looking every second of her un-earned, ninety-something years. "You told her she could return to her family."

"I did and she can—"

"Because I believed *you*, she believed *me* and followed—"

"Admittedly, when I said that, I *did* think that her family would likely be dead—" He hissed as she twisted the knife's handle. His hand went to her wrist, but he didn't stop her.

"*None* of us are any more free than when we went into that damn Moon Dark Sea—all we've done is extend the cage."

"I didn't lie." He breathed the illusion of life out of him. She must know that beneath his shirt, the knife pointed into the open hole in his chest, but she kept it there as even his sunken eyes grew sullen. Vivian backed into the wall. I let her pull me with her, but I'd already seen this show.

"I didn't *trick*. I gambled." He stepped back from the blade and released her wrist, ending their stalemate. "But it seems the Queen of Dawn was willing to do the same and stooped to parlay with Orias himself. She's *allowing* him this plot of your Ruined World so he'll send his minions to fetch me on her behalf. I knew she just wouldn't let me go, but this is treacherous—even for her."

"I see." Her tone was sharper than the blade she lowered. "So later she can deny she was behind any of it. Your mother will *always* get her way in the end."

"Your...mother?" I asked from where I hadn't moved from the door

"You sound surprised. I *do* have one," he said without a glance my way. "Did you think faery were born from dew drops and rosebuds? Or that every time a bell rings we spring forth fully formed from the trees?"

"Don't be an ass," Mom told him. "The Queen of Dawn is his mother—and a truly wicked piece of work."

"But...wouldn't that make you some kind of....prince?"

"Well now, that shouldn't be surprising at all." He smirked my way now with his ashen skin and colorless lips. "Am I not regal?

So, not a criminal...literally a prince *charming*. I cringed. And he'd been slumming it over on our side of the Veil and even falling for its natives. No wonder his mom wanted to ground him. And if his freedom somehow relied on his heart, no wonder it mattered so much to everyone.

"You're an *ass,*" Mom said with authority.

Well, almost everyone.

"Isn't he some kind of pirate?" Vivian whispered. "I thought he was some kind of pirate."

I sighed, brushing her question off in favor of the one I was almost too afraid to ask. "Hawthorne...what happened to Shane and Lydia?"

"Ah, well there was a bit of a shootout. Our hero won, obviously." He nodded at the body on the floor. "But the grandame was pulled away by something that didn't mind the metal of bullets, and the noble fool, he ran after her while I dealt with..."

"If we've been found out, then what good is this now?" Mom ignored the pained look in his eyes as he looked at the place where the ort had fallen and pulled out the pouch. Thankfully it hadn't reverted back to its true form. I wasn't sure Vivian could have handled that.

"What good? It broke the curse over you," he said softly, making no motion to take it. "*That* was good. It kept me from being found until I could be here, with you. *That* was good. Without it, I am useless to the Dawn Lands, which *would* be good, only they haven't yet learned that I'm no longer one with the thing. But since whatever demon had been paving the way for Midnight to come here after me was *summoned* by that now lucky dead man there, it may well be out of *good.*"

So that's what Noc had meant about Wes Samuel being useful. Being summoned was always his plan. I'd just been a backup.

"So, no happy ever after then?" Mom said flatly.

"Not for me." He stepped back and scooped up his sword. "Nor for you. But I did warn you of that."

"It was too late for that anyway." She looked drained. "But all of *this* can't be the work of one summoned demon, can it?"

"Not your average summoned demon, no. But one on a mission from Orias himself? One that was granted a boon of power to complete it? That *might* explain how it was able to tear the Veil open wide enough so that anything near it...tumbled in."

Her eyes widened and I didn't think it was possible for her to look any paler. "Oh...no..."

"I don't understand," I said. "What does that mean?"

"It means"—Hawthorne twirled the sword handle in his hand—"welcome to the Everlands, ladies."

36

The Midnight Door

From where I stood, the sky wasn't as dark as I would've thought it would be for a land called Midnight. The dusky light that came in through the window was more like the purple-red hue of a deepening bruise.

"I didn't feel anything 'tumble'," I said.

"You were preoccupied." He glowered at me. "And the ripple was slight. I knew when Kehente gave you my heart and knew what you might do with it, but I gambled that however much sense you lacked, you would make up for it in the love for your mother." He tilted his head toward her. "And you *do* love her, don't you?"

She glared at him but said nothing.

"Well. All isn't lost. Not yet at least. I may still be able to right this." He sheathed his sword. "I mean to go after your friends, and then I'll deal with your demon—though I suspect they won't be far from one another."

"He's not *my* demon. And don't you need...*that*?" I pointed at the pouch.

Noticing how Mom seized her hand over it in a panic, he told her, rather sadly, "It's *yours*. I promised you. Hold it until you're all the way free. Until you feel safe. Hold it forever, if you like."

"Wait, no, you said you needed it to not be all..." I gestured at his deathlike physique.

"Oh, but this is much better suited for the territory." He winked, which looked as creepy as you'd imagine coming from a near-corpse. "This is more *my* land than yours now—not quite Midnight yet, but close enough for me to draw from when I make my own bargain with this demon to undo this mess."

"What—? No. No, no. You do *not* want to bargain with him, first of all. He went through all the tricks and trouble to manipulate me into stealing *that* thing so he could capture you. You *have* to take it back while you can."

He held up his hand; his laugh was breathy and unnerving. "He. Him. *Who*?"

"*Noc*," I confessed in a whisper, half convinced that my saying his name would make him pop out of the refrigerator or something.

"Ah." He raised a brow and sucked in a breath. "The Archcarver. That's a...larger problem. But at least that explains a few things." Before I could ask him to share them—literally ANY of them—with the rest of us, he turned to Mom abruptly. "I know his games. If you care to stay safe, stay *here* until I return and if I don't—"

"Then it doesn't matter," she said flatly.

"Well." He lifted her chin. "I will just have to return then."

"Wait—" I began, but he was already darting out the door.

I started to follow after him, but the barking caught my ear. It was distant, but it was definitely barking. Leaning into the hallway behind me, I listened. It was coming from the black of the dividing door.

Kehente's hand was on my shoulder the second I moved toward the sound. She held up a finger and waved it from side to side.

"I think my friend is there," I told her.

"Then she's not coming back," Mom said. "And if you go in there will be no one to save you."

At this point, I was almost choking on all of the questions I wanted to ask. Instead, I only reminded her, "Someone saved *you*."

"Yes, and you see how well that's gone for everyone." She pointed around with the knife. "You may not think we could be more deeply damned than we already are, but this is just a *layer*. The first thin, creeping, dark wave on the shore of a place that is soon to drown. Let me be the warning I wish I'd had: there is *nothing* worth going into that place for. Nothing and no one. If I'd thought there was even a chance that you—" A low dragging sound came from upstairs that no one directly acknowledged, but she waited for it to stop before she continued without bothering to hide the disappointment in her voice. "I just...I didn't think I'd ever *see* you again."

That stung. Sure, all the years she missed were a lot to process, but that she didn't seem even a little happy to see me was starting to salt the wound.

"I recognize that tone." Vivian still leaned against the wall clutching the copper frying pan to her chest. "That's Nicolette."

"And you, Mother, I didn't ever *want* to see again." She sighed.

"I wanted to see you again," I told her, my voice wavering, wishing my heart could exist outside my own body like Hawthorne's. "And there's people that want to see Mattie again. I can't leave her behind in there anymore than I could leave you, and Mom...real soon I hope to tell you all the ways I could never leave you behind, in all these years. I even made a deal with an *actual demon*—"

"Oh, you didn't," she gasped with a roll of her eyes. "You didn't make *a bargain* did you?"

"A bargain with who?" asked Vivian.

"With any of them!" Mom was incredulous.

"Well, I *thought* I was helping. You know the games they play. He knew what to say. What would matter."

"They always do." Mom scoffed.

"Will someone please tell me what you're talking about? Who is Mattie? And who is this? *Who*"—Vivian poked her pan at Kehente, who was fiddling with one of her disheveled braids—"are you??"

"She's with Mom, Vivian. They both escaped here from a world that's now eating ours because I accidentally helped a demon lure some apparently half-dead criminal faery here to be captured in exchange for Elmwood and everyone in it."

Vivian blinked at me, lowering the pan.

"I don't think that's what's happening," Mom said.

"I..." I rubbed my temple to draw focus away from my own growing frustration. She hadn't even been coherent until less than an hour ago. Kehente had been sheltered at Shane's, and Vivian...well, I was pretty sure I had the best clue of all of them as to what was happening here.

The barking came again.

"Look, I'm going after my friend."

"But that prince pirate said to stay." Vivian's eyes darted to each of us. "He...he had a sword."

"Yeah well, listening to him hasn't always been the best idea in my experience." I looked around the floor for anything that could be a weapon and saw the knife block where it had fallen.

"What is your experience?" I couldn't tell if it was suspicion or concern in Mom's voice.

I helped Kehente flip the chair she was struggling with upright so she could sit down, then tried to find anything larger than a steak knife. "He showed up looking for me. To get to you. He thinks you were stolen from him."

"I was."

"Mom?" I asked, drawing a breath. "You have to know by now that he tricked you."

"That's what they all do." She ran her thumb over the pouch. "But at least I knew what Hawthorne was. I didn't pine for him after I ran off with Richard. But that life never felt like mine. So, I came back."

My heart turned ice-heavy, and before I could stop myself, I asked what I knew I really didn't want to know. "Is Hawthorne why you left me?"

"I left..." Her face stayed neutral, but I caught the pain-tinged panic in her eyes before she hastily turned away. "You were better off without me."

"No. I wasn't." I could feel the tears, the exhausted tears, fill my eyes. "Mom, I really wasn't."

"You can't understand." She flinched then. "Whatever was wrong in me...I didn't want to be wrong in you. I knew if I stayed, I would only ruin you."

"You were depressed. It messes with how you see things. And yourself. If you got help—"

"I wasn't depressed. I was trapped."

I hated my tears as they started to fall. I hated them for how they were making her look at me. It wasn't with empathy. She looked *uncomfortable*. As though I were a stranger accosting her at a party. "So, you ran off with...what? An old woodland boyfriend? Who wasn't even human? Rather than stay with your six-year-old daughter who needed you?"

"You didn't.... *I* didn't belong here. I never fit." She shook her head and slid back down the cabinets so that she was sitting with her knees up on the floor, holding the holly knife and her lover's heart in her hands. "But I didn't mean to just disappear. I thought I would visit, but things—"

"*Visit*?" The word was sour in my mouth.

"There were monsters in the garden...." Vivian said suddenly, her eyes drifting unfocused toward the window. "They ate up every tho ught.".

"Yeah, Vivian.," I snapped, wiping my eyes with my sleeve, "I know. We've kind of been through this." But she began to hum and sway, handing me the pan in favor of grabbing the broom from the corner. She began to sweep while she danced, making a futile attempt at the glass.

"Vivian?" I asked as she began sweeping up the blood. The bristles only acted as a brush, painting in gory half circles.

"I dreamt I killed Nicolette again," she said to no one in particular.

"Excuse me?" Mom asked.

"It wasn't you," I told her dumbly. "I mean, obviously. It was some sort of sad, cursed woman that I'm not sure was really a person anymore."

"I dreamt she came back." Vivian swept the blood close to Kehente, who shot an irritated glance at her as she raised her feet out of the broom's path.

"She didn't," I said, looking at Mom.

"Huh, so *that* was Joanna then." She looked to the spot where the ort had fallen. "Well, no one would ever accuse Noc of being boring."

"You *know* him?" I asked, but she looked at me and everything rippled around her, like a stone had fallen into a pond we were reflected in. I turned and the edges of things seemed to take a second to catch up. This...this was another of Noc's illusions? No, not an illusion—a dream.

My lazy gaze fell on a hand that touched my arm; I followed it up to Mom's face. She was looking up. I shook my head to clear it, which helped—for a few moments anyway as far as I could tell. Unless there were *not* little mushroom creatures with bioluminescent veins crawling along the roots that covered the ceiling—in which case it actually made it worse. Assuming they *were* there, however, then so were the pale bulbs of bluish flowers. They were shaking, causing fine powder to rain down.

"Blurring things..." I said, my voice thick and slow.

"Yes, they do that," Mom said. "Mostly at the openings. The little *kindraug*. They make people unaware. It's a mercy really, one of the only ones you'll get as you go deeper into his realm."

There was a flash of light behind my eyes and hot pain on my face as she casually slapped me. "Hey!" I yelled, holding my cheek.

"You're fine," she said, and gave Vivian an enthusiastic, head-turning slap.

"Why are you—? Ooh," I said, realizing that everything was clear again.

She looked at Kehente, heavy-lidded in a chair, and hesitated. "Poor kid. Maybe it'd be best to let her dream for a bit."

I looked up again. The chubby white bodies with their wide-capped heads were almost cherubic until one turned to me with its faintly glowing, dead blue eyes. "I...don't think we should stay here. If we're just at an opening, then maybe we can make it back to our side."

"Maybe you can," Mom said.

Vivian, still holding the broom, now clutched one of her gemstone necklaces as she slowly turned around the room. "I'm not leaving my home," she said defiantly—if nonsensically.

"This isn't your home anymore, Mother. In fact, this house was never really anyone's home."

"Hawthorne said there's a chance to undo this, so that means we have a chance of making it," I told them, unsure if I even believed it. But I was done giving up on myself. And I wasn't giving up on anyone else either. The barking coming from the hallway had an echo now.

"I'm going after Mattie," I said resolutely, but the walls began to waver, so I put my hand out to keep me steady, but it was wavy too. The slap was a bit more welcome this time, even if I didn't see it coming.

"Talia." Mom's dark eyes stayed on mine. "Don't."

"I guess you really can't understand," I told her with my hand back on my cheek. Crouching down, I opened the cabinets under the sink, relieved to see that no *kindraug* guarded the ancient flashlight, and that it hadn't been replaced by a slab of petrified wood or a flashlight-shaped mound of moss. I hit it on my palm to get it to flicker on. The three women all watched me with varying degrees of concern. "I can't leave people I care about."

I wasn't surprised that the light illuminated nothing in the doorway. I was a little surprised that when I slid my hand into the cool darkness to feel for a wall, nothing felt me back.

"Mattie?" I whispered as loud as I could while still being considered whispering.

Behind me, Vivian's face peered around the kitchen door, her hand pressed to the wall. Her expression told me she thought what I was doing was either very stupid or very brave. Or both. Her expression wasn't wrong. However, the alternative was being smacked around the kitchen while waiting for Hawthorne to sort my fate out—something that didn't fill me with the most confidence.

I took a steadying breath just as the house clocks began their disjointed chime. Then I stepped into silence and shadows enfolded me.

It was like a strange gravity pulled me forward—a force that propelled my legs to keep moving. Then there was ground under my feet, but the flashlight shone into the dark without landing on anything. It reminded me of those haunted houses old strip malls would transform into at Halloween where you'd pay ten bucks to go into pure blackness, following little lights on the walls while people in Party City costumes grabbed at you until you made it to the next lit room of themed horror vignettes.

This, though, kept going into a midnight-with-no-moon darkness, and before my eyes could try and focus on the shapes around me, there were whispers. I couldn't tell if they were words or the rustling of dry things against each other, but they came from all around. Something that must've been in the loon family called mournfully in the distance, answered by a chorus of more.

My foot struck something hard. I shone the weak light down to a raised, flat stone, then to another above it. Stairs. Upward I went. Until I saw a flicker of light. Not fire, something colder was beyond the last stair, and once I reached the top, I gasped at the sight in the distance below me.

Stretching into nothingness, a shining, silver sea.

It was terrifying, but strangely—almost impossibly—it was beautiful too. The ragged faces of surrounding mountains were lit with its glow. Dark spots that could be islands broke up the surface. I couldn't gauge how far it was, but it illuminated the massive shape of what seemed to be a forest that stood between me and its shores. A breeze carried the familiar scent of rain mingled with soft evergreen things and a touch of sulfur.

The sky above it was flecked with purple and gold dots of light I knew couldn't be stars, at least not stars as I knew them. If this place didn't look up to the same space, then it wasn't of the same galaxy, and I wasn't ready to know that yet. But if I figured the alternative was that they weren't stars at all, but hundreds of eyes looking back down, then just being stars in an alien sky didn't seem as bad.

I jumped at the movement out of the corner of my eye, turning toward a swirl of light hanging in the air. It hovered, wavering like a living thing but it had no features, no face. Just a pulse. As I watched, another appeared just beyond it.

I looked at the black I'd just come from and the unreachable sea ahead. Following the ghost lights seemed both the dumbest and best option. The barking came again. Something as common as a dog didn't strike me as native to this place. It *had* to be Cinder. Or something that was enough like her to try and fool me. I sighed and clung to my hope as I walked toward the lights.

Blue grass grew wild along the hardly used path. More lights appeared as I went. The trees around me were too tall to see the tops of and each wider than the length of a truck. The path went straight for a while, and it was when it began to curve slightly down that I heard the distant but unmistakable rippling soundwave of a violin. A different kind of fear cut through me, and I sped up as the notes, rich, melancholy, and familiar, trembled through me the closer I got, panic closing my throat.

The path began to widen to a clearing of some kind. A circle of stones marked the place off from the woods. I smelled smoke and saw the orange glow from around a strangely constructed structure that could have been described as an ongoing shack for all the odd angles. I ran around it, holding the useless flashlight with both hands as though

I could will it to be a weapon, tears tugging at the corners of my eyes and the music overwhelming me.

I saw him then, sitting on a log playing music so hauntingly sad it could have made the shadows weep, though the ones surrounding him only sat like faceless acolytes, shuddering with the tremble of each note he played. His red hair falling over the instrument, his mouth set in concentration above the copper beard, then he stopped and, seeing me, smiled.

"Hey there, Doodlebug."

37

The Lost

"Dad?" Before he could answer, I was throwing my arms around him like I did when I was a child, my face pressing into his chest. The violin poked into my arm as he returned the hug. The circle of his shadow audience dissolved around us with hisses, but I didn't let go. I didn't want to let go of these few precious seconds of comfort.

"How are you here?" I asked, my voice half muffled by his shirt. "*Why* are you here?"

"I'm not sure," he said, gently pulling away and looking down at my face. He looked tired, but surprisingly calm. "I was trying to bring you another phone, like I said I would. It was dark by the time I got back to town, but I came straight to the house. Or I thought I did. I know these roads, but somehow, when I turned toward Vivian's place, I got lost. The curve in the driveway...kept going, then it started to rain, and I don't remember being tired, but I must've fallen asleep or something because...I feel like I'm missing time."

"Where's your car?" I asked, letting myself imagine for a second that we could just hop in and drive out of here.

"You know, I don't know?" This fact seemed to impress him. "I was driving and then...I wasn't. I was here. And there was a strange man." His face fell from dreamy uncertainty into apprehension. "He told me something that I thought was important. I can't remember..." His hand ran down his beard as he tried to grasp the tail of the memory.

I knew that strange man was no man at all. Dad had been *addled*, maybe by mushroom things or a curse, but he was obviously not thinking clearly.

"It doesn't matter now. We're not far from the door out of here, but I'm looking for my friend. And her dog. I don't suppose you've seen a hopefully still armed goth girl wandering around?"

"I don't think so. Just the people here...oh." He looked around us. "I guess they left."

"You mean those shadows—"

"The stars are beautiful here," he said, as though he were in the middle of an entirely different conversation.

I gestured at the now empty places around the fire. "You saw *people*?"

"Yeah. They were quiet. Seemed tired. It didn't occur to me to stop and talk to them. I was kind of in the moment, you know?"

"Um, sure." A bird's strangled cry sounded in the distance. I hoped it was a bird. "We should go. I'm starting to think being here too long might have an...effect on people"

"Go where?"

"Back to the house. To Mom. She's better now. She remembers. Maybe I should just explain on the way. Hopefully we can just go back the way I came—"

"Talia." His cool hands took mine, his eyes suddenly focused. "There's something I *need* to tell you. Something I should've told you a long time ago."

My gaze flicked around us as he spoke, making sure the only shadows cast by the flicker of the fire were ours. "Okay..."

"I thought it was better if you didn't remember a lot of things about your mother. You were so little when she left, and it seemed like you only managed to hold on to the good memories, but I was always afraid that the bad ones were lodged deep too. When you would get down for those long stretches and then when you...when things got really bad, I thought it was like a seed those memories had planted."

"What are you talking about?" A branch snapped nearby. I gripped the flashlight like a baton, straining to see any movement in the dark. "I do remember. She was depressed. Like me."

"No. It was more than that. I was afraid to leave her alone with you."

"That's...no. You don't get what it's like to struggle with yourself. She was probably doing her best."

"Talia..." He hesitated. "She once left you in the house with the gas on while she sat outside picking flowers."

"Well, that...just *shows* that she was struggling," I said automatically, dimly aware that I was defending her by default.

He looked at me sadly. "She *pushed* you."

"What?"

"I think...she pushed you into the lake that day. You remember that I pulled you out, not how you wound up there. But I saw you in the water and her standing still over you as you went under, not moving a muscle to help you. Later she said she panicked, but a few people saw the whole thing and told me what she'd done....that it was on purpose."

"Oh, come on—you don't really think that." I tried to sound dismissive, but the words came out as brittle.

"You're right, she'd struggled. Even before you were born. I began to worry it made her not bond properly with you. She could be so loving with you sometimes, but when she fell into her moods...she went really *dark*.

"I blamed myself for not being there and...our relationship was complicated. But that last year, it was really bad. I loved her. I didn't want to leave her, but after the lake, I knew I'd have to do something to keep you safe. But then she just...left.

"I wanted her to get help and come back, but...how she was when I saw her in the hospital...there was something familiar about the *coldness* in her that made me worry that she was still the same. Or worse."

I pulled my hands from his and turned, taking a deep breath of the smoke scented air. I walked in a small circle, pressing smaller circles into my temple with my fingers. She said she had left to be with Hawthorne, but what prompted her into thinking that was a good idea?

Whatever was wrong in me, I didn't want it to be wrong in you.

The fire crackled and a log dropped down, sending orange embers up into the smoke. Only they didn't disappear. They swirled into shapes, curled like tiny kittens with opened mouths that let loose a high-pitched chorus of mews, then drifted sideways and glided away into the dark.

"The stars are beautiful here." He was smiling up at the sky, as though the gravity of what he had just told me had washed away from him.

I turned back to the fire. We had to go. I had to find Mattie and now tow my addled father along as well. Once we got him back to the house, maybe I could slap him back to himself. And when this was over, if Hawthorne pulled off getting us all out of this, and Mom was no longer wielding a knife, we were going to *all* have a long uncomfortable talk about a lot of things. Then...I would go away.

Somewhere. Anywhere. What was wrong in Mom was *not* wrong in me. Something in me laid down its sword, and I felt a strange relief. Followed by an intense wave of nausea. I could never do what she did. Any of it. I might've been fucked up, but I knew now I wasn't *that* fucked up.

A howl echoed through the woods, loud enough, close enough, to make my blood go cold. "Dad?" I said with my eyes on the orange-lit trees.

"Yeah..."

"We've gotta go." I glanced at him, relieved that he had snapped out of it too and was also watching the forest.

"Anywhere that's away from whatever *that* was is a great idea," he said. "Stay close."

In the firelight, our shadows were long as we started back in the direction I'd come from. I looked behind me for just a second, and it took just that second for my heart to break.

As I took a step, my shadow moved.

His didn't.

I stared as he went ahead with his hand reaching back for me, leaving his shadow standing with mine. I waved my arm to the side; my shadow obeyed. His waved back. Then it walked away in the opposite direction, quickly swallowed by the dark beyond the fire.

"What are you doing?" he asked when I hadn't taken his hand. He was about ten feet away, and the only shadow cast from him came from the violin.

"Dad..."

"Oh, hey, it'll be alright." His hand on my arm was supposed to be reassuring, but his eyes, which were still the same storm gray as mine, looked back at me with a sadness that took a bit to weigh down his smile. "Oh." He realized. "I can't go, can I?"

I gripped onto his cool hand, unable to speak

"I'm—" He closed his eyes and when they opened, they were wet. "I'm so sorry."

I threw my arms around him again, squeezing as tight as I could as though I could hold him together, force him to be whole. To be *alive*. Because, I realized with a shocked, shuddering sob...that he wasn't.

He'd seen those shadows as people because they were like him. Remnants. *Ghosts.* The only reason I could see him was likely because Noc had made him that way. Carved him that way.

Demons delight in such cruelties.

"I'm so sorry," he whispered again, his cheek resting on the top of my head as he smoothed away the hair from my face, like he used to when I was small. "We should have—*I* should've made you come home before."

I wanted to tell him that it wasn't his fault, that I wouldn't have gone, but all I could do was weep. All the pain and confusion I'd gone through the past couple of days merged with all I'd gone through the last couple of years, and behind that, the surge of all of the pain of the last decade, it all released in the tears that soaked the front of his shirt.

I don't know how long I cried, but my head was starting to ache along with my throat by the time it subsided. I wanted to close my eyes. To sleep. To have all this be a nightmare.

"We could be together now," Dad said quietly.

"What do you mean?"

"If you stay here. With me."

I released him, stepping back. His eyes reflected the fire more as they grew darker. Horror mixed with devastation, because either he didn't understand what he was suggesting...or he did.

"No. I can't." My voice cracked. "Dad, I can't stay here."

"It's not safe for you. Alone," he said in a voice that started out as his, but slowed, stretched deeper, "*And it's so cold in the dark.*"

No.

I couldn't bear to watch him twist and change into something horrible like Maevyn had. If I had to watch that, I wouldn't come back from it. I took in the sight of him there, while he still looked like *him*, and ran.

The ghost-lit path was still there so I followed it. I had no plan. I didn't even know if I was being chased. All I could see was the image of my father with the fire behind him, holding his violin in one hand and reaching for me with the other. My mind became a wind tunnel of my own screams until something snarled from the dark in front of me, and without thinking, I turned, running between the giant trunks of trees and into the forest.

I didn't get far before reason snapped back into me, stopping me in my tracks with a few fun facts about my situation. I was now lost in a dark forest. The forest was in another realm. The other realm was filled with ghosts and demons. And something was after me.

I could hear it moving through the undergrowth, its high pitched whine. Something cold and wet touched my fingers. I flinched, but then reached out my hand and felt the familiar soft fur. "*Cinder?*"

She whined again, and my eyes adjusted enough to see her shape. I ran my hand over her side. "Was that you growling earlier?" I whispered, my throat still raw.

As if in answer, the howling from earlier came again, but further away. Now that my eyes adjusted, there was a very slight blue glow to the place, perhaps from the silver sea.

I crouched down, petting the scruff of her neck with both hands. I didn't know if orts could be made with dog's shadows. But the way she was shaking, I doubted she was anything that belonged here.

"Can you take me to Mattie?" I asked, realizing as soon as I did so that I probably didn't really know how dogs worked. "Cinder," I said with hopefully enough authority, then clicked my tongue like I would when calling a cat, "ride?"

I could just make out the swishing of her tail and the white of her teeth. I hit the flashlight on and kept my hand on her as she started to lead me to an opening in the trees, but the path there was not the one I'd run from. It was narrower and partly overgrown.

"I'm really trusting you here," I told the dog, but she was the only one of us that seemed confident of where we were heading.

Eventually, the sky lightened from black into a deep bluish gray, and the path transitioned from dirt to half-buried cobblestones. The sulfur smell still lingered, but the air around it was crisper. The trees became smaller but more dense until they ran together, the ground smoothed into wood. I could see, thanks to the familiar golden light that emanated from above, that I'd come full circle.

I stood in the library of the Adair house.

It was the layout that gave it away. I'd certainly never seen it this well lit before, but the same mysterious glow that had illuminated the house earlier was here as well. Some creeping, blue-green vines with iridescent leaves covered much of the walls and shutters. Moss grew like mold along soft surfaces. Behind me, the space I'd entered was a random opening at the end of the room where I'd guess an outer wall used to be. Still, it wasn't quite as transformed as the other side of the house had been.

Logically, I knew that if I went into the hall, there should be the dividing door, and going through it *should* lead to the wall along the stairway then the kitchen door where I'd left two generations of my Adair family and one lost elderly child. But I strongly suspected that beyond the door here was the darkness that led deeper into Midnight.

So effectively, the place I'd just found my way out of was also in front of me.

The stack of books and cassette player still sat under the desk, now coated green. The place where I'd spotted the box that I now knew had contained the knife— a gift from Hawthorne to Mom apparently—was empty. I knew there was a back staircase, probably at the other end of this side of the hall, which would lead to the dividing door upstairs...which likely also led back to the dark.

Cinder sniffed along the furniture. She'd been right so far, so I followed her to the next room, once again jumping at my own reflection in the mirror as I passed it.

Only this time, the reflection wasn't mine.

With a hand on either side of the mantle, she leaned forward, scrutinizing, hazel eyes rimmed in the residual smear of black eyeliner, staring into the library where I was from its twin where she stood. She saw me, then pointed with her chin to where Cinder's tail disappeared down the hall.

"Can't get out that way," Mattie said warily. "You can't get out any way."

38

Parting Glass

Hearing Mattie, Cinder came bounding back into the room. She stopped beneath the mirror and jumped up, knocking a few knick-knacks off the mantle with her paws, tail wagging.

"Hey girl!" Mattie's voice went up the way people's tend to when talking to animals or small children, and a smile spread up her cracked lips as she placed her hands on the glass. "I told you to stay, didn't I? Yes, *I fucking did!*"

Cinder whined happily at the mirror a couple more times before I knelt to pat her sides. "Hush. She's okay. You *are* okay," I said to Mattie. "Aren't you?"

"Well, Talia. One of us appears to be stuck in a mirror, and I'm kinda worried that it's me."

"I don't know. I think it might be both of us. Which makes no sense, but this place..." I stood and got a better look at her. "Wait, so you are *you*, right?"

She tilted her head. "I could ask you the same thing. What a *fun* game we don't have time for."

"It's just I've seen—"

"Oh, *you've* seen?" She went suddenly shrill. "Hey, you remember how I didn't want to have to shoot your grandma earlier?"

"Uh..."

"I just want you to remember how *against* gunning down your relatives I was when I tell you I kinda had to shoot your mom. Oh, but don't worry"—I caught the ragged edge to her voice as she ran her fingers up her face and folded them together at the top of her head—"it didn't bother her in the *slightest*."

"Right. Mattie, that wasn't her. It was...a trick." It was at the tip of my tongue to tell her about my dad, but tears threatened to come as soon as I even cracked the door of that recent memory open. "What you saw was a trick. Mom is with Vivian and Kehente over...somewhere." I pointed my thumb at the wall. "I gave her his heart, and Hawthorne had no doubt she was the real thing, and he knew her better than I ever did."

"Well fantastic. You wouldn't want to be a part of whatever gene pool that thing belonged to." She paced in a circle. "By the way, you were right; my gun *is* useless against these things. But it's great for opening doors in dire situations apparently. I set it down once I got clear of...upstairs, and"—she reached down and came up with a green shotgun-shaped stick—"now it's even more useless. Though I guess, if whatever I hear in the walls decides to come in, I can try throwing this at it."

"But how did you end up here?"

"The short answer is that I'm an idiot. I went to follow you once everyone was distracted by what was happening outside. And I thought I saw...but of course I knew it couldn't have been. But seeing him..."

"*Who?*"

"My brother. He...drowned." The word sank in her throat. "A few years back. But I thought, well, everything being weird as it is, maybe it *could* be him. His spirit. Ghost. Whatever. Maybe he needed to tell me something. I guess spending all that time not looking at the past gave me some blind spots about myself because I didn't recognize the desperate part of me that took over. So I followed him up those stairs until he disappeared down the hall, then I started trying doors. Only the last one opened and I went inside, like *an idiot*—"

"I know," I said, seeing the look in her eyes and wanting to save her from reliving it. "I saw her. *It.*"

"Talia"—she rested her arms on the mantle and closed her eyes—"*Did* you make some deal with a demon? Is that why this is happening?"

"I didn't have a choice." Each syllable was wrapped in shame as I spoke. "And if I told anyone about it, I would've been cursed, and I thought my mom would have been lost. But...no. This is happening because Hawthorne is some prince who tried to escape the Everlands. And because of some deal between his queen mother and the demon king. And other alien politics I don't understand."

"So. Many. Questions," she said, punctuating each word with a soft thump of her head on the backs of her folded hands.

"And"—I sighed, tapping my finger on the cool glass—"it's happening *here* because I wouldn't let Vivian send Mom away. Because of that bargain I made. Or thought I'd made. Not surprising that making a deal with a demon comes out pretty one-sided in their favor. So Hawthorne was right, the demon had been protecting me as long as I did what I was told to tried and get his heart. I just didn't realize...I didn't realize a lot of things until it was too late. I'm..." I could feel the lump forming in my throat, the sting of tears starting again. "I'm really sorry for all of it."

"So...you *did* give Hawthorne's heart to your mom, and it fixed her?"

"Yeah."

"Was that what the demon told you to do?"

"No...he was *pretty* insistent that I give it to him."

"Okay, but you didn't? So would this King of Midnight...*not* have taken over this place if you *had* given the thing to this demon?"

"Well no, it sounded like that was always on his agenda."

"Then...it doesn't sound like this has much to do with you."

"But if Mom had been sent to Stillview or wherever instead of here—"

"This place is a fold in the Veil, like Hawthorne said, remember? She probably couldn't have left if she tried. Elmwood has a way of making people stay."

"I...hadn't thought that."

"Well, bask away in the warm glow of my absolution. You didn't do this. I hate to tell you more bad news here, but you're just a girl. An exceedingly unlucky one, but still just a girl. And probably also an idiot. Just like me. But bad luck and gullibility aside, if you don't figure out a way to get yourself out of there, then neither one of us has a chance."

"You said there was no way out of here."

"Yeah. But now I'm wondering if that's just on my side." She exhaled shakily. "There's something over here, Talia. With me. Not just whatever I hear groaning in the walls, I hear...things. Outside. If *your* side is where everyone else is, then I think maybe...you're in the *real* house. Which means you have a *real* chance to escape that I don't."

"I'm not sure that's how things work."

"Look, over here, if you open that door, it leads to a version of your house that is quiet and empty. It feels *lonely.* Not just in that it's missing people. It looks like the house we all walked into, but it's like a doll house, it's...fake. I think that if I were to open these shutters, I wouldn't see the same thing you would there. And not only would I wish I hadn't seen it, the things I'm hearing out there would rush in."

She winced at the thought. "Or maybe I *am* one of those shadowlings. Didn't Hawthorne say they were all crazy? Because the way I feel—"

"You're not crazy," I told her. "You're in the Midnight Lands. It messes with people."

The way this place worked, I knew I couldn't know where she was in terms of distance. She looked only a few feet from me, but she might really be miles away. But she was right. She had been led somewhere the rest of us weren't.

Noc had put her in some kind of cage.

"Cinder might be able to sniff out an exit, then you can find Shane, and do whatever it takes to get everyone out of this Hellscape." The fear in her eyes betrayed the steadiness of her voice, and seeing it there made me resolute.

"You're getting out of here. Hawthorne said he was going to make a bargain to undo what happened. Just...look. This?" I waved my hand at the glass. "Obviously it isn't really a mirror. It's a window. So, what if we just break it?"

"NO." Mattie's eyes grew wider. "Absolutely *no*. I thought of that too but couldn't get past the idea that behind the glass is only more of that awful dark. Or worse."

"We could—" I lost whatever not-very-good idea I'd been about to suggest when the sound of twisting, splintering wood fell from somewhere above.

Mattie and I both looked up. There was nothing, well, nothing *new*, happening on the ceiling here. But Mattie hadn't looked away from whatever was above her.

"What is it?" I asked, trying to angle myself against the glass to see what she was seeing.

She took a few more seconds before lowering her eyes to meet mine and forcing a smile. "Nothing it...it's been doing that."

"Mattie?"

"You said Hawthorne has some sort of plan?"

"Some sort, but it's *Hawthorne*, so..."

"Then find him. If that hallway door doesn't work, you might as well try the windows, but I think it's a really, *really* good idea to get the fuck out of this house, all versions of it. Now."

"I can't just *leave* you here."

"Oh, you're not. You're getting help. Big difference."

The cracking came again, and this time she backed away from the mantle with her moss shotgun in hand. Her eyes glared up at the ceiling, and without looking away, she said, "Gwen and Tomas Pratt."

"What?"

"You get out, steal someone's heart like your mom did if you have to, but if this cursed hole of a town is lost. *You* get out. Hopefully with Shane and the others, hopefully not aged a hundred years. You get out and find my parents, Gwen and Tomas Pratt. Tell them some happier version of what happened to me, but Talia, you promise me that they *know* I'm dead."

"You are *not* going to die," I snapped.

"That's the spirit." She wobbled on her feet as the building she was in shook, books tumbled, picture frames shattered. "But unless I escape with you, you'll never know whether that's true or not, and I need you to tell them I'm dead. Please. They will never stop looking for me if they think I'm lost, and if they look enough, they could end up here and I can't....*I can't...*"

"I promise," I said, and this one felt so much worse than the ones I'd made to the demon or the faery. "I'll tell them."

"I'm trusting you." She managed a tight, grateful smile. "I told you Cinder was a good judge of character—"

We both yelped and jumped back as a root nearly the size of a telephone pole exploded straight through the floor on her side, sending wood boards flying as it unfurled itself across the room.

"It's changing." She turned back to me while taking in the still-settling room. "This place is...*shifting*. Maybe something else has opened up somewhere then. Look, I'm going to keep trying to find my way around. I don't think it's safe to stay here."

"Probably not." I wanted to say something empowering, something optimistic, something that would make her feel less alone. Instead I went with, "Don't die."

"Back atcha." Her chin trembled a bit as she looked at her dog. "Keep her safe, okay?"

"I will," I said over the lump still in my throat.

"I wasn't talking to you," she said over her shoulder, then she was gone out of sight.

Cinder was barking again, but not because of Mattie. She was barking at the dividing door. I backed away from the mantle as her barks turned to growls. The hallway was darker than the library, but I could still see the door clear enough. It was just a door, not opened to the dark, with a skeleton key in its lock that was unbothered when the door handle turned above it—the brass oval moving just a bit one way, then the other, as though something with small hands were trying to figure out how the thing worked.

I ran forward and turned the key.

Guess I wasn't going that way.

I looked at the mirror, now just with only me in its frame. Cinder was still growling at the door. I pulled at the shutters on the nearest window as a *thud* came from behind me. It didn't budge. Cinder's growl turned to threatening barks. Another *thud*. Something was trying to break its way in. I noticed the latch and I flipped it, then pulled the shutter open.

The sky was the same discolored one I'd left behind when I went through the dark, but the outside wasn't the same at all. At least, I didn't think it was. Instead of the side yard, there were trees, pale and slender, coming right up to the house as though it was in their way.

The thudding became louder, more insistent.

Thankfully, the window ledge was low. I slapped my hands on my legs to call for Cinder, who hesitated for a couple of more barks, before following me over it. I didn't turn to see what burst into the room as I ran into the trees.

My just-made-exactly-right-now plan was to circle back to the front of the house to hopefully give me some semblance of my bearings. But I didn't want to go back inside of it at all. Not yet. I wasn't ready to confront what Dad had told me, and I wasn't ready to have to tell anyone what had happened to him. Not only because I didn't think I could say it out loud, to make it real, but because I didn't think I could handle them not caring.

Going by all the Midnight Lands I was still making my way through, I knew Hawthorne's plan hadn't worked. Maybe he just hadn't found Noc yet, but even still, I couldn't guess at what bargain he meant to strike with the demon.

If it weren't for the fact that Mom still held his heart, literally and figuratively, I might have suspected Hawthorne had lied to us and maybe just fled to save himself. But he cared about her more than himself it seemed. I wondered what it would be like to carve your own heart out, only half dying in the process. How much it must have hurt. Or how much it might have numbed. Or what it would be like to love someone enough to do it for in the first place.

My own heart hardened with each beat.

I had nothing worth carving out of me to offer in exchange for escape, but I had something I could *steal*. Noc hadn't cared if Hawthorne's "talisman" was given to me or if I'd come across it discarded on the ground. He wasn't trying to keep its power intact, he just wanted to keep it from Hawthorne.

He wanted *Hawthorne*. For his errand to be complete.

My stomach twisted with the realization that maybe I was more like my mother than I thought. That coldness that moved through me so often, always mingled with anxiety and fear, maybe that was the same sort of cold that lived in her and allowed her to do what she did to me.

I tried to tell myself that Hawthorne deserved to be betrayed, but I didn't believe that. The guy from folklore, Thorny Jack, Ruiner, and...fuck faery, that didn't seem like the same guy who had rescued Mom and Kehente. Who didn't give up on breaking her curse. Who had run off toward the sound of danger to help Shane and Lydia.

I didn't know if I could barter for all of Elmwood to be free from the Midnight Lands. I didn't even know how much of the town was left to barter for. But for Mattie, Shane, Lydia. For Kehente. For Vivian. For Mom. I believed they could still be freed from this place for the right price.

I slowed. Cinder stayed at my side, not venturing ahead. She'd probably given up on sniffing out anything familiar. It was an unsettling reminder that I was supposed to be in charge. That I was supposed to know what I was doing.

I guessed that if I went into what felt like a safe enough distance straight from where we'd fled through the window and then arched right, it *should l*ead me back to the driveway. I knew better than to actually expect that to happen in this shifting place, but it was better than wandering aimlessly.

Only, it turned out, I hadn't been.

When the white of the vine-wrapped walls of the house first peeked through the branches ahead, I knew I'd have ended up standing before it no matter which way I'd gone. There was nothing beyond it but the purple-stained sky above an insurmountable fence of those enormous pale trees, the tops of which were swallowed by darkening clouds.

The black of Midnight was forming in blotches along what I could see of the horizon through the branches around me, like a watercolor brush pressed against it wielded by some cosmic giant with no talent for symmetry.

It's stitching deeper into this place. There'd been a sense of permanence in the pitch of the sky flecked with those foreign stars above the silver sea. I had the terrible thought that once those stars began to shine over me, over Elmwood, there would be no undoing it.

Hawthorne was running out of time. Which meant I needed to take his heart from Mom somehow to end this. I already hated myself for it. For the very idea of doing something that would satisfy Noc, no matter the reason.

Set in my resolve, I moved toward the porch, not at all anticipating being knocked to the ground by what seemed to be a wall of smoke.

39

Eaten

I flailed my limbs to scramble out from under it, or tried to. It wasn't exactly solid, but it was somehow still heavy—hovering just inches above me. Like fighting a cloud, my fingers would break through a gap in its fluctuating mass only to have it push my hand back down as it closed itself over it. I was quickly figuring out that it wasn't as huge as it felt at first as it drew itself more compact where I kept struggling against it. I kept at it until its forced shape was enough like mine, so I eventually had something solid enough to push away from.

With a growl Cinder dove at it then, snapping her teeth at the air it became, driving it back.

I turned to run for the house, but was met by more smoke. Smoke that didn't have a scent and was cool to the touch. It broke into inky clouds that quickly became more defined, until dozens of human forms stood in front of the house and along the trees. But I knew they were not shaped of clouds of smoke.

They were shaped of *shadows*.

Adults. Children. And I realized not only human ones. Some were tiny, wispy things floating above the rest. Some towering. Some mis-shapen. All creatures that were once living, carved away from who they had been. Now remnants. Ghosts. All still as stone, pointing their incorporeal fingers in the same direction. A silent, faceless choir with a single command as its song.

So Noc wasn't quite done with me yet. The trees I was being pointed towards had parted to form what seemed to be the only way I'd be allowed to go. Behind me Cinder had backed away from the shadow she had attacked as it dissipated, reforming near the rest of them.

I reached back and lightly tugged the scruff of her neck along as I started down the path, having no doubt who I would find at the end of it.

"*His name, Tali.*" A whisper broke from somewhere in the throng of dead.

"Dad?" Nothing answered me back. Not one of the phantoms moved. My chest tightened. I kept walking.

The hazy amethyst light of the forest was bright enough for me to see the path was formed on autumn leaves pressed into the ground, but I couldn't see much beyond that. I realized, since fleeing the house with Cinder, not a bird or a single scurrying thing had made a sound. The whole place had been silent as shadows, which was why the sudden rustling ahead was so jarring, but the figures emerging from the trees were blessedly familiar.

Shane was using a long stick as a walking staff. His forearm was wrapped with a makeshift bandage made from the sleeve of his shirt. The dark splotches that bloomed on it matched the streaks on the front of his jeans. Lydia held his arm and a staff of her own to help her walk. Her hair was a salt and pepper cascade around her shoulders. Dried blood stained her forehead.

Surprise morphed into worry when he saw me with Cinder. "Where is everyone?" he whispered.

"Nowhere we can get to, and nowhere safe, just like us. I take it Hawthorne didn't find you."

"We've just been trying to get back to the house, but...it keeps circling us. Driving us further away. This is at least new," he said of the path, then furrowed his brow at me. "Are you alright?"

I dodged the question. "Are *you* guys?"

"We will be better when we get back to our own soil." Lydia spoke with certainty, though her voice shook.

I nodded. "Do I want to know what 'it' is?"

Shane's eyes were wide. "*No.*"

"That's your gun?" I pointed to the stick.

"No..." He looked at me strangely. "My gun was—"

The rumble came like ground thunder, reverberating through my bones. Cinder growled as the singing began. Maevyn's soft voice came from close by in a slow, sad melody that could be a lullaby, a likely terrifying one given the source, but thankfully I didn't know the language of this one.

"—eaten," Shane continued, ignoring the song. "My gun. It was *eaten.* It could have done the same to us, but it just keeps *herding* us."

"I'm guessing it's no accident that you found me now then. I think we've been rounded up, and now we're being led to him."

"Who?"

"The demon after Hawthorne."

"That would be the same thing that Wes called up right before hell broke all the way loose?" he asked.

"Yep."

He gave one short but firm shake of his head. "Yeah, no, we're not doing that."

A child's laughter, also from Maevyn, came from the other side of the trees.

"I think you'll see we don't have a choice," I sighed.

"Does this path lead back to the house?" he asked.

"It did when I got on it. Now? Who knows? The house is be-ing...guarded anyway."

"How guarded?"

"Like, no-hope-of-getting-in guarded."

"This is no place for hope at all," Lydia snipped impatiently. "Was she healed? Your mother?"

I gritted my teeth and nodded. "Yeah."

"And?" she pressed. "What about Hawthorne?"

"Didn't want to be. He said that since we all sank into the Midnight Lands, it was better to stay as he was here. He wanted to strike some bargain to end all of this, so either he hasn't found the demon yet...or he didn't have anything that the demon wanted more than him."

"Hawthorne's the closest thing we have to a native ally here, which makes him our best shot at escaping this," Shane said carefully. "Cole's still in the house?"

"Last I knew everyone was still in *some* version of the house."

"That's why it's guarded then." He nodded. "He would come back for her, and it seems like nothing here wants that to happen."

The growl came again, wrapping around us from all directions. I shushed Cinder when she began to bark, and surprisingly, she obeyed. "I take it that whatever is making that sound is your stalker?"

"Yeah," he said flatly, his eyes set on something behind me. "But I think this other one is yours."

Maevyn stood on the path about twenty trees away, wound back down to look the same as she had when I first met her on the path—a harmless little girl in a little green dress, little black shoes, and little hair ribbon all perfectly in place.

"Miss, there is danger in dallying here," she said, her little voice sweet. A surprising sadness rolled over me. Maevyn had been a real child once. Eaten by the Everlands, carved away from her shadow so that echoes of her could be stitched together with other remnants of once real people so that she could ensnare others to the same fate. Others, like my father.

"I'm pretty sure *here's* not where the danger is, Maevyn. What if...what if I helped you find Starry Anna now?" I asked, an idea forming. "You remember her, don't you? You lost her. When you lost your mom."

She tilted her head. "That...was before."

"But, I'll bet you still want your doll back, don't you? And you still want to find your mom."

"Talia..." Shane warned.

"I...I *do*!" Her little voice cried out, seeming to surprise even herself. Her hands clasped together, and she looked quickly from side to side. For a second, she looked like the lost child she had once been, then she lowered her chin, looking up at me, eyes cold. Her voice went guttural. *"I don't like this game."*

"Talia, we need to *go*." Shane tried to pull me back, but I pushed his hand away and stepped toward the girl.

"Maevyn, you can remember. It's all right." I was hooked now by the desperate thought that if I could make her focus on who she had been, then the more disturbing, murder-ballad loving shadow she's been stitched to might not be able to take over. Then there would be no more dutiful ort.

A fine theory, only in theory, I thought when her green eyes blackened and her body began to quickly morph larger—dark cracks breaking it apart. Her small face locked into wide-eyed terror as it twisted back, and the other Maevyn's head came around the other side with his lopsided smile—eyes black beneath his floppy, sandy hair as his wiry frame stepped forward.

"Little dove, little dove..." he crooned. "Come back to a path, different but the same. And once again we have parts to play in my master's game."

"I suppose this time you're here to keep me on this path then?"

"Mercy me, miss. But our part has changed. Now we're to play a siren song, and you"—he drew the dagger from his belt and started toward me—"could help marvelous much there."

"Wait—" I began, but Shane yanked me by my shoulder, stepping in front of me with his staff raised like a bat despite his injured arm.

"Go. Find Hawthorne," he said without turning.

Before I could argue that, unless he was secretly a wizard, that staff wasn't going to help him much, Lydia yanked me back, harder than her grandson had, knocking me to the ground. She limped off to the side of the path, waving her arms and calling like a bird, trying to draw Maevyn's attention.

"Gran—no."

"Oh, where do you think you got your courage?" she called. "You go."

Maevyn looked annoyed at first, then grinned wider. As he turned to her, Shane rushed forward and landed a blow to the back of his knees.

He didn't buckle, only stopped and looked at Shane with disdain. "You struck me."

Shit. I braced myself for him to mutate into the stretched out horror show he had become before, but instead he twirled the dagger, gripping the handle to angle the blade to its side and spun at Shane.

I watched uselessly as Shane blocked the first downward swing from landing in his chest. Maevyn quickly circled his free hand up to swat the end of the staff away and swipe the dagger around it.

Just before the blade could stick his side, Shane pivoted and managed to elbow him hard in the chin, gaining back some of the distance he needed to take the swift, controlled jab of the staff that connected with Maevyn's chest, sending him staggering back a few feet.

Maevyn smiled.

In one fluid motion, he switched the dagger to his other hand while spinning at Shane, deflecting the staff that cracked his forearm by forcing it down. Once again, he was poised to stab the blade into Shane's chest when something struck him hard in the face, tearing a dark hole across his cheek.

It had been a rock, aimed by Lydia who stood with another one already in hand.

The distraction was enough for Shane to twist the staff into Maevyn's wrist before the blade could land, then smoothly ram the stick into his chest once again, shoving him further back.

This time Maevyn didn't smile. His hand went to the hole in his cheek and his eyes went to Lydia. Shane wasted no time, swinging to club the dagger from the ort's hand, but quicker than I could register what was happening, Maevyn grabbed the staff, yanking it—and Shane—toward him, driving the blade into his center.

I thought the scream was Lydia's—it was mine. Everything went slow and quiet. Maevyn slid the glistening red blade from Shane as he fell, his eyes on Lydia as she ran to her grandson, a grin crawling up his cracked face.

I hurtled to stop her, knowing I'd be too late, but it seemed Maevyn heard the same shrill cry just as I did, both of us turning to see a young girl running up the path just as she leapt at him. I recognized the shape of the knife she held in the moment just before the silver of it sliced into Maevyn's neck and lodged there. I recognized the girl the moment after, but only by what she wore: the brightly colored housedress beneath Shane's denim jacket—now rolled up to her elbows.

Kehente, her disheveled braids now jet-back and her smooth face flushed, glowered at the ort as he dropped, his head dangling as black streams cascaded from the wound. She watched him, still panting, as though she needed to make sure he was dead.

Lydia didn't seem to notice any of this, rolling Shane over by his shoulders and pressing her hands on his sternum, blood spilling over her fingers, spreading over the gray of his shirt. His eyes were blinking, but his face had gone colorless, except for the red he sputtered through his lips.

"Don't try to talk," Lydia ordered gently. "Do not try to move."

"He's not gone yet," Kehente said in what I knew wasn't English, but maybe because of this place, I still understood. It took me a second to realize who she meant.

Maevyn hadn't quite made it to the ground, suspended in the air by the tendrils of falling shadow. I shoved him, and he drifted like a balloon toward the trees. Not knowing what else to do, I slipped off my cardigan and handed it down. Lydia took it with barely a glance and pressed it to the wound with Kehente's smaller hands joining hers in trying to keep Shane from bleeding out.

A crackling sound came from where Maevyn was crumpling like a wad of paper. The odd jumble of him was propelled by the smoke that had begun to billow from his edges, wrapping and enveloping what was left of him, until with a howl of wind, he shot straight above us, snapping away branches and whipping up the leaves from the ground.

I threw my arm over my face, dropping down to help Kehente and Lydia in trying to shelter Shane from the debris, horrifyingly aware of how helpless we were as the black mass that had begun as Maevyn began to swirl down like a funnel. I squeezed my eyes shut against the wind, opening them only when it ceased, and saw the shadows had settled into the shape of a *monstrously* giant wolf.

It was tattered, as though it had run out of flesh for its edges. Fangs the size of children's hands sat in its exposed jawbone; claws attached to the protruding bones of its paws sat on either side of the path, blocking it. But its eyes...were moons in a midnight sky.

Fear lanced through me.

"Leave them," a bored voice called.

40

Twilight

Hawthorne swaggered out of the trees behind us with a twirl of his sword. Beneath his green coat, thorny vines wrapped around his chest like armor. The pallor of his skin was still there, but the sickly frailty was not. At his side was Cinder. It was only then I realized she'd slipped away in the commotion. "You have enough new playthings, and I'm the one you're after anyway."

I could have sworn the beast laughed. I knew he could lock me in another illusion or, considering his shoulders alone stood taller than I did, even bite me in half with one snap of his jaws. I knew I should probably be cowering, but at this moment, my sense of self-preservation was at war with my useless rage. I wanted to do something, anything, to *hurt* him.

"My, you have to admire his commitment to that heroism," Hawthrone said, pausing at Shane's body.

"He will not end here," Lydia said without taking her eyes from her grandson's face. "*You* will get him back to our ground."

To end there, I knew was what she didn't say.

"He will be at peace, grandame," he said quietly. With a glance my way, I saw the green was gone from his eyes, replaced with a crow-black that now sat above the blue. With a familiar flash of gold along his irises, darkness began to cover Shane's chest, filling the wound like a plug.

"You took back your heart?" If so, my plan to hand it over had just been foiled, so the relief in my voice surprised even me. Apparently, I wasn't as cold as I thought.

"How many times must I say it?" He half grinned. "It isn't mine anymore."

"Well. You," came Noc's voice from the depths of the wolf, "have almost managed to be surprising, Heir of Shadows."

"Noc." Hawthorne sheathed his sword. "I can't say I was entirely surprised that you were the one meddling with my escape."

"It was not your escape I was meddling with."

"You know, you aren't nearly as mad as Orias. Conniving? Sure. Vindictive? Absolutely. Cruel? Without a doubt. But not *mad*. I suppose that's why I was shocked at your recklessness in this."

"*My* recklessness?" echoed Noc's voice. "You thought to abdicate yourself, Prince of Dawn. By carving out your living heart to dwell in the Ruined World with your latest human lover. Dramatic even for you. Think of your dear mother."

"I've thought of her better than she's ever thought of me. A son of Dawn with a heart of Midnight? I agree with any that call me an abomination. I never understood why you took *my* curse so personally, but Cousin, this could have been your chance to be *rid* of me."

"I might have been glad of it"—the wolf's eyes lowered—"had you given up your *shadow* heart instead."

"And give up these new talents?" He waved his hand and formless dark shifted and stretched from the trees into the path before receding.

So, that was what he'd meant by being able to draw from this place. Hawthorne was, as Noc said, a dual creature. The heart he'd cut out belonged to Dawn...but he'd had another. And things were more powerful where they belonged.

Noc's wolf head tilted. "Yes. What a wonder you've so long dodged ascending to a fate that would've allowed you to master those ill-gotten gifts."

"True. *So* irresponsible of me. What a scoundrel I am to not want to be forever caught between Orias and *Mother*. But the one thing they both agreed on was that my curse means I'm destined to rule in Twilight. Maybe Orias can tell me himself how appalled he is at what I did to avoid it, or how impressed. One never knows with him. But I'm just on my way to Midnight to discuss terms with him."

"And what would you say to my grim liege?" There was a bite in Noc's voice.

"That his ArchCarver has gone rogue for one. It seemed a stretch that Orias would deal with Dawn, but as soon as I knew you were the one entangling things, I knew it was *you* that plotted with the Queen. Mad as he may be, Orias never matched your enthusiasm for vexing me, and he is not half as ambitious."

There was a creak of wood and whisper of leaves as the trees parted, and Mom, along with a bewildered looking Vivian, wandered out. Mom glanced at Noc without so much as a shudder. Vivian, her white-gold hair loose and wild, clutched her stone pendant with one hand and her mouth with the other as she backed away from the wolf creature, nearly tripping over Shane's legs.

Without looking, Mom grabbed her arm to stop her from doing so. My warm memories of her were battling the idea of who Dad had told me she really had been. The memories were losing.

"Ah." Noc angled his head at the women. "And that is why you have called the shadows to reshape my path? To tattle?"

"I've just been rearranging the playing board you've set up so that it now goes *straight* to Orias' Keep." As Hawthorne spoke, light began to filter in through a nearby section of forest. The trees there became familiar, so did the golden fall sky behind them. And the unmistakable sound of cars whizzing down a road. "Apparently mastery comes easy when something is innate, so I've also made this other path for my brief companions. They're returning to their realm."

Noc sniffed the air. "The man is nearly a part of no one's realm. And that small one was claimed by *mine*."

Kehente's eyes were the one thing about her that hadn't changed at all, still holding that spark of defiance even as she trembled under his gaze. Seeing her as the child she had been all along, as the little girl who had her life stolen away, made my heart ache.

"Not anymore." Hawthorne offered her his hand and pulled her up beside him. "And this isn't your dominion entirely, is it? Not yet. This place is still in Twilight."

Thunder sat low in Noc's throat as he lowered his wolf head. "Still closer to my realm than Dawn, Prince of Briars. But I will *allow* the old and the dying to leave."

Hawthorne leaned toward Noc's jaw. "You can take off the illusion of authority along with that ort suit. As it sits, Twilight is in essence neutral ground, which makes you and I evenly matched here."

"A shadow heart beating in you does not give you power over *me*, boy," Noc rumbled. "Nor does it give you rule in Midnight, and night does fall *quick*. The old and the dying only."

"That means you, Mother," Mom said nonchalantly.

"Nonsense," Vivian said, her terror obvious but still managing a tsk. She came to me and brushed my hair back from my shoulders. "I'm not leaving you."

"If you stay, he will only use you to hurt her," Mom said. "That's what he does."

Knowing how right Mom was allowed me to infuse a false calm into my voice. I took Vivian's hands. "I need you to help the others get to safety. Hawthorne will get Mom and I out, but your chance is now."

"I'll be old again, won't I?" Kehente asked, looking mournfully at the door. "If I go back to my own soil, I'll get buried in all the years I missed."

"Yes," Hawthorne answered softly.

I watched in a detached kind of way as Mom wrapped the child in the hug I'd been longing for. "If I can, I'll help you find your family," she told her. "I'll make sure they know what happened to you. To us."

"The only story you could tell is how I became a ghost. That's all they are now too. My parents and sisters." She looked at Noc, then down at Shane. "Still, better to be a ghost out there, than what here makes you."

"Well," Hawthorne said, crouching down, "you're not wrong."

"I know him." Mom pointed at Shane. "Don't I?"

Shane only squinted at her, looking better but far from well, groaning as Hawthorne pulled him up. His eyes went wide at the sight of Noc, then he looked to the girl wearing his jacket. "Who...?" he asked weakly, glancing over all our faces. "Where's Mattie?"

"Right behind you," I lied.

"Come grandame," Hawthorne told Vivian with a wink and a grin that still managed to be charming. "I'm actually trying to be quite gallant here, but it's not my strong suit. Help me help them."

"It'll be okay," I told her and hoped what was meant to be a reassuring smile didn't come out as grim.

Hawthorne transferred Shane's arm from his shoulders to Vivian's, patting his back. "Live to die another day, friend."

Lydia leaned heavily on her staff as she limped, so I took her arm and led her to the door. "Don't hold on to false hope. When you get the chance to escape from this place, take it," she told me and, with a last squeeze of her hand, followed Vivian and Shane over the threshold between worlds.

I could smell the fresh chill of the air from my world, hear the signs of life. From my side came a whine. I knelt, and with a voice higher than usual, asked Cinder, "Hey. You wanna go on a ride?"

Her tongue immediately fell out of her mouth; her tail swished. I thought of how much Mattie probably missed her right now, how alone she must feel stuck wandering her house-shaped cage. Even if she didn't blame me for her being there, I did.

"Go on." I snapped my fingers toward the door, but she hesitated, her brown eyes looking up at me expectantly until Lydia whistled for her. She reluctantly went to her, nose down, stopping once over the threshold to look at me with her ears pulled back just as the trees were pressing back together.

I shivered in my short-sleeved dress but left my bloody cardigan on the ground.

"Now," Noc said. "Cole will return to the Midnight Lands with me."

"What?" I whipped around, the panic sharp and sudden.

"Hmm. Interesting play." Hawthorne strolled up beside Mom. "But, I think not. If Orias wanted her, he'd have to reclaim her himself. Once she was freed, her will was her own. He knows this. And so do you."

"Fine and fair," Noc considered. "Yet. A debt is owed, and her place will be taken. As *you* know." When he looked at me, the whispering of the leaves grew louder from the forest. "So the daughter must come if the lady will not."

"Um—" I began, but the "Grownups Are Talking" look from Mom shut me up.

"Oh, always playing the loyal servant, Noc. But I know the truth of you." Hawthorne rolled his newly dark eyes my way and pulled Mom behind him. "This isn't about the tithe or whatever you've promised the Dawn Queen, but If you want to pretend it is, fine. Let's get on with it. Take *me* to Orias."

"So noble a sacrifice. Though you would make a poor wife." Noc pulled his upper lips further away from the bones of his teeth in some malformation of a sneer aimed at Mom. "Your loathsome husband awaits in his loathsome lands, *my lady*."

"Husband?" My eyes popped at Mom, but she looked away.

Hawthorne drew his finger across her chin until her sad eyes met his gaze. "Orias is tithed a wife of his choosing," he said softly. "A wife to replace the one he lost. And each he loses after. Even if she was unwilling. Even if she was already chosen."

"You were *married*...to the King of Midnight?" The look on her face was confirmation enough. I glared at Hawthorne. "And *you* didn't think to mention this until now?"

"Oh, it hardly mattered." He cut his eyes at me. "Orias loses every wife, most soon after the wedding night. Or during. Which is why it seemed so odd that he would bother with coming after her. And to do all of *this*? The idea that he would conspire with Dawn, for *any* reason, was suspicious...but of course he didn't. The Grim King isn't a *bad* king. None of this was worth risking upsetting the Dark.

"But his Archcarver here, who he always knew to keep leashed, had other ideas. Had Noc gotten my heart, he would have a powerful bit of collateral while he was off roaming your world, delighting in the damage he does there untethered by the laws of Midnight. But since you were *at least* smart enough not to give it to him, now he needs some other leverage for when Orias seeks him out for all of that treachery. Like his escaped wife."

"Or her replacement," Noc growled. "The lady's will *is* her own, but that doesn't stop her from being part of Midnight as the wife of its king. As long as she chooses to live outside of it, then the Rule of Blood comes into play. This one"—he lowered his head so his eyes were level with mine—"is of her blood. Thus. *Suitable*."

I stepped back, the contents of my stomach curdling. Mom looked at me and shook her head in warning.

"Yes, Orias will be pleased. And was my heart to be a wedding gift?" Hawthorne mused. "Only, neither my heart nor a bride outweighs what I can offer Orias in return for his rolling Midnight back and freeing this town."

"Which is?" Noc asked, bored.

He pressed his forehead to Mom's for a few moments before turning to me. "Oh, I'll give him what both he and the Queen of Dawn have always wanted. What you no doubt promised to deliver. I will not only return, I will bind myself to the Twilight Lands willingly."

"No." Mom grabbed his shoulder. "If he wants a replacement, he can have my mother."

"Mom!" I gasped, realizing that she meant it.

Noc definitely laughed that time, a nightmarish sound coming from a ten-foot-tall monster wolf. The shadows began to shimmer. "So, you would finally end your roving ways and take on the mantle of rule. I don't care if you sit on the throne of Twilight or a barstool in—"

The shadows sighed in a chorus around me, and I could no longer make out what Noc was saying. In a breath, things were suddenly very wrong. Mom and Hawthorne stilled. Everything went dim, and what started as a whispering swelled into an indecipherable rush of sound.

My vision went black and I felt a dizzying swirl, but I didn't even have time to panic before it all began to recede.

"Did you not favor my realm?" Noc's voice asked, softer and more human.

The black faded into color, and I found myself standing on the bank of a familiar, murky river. Noc was in the middle of it, standing on the water. No longer a wolf, but the gentleman-thing he had been before. Above us the sky was dull, yellow tinged with the rose of the incoming sunset. The air nipped at the bare skin of my arms, waking my bandaged cut up with a throb. In the distance I could see the line of a bridge crossing the water.

This was Elmwood.

41

Bargains

"I thought to make a place for you in it that you could call home."
The water lapped at Noc's boots as he continued on as though there
was nothing odd about him walking on it. "I even left you a gift."

"A gift." I stared unflinching into the cold center of his eyes. "Is that
what you call what you did to my father?"

"Well, yes." He tilted his head. "You are quite possessive of people,
you know. Unwise. People are fickle. Even your mother. I told you she
was never yours and it...bothered you. So, I made you someone you
could keep. If you stayed."

"You...*murdered* my father..." I couldn't tell if I was shaking because of the cold, or out of fear or anger, but I wanted to throw up
either way. "And thought I'd be grateful?"

"I thought to make you stay," he said with sincerity I couldn't trust.
"*He* did not want you to be alone. As you are now. In a world that is
so very cruel."

"My world is no crueler than yours, and I don't want to be in a place
where a *thing* like you *exists*," I spat.

"I exist. *Everywhere.* My cruelty is natural. It's a choice with *your*
kind, yet still so prevalent. Especially in those who you love."

I tried to focus on pushing away the illusion I knew I must be in,
glad he was keeping his distance for this one. But it was sticking. So I

just tried to ignore his words, not because I knew they were attempts to manipulate me, but for the truth I knew they were laced with. "Hawthorne was right then? I'm leverage now to keep you safe from your boss?"

"Perhaps not. Perhaps Hawthorne will come rescue you. Though if we're being honest..." The water splashed at his boots as he began to leisurely pace. "He would have no reason to, would he? Not unless *she* urges him to, of course. But we are not being honest, you prefer to pretend. So let's *pretend* that she would do so. That she *would* come back for you, when she could take this interlude as her chance to escape, to run off with Hawthorne. Again."

As soon as he said it, I felt the dread roll up into my chest, letting me know I did actually suspect, with no small amount of pure misery, that Mom might just let me rot there. "And why would you just allow that?"

His smile then was viscous as he turned to me. "Would you like to know a secret?"

"God, no. No more secrets or bargains or promises—"

"I was never here for Hawthorne."

"Well, of course not. You just gave him a chance to escape while you do...whatever *this* is. Oh, let me guess, you're going to say you came here for me now."

He stepped closer to the muddy bank. "You? Dear Talia, if I had come for you, I would have already *had* you. My errand has truly been *Cole*. To return her to Midnight."

"Was it?" I said, feigning ignorance in the way he seemed to prefer doing. "*Awfully* odd choice then, to get her just short of your Midnight Lands just to leave her a chance to escape too. Come to think of it, it kind of seems like you could have finished your 'errand' at any time, if it were truly her."

He stopped mid step. "She was wedded to the Midnight King, do you know what that makes her?"

Oh. The shock hadn't allowed it to dawn on me before. "Queen?"

He looked to the sky as he resumed his pacing. *"Untouchable.* She is protected by Midnight. It's very old magic that binds that protection to her. Even I cannot break it. As Hawthorne said, none from my Lands can harm her or steal her. So. I waited. I watched. I listened. I spoke to her from the walls while I made the bridge between our realms. I told her beautiful tales of where she belongs—"

"Keeping her more confused and scared."

"No. It was her journey through the Sea that addled her, not me. I only adapted my plan to her state of mind to keep her from fleeing further."

"You told me holding his heart is what 'addled' her. Another lie. Hawthorne told me it was Orias that cursed her."

"Why would Orias curse her into forgetting she was his?" He glanced my way without turning. "The Moon Dark Sea of Midnight is protective and brutal. At its darkest phase, it is most...unpredictable. The journey over it had never been made before by a human. But then...carving one's heart out and presenting it as a talisman had also never been done before either. The handmaiden survived the journey because she held the heart of a faery, but not Cole. It washed away her mind."

"Then why did Hawthorne's heart fix it?"

"That I cannot say. Perhaps...because it was forged with the same dark and brutal magic as the Sea itself. Truly, I didn't yet know what he had given her at first, or what it might do to her if she were to get it back. So, I kept it apart from her. And in the meanwhile, I laid the groundwork with that broken boy to ensure he would play the part of summoning me. Yet. I would have rather it had been *you* that brought me here."

"That 'broken boy' ended up bleeding out on my kitchen floor."

He shrugged. "His desires were met as quickly as his usefulness expired. *Our* allegiance would have been far more...fruitful."

A chill moved through me at the thought of what that could have meant.

"You were almost correct before. At first, I did think of taking you as a lure. 'Bait' as you called it. But my ort was thwarted."

"Right. The birds you lied about sending to save me from that 'well-crafted ort'...that *you* crafted."

He shook his head. "Those bothersome Stitches. I had hoped I had given them enough diversions to keep them occupied elsewhere, but they were not just on the watch for the odd shadow kin. They were *searching* for something. Had I known what for, I would have changed my design for what needed to be done. But it was not until you revealed Hawthorne's weakened state and what he had told you about its corrosive nature that I began to realize what the talisman he'd fashioned must truly be: his own faery heart. Quite impressive. For him."

"I don't know if 'impressive' is the word I'd choose."

"Then you lack imagination. It was then I knew the Queen of Morning too had pieced together that her wayward prince was trying to break away, quite literally cutting what tethered him to her lands. Cutting away what made him hers. I knew he meant to live as some sort of...aberration. Here. With the wife of the Grim King." He tsked and waved his finger. "That walked precariously close to breaking the ancient truce between our lands. So I offered her a trade: I would retrieve her his heart, the prince himself to follow it. And as for the woman he was set to hide away with, well. I said I would return her to her place. And if the Dawn Lands were to...look away...while Midnight overflowed where she had walked, all *trace* of her would be washed away from him should he come looking for her again. And I assured the Queen that Orias would be none the wiser."

"So...you tattled first," I said and he chuckled. "Dawn didn't want Orias to know what her son was up to, so she made a deal with a worse devil?"

"Orias...*forbade* any dealings with Dawn. Bad blood there. Much of it mingled with spilled blood of war. And moving our borders over the Veil causes...reverberations. Though mad, he would do nothing to risk such a thing as waking the Slumbering Dark." His sharp teeth flashed. "But I did it anyway. I reached over with the hand of Midnight and wrapped it around Cole. I lined up the players and the pieces that all landed correctly. Now, I freely walk your world. *Untethered*—as Hawthorne gathered.

"But that isn't why I did any of it. Being summoned was just another way of boxing her in—to stop her from being able to escape me. As was collecting Hawthorne's heart. It would have occurred to your clever mother that, as impressive as it was, he can't repeat *that* trick, and she wouldn't be able to escape Midnight again without it should his gamble to trade himself to Orias fail. Which it will."

"Because you're cheating." The water began to churn, spilling waves onto the shore that spilled out splashes of shadow that branched into those familiar vines. I backed away as they reached my boots.

"Because I'm a better player. I *allowed* Hawthorne to make that path to Orias. It is open, unguarded. He is free to cross into Midnight and propose his bargain. Sacrificing his freedom for a few humans and some land. Or. He'll dodge that fate. He'll use his shadow heart to make a path out of the Twilight place I left them in...to restart himself here. With her. Knowing that would mean *you* would belong to Midnight. And she will allow it, Talia Adair. She *will* allow you to replace her."

I hugged my arms tightly around my chest, shaking my head. I knew he was trying to twist me, to hurt me, to manipulate me. I wasn't going to give him the satisfaction of showing him that it was working.

"But you will see, I've already laid the trap. The path to Midnight *will* take him there if he chooses it. But. If he tries to open a path through the Veil to escape, *my* shadows will pull at it and redirect them here instead." He narrowed his eyes as beside me there came a whooshing sound, a ripple appearing in the air. "*There,* to be precise. I already know what she will choose. I want you to know it too."

"Why?" I snapped.

He studied me for a few moments, folding his hands in front of him. "When I realized what Hawthorne had done, I knew that if she regained her mind she would not choose to return with me. If I'd convinced you to give me his heart, and I'd imprisoned him in Midnight, I was curious to see if she would return to it then, to save him. Howbeit, I've come to realize that your mother would not have acted to save anyone. Not him. Not you.

Your longing for who you thought she was has shaped your short life. I merely want you to see her for who she truly is. So that hereafter, you can shape yourself...differently."

He might well be lying, but the fact that I was looking at the ripple, fearing that she might step out of it at any time, told me how much I suspected he wasn't.

"Speaking of reshaping I do...rather like her. Your friend. Matilda Pratt." My eyes shot to his. "She's proving challenging. She caught on quickly after the first trick. She told my ort to, 'Go fuck itself.' The thing was only trying to do what it was sent to. But I had it do as she requested instead."

"Oh...no...".

"Yet. She didn't seem to like that much either." He rested his hand on his cheek. "No. Not *at all*."

"Okay," I said, throwing my hands up. "What do you want?"

"A bargain."

Of course he fucking did. "What do you *want*?" I repeated through my teeth.

"If Cole refuses to return with me, then I will have you *and* her lover's beating heart in my hands. I want you to bring it to me."

Well, at least he was consistent.

"Putting aside that you know I don't have it..."

"Convince her to give it over, as a parting gift to you."

"To appease Dawn? Orias? Or...you?"

"Oh. I suppose I could share more of my motives. For a cos—"

"JESUS—*no*. Look, if she were willing to let me be swept off to the Midnight Lands, to be forced to marry the Jolly Grim Nightmare King of Shadows and All Things Terrible in her place, she sure isn't going to turn around and betray the guy she would be doing that for. I think you just want to bask in my misery."

"Why would I wish to do that?"

"BECAUSE YOU'RE A DEMON."

His lips parted but then curled to a grin as beside me, with the tinkling sound of a breaking crystal and a slight smell of rain-tinged sulfur, my mother and Hawthorne emerged.

My crushing disappointment was tempered only by my bitterness.

Hawthorne's surprise at where they'd ended up was extremely short-lived. His eyes narrowed at Noc. He sighed. "Never a bore, are you?"

"And your predictability also remains an amusement, Prince of Morning."

Mom stepped back, taking in where she was and quickly seeming to gather what it meant. "I told you it wouldn't be so simple."

"And I told you"—Hawthorne nodded to me—"this wasn't the way."

Her shoulders dropped a bit when she saw me. "No. I suppose it wasn't."

"Tell her," Noc urged. "Tell *your daughter* of how you were on your way to escape. Tell her you were going to leave her to Orias."

"I was *going* to come back—"

"Really?" Noc was relishing this. "How?"

"I—" She glared at Noc, then turned to me, slightly pleading, "I...Talia, he's just trying to use you, whatever he's told you, don't believe it. Hawthorne would have still freed you once he got me safe enough—"

"A *gamble*? You were going to risk my life on one of his gambles?"

"In fairness, my gambles *have* worked well enough..." Hawthorne broke off with a breath, seeming to take in that this was not about him.

She shook her head. "I know how it looks, but I was trying to make it so we could *all* be free."

"But if not...then you. *You* would at least be free, right?" A hollow laugh fell from my mouth. "And you weren't even going to say good-bye. I should be used to that from you."

Her mouth dropped open.

"I would have come for you." Hawthorne spoke up, locking his eyes on mine. I could feel a shift in the air between us. He was trying to sway me. "*Understand*. I needed to be sure of what I would face to do so first. Or who."

Noc's voice moved through me like a whisper, severing Hawthorne's pull. "*The next shadow I send to torment Matilda Pratt, I'll carve to look just like you.*"

"Enough." I held my palms against my temples and turned away, fixing my focus on the darkening water of the river. Whatever Noc planned to really do with me, Mom didn't care enough to stop. Hawthorne wasn't strong enough here to try. I pressed my hand over the fracture cutting into my heart to quiet the sensation of everything collapsing inside of it. "If you're going, go then. But...leave *me* his heart. "

I didn't have to see Noc to know his smile got sharper right then.

"Why would you want such a thing?" Hawthorne asked softly.

"Same as everyone: collateral. " I shrugged. "*Cole* doesn't need it if she can't be stolen back again. And, as you keep telling me, it isn't yours, so why does it matter?"

"Yes, why *does* it matter?" he said, stepping in front of my view, holding Mom's pale hand in his. "Talia...you don't trust me but—"

"There have been literal ballads written about what happens to girls that do," I snipped.

"And who wrote them, I wonder? Until I saw what became of Joanna, I thought Noc's ire only harmed *me*. Apparently, I underestimated his ambition too. I'm afraid I opened a very dangerous door when I divided my heart, and I mean to close it."

He closed his other hand over Mom's and she nodded up at him, pulling her hand away, and there it was: his heart. Finally and willfully returned to him. It was beating, streaked with shimmery green...and quickly forced into the hole in his chest with a sickening *squelch*. Hawthorne's eyelids fluttered as his bones cracked themselves closed. He rolled his neck, then his shoulders. Then he looked at me, the black draining from his eyes and the green replacing it.

As though a light had been flicked on within him, his entire presence shifted into something more commanding, more *regal*.

I had the sense that if he tried to charm me now, I'd be helpless to stop him.

"Oh, abandoning the fantasy of escape, are we?" Noc kept his distance, but the water began to reverse its churning.

"Much as I loathe it, it's my curse that makes me whole. I realize that it's the lesser evil while *you* are free."

Noc laughed. "And you think you can remedy that. Drive me out?"

"We'll see, Cousin." And he pulled out his sword. "But you're not taking anyone this day."

Noc dragged his tongue along the inside of his cheek and with another glance to the sky and a shake of his head, he flicked his wrist.

I didn't even have time to register the yanking of my feet out from under me before I smashed into the ground sideways, only barely getting my hands in front of my head to cushion it from the blow, but it still dazed me enough to not be able to attempt to grab onto something before I was pulled into the water.

42

Beasts of Old

A memory I would not look at surfaced as I went under. Blurry, feral fear and panic. A sunny day, the shape of my mother above me, the musty smell of old water clogging my nose, burning as I gulped it down my throat.

I was pulled from the river with Noc's hand gripping the back of my neck as I sputtered out the breath I'd managed to hold. He pulled me to him by my waist. The land I'd been snatched from was maybe twenty feet away, but the water I was held over was at least just as deep.

On land, Mom's hand was at her throat, the other on Hawthorne's arm. He held the sword away, the vines creeping on the ground shriveling where he stood, braced as though Noc might hurl me at him at any second—which I couldn't be sure he wouldn't do.

"I cannot kill the Prince of Morning." Noc pulled me close, relaxing his hold on my neck, but tilting my ear to his mouth as he whispered into it. "Not without risking war. So. I wished to give him back his bleeding heart so if he were ever to come to rescue anyone again, I could carve his shadow heart out of him *myself*. It belongs in Midnight. And Midnight always claims what it is owed."

I heard the crushed-glass sound of the Veil tearing again, but before he could drag me through, something began thwapping against my waterlogged boots and up my calves. Noc growled as he kicked what looked to be a fish, then another, which landed on the shore. As it flopped there, I saw it wasn't a fish at all. It was covered in bluish-silver scales, had shelled legs, and human-like arms; its narrow, froggish head had eyes the color of dimes. It hissed, diving back in to rejoin the rest as they climbed Noc's legs, trying to pull him beneath the water—and me with him.

I took this chance to grab his wrist and try pulling it from my neck, but a cocoon of black water, thick and cold, slid up my legs, my torso, over my arms. Panicking, I looked to land to see Hawthorne charge forward on a bridge of some pale, large thing that undulated beneath the water. Just before he reached me, a wall of shadow smoke erupted between us.

There were subdued, burbling cries of defeat from below as the aqua fae things were washed away by the same sort of black water that now enveloped me up to my neck. My body shivered uncontrollably as the chill of it bit in deeper.

Noc brushed the sleeve of his jacket, a glimpse of maniacal glee on his face and a faint red glow in his eyes. "I did think he wouldn't put up such a fight, but I like this better."

"So glad...you're having a good time," I said through my chattering teeth. "If you don't put me back on the land while you guys measure swords...you're going to get me drowned."

"That would be...unfortunate." He wiped the strands of wet hair that were plastered to my cheeks back and gazed down at me for too long to be comfortable. His moon-like irises, softly gray at their edges and flecked with silver, seemed to be considering something, and that worried me very much. He blinked whatever it was away and forced out a chuckle. "Well. Better to put you out of harm's way then."

Stale air that smelled of rain and sulfur breathed out as he began to pull me toward the ripple in the air that led, I knew, to the exact *opposite* of "out of harm's way".

"I guess...this means you give up," I tried. "No retrieved bride...no heart...just me as a consolation prize for...Orias."

"Oh, you sweeting thing. You will not console Orias." With a flick of his fingers the ripple tore wider. Fortunately, before I could be tossed into my new life as a shotgun queen to this unseen King of Nightmares, blades of light pierced the shadow wall.

"Well. He's surely spry," Noc mused.

Hawthorne stood with his arms crossed in a halo of sunset as the shadows dissolved. "By the Dark, *why* won't you just let this go? Let *her* go? Enjoy being a thorn in the world while you can?"

Noc matched his pose, but his answer came in Mom's shrieks from land. Hawthorne turned, having enough time to see the rising black tide of beetles, millipedes, and other small dark things as they surged up from the ground before whatever had been keeping him above the water disappeared, dropping him into it.

The countless number of insects was enough to let me hear the chittering of thousands of legs moving up the rocks, up the trees, Rapunzelling their way up Mom's hair as she futilely tried to bat them away—wisely ceasing her screams before they reached her mouth.

"I thought you couldn't harm her??" I yelled to Noc.

"She is fine. Though I expect she'll want a bath. Oh bother," he said as a shadow fell over his face.

I looked up as birds began to swoop down in the dozens. Above, a swarm of hundreds more of the Stitches circled in an intricate pattern. Mom covered her face as they began decimating the insects around her by the iridescent little riders hurling something that exploded in flashes of color on the ground.

The water seemed to respond to Noc's clenching fists, squeezing me tighter. I gasped and it began to rise up my chin, over my lips, but just as it reached my nose, Hawthorne rose out of the water in front of me, his eyes glowing gold at the edges. He uttered something foreign before Noc could react, and the demon was suddenly besieged from behind by beaks, talons, and those incendiary rainbows.

The water holding me collapsed. Hawthorne plucked me up in his arms before I fell back into it. The thing under his feet keeping him on the water whisked us both back to shore. Over his shoulder, I saw Noc cross his wrists over his horns, his forearms shielding his face from the onslaught. For that second, I had a glimmer of hope that he could be driven back, at least long enough for us to escape.

That glimmer faded as he threw his hands down, and the shadows of anything around us that stood tall enough to cast one, spiked upward, impaling a good number of the birds—a sudden flurry of black feathers falling around us.

I was wet, wobbly, and freezing as we were launched onto the ground. I wanted to stay there but thought better of it when one of the beetles scurried over my boot.

"Take her and go." Hawthorne hauled me up and thrust me towards Mom,

"He'll just find me again." I shoved his hands away. "He'll...*hurt* whoever is around me."

"She's right." Mom was still slapping invisible bugs from her head. "He won't stop until he's cast out."

"Love, what do you think I'm trying to *do*?" he said.

Before she could respond a sudden wind whipped her hair over her face. She fought to rake it away with her fingers, and I caught the heavy scent of rain just before a strangely fractured thunder boomed.

Noc was gone.

In his place, the water of the river rose in thick, dark tendrils weaving in and out of each other. A dense cloud, carrying twin moons crackling with lightning spilled over the sky just over our heads.

"Oh, good," I said to no one in particular. "Good. He's a storm now."

Mom was tying all of the hair she could capture in a knot to the side. "Oh, he *would.*"

"Well then." Hawthorne tapped his fingers on his bottom lip for a few moments. "Now that we're done being subtle..."

The violent sound of twisting, groaning wood beginning to snap from behind me was almost not enough to make me look away from the living storm that was Noc. But I'm *so* glad I did, otherwise I might not have had the sight of rows of trees pulling themselves out of the ground as the bark of their skin took on the vague appearance of distorted faces to haunt me for the rest of my days.

"Stay close, those are mine." Hawthorne pulled Mom to him and me too by the fact that she held my arm.

"What does that even *mean?*" I yelled.

Hawthorne ignored me and held his sword up and called, "So how many of these cranky beasts of old do I have to wake before you'll stop this?"

The water lashed, crashing through one of the trees in response. I ducked as wood debris shot forward, but it was blown to safety by a gust of wind. My relief was short lived as that same wind knocked me in the path of another tendril of water plunging toward me. Hawthorne's sword gleamed with light as it sliced through it, the splash of it falling over us was heavy enough to knock the air out of me.

Around us, the trees moved surprisingly quickly for perennials as they ran to the riverbed. The thunder roared as they shot their spindly arms forward, weaving together to dam the water as thin bolts of unbearably loud and blinding lightning began to strike at them from above. My hands were over my ears as Hawthorne pulled us back into the remaining forest. Every instinct told me to take this opportunity to run, but I knew there was nowhere to go.

"*Thorny Jack. You aren't trying to flee, are you?*"

"Oh. 'Thorny Jack'," Hawthorne said without stopping. "I always hated that one."

"He knows," Mom assured him.

With an abrupt half spin, he gracefully sidestepped us onto a path of reddish clay that stood out starkly against gray trees. There hadn't been any sounds of an opening portal, no ripple. Behind us, the forest was still there, only at a slightly different...angle. Ahead the path was lined with wildflowers, and it was blessedly warm, as though we had walked into a completely different season.

This must be a fold in the Veil. I had to wonder how many of these existed and if they were confined to forests. Could you be in the cereal aisle and accidentally wind up in some flowering nightmare of a place? Could you turn a corner in a library and be on the shore of some silver sea aching to swallow you whole? Could you step too far back in your wardrobe and end up in the "underburg" of Hell?

"No." Mom put her arm in front of me, halting us both. "No. Not the Dawn Lands."

"It's the only—"

With a sound not unlike rats gnawing on a shoebox, the ground before us began to shudder, then sink, as the now familiar bugs burst from the dirt in front of us, scurrying along the flowers, their shiny exoskeletons quickly turning the path black. Something slid along my boots, and I jumped back with an instinctual kick landing on the side of the writhing pile of snakes that had begun spilling out of the ground like oil. The mass of them slithered right for me. I stumbled back, tripping over my feet until an arm scooped me up around the waist.

Turning, Mom looked so utterly *annoyed* to see Noc holding me to him.

"You wound me with your lack of decorum, *Gancanagh*," he said from my side. He was somehow dry and still smelled like a stick of incense. "Running back to your mother."

"I take it back." Hawthorne spun on his boot. "You *are* a bore."

"Oh, I don't think the women would agree." He gave my waist a squeeze, I didn't even bother to try prying his hand away. "You and I can keep at it until one of them falls, Son of Morning, or you can lower your sword. I'm giving you this last chance to stand aside and let me claim what is *owed, Knave* of the Wood. "

"Good god," I said, my fear and frustration having rubbed together long enough to spawn my old friend: irrational anger. "'Green Man', 'Thorny Jack', 'Knave of ... Whatever'. What is the *point* of so many..."

It hit me like a swerving car being driven by a baby. His fucking name.

43

Twist

"*Enough*, Noc," Mom said, her voice solemn. "You win. I will return with you."

"As fickle as a fae you are. No, you will *not*," Hawthorne told her.

"Actually," Noc sighed, running the back of his fingers down my cheek, " I rather prefer the girl."

I flinched, trying to focus. I both knew and did *not* know Noc's true name. It was in my head somewhere, a slippery little thought that dodged all attempts to hold it.

Mom's eyes were daggers. "You don't *need* her if you have me. You just went on and on about—"

"I've taken a *liking*."

If giving your name lets faeries some measure of power over you, given how all of these *Neighbors* had, like, seventy-five worthless names a piece to better hide their true one, then it probably was even more important to keep their own hidden from each other. It could give Hawthorne an advantage, hopefully enough of one to shove Noc back to Midnight empty-handed.

You will not know it until you need it. Once you speak it, it will be gone.

I wasn't sure how to speak without words preloaded on my tongue, and I was aware that Noc telling me I had it at all could have been just another one of his many tricks. But I cleared my head and commanded myself to open my mouth to see what might fall out. I felt something begin to break free in the back of my mind—just as Noc's hand clamped over my mouth.

"Wait." His voice was low in my ear, seeming to sense what I meant to do. "Return it to me, and I'll release your friend."

"Talia..." Hawthorne's eyes bounced from me to Noc, trying to work out what was happening between us.

"I will withdraw from your land, go back to Midnight, along with all of its brethren."

Hawthorne raised a finger at me. "Do *not* believe anything he tells you."

"I'll cut the remnants of your father free."

"Her father..." Mom looked at me—a terrible understanding falling over her. "Oh no..."

I didn't want to share my grief with her. I thought of all of those pictures, ones that existed in a shoebox in an apartment he would never return to, and tried to blink away the tears that came, but that only made them fall fast in burning streaks down my still-cold skin. *Not yet.* I dug my nails into my palm.

If Noc was willing to offer me these things for his name back, then I must be right about what it could do. So now the choice was giving it to Hawthorne and buying myself more time...or freeing everyone else instead. My father's spirit. My friend's life. Over my own freedom. And the freedom of the mother that had walked out on her world. On me. It was an obvious choice.

She seemed to have come to the same conclusion. With a nod, she looked down at her hands, then back to me, but said nothing. I was grateful at least for that.

"Choose," Noc whispered and removed his hand, "wisely."

I glared up at him as he let me go. His face impassive, his eyes unreadable. But he already knew what I'd decided. He was simply waiting for me to say it, wanting me to give in to him in any way.

"Talia, whatever he wants, you would be *mad* to give it to him now." Hawthorne implored me, then turned to Noc. "Just take me and let your king sort this out. He's had at least hundreds of wives. I don't believe for a moment that he finds this one worth all of this trouble."

"Oh. Orias isn't troubled by much these days." Noc glanced disinterestedly in Hawthorne. "What a pity that you would find him a grave man of late..."

Something hung in the air between them before, with a sharp inhale, Hawthorne stepped back with a look of horror.

Mom took his arm. "What is it?"

"He...he seems to wish for me to believe that the King of Midnight...is *dead*."

She spun to Hawthorne. "You *killed* him?"

"That *is* the story I'll be sticking to." Noc shrugged.

"No." She shook her head. Apparently she'd picked up quite a bit of their rules during her time over the Veil. "You are bound to him, Noc, you couldn't have..."

"I serve no *king*, lady. I serve the heart of Midnight itself. True, none would defy him, none would challenge him. At least...not with no one to supplant him."

"Okay, unless things work even weirder over there than I thought..." My fingers automatically pressed into my temple. "If he were dead, wouldn't that make him not need a wife, or a replacement for one, then?

"The Everlands are ruled by a bloodline," Noc said placidly. "And while Orias has had many wives...he had zero heirs. Until now."

Hawthorne's eyes snapped to Mom who stood there agape with shock that bordered on horror.

"An heir..." I repeated while dissecting what that meant. "No. Another trick. They would've been able to tell if she was *pregnant* when she was in the hospital."

"Perhaps they could. Were it not a creature of Midnight's blood she carries in the pit of her," Noc said.

"You knew all along." She locked eyes with the demon.

"As did some part of you," he told her.

"That's how you were able to cross the Moon Dark Sea without the heart of a faery and live." Hawthorne tapped his fingers along his lip but, for the first time in our short relationship, looked defeated. Gone was the winking, playful charm. He now looked like he was slowly turning to stone inside. "This is why Midnight has been able to run amok. It's nothing for Midnight to lose another Queen, but it's heir..."

"*The* heir," Noc corrected. "I didn't argue when you said Orias was mad. He was. But it suited his part...to a point. Perhaps the new king can be shaped...better."

"By you." Mom barely breathed the words out.

Noc stared back at her for a few long moments. "*You* have already made your choice," he said, turning away from her with a wave of his hand. "You can have her, Prince of Briars, the *Lady* of Midnight. Take her and live as happily as you dare, until the babe comes. Unless you tire of her before then. As for *you*, Talia Adair, my offer stands on frail legs. You're mine, either way."

"Noc—" Mom warned.

"But *I'm* not the merry widow here!" I protested "*I'm* not carrying a junior King of Nightmares. There can't be a point in me taking her place now."

"Would that be a no then?" he said icily.

"What game is this?" Hawthorne's voice was thin. "Why refuse what you've been after all along?"

"Because I know his true name," I admitted wearily.

"Does she now?" Hawthorne's eyes sparked.

Noc curled his tongue along the corner of his mouth and let out an annoyed sigh. "If anyone is going to have even a small amount of power over me, I'd rather she be at my side where I can also have power over her. Moreover, darkness made its home in the girl long before now. One that houses darkness will always turn to it in the end."

"Talia, give him his name so he has no reason to find you again," Mom said as though I had stolen another child's toy on the playground.

"If I give it back, how do I know you'll do as you promise?"

"Well. There is *no* chance I will, if you do not."

"He'll do it," Mom said. "I'll make sure of it."

"Oh?" He looked at her coolly. "How will you do that, safe from *his* bed?"

She raised her brows at him. "Because I'll be queen—or something like it—when you bring me back home with you."

"Cole..." Hawthorne began.

"Certainly, you will come willingly now only to plot your escape with him. Again. Despite any promises." He raised his chin at me. "*She* is, so far, much less conniving."

"Uh-uh. No. I know what you're doing. You're trying to make me beg for something you need me to want. What are you going to do? Force *her* to raise this heir out of stubborn spite? Midnight is owed a queen, and *I* have the blood of Midnight already inside of me."

"Hmm. The *widowed* Queen would be more of a cipher." His voice was tarnished silver. "*I* will rule as regent king until the heir comes of age."

Hawthorne looked appalled. "*No.*"

"I am the ArchCarver. Midnight is made of shadows, and the shadows already obey me."

"Mom..." Despite everything, I wanted her to stay as much as I wanted her to go. Noc was right. She was never entirely my mother. Part of her was something darker. She turned to me as she walked past with a plea ghosting its way through her eyes that told me, "*Don't.*"

"She's a broken girl. I know how many amusements that may give you for a time, but you would rather have me at your side. And the heir is *my* child," she implored him, but stole a glance at me. "Children need their mothers."

"Such as they are," I whispered.

Seeing her there, with her tangles of white hair clinging to her frayed black sweater alongside Noc, I sensed a likeness there that unnerved me. Maybe she had always carried some of that same darkness that made him up, the kind that reaches into you, soft as shadows, and twists.

Hawthorne placed his hand firmly on my shoulder. The column of his throat rose and fell as he swallowed down all the words he didn't say. I think even he knew to let her go. She was like him too. A dual creature. One that didn't belong anywhere.

"Perhaps..." Noc's eyes shifted from my face to hers. "You will have your daughter join you?"

"I didn't want her then," she said flatly, looking through me. "I don't now."

The thorn in my heart twisted. Hawthorne's hand became steadying on my shoulder. I was grateful for it.

"Very well." Noc's fingers rested on the sides of her face as he peered down, tilting it, assessing her, before drawing in close, whispering something in her ear. She closed her eyes, then turned away with disdain.

The corners of his lips curved upward as he held out his hand and beckoned me to him, all the while watching her walk to where the trees slanted to the fold between our worlds.

"Take care, little fox," Hawthorne cautioned, his gaze lingering on Mom a few seconds more before turning to me with the duelling colors of his eyes. I thought he would say something more, but he let me walk away.

Noc swept his eyes over my like he did when we first met as I approached. I wondered if he found me any different now. I wondered if I was.

I didn't even flinch this time as the world dimmed and shadows rose again, or even when they faded and I found myself on the bridge overlooking the river, a full, rose-gold moon hanging low in the sky.

"What now?" I asked numbly.

He clasped his hands behind him and stood next to me. The moon's reflection, allowing me to see the profile of his face. "You return my name—I return your friend to her realm, free your father's shadow from mine, and leave you to your world."

"And you keep to yours?"

He smiled. "I do expect to be quite busy there."

"Right." I rested my arms on the stone wall that ran along the bridge, watching the moon wobble in the current below. "Let's get this over with."

"Look at me."

I did, and he smoothly cupped my chin, raising it so that my lips met his and I had to force myself to not recoil, resigning myself to whatever needed to happen to make this all be over.

He kissed me *deeply* and tasted like rain just before it turned to snow. It seemed his tongue searched my mouth for his name. After the moment stretched longer than I could bear, I pushed him back from me.

"Why isn't it working?" I spat, wiped my lips with the back of my hand.

"Why isn't what working?"

"You taking your—Oh, fuck y—" I clamped my mouth down over what he would likely take as an invitation.

He chuckled. "Merely passing the time while I wait for *you* to give me what is mine."

"*How?*"

"Just think of me, with intention, and...say it."

My "intention" was to cause him bodily harm, but I refocused it, glaring into him how much I wanted him gone. When I opened my mouth, I felt something lift out of me like a wave, brushing against every secret on its way out. The voice that spoke was mine, but I heard it as though I were listening through someone else. The name it spoke evaporated into the night air before I could remember it. I only knew the sound was beautiful and terrible at once.

Overcome with dizziness and intense nausea, I shot my hand out to grab the railing as my knees folded. Noc's hands were on my shoulders, gently pulling me up, but that only made it worse.

"May we meet again in darker times, Talia Adair."

His eyes flashed silver, the points of his teeth gleamed white, as he shoved me over the railing.

I had barely let out a scream before I crashed into the merciless cold of the water below.

44

At the End of the Day

Shane recovered quicker than the doctors expected, and Lydia's injuries weren't as serious. They'd stumbled out of the woods twenty miles from where they'd gone into them and managed to flag down a car. When asked at the hospital how Officer Shane Walker had come to have a stab wound in the torso, there was an awkward silence before Shane said it had been an accident while Vivian simultaneously declared it was "vagrants".

There were a lot more questions after that and due diligence led investigators down a pretty weird road.

The town of Elmwood had been all but entombed by waves of webbing. The gossamer blanketing of the fields and forest resembled a thick, frozen fog. It was eventually explained away as having been the work of thousands of some sort of ballooning spiders that had likely been driven there by extreme changes in the weather. But that didn't explain the fine layer of soot that covered the buildings and cars, or the more viscous black membranes of mold that stretched along the ground and around houses.

If you asked any of the town's residents about what had happened on the day Shane Walker was stabbed, you'd find there was a collective, if vague, memory of a storm that must have knocked out power and cell phone towers that somehow also accounted for the missing time as well—some sort of weather-induced sickness that must have led to a town-wide nap.

The event even led to a few of their neighbors, like Wes Samuel, to up and leave town without a trace,

They didn't find Mattie for two weeks. It may have been sheer luck that a cruise ship spotted her bobbing in the ocean two miles off the Irish coast. Luckily for her, neither hypothermia nor sharks got to her before the rescue boat did. There were a lot of questions there too. After a while of her not being able to give them any answers, she was reunited with her parents, more or less physically fine. "Nothing that wouldn't scab over," she'd told them.

It was the same response she'd given Shane weeks later when he'd asked her how she was handling everything.

Nothing that wouldn't scab over.

He didn't believe her.

They didn't find me at all.

I woke up in a bed in Stillview. In a private room. With a door that was kept locked "for my own safety" I was assured by the overly well-kept doctor who first came and stood over me with a folder and notepad in his hand.

He tried to have me answer my own questions, as these types of doctors tend to do. *How do you think you got here?* And I genuinely didn't know, which, with a click of his gold pen, he made a long note of. *Well. What was your last memory?* I didn't know what to say to that either when I certainly couldn't tell him the truth, so I said nothing—and that pen kept scrolling along.

The tears came mostly at night when I was alone. Eventually I decided to tell the doctor everything, partially because the tangle of it was only getting tighter in my head, so I may as well let someone else try to sort it out. Besides, I could always change up the presumed disorder later and tell him I'd made it all up.

The clicking of that pen as I spoke followed me into my dreams.

The doctor (god, what *was* his name?) always wore these perfectly manicured suits and colorful ties that all looked very expensive, so I thought maybe he might be some specialist, sent in to deal with the special headcase. Surprisingly, he didn't try to medicate me at all even after hearing what I had to say. He asked questions as though he were truly interested in my story as something more than the absolute delusion I knew he must think it was. With all the pages he filled in his notebook, maybe he planned to write a research paper about me. Or a whole book.

Once on his way out he asked what if this "demon" (I never named Noc—just to be on the safe side) had been driven away and I'd been free to leave with my mother, what kind of relationship would I have wished to have with her?

"None," I told him. "Some people hurt too much to love."

"How curious," he said and clicked his pen without writing a thing.

Soon after this, a breathless young nurse woke me in the middle of the night, telling me I'd been discharged. That there had been a mix-up in the paperwork, some miscommunication in administration, and other things that I was too groggy to catch. But she said there was a car waiting to take me home, so I dressed in the sweatpants and hoodie she gave me, shoved my feet into boots that were too big, and followed her to the courtyard where she pointed me to the unlocked gate.

She didn't walk me out. As the cold night air hit me and I became begrudgingly more alert, I realized how strange that was. I was even more confused when I opened the gate to find nothing there but an empty street. A fleck of ice landed on my hand, then another, as the year's first snow began to fall. When I went to put my hands in my pockets, my fingers fumbled over what felt like a pointed rock. Gingerly, I took the thing out and held it in my palm: a perfectly carved little wooden fox.

I looked around me for a green-jacketed man who looked like he had wandered too far from the Ren faire, but all was still and quiet. I pulled up my hood and started walking.

The key was under the mat, the girlfriend wasn't there. I went to my old room, thinking I would grab some more things, a change of clothes at least, but as I stood in the doorway, I realized I didn't want any of it. Not the clothes, not the pictures, not the art supplies.

I ignored the sprays of women's clothing strewn about my father's room and opened the drawer where he kept emergency cash and shoved that into my pocket alongside the fox. I paused by the closet door when I saw his favorite scarf: soft gray like his eyes and still smelling of coffee and his cologne, of the long walks around the holiday light show every year, of the day he took me to my first grownup painting class when I was thirteen.

I wrapped it around my neck and flagged down a cab.

"You didn't die," I pointed out to Mattie months later in the sun-bathed New York City loft where I had gone to live with Vivian. It was modern and uncluttered, on loan to us indefinitely by one of my grandmother's old comrades from her model days.

"I do not ignore sound advice," she said.

She had come out to visit me before heading to the Caribbean. Something about the joyous reunion of my mother and I had inspired her to find out about her own birth family, I guess, and that's where it led her so far. Her travel expenses were covered thanks to someone buying her old truck for an exorbitant amount of money.

"It was the goddamn weirdest thing," she told me. "I went to campus to sell back some books since I was taking a hiatus from classes and this bougie blond woman shows up out of nowhere in the parking lot and tells me she's been looking for that exact model for a long time. Sentimental reasons, she said. I told her it wasn't in the best shape...or technically street legal, but she insisted she had to have it. Literally gave me *a bag* of cash—and some of that cash was old. *Really* old, a few of the loose coins in that bag were actually ancient and fucking valuable."

Rare, good fortune was a suspicious trend in our little Everlands survivors group. Some guy came looking for Shane inquiring about his tinker car, said he'd heard about it from someone, but couldn't remember who. He offered five times more than it was worth—an offer Shane refused. A few days later, a realtor called him out of the blue to say someone was very interested in purchasing his house, cash up front, and asked if he'd consider selling. He is still considering it. He's the only one of us that returned to Elmwood.

Kehente had left her youth in the Everlands and was an old woman again by the time they left the woods, but Lydia had managed to find one of her equally elderly sisters living on some reservation. After reuniting them, they discovered that the Scanadoah family had been given a huge sum of money by a supposedly long-lost relative no one had heard of. It had been more confusing to them before Kehente showed up because it was specifically in her name, and they had long thought her dead.

Vivian never returned to the house.

Eventually, Shane did it for her. From the pictures he showed us, you'd think a flood had receded there. In addition to the wreckage, black markings you might assume were mold lined the walls, and that viscous slime was everywhere downstairs. But some of her more personal belongings, artwork and photos, were able to be salvaged, and wouldn't you know—some of it turned out to be worth quite a lot of money.

She slid back into the life she had put down over forty years ago with catlike grace. Her aged, wealthy, art-scene friends, her theater nights and afternoon brunches. But she had kept true to who she had become too. She stayed sober and grew a potted garden on the terrace and a pot garden on the windowsill.

Speaking of art, my creativity came roaring back one day and hasn't let up. Vivian...well, she restrained herself and kept to only a light tsking when I left smudges over the edges of counters and chairs or made a mess of the sink, until she finally decided to call in another favor, and I was given use of one of her friend's studios–a connection which led to some big gallery owner taking interest in what I was doing.

So I decided to skip art school.

"My granddaughter." Vivan would always introduce me this way and smile, proudly. But I still couldn't call her grandmother, or any of its derivatives.

"It's dark. And Angry. And sad. It's violently...beautiful," Mattie said as she scrolled through my portfolio. "Remember me when you're famous."

They found Dad's car in spring.

Hunters came upon it in the middle of the woods with a full tree growing through it as though it had been there for years, but with a new cell phone still in its box in the passenger's seat. He'd been reported missing by the girlfriend, and his disappearance made a tiny dent in the news, which I imagine is what prompted Ashley to message me after nearly three years of ice-cold silence: So *sorry to hear about your dad! I'm always here for you if you want to talk—hope you're doing okay.* She may have been sincere, I mean, she added a heart emoji and everything, but I figured she was just in between boyfriends. And the thing is, I didn't *care.* I now found the loss of her friendship was so completely underwhelming that it no longer even registered.

One night, I saw my father in a dream. In it, I was arguing with Mattie about whether mermaids count as seafood or if it would be straight cannibalism, and he was just *there.* He felt *apart* from the dream— like everything around us was black and white and he was in color. I was happy he was there, no tears, just...happy. We hugged then we talked, the conversation I remembered so clearly when I woke, but faded by the time I got out of my morning shower.

I do remember that the look in his eyes was warm and so full of love. It felt so real. I can't see the harm in believing it was.

And sometimes, I'd think of my mother.

Vivian confessed, when we had finally started talking about things, that my father had called before Mom left to say that he was worried about her. And that he thought she might hurt me. He'd wanted to know if there had been anything in Mom's family history he should know about. But Vivian brushed him off. He never forgave her for that.

I know that my mother was broken. I would have loved her forever anyway. But that wasn't our story. And the more time that passed after she left the second time, the more she felt like only a character in some book I'd read a long time ago. I wasn't tethered to the pain of her anymore. No more grief ambushed me and I hadn't had a panic attack since Elmwood. A scar finally formed over the wound she left in me, and maybe in a few years...it'll hardly be a scar at all.

I pictured her there in the Night Lands. Living so close to Hell with Noc and some demon half-sibling, a crown made of creature teeth and bones on her head, wearing a rage red gown that wraps her body like a membrane as she sits on her Midnight throne. Maybe it was my renewed creativity that makes the image so vivid, but when I imagined her like this, she looked like she was where she belonged after all.

It's a reminder that I'm somewhere I belong too. And that's a comfort.

However cold.

About the author

Rhiannon Blackwood lives in New Orleans and writes mostly for revenge.